phacp

"The magical land Johns[obscured] whimsical treat, and the brothers are a joy to b[obscured] more in the Sons of Dest[obscured]

More pra[obscured]
and th[obscured]

"Enchantments, amusement, eight hunks, and one bewitching woman make for a fun romantic fantasy . . . Humorous and magical. A delightful charmer." —*Midwest Book Review*

"A must-read for those who enjoy fantasy and romance. I so thoroughly enjoyed this wonderful . . . novel and eagerly look forward to each of the other brothers' stories. Jean Johnson can't write them fast enough for me!" —*The Best Reviews*

"I love this world and the heroes and heroines who reside there . . . A lively, wonderful, and oh-so-satisfying book. It is long, beautifully written, and entertaining. Light and dark magic are everywhere . . . Fantasy romance at its best." —*Romance Reviews Today*

"A complex fantasy-romance series." —*Booklist*

"A fun story. I look forward to seeing how these alpha males find their soul mates in the remaining books." —*The Eternal Night*

"An intriguing world . . . an enjoyable hero . . . an enjoyable showcase for an inventive new author. Jean Johnson brings a welcome voice to the romance genre, and she's assured of a warm welcome." —*The Romance Reader*

"An intriguing and entertaining tale of another dimension . . . Quite entertaining. It will be fun to see how the prophecy turns out for the rest of the brothers." —*Fresh Fiction*

Titles by Jean Johnson

SHIFTING PLAINS

The Sons of Destiny

THE SWORD
THE WOLF
THE MASTER
THE SONG
THE CAT
THE STORM
THE FLAME
THE MAGE

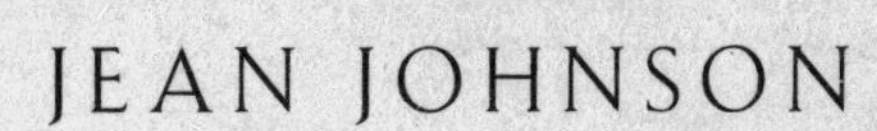

BERKLEY SENSATION, NEW YORK

THE BERKLEY PUBLISHING GROUP
Published by the Penguin Group
Penguin Group (USA) Inc.
375 Hudson Street, New York, New York 10014, USA
Penguin Group (Canada), 90 Eglinton Avenue East, Suite 700, Toronto, Ontario M4P 2Y3, Canada
(a division of Pearson Penguin Canada Inc.)
Penguin Books Ltd., 80 Strand, London WC2R 0RL, England
Penguin Group Ireland, 25 St. Stephen's Green, Dublin 2, Ireland (a division of Penguin Books Ltd.)
Penguin Group (Australia), 250 Camberwell Road, Camberwell, Victoria 3124, Australia
(a division of Pearson Australia Group Pty. Ltd.)
Penguin Books India Pvt. Ltd., 11 Community Centre, Panchsheel Park, New Delhi—110 017, India
Penguin Group (NZ), 67 Apollo Drive, Rosedale, North Shore 0632, New Zealand
(a division of Pearson New Zealand Ltd.)
Penguin Books (South Africa) (Pty.) Ltd., 24 Sturdee Avenue, Rosebank, Johannesburg 2196,
South Africa

Penguin Books Ltd., Registered Offices: 80 Strand, London WC2R 0RL, England

THE STORM

A Berkley Sensation Book / published by arrangement with the author

PRINTING HISTORY
Berkley Sensation trade edition / September 2008
Berkley Sensation mass-market edition / May 2010

Cover art by Aleta Rafton.
Cover design by Annette Fiore DeFex.
Interior text design by Kristin del Rosario.

For information, address: The Berkley Publishing Group,
a division of Penguin Group (USA) Inc.,
375 Hudson Street, New York, New York 10014.

ISBN: 978-0-425-23471-6

BERKLEY® SENSATION
Berkley Sensation Books are published by The Berkley Publishing Group,
a division of Penguin Group (USA) Inc.,
375 Hudson Street, New York, New York 10014.
BERKLEY® SENSATION and the "B" design are trademarks of Penguin Group (USA) Inc.

PRINTED IN THE UNITED STATES OF AMERICA

10 9 8 7 6 5 4 3 2 1

ACKNOWLEDGMENTS

Stormi, NotSoSaintly, Alienor, Alexandra . . . gems. Absolute gems. You help give me the polish that makes my work shine. (Ooh, shiny!) My gratitude goes out to my family for their patient support, my appreciation for their tolerance to all the online friends I ambushed with little wadded-up ideas I wanted to bounce off their foreheads . . . and my deepest thanks to SoulBound, Terry, and Qestral for cold-reading this novel. This was the other half of a very complex pair of stories I wanted to write, and Terry and Qestral in particular made sure that they would still make sense, even if readers picked up *The Storm* before picking up *The Cat*.

Anyway, if you're looking for more of my books, or for a forum to leave a comment or just chat, you can check out my website at: www.JeanJohnson.net (managed by the multitalented Stormi). We try to keep it tidy and family friendly, so definitely drop by! If you're eighteen or older, feel free to gawk at the Mob of Irate Torch-Wielding Fans, which is here: http://groups.yahoo.com/group/MoITWF.

AUTHOR'S NOTE

This book, and the one preceding it, The Cat, *have been written from two separate sets of perspectives. They cover two different stories, with two different plots, but they also cover many of the same incidents, as the two stories take place more or less simultaneously. There will be certain differences because of these separate viewpoints in those parts where the two tales coincide, in dialogue as well as other areas.*

Ask two people who have just had a conversation to recite exactly what was said on both sides during that conversation and you'll get two slightly different answers, because of those differences. Ask two witnesses to a car accident exactly what happened, and you'll get two similar but still somewhat different accounts of what took place. This will usually be determined by what each person was focused on at the time and how much they could personally see from their individual vantage points.

I hope you'll enjoy these two stories both for their similarities and for their differences.

Thank you for reading,

~Jean

ONE

The Sixth Son shall draw the line:
Shun the day and rule the night
Your reign's end shall come at light
When Dawn steals into your hall
Bride of Storm shall be your fall

Tired. Rora was very, very tired. Exhausted. Weary even, and ready to rest.

Not physically; her twin was doing all the physical work. Rora was cold, and tired of being periodically wet, but mostly she was emotionally and mentally exhausted. Being constantly on guard around strangers who might be able to divine her secrets had been bad enough, before the shipwreck. Having to endure her sister's resentments—however silent—over their current predicament with nothing to do but travel south over endless miles of water and no one to distract from those resentments building up . . .

They were both tired of being chased, but Rora was particularly tired of being wanted for what she could do, never for who she was. Tired to the point of feeling cranky, an unpleasant emotion to suffer, whether first- or secondhand. Tired of holding it all in, always being calm, always being rational and polite. Tired of never getting to throw a tantrum, because tantrums were a loss of self-control, and losing self-control was dangerous. She was tired of being different, tired of being hunted, tired of being strange—tired enough to scream, though the only one around to hear it would be her sister.

But even though she was tired enough to scream, she didn't dare. Her sister, shaped into a sea creature strong enough to pull on the rope attached to Rora's makeshift raft, was all she had to rescue herself . . . and for that, Rora was tired of not being able to *do* anything about what she was. Nothing overt, that was. She could feed her sister encouragement and energy, but that was it.

She had great potential within her, but that potential had to be developed through training . . . and those she had met who could have taught her how to properly wield her powers had wound up coveting those powers instead. That left Rora and her sister as fugitives, constantly on the run in search of a place where no one would want to harm them or steal from them. When Rora had bent her powers to that thought, the aura had appeared. Faint at first on the otherwise featureless horizon, it had drawn her southward.

Well, there were two auras, but one had been almost directly beneath them, unfathomably deep, and not nearly as appealing as the one on the horizon. Mara could shift her shape, growing gills to breathe water, but Rora couldn't do that. What little training Rora had cobbled together for herself hadn't included shapechanging, though she had tried for years. The aura on the horizon was bright and clear and seemed to say "land" to her. And it said "home."

So, southward they had fled.

Being unable to see the auras herself, but knowing that Rora could see them, Mara had agreed to swim in that direction, for lack of any better idea. It had taken more than a week for the aura to start growing perceptibly, to brighten and strengthen with increasing proximity. And in the last day or so, it had slowly divided into distinct emanations. Pastel hues, with hints of jewel tones, vivid whites, and scintillating golds . . . Good colors, coming from a good place to live. A safe haven waited for them; she just knew it. She couldn't see the details of how they were to make their living, or where they would reside, or who might be waiting for them . . . but she had concentrated on finding a home for her and her sister.

Darker-haired, pragmatic Mara didn't understand, but then Rora didn't expect her to; no one else saw the world quite the way Rora did. Her twin was concerned with protecting her—and it was necessary; Rora didn't deny that—but she had other concerns on her mind. The place where those auras flared, some of them like towering pillars of fire, a cloud-piercing beacon of hope, loomed very close now.

Blinking twice to restore normal sight, Rora squinted through the haze covering the sea. A chilly morning fog had started to rise. The water was now cold enough to be a threat to her health and had been for the last handful of days, though the sturdy, high-floating planks kept her mostly dry. Up north, it was the start of summer. Down here . . . well, she'd *heard* the southern lands below Sun's Belt were backward, but hadn't believed it. Not until after suffering too many days of increasingly cold weather, forcing her to believe the craziness of it.

The sun still rose in the east and set in the west, but it passed across the sky to the north, not to the south, and the season was all wrong. Being clad in extra layers of clothing didn't help, for that clothing was summer-weight, suitable for the climate north of Sun's Belt. Summer-weight meant leather and linen, not heat-retaining wool and fur.

The half-barrel would have kept her even drier, despite its broken edges, but she needed it more for the remaining few handfuls of rainwater it held. It hadn't rained in the last few days, which was a mixed blessing at best. Her sister could shape her insides to tolerate the salty nature of the ocean, even shape extra layers of fat to insulate herself against the chilly water, but Rora couldn't do that. Rainwater was all she had to drink, carefully hoarded since first lashing the barrel onto the section of hull supporting her. But if the land that held those auras was close enough to dazzle her othersight . . .

Her sister shied to one side, tugging the raft to the left. A moment later, she saw the cause for the sudden deviation; a rock thrust up out of the swirling water. Land *was* near! Squinting, she couldn't see anything physically through the fog, but a double-blink shifted her sight into the thermal range. The cold blues of fog and water differed only by a little bit . . . but there was a glow of something ahead. Something in the shape of trees on a shoreline.

Her sister's horned, blunt, sea creature head surfaced just ahead of her. Rora knew what Mara wanted and called out to her. "I *knew* there was land in this direction! Keep swimming, ahead and just to your right, if you can. I think I see trees in the distance."

"I zzee it," her twin agreed, her voice slow and thick, thanks to the overly large mouth and tongue she currently had. "I zzhall aimm vor it!"

It wasn't overly encouraged for a Shifterai to speak like a human when in an animal shape, but there were exceptions to the rule. Combat was one instance, and awkward circumstances was another. Rora could only imagine just how awkward it was for her sister to be a sea creature, let alone attempt to talk in the middle of all that salt water.

Mara ducked under the rippling surface. Rora focused her attention ahead and heard a hissing sound in the distance. It took her a couple of moments to make sense of it, until she realized she was hearing waves curling onto some sort of shore. Not since they had left the reefs at Sun's Belt too many days ago had she heard that sound. It had been roughly two weeks since the shipwreck had happened, tossing her into the water and forcing her and her sister to flee south instead of east in such an unconventional manner.

They had originally decided to aim for the far-distant land of Fortuna. The two of them had hoped that there, in the most ancient and powerful of all Empires, *some* sort of viable solution to Rora's problem could be found. Mara hadn't been happy about the solution, but it had been the best idea they could think of until Fortuna's own Patron, the Threefold God of Fate, decided to lob not only a couple of extra ships their way but a storm as well.

The ships could have been pirates; the captain of their vessel had taken them for such and had ordered evasive sailing. Rora's opinion, kept quiet since it would have invited too many questions of *why*, was that those two pursuing ships had contained mages, not pirates—mages who were overly eager to get their hands on her; Mara had agreed. The two of them had fled their homeland in the need to avoid that very problem . . . and both of them were very tired of running.

Though she could now hide her true nature, and hide it completely from prying mage eyes, Rora didn't know how to hide herself from a simple touch. She hadn't told Mara, but she was fairly sure she had brushed past at least one mage on the docks of that last city. Not all mages were after her for her abilities. Just the selfish, greedy, troublesome ones.

A wall of glowing, whitish mist loomed through the fog. It wasn't a physical wall; it was magic, a barrier of some sort. No, not a barrier, Rora decided; barriers were for keeping things out. This was a lighter warding, one designed to alert its caster of something. Such as the two of them crossing through it. Clamping down on her mental walls, she barricaded herself in a pretense of nonexistence.

The wall trembled, shivering as her sister passed through it, but it didn't react to her own presence. Good. That meant whoever set the ward didn't know there were two people approaching their land, just one. As good and kind as those auras seemed to be, Rora had suffered too much curiosity from those around her not to be wary of strangers right now. They *could* be as trustworthy as their auras suggested, but *could* wasn't the same as *would*.

And Mara doesn't think I'm paranoid enough, Rora thought with a wry twist of her wind-chapped lips. *Of course, right now I'd welcome even the attentions of a power-hungry mage, like that Xenos, if it meant being warm, dry, and free to eat as many fruits, vegetables, and* cooked *meats as possible, instead of our recent diet of water and raw fish . . . I wouldn't welcome them for long, but I would welcome the rest of it with open arms.*

Not the blond one, whoever he was; he frightened me when I Looked at his emotions. There was just something wrong with that Mornai mage. The Verenai one seemed worse on the surface, and we were right to flee him, but I think Xenos would be content with grabbing power wherever he could find it—may the Gods let him find a different power to grab, and may he get thrashed for it. If he survived the reefs, if he followed us here, at least there's enough magic in this land that he might be distracted by it. The blond one . . . he mostly just wanted to hurt me. Control me . . . and he would have enjoyed breaking me, I think.

The breaking curls of waves emerged from the fog, rippling white lines that formed and receded into the chilly mist. The rushing of the surf met her ears, insistently loud, increasingly loud. Immediately loud, she realized, as Mara surfaced with a puff of her own spray, shifting from the efficiency of gills to the need for lungs and the need to clear water from those lungs. She wasn't exactly pretty in this form, being scaly, grayish, and sort of elongated and bulbous. She wasn't even vaguely human looking.

Rora didn't flinch, though; she watched her sister's body shift shape, forming pseudopods that grabbed the towrope from the rapidly retreating horn, as well as a pair of stoutly muscled legs that allowed Mara to drag the makeshift raft up through the curling waves, onto a beach that was half tumbled rock, half pebbled sand. When the planks jerked, hitting the sand, Rora clung to the raft while her sister increased her size and mass, forming oversized arms and legs; her skin was still scaled and gray, thick with insulating blubber, but within moments she looked mostly human in her general shape.

Not in her size, though; by shifting herself into a larger mass, Mara was able to pull the raft well above the tide line, while Rora held tight for the jerky ride. After two weeks of not being able to stand or even move very well, she didn't trust her limbs for walking just yet. If her sister wanted to haul the raft all the way to the grass line, Rora was happy to wait.

Mara hauled them into the shelter of some trees and thumped onto her scaled rump beside her twin, reshaping herself back to an approximation of her normal self, albeit still clad in seaworthy skin. "No farther," the black-haired woman panted once her mouth was more or less normal again. "I can't go any farther . . ."

Rora patted her twin on the shoulder, then used it to shove to her feet. "Then rest. I'll look for something edible. *Without* any fins."

"Mother bless your quest," Mara groaned, easing onto her naked, scaled back. "Wait—don't go far. We don't know if this place is inhabited."

Waving negligently, Rora double-blinked her eyes, enhancing her vision away from heat sensitivity so that she could see details more clearly through the gloom of predawn. Not with quite the same set of colors, of course, or with the thermal sensitivity from earlier, since it wasn't needed. No, when she concentrated, she could enhance her vision to pick up whatever she *willed* herself to see. In this case, she was on a quest for edibility as well as visibility.

Right now, everything was cast in various dull shades of blues, greens, browns, and grays, save for several brightly glowing, yellow-hued clusters. Berries, she decided, though she couldn't tell if they were familiar without altering her vision further. Doing that too often in a short span of time left her eyes and head aching, something she was too tired and hungry to endure right now.

Reaching for the glowing nubs gingerly with outstretched fingers, Rora identified them by touch as berries. Slightly squishy with over-ripeness, possibly some relative of a grape, but definitely edible according to their bright, cheerful glow. Lifting one to her nose, she eyed the bright-glowing fruit, sniffed, and popped it between her lips. Definitely overripe. A grin split her sea-weathered lips. Licking them, Rora tossed several more of the odd southland fruits into her mouth, chewing and enjoying the slight, natural fermentation.

Clad as she was in two layers of clothes—literally, for she wore everything her sister had worn before being dumped overboard from the storm, save for the extra pair of boots lashed to the raft—Rora had plenty of room in the gathered sleeves of her two blouses to stuff in more of the fruits. Stains weren't a concern at the moment; survival was far more important. Just because the glow of this land was a good and friendly one didn't guarantee they would always be able to find food this quickly.

Off to the side, leaves from something low-growing attracted her next. They glowed a paler yellow, not high in caloric value, but rich enough in nutrients. Rora found them growing under a tree with nutlike things in a lurid shade of red. The nutlike things were to be avoided, but the leaves looked reasonably edible, based on their hue.

In fact, they were something spinachlike, Rora decided,

after plucking one and giving it a cautious nibble. Adding that to her forage, she found roots next, mainly by the shading of their shoots. The leafy tops weren't edible, but the purple hue she saw with her altered vision led to brightly green-glowing, tapered things that tasted like carrots.

Red meant danger in any form, orange meant it could only be eaten in small amounts, yellow meant delicious when raw, green meant she could eat it raw or cooked, blue meant best when cooked, and purple meant something that was attached to that plant but buried underground or hidden within a husk or pod was potentially edible. It was a system Rora had come up with years ago, and it could be applied to anything potentially edible.

As a child, learning how to tell edible food from inedible when her Family had roamed around the Shifting Plains from spring to autumn had been useful. When she and her twin had been forced to flee the Plains, it had proven useful again in identifying foreign foods, and in catching sight of harmful potions others had attempted to mix into their food in order to knock them unconscious for an easier capture. Now it was useful for identifying edible food in a land so far from home that very few of the bushes, grasses, and trees looked familiar.

Not wanting to go far, Rora retraced her steps back to her sister, double-blinking to restore plain, regular vision. It was still dark out, but she could see everything around her and didn't need her special sight anymore. If she'd been taught how to use her abilities, she could have literally transformed rocks into bread—at least, according to the legends of how real magic worked—but it was all she could do to hide herself and See things a little oddly now and again.

Rora shivered a little as she reached her sister's side. The fog was seeping onto shore, following them with its damp, pervasive chill. Mara, sitting up, noticed her twin's discomfort.

"Here, sit by me; I'll wrap myself in fur to warm up both of us."

Grateful, Rora settled against her twin, used to the rippling feel of shapeshifting flesh. In moments, Mara had conjured odd, fur-covered flaps, sort of like wings, to enfold her twin. In return, Rora fed her sister her share of their bounty, shivering as her body slowly warmed in her sister's embrace. The food didn't last long, but it was enough to sate them for now.

Rora was aware that her sister's presence, at least, had been spotted by the inhabitants of this place. On and near the Shifting Plains, people knew what her sister was, but the farther from the heart of Aiar they had traveled, the fewer people had understood what she was and what she could do. Those that thought they knew . . . well, Rora wasn't the only one who had found herself pursued. Of course, Mara had been pursued back home for her political power as a marriageable maiden, which wasn't quite the same, but there had been talk among the Shifterai. Outlander mages sometimes tried to figure out how the shapeshifters of the Plains changed their bodies, and they weren't always polite when doing so.

The people of this strange southern land were even more ignorant than those of Shattered Aiar. They would eventually come looking for the intruder in question; being caught literally with her pants off would not sit well with her twin's pricklish sense of status and dignity, but it was nothing compared to the potential embarrassment, confusion, or even possible disgust their hosts might experience at seeing her quasi-animal state. Not to mention Mara prided herself on the perfection of her full animal forms; these half-forms were undeniably useful, but they were considered sloppy by a true Shifterai.

"I should give you back your clothes," she offered her twin tentatively. Rora didn't offer to hand over the one knife they had between the two of them; Mara didn't really need a knife, unless she needed to slice something cleanly.

"Keep them for the moment," Mara returned lightly, swallowing the last of the overripe berries. "At least, until we can find a stream or something to wash them in and a way to create a fire to dry them again. Not to mention a fire to keep *you* warm."

"Well, I know how you hate half-forms," Rora reminded her sister.

"Even the most picky of our people would be lenient, under the circumstances," Mara told her. "I'll be fine. You need clothes more than I do right now. Come on, let's get some rest."

Rora nodded, somewhat grateful the offer hadn't been accepted. They *were* her sister's clothes, but two layers were better than one. In many ways, it would be so much simpler had she been born an actual, normal, regular mage, a rare thing in Shattered Aiar these days. But she hadn't been. Her only hope was that distant Fortuna held a record of someone else being born like her at some point in the past . . . and that someone in Fate's Empire would be more interested in teaching her how to use her power than in trying to steal it from her.

But Fortuna lay far to the north and east of this place, and *this* was where her other senses had drawn her. Wrapped in her sister's embrace, Rora slowly warmed and relaxed. Whatever would happen, they were on solid, safe ground, with food that wasn't raw fish. Right now, she—and Mara—needed sleep.

She was tired, as was her twin. Tired of running, tired of hiding, tired of being hunted just because they were different from everyone else—and the farther from the Shifting Plains they had traveled, the more Mara herself had been sought for her own abilities. Nudging her sister, Rora stretched out on the planks, letting Mara adjust her furry wings for better coverage. She couldn't do anything about the reactions of others, save hide her abilities and reduce the need for her sister to display her own, but Rora could ensure that the two of them were physically rested, at the very least.

Grateful when Mara complied, Rora snuggled against her sister and relaxed. Finding out where they were and what kind of people lived here could wait a little longer. Sleep could not.

Rydan stepped back from his latest effort, lifting one wrist to rub at the sweat and grime that had beaded on his brow. All that did was smear it around. Wrinkling his lip, he extended his hand. The towel set on the floor a few yards away—far enough back to avoid any shards of stone—flew into his grasp. Mopping his face, he ran the nubbly fabric down onto his bared chest. It might be winter and thus cold outside, but he was buried deep inside the northern mountain range, in the catacombs he had carved yard by painstaking, driven yard. It was cool down here, neither warm nor cold, but he had built up a definite sweat.

This was his refuge, his sanctuary, his catharsis. His place to hide and be free.

It wasn't that he *wanted* to be alone, but compared to the alternative, he was used to it by now. Going out among his brothers had been bad enough during their exile, like being smothered in layers of patchwork blankets. Rough, smooth, scratchy, smothering, fluffy, damp and mildewy, hot and smoky . . . It was difficult to describe the feeling, when he surfaced for some "mandatory socializing," as his eldest brother, Saber, had once called it. Like he was suffocating, being forced to crawl on land instead of swim.

Then there were his new sisters-in-law. The towel slowed in his hands, distaste distracting him. Women on the island. Being exiled hadn't been as torturous for him as it had been for most of his seven brothers; it had allowed Rydan to legitimately escape the increasing chaos and social pressure of life on the mainland. And though his next-youngest brother, Koranen, was the only virgin left of the eight of them and thus literally didn't know what he was missing, it had been far easier for Rydan to give up sex.

He couldn't even call it lovemaking. Women had seen his increasing moodiness as a challenge, as if it were something that had to be soothed away. On the surface, it had worked for a little while . . . but it had felt hollow. Having sex with someone who considered him a *project* in need of fixing hadn't been enjoyable. Or worse, a man to bend to their own selfish whims, and then to rail at when he called them on it.

Scrubbing hard at his skin, Rydan tossed the towel aside, returning his attention to his latest sculpture. It was his outlet, his release from the turmoil within him. Like a sponge absorbing the moods of the sea, he absorbed his family's passions and wrung them from his body and mind down here, surrounded by the quiet peace of stone. Room after room, hall after hall, chamber after chamber, he carved out the demons and the delights and the dreams trapped within him.

Sometimes, he didn't even know *what* he was carving until he stepped back and saw it with his outer eyes, instead of his inner ones. This was one of those times. Eyeing the bas-relief,

Rydan traced the lines of the fantastical, underwater world he had chiseled. Domed cities surrounded by swimming fish, forests of kelp, and gardens of coral. If such a place existed, he hadn't heard of it, but it was in his heart and in his head, and thus came out of his hands.

A benign image, then. Rubbing at the curves and angles, Rydan was grateful for that. Sometimes, some of the things he carved while in his trances were disturbing. Images of chaos and destruction, of torture and death. Nor did he always carve such things when he was himself disturbed and feeling chaotic . . . which made it all the more disturbing. Of course, the other side of that coin was that sometimes, just sometimes, when he was at his most frustrated and tumultuous, raging with an inner storm no rain, wind, or lightning could release, he would wake from his trances and find he had carved visages of such beauty and longing that it physically hurt to look upon them.

But tonight's image was calm. Serene. Benign. After the rush of getting the crystal towers erected for their communication needs, the shock of the Council coming to the Isle, and of his eldest sister-in-law successfully summoning the attention of the Gods in the quest to make their little island exile into an independent nation, he had found himself carving calm images. Rydan didn't know how long such sculptural tranquility would last, but he would enjoy it while it did.

It was almost time to start breakfast. That was his chore, most mornings. Sweeping his hand over the grit and shards on the floor, he gathered them with his magic, sending them into the bed of the wagon-cart. A flick of his hand enchanted it into action, floating silently away toward the main corridor where it would self-propel all the way to its designated dumping ground, then return to this spot, obedient to his spell.

There was a chasm at the northern end of the island where he was currently dumping the tailings of his stonecutting efforts. Actually, there had been more than one rift in the earth that he had filled this way over the last three and a half years; carving the walls of all these chambers and passageways had its own consequences, after all, in that the rubble created had to go *somewhere*. In fact, he was now running out of places to dump the smaller and therefore useless shards of granite wrested from the surfaces of his creations.

Unless, of course, Her Majesty wants crushed stone to pave the paths with, he thought with a touch of humor. *I suppose I could pulverize it and round off the sharp edges for pea gravel with just a spell or two . . .*

His first sister-in-law was a contradiction. Kelly was a passionate woman, a redhead with a redhead's temper. She would debate and argue with anyone and had even gone toe-to-toe with the King of Katan and half his Council—all of whom were powerful mages, while she herself had no magic. The outworlder woman had done so with a breath-stealing cleverness and a distinct fearlessness, too. Yet around Rydan, she muted that side of herself. Not around her husband, Saber, eldest of the eight brothers and a man who thrived on her passion, but for Rydan's sake, she curbed her temper and curbed her tongue and spoke calmly with him. Rationally, even.

Well, sort of. Lately, she had managed to get him to do what she wanted by poking at his sense of duty and honor. It was a subtle form of manipulation, yet her requests were undeniably sincere and logical enough not to be easily set aside. Rydan had felt disarmed in the face of such focused sincerity.

By comparison, Alys—wife of his secondborn brother, Wolfer—was like a pressure spell. She seemed quiet on the surface, but roiled underneath with a tumult of feelings, with her courage and curiosity at war with her shyness and fear. The curly-haired woman, a childhood friend of his family, had calmed somewhat, now that both of her uncles and her cousin were dead and thus incapable of harming anyone she cared about anymore, but she still vacillated between advancing and retreating in all that she did.

Rydan snorted at the thought of his third sister-in-law as he traced his way through the underground maze of chambers and passages to the entrance he used most, the one hidden in his tower at the palace where his brothers lived. Serina. Now there was a woman who was even more ambiguous than Kelly.

When she had merely been the Guardian of a Fountain, a voice heard in the distance, Serina had been all business.

Efficiency had been her nickname. The reality was anything but businesslike. Scatterbrained was more like it; if his third-born brother, Dominor, wanted a challenge, she was definitely it. When she was working on her arithmantic equations, the tall, pale-haired mage was as focused as a mountain and just as immovable: efficient. When she wasn't, however, her mind leaped and scattered in a hundred different directions, like a goat leaping around the rocks and crags of mountain peaks, constantly risking the perils of chaos and threatening everyone around her with an impending avalanche of confusion.

Rydan's greatest relief was that Serina had suffered the nausea of her delicate condition in the hours when *he* was deeply asleep. A sick, scatterbrained mathemagician wasn't something he cared to experience. By comparison, their newest female on the island, Mariel, was calm and motherly. He liked her a little more than the others for it. But she was part of a package deal with her young son, Mikor, an exhausting bundle of energetic curiosity and youthful thoughtlessness who had only been here for less than a turning of Sister Moon, yet had managed to get himself into an amazing amount of trouble. Including being captured by the Katani Council of Mages during their invasive, aborted visit a little while ago.

But Mikor was now Evanor's problem, since Evanor had married his mother. They were still trying to come up with a marriage ceremony that would be appropriate for the new kingdom they were trying to form, something that wasn't Katani, since they had split off from the mainland and had to come up with their own ways of doing things, yet wasn't Natallian or Moonlander or outworlder, either. Koranen had pointed out that, without a Patron Deity, they couldn't sanctify the marriage with a religious blessing, while Kelly had argued that marriages were predominantly a legal matter and had given the couple a "civil union" ceremony and decreed it perfectly acceptable to be married on Nightfall without the blessing of any Gods.

This, of course, had turned out only somewhat satisfactory to everyone involved. The newest happy couple on the island was therefore still doing research on marriage ceremonies. As were Dominor and Serina, consulting with the Nuns of Koraltai over in the kingdom of Natallia, the place where Serina,

Mariel, and Mikor had lived before coming to Nightfall. The nuns had gathered a great deal of information from several kingdoms in their archives. They traded that knowledge with Nightfall for food—mostly, they wanted fresh-caught seafood, given how they lived in a mountain range far from any shore.

It was Rydan's responsibility to assist in the exchange of barrels of fish for scrolls and tomes of copied customs and old magics. Rydan's headache, too. For roughly three years, he had kept the existence of the Fountain of Nightfall a secret, and for very good reason. Fountains were wellsprings of immense magical power and were not to be used lightly or casually. In fact, Serina was in the middle of correcting a centuries-old problem in Natallia because of just such a casual, careless, unthinking use of the Fountain in her former care.

His brothers and sisters-in-law wanted him to use the vast power and majesty of *his* Fountain for a delivery service.

With his inner peace soured just a little at that mental reminder, Rydan finished mounting the stairs to the trapdoor in the base of his tower, one of eight ringing the great wall encircling the palace compound. It wasn't the only entrance to his stone-carved little empire, but he preferred not to let the others know the carefully concealed locations of the others. Some, he had created. Others had been in place long before his arrival and his subsequent discovery of the first of them.

But his brothers were falling, one after another. His next-eldest sibling and twin was due to be the next to meet his mate and fall in love . . . and then it would be *his* turn. The Curse of the Sons of Destiny decreed that Rydan would lose all that he ruled over, that he would be felled by his Destined bride, somehow. As happy as his elder brothers were with their wives, Rydan couldn't imagine how *he* could be happy losing everything he had built up to protect himself.

As he did every morning, Rydan climbed the spiraling stairs leading to the ramparts built into the top of the guard wall. Once outside in the cold, damp morning air, a glance to the east showed the world a fuzzy, patchy gray below the tops of the trees, thanks to a heavy morning mist that had rolled in from the ocean. Descending the outer stairs, he crossed the courtyard, striding between the two split wings of the northernmost spoke of the sprawling, castlelike palace that formed their home.

He could tell without having to physically see that his next-eldest brother was awake, and that Trevan was bothered about something; he had always been able to tell what condition his twin was in whenever he concentrated, though exact details were difficult to discern. His next-youngest brother, Koranen, was also awake and upset.

Of course, the reason didn't require any special divinatory powers; they weren't getting any feminine companionship. Rydan wasn't, either, but he wasn't going to complain. Women had always been more bother than they were worth, always demanding things from him, things he couldn't provide, or didn't want to provide. Sometimes he wondered if a woman would ever *give* him something he both wanted and needed, and give it to him without being asked, but based on the past, that didn't seem likely.

The last three years—before Kelly's arrival—had been relatively peaceful. Now things were churning up all around him, making him want to retreat back to his underground realm and stay there. At least no one bothered him down there.

Except when they wanted to trade with far-off Natallia.

Not for the first time in recent months, Rydan wished Serina hadn't sent Dominor home through the Fountainway, returning the thirdborn brother to his family after having been stolen away by the Mandarites, sworn enemies of the Natallians. Doing so had alerted his family to the fact of his own Guardianship, and that they *could* trade safely with the other continent, despite the brutal, ongoing civil war between Natallia and Mandare, a war that had ruined opportunities for more normal, seafaring trade.

If he weren't required by his assigned chore, three and a half years of tradition, and family pressure, Rydan would have turned around and gone straight to bed. Or even grabbed his bedding and retreated to his hidden lair to sleep. He was tired of all the upheavals in his life among his family, the demands on his time, the drains on his energy, the taxations of his patience . . . and the flinchings whenever he was forced to see his brothers being happy. *They* didn't have to worry about losing anything when they fell in love.

Alright, so Saber did have to worry about Katan falling under his Prophesied Disaster all those years, he allowed grudgingly. *But Kelly proved it was just a misunderstanding. That in exiling us here, Katan* failed *to aid us in* our *moments of Disaster. But I'm supposed to lose everything—and if I do, who will be the Guardian of the Nightfall Fountain? Dominor? Serina? Morganen?*

He didn't trust any of them with the Fountain. Or he did, in a way; none of them were *bad* people, nor would they misuse all that magical energy. He just didn't trust the thought of anyone invading the underground palace surrounding that Fountain. Not after having spent so long laboring to make it his personal haven.

I think I will retreat there, when I go to sleep this time, Rydan decided, sensing the way Kelly and Saber woke each other this morning, far overhead in their room above the dome of the donjon hall at the center of the castle. There was just too much *love* and *passion* in the air . . . all of it for others, and all of it irritating him.

There were days when Rydan wished he could just blithely ignore the others copulating all over the island, as his twin—lusty though Trevan was—somehow managed to do.

TWO

Rydan's hesitant resolve to hide in his underground lair while he slept today solidified at breakfast. Normally, he tried to ignore the minor squabbles of his growing family, but it wasn't always easy. Today was no exception, unless it was an exception in the wrong direction.

It began with his twin's carefully couched request to *record* the sexual responses of his sisters-in-law, in order to create more realistic, responsive, illusionary women to interact with, carnally. Apparently, the versions Trevan had created so far weren't adequate for his and Koranen's needs. Of course, despite the politely phrased request, the married members of the family weren't very interested in cooperating. Not that he could blame them; even indirectly recorded, it would still be a violation of their privacy.

The tension rose further until Koranen—Trevan's co-conspirator—stormed out of the chamber. He was followed a few moments later by Trevan himself, just as visibly frustrated, and just as much in pain. His parting words all but echoed in Rydan's head:

"Go ahead! Refuse to help us solve our immediate problem—who gives a damn if Koranen and I suffer until the end of time, selfishly waiting for our Destinies? Not so long

as you *can be selfishly happy, with or without women in your lives!"*

Vibrating inside from the unpleasantness, unable to help his twin, Rydan buried his grimace in his cup. He grimaced a second time, swallowing quickly. Morg had topped up his goblet, but with a different fruit juice than the one he had been drinking. The two flavors were unexpected and thus a little odd. Not bad, just odd, mixed together like that. With the addition of four ladies to the island and an impressionable young boy, the brothers' home-brewed stout had been replaced by fruit juices and milk for their breakfast drinks.

So long as you *can be selfishly happy, with or* without *women in your lives . . . with or* without *women in your lives . . . selfishly* happy . . .

Who said I was happy*?* he demanded silently, drinking more of the juice to give himself something peaceful to do.

Not that he couldn't slam the goblet on the table as an outlet for his own frustrations, as his brother had chosen to slap his napkin, but that would be displaying a loss of control. One that should not be present in the Guardian of a Fountain. Even if he had stumbled across the Guardianship of that Fountain by accident, Rydan had painstakingly learned the necessary discipline. Mages who let their tempers get the better of them weren't capable of guarding that much power.

But his family did provoke him at times. Or rather, they provoked his beast. He took another sip to calm himself, making it almost a ritual of lifting the cup to his lips, tipping a bit of the intermingled juices into his mouth, sampling the combined tastes, and swallowing it down. Really, it wasn't bad; kind of tart-sweet, with a hint of spiciness. And a little herby; Trevan must have put some mint into the *toska* juice, or something.

"Well." Kelly's voice dropped into the uncomfortable silence at the breakfast table. "That *was* spectacularly selfish of us, wasn't it?"

"Kelly, I am *not* going to allow them to record your responses while making love!" Saber protested. "I don't care *how* desperate they're getting for companionship—"

His wife cut him off by raising her hand.

"—I'm not *asking* you to go against your feelings on the

matter, Saber. But it *is* something that needs to be rectified." Kelly looked around at the brothers remaining at the table, her tone droll, her freckled cheeks quirked on one side. "Actually, I'm surprised the bunch of you didn't think of trying such a thing yourselves, right after you were exiled here."

"*I* did," Dominor admitted frankly, lifting his own cup of juice for a casual-seeming sip.

Rydan thought his elder brother must have been studying him, to look so unconcerned in the face of his siblings' shock.

"And you didn't *share* your idea?" Wolfer rumbled at him. Next to the secondborn brother, his wife, Alys, whapped him on the arm with the back of her hand. He gave her a mock-innocent look, golden eyes wide. "What? Like *you* didn't visit with a tavern wench before coming here, asking her all manner of things?"

"*Wolfer*," Alys muttered, blushing fiercely. The curly-haired young woman whapped him a second time.

"I did think of it, but I ran into the same problem they did," Dom admitted. "I certainly wasn't going to tell any of you about my attempts until I had a viable prototype, but since I couldn't come up with one, I abandoned the project. If I had known that was what those two have been up to lately, I could have told them it was futile and saved them the trouble."

Rydan noticed Kelly's attention sharpening. She eyed her youngest sister-in-law speculatively, then addressed the others. For all she could be abrasively forward and outworlderish in how she presented herself, Kelly of Doyle was undeniably intelligent. Whatever was going on behind those aquamarine eyes of hers would bear studying. Her words were carefully considered.

"I suggest that we who are married tread with a little more respect around those who are not, for the time being. And, for that time being, we have another, more pressing problem to consider. Katan is still being stubborn about letting people come here freely, and is supposed to be letting us develop as our own nation. We have less than a year and a day to prove ourselves as a nation . . . but a nation of just thirteen people isn't exactly a nation, not even in my book," she finished dryly.

"We *will* be a nation when we have a God to worship," Rydan pointed out, compelled to remind her of that fact. "The size of our population base will not matter, if we can achieve that."

"The size of our population base is what will *create* ourselves a God or Goddess, Rydan," Evanor countered, addressing his younger sibling. "Right now, most of us still have ties to Jinga and Kata, but they're the Patrons of Katan, not of Nightfall. If we want our independence, we have to break away from the Empire's Patronage."

"So then we'll just import more settlers from Natallia," Dominor countered, addressing his twin. "And from Guchere, and from far-flung Mendhi, if we can. If we get a large enough population base, we'll be able to vote on what or whom we should worship."

Rydan had heard enough. This argument was one that would wobble back and forth between the need for more settlers and the need for a Patron Deity. Draining his cup, he set it on the table and slipped free of his chair, while Saber spoke, distracting the others from their discussion.

"As lovely as this headache-inducing topic may be, hashed and rehashed a hundred times, I'll remind all of you that Captain Melkin is due to make landfall sometime today or tomorrow with the latest in 'free-trade' goods. More trade with both Natallia and Katan means that *we* have to produce or acquire more products. Even if we're mostly doing it through Katani smugglers and Natallian nuns at the moment. I *suggest* that we try to find something valuable enough among our combined stock of supplies to induce the good captain to smuggle us a few more settlers from the mainland."

"We have already cleared some patches of land for eventually housing those who want their own farmland, but we should start planning an actual city and put everyone who comes here in that city, to begin with," Wolfer added, surprising even Rydan with that observation. He shrugged his broad shoulders, accepting the startled looks from the others. "*I* was thinking, if we're going to be bringing settlers here, some of them will want their own homes. For that matter, do we really *want* strangers settling in the palace, strangers who will be working *outside* the castle?

"We're building a nation, not a refugee settlement," the muscular mage continued, reminding his siblings and sisters-in-law of the sharp intelligence lurking inside his large frame. Rydan paused by the door to listen to him. "We won't know the mettle of the people brought to live here until they have been here for a while, long enough to have proven their true selves. But as much care as we may take in the selection process, some of the incoming settlers may be thieves in disguise, or worse. I would rather they were given their own homes somewhere outside these walls."

"He has a point," Kelly admitted. The others nodded in agreement. Wolfer sat back, looking pleased at the value of his contribution.

Rydan certainly didn't like the thought of strangers wandering through these halls, strangers who might accidentally stumble upon the entrance to his private lair, as he had once done. He lingered by the doorway to hear more. *When* she was being levelheaded—and not a virago—the first of his sisters-in-law was quite logical in her thoughts and observations.

The freckled outworlder continued her point. "I think it would also be a better inducement for bringing people here, and a punishment to hold over their heads. We'll give them their own homes, a good roof over their heads, running freshwater in their kitchens and refreshing rooms . . . and expect them to work hard to contribute to the island's economy, to repay our generosity."

"I find myself hesitant to give away that much land to strangers, actually," Serina said, wincing a little. "Land is revenue, and this kingdom is still quite poor. One of the few resources we have *is* land. If you sell that land to incoming settlers, yes, you'll have a fair amount of capital coming in initially . . . but then it'll dry up once all the land is sold. I would suggest *renting* the land and retaining full control of the island's physical resources for as long as possible."

"Renting versus selling is a good idea," Saber agreed, "but in order to entice people into living here, we first need those houses constructed. I'm with my twin; I'd rather not invite random strangers to come into our home, here in the castle. Pre-Destined wives, yes. Those who are skilled in household management and its tasks, perhaps. But we need farmers and fisher-folk, craftsmen and herders far more than we need palace staff. Those sorts of people do need somewhere else to live. All we have are crumbling ruins left over from the duchy when it collapsed two centuries ago, and most of that was swallowed by the jungle. Clearing land is within our scope, but need I remind you all that none of us trained to be a house builder?"

"Actually, I have an idea about that, and I'll need *your* help, Morganen. Yours, and Hope's," Kelly stated, catching their attention. "We need to build ourselves a new city, and I'd like it to have a distinct look to it, one that says 'Nightfall,' not 'ex-Katani.' The easiest way to do that would be to go to an outside source for building plans . . . and there's nothing more 'outside' than hiring an architectural firm from another world. But first . . . I need to have a word with Alys right after breakfast for another idea I have in mind. Can you spare the time?"

"I have to feed the chickens right after breakfast," Alys warned her. "You can come with me, but . . ."

Kelly winced at that, and Rydan slipped out of the room before he gave in to the urge to grin. Their incipient queen's dislike of the island's poultry was legendary. Then again, so was the ferocity of said poultry. He and his brothers all firmly believed the Council had exiled them with the orneriest chickens in all of Katan as further punishment for the mere crime of being born.

As much as he wanted to head straight for his bed, Rydan couldn't shake the way his skin crawled at the thought of yet more strangers roaming the palace. He called it his beast, though it took no corporeal form, unlike his twin's shapeshifting spells. Rydan had warded the hidden entrances to his sprawling, stone-wrapped sanctuary against discovery when he had first realized what lay beneath the mountains to the north. Doing so had given him a sanctuary far from the others, where they could not come and make his nerves twinge at their proximity.

But someone with a strong gift hidden in their blood might be able to circumvent his wards, especially if it was a settler from a land with a discipline of magic unfamiliar to him.

It always took him a few minutes to get from his rooms

in the palace to the Fountain chamber, even if he shadow-ran the distance, mainly because of the lightglobes and suncrystals illuminating most of the path. If he slept under the mountain, however, he would be mere moments away from defending the Fountain . . . and far from the turmoil of his family. If they didn't find him in his bedroom, they would just go ring the gong in his tower. But that always woke him roughly. *Perhaps an alert-ward on my door?*

Or perhaps he would just make them call him on his communication cryslet and let its recording function accept their incoming messages whenever he wanted to sleep. Ideally, he would just turn off the enchanted scrying bracelet and ignore his family. If it were a true emergency, they'd ring the gong. Otherwise . . . they could just suffer without him.

He was supposed to join some of his siblings in the palace salle for a weapons practice, too, but Rydan wasn't in the mood to fight. At least, not a practice fight. He could afford to skip a day or two—Saber wouldn't be happy if he skipped too many sessions—but his best defensive skills lay in magic, anyway.

He didn't need much from his quarters, just his favorite pillow and a few extra blankets. Rydan had sculpted a suite for himself beneath the mountains in their first year on the island. Only habit and the need to keep himself available for his brothers in an emergency had kept him sleeping in the bedroom he had chosen three and a half years ago, up in the northwestern wing of the palace.

For a long time, they had been besieged by magical beasts sent to them by a previously unknown foe—who had turned out to be their own uncle-in-law, Broger of Devries—and he hadn't felt right leaving his brothers one mage short in watching for the creatures. But that foe had been defeated months ago; there was little need for him to stay available during daylight hours. No, he would get a restful, tranquil day's sleep safely underground.

Away from the chance of being found by some random, Prophesied female. The next one would be Destined for his elder twin, given the progression of how his first four siblings fell, but after that . . . No, Rydan would not make it that easy for the Gods to ruin his life, throwing some emotional, irrational, demanding female into his constant proximity. Not when his life was barely tolerable as it was.

Rora woke gradually, deliciously warm for the first time in days. As reluctant as she was to move—doubly so, since not only did it mean leaving the warmth cocooning her, it meant waking her sister, the source of that warmth—she really, really needed to use the bushes. And, as paradoxical as it might have been, she was also really, really thirsty and needed to find a source of water. From the shadows cast by the trees, they had slept until midday, but not past it. There would be plenty of daylight left in which to explore this new shore, including looking for more edible plants as well as potable water.

But since her sister would fuss if she tried to slip off on her own, Rora didn't try to stealthily ease her way out of the layers of fur and skin blanketing her. Instead, she matter-of-factly pushed Mara's arm out of her way and rolled onto her hands and knees, out of her sister's embrace. Sure enough, Mara woke and squinted, peering first at her twin, then at the sunlight-dappled forest sheltering them, checking for danger. She grunted in inquiry, but otherwise didn't move.

"Relax; I just need to use the bushes . . . and look for something to drink. We used up most of the freshwater last night," Rora reminded her sister. Mara was amusingly sluggish when she woke up. Usually full of intense energy at other times, this was one of the few times Rora ever saw her twin lazy and vulnerable.

Mara grunted and closed her eyes again, relaxing onto the weathered planks of their makeshift bed. She tensed a moment later. "Don't go far, and don't go out of my hearing range."

Rora rolled her eyes. Sometimes her sister's protectiveness bordered on chafing. "Spoilsport. A whole new land, and *you* won't let me play."

"You think this is a lark?" Mara challenged her twin, opening her eyes and lifting her head a little. "We don't know *anything* about this island, *or* its inhabitants."

Impatience threatened to color her voice. Rora spoke as calmly and logically as she could. "Mara, when I Looked for a land after the shipwreck, I specified a place we could reach where we would be *safe*. A *home*. Somewhere that we could stop running. You say you trust in my powers, whatever they are—so *trust* in them! They didn't guide us wrong."

The slight twitch to her sister's facial muscles told Rora that Mara was suppressing a sarcastic urge to roll her golden eyes. Sighing, Rora moved away from her twin. If Mara wanted to play paranoid nursemaid, her twin could do so. *She* needed a shrub with soft leaves. When that was handled, she joined her sister, who had finally risen and was beginning to look more alert than disgruntled.

Water flowed downhill, which meant it inevitably poured into the sea. Even coming from as landlocked a location as the Shifting Plains, she and Mara knew that much. So, to find freshwater, they needed merely to find a stream spilling into the surf and follow it upstream until it was higher than that surf and thus not salty.

The sun had burned off most of the morning fog while they slept and left a slightly hazy but mostly blue sky overhead. Rora enjoyed the warmth of the sun, tipping her suntanned face up to its rays. If they could just find a bit of water to wash as well as drink, she might even be able to rinse the salt from her and her sister's clothes, removing the persistent, annoying itch against her skin. In the meantime, she distracted herself by listening to the waves rushing rhythmically against the beach and watching the seabirds sailing overhead on the steady wind.

"Water!" Hurrying ahead, Mara reached the top of the little ravine cut through the sand dunes. She turned back to her sister with a grin, the first sign of happiness Rora had seen in her twin all morning. Turning upstream, the pair picked their way through the forested shore, until the sound of the surf receded behind them.

Another sound impinged on Rora's ears, a rushing of water that came from ahead of them. "Is that more ocean, up ahead?"

"I don't think so," Mara replied doubtfully. They glanced hopefully at each other and continued on, until the thick brush keeping them away from the stream opened up into a broad pool. At the far end, the source of the noise proved to be a cascade of water falling down a very steep slope, the last twelve or so feet of which were distinctly clifflike.

Rora eyed the mossy bank off to the right of the pool with pleasure; there were leafy bushes perfect for spreading out the clothes she wore, and enough room to stretch out and relax. Her scaled and furred twin waded into the stream, tasting the water in her cupped hands. When she saw Mara's shoulders relax and her enthusiasm for more of the water, Rora removed her boots, tied the laces together so she could sling them over her shoulder, stuffed her socks into them, and waded into the pool. Between that mossy stretch—sized large enough to erect a decent, if makeshift, shelter—and the water, and the twitching of her vision that allowed her to locate edible foods, this was a far better location than their rough camp by the shore.

"This place is perfect! Look, there's edible fruit over there, and I think that one's a relative of soapweed," Rora told her sister, wading deeper into the cool—thankfully not cold—water of the pond. Already she was imagining how good it would feel to get her double layer of clothing scrubbed clean. Stooping, she scooped up a palmful of water, enjoying the clean, sweet flavor of the pool.

"Be careful," her twin ordered her. At Rora's wry, eye-rolling glance, Mara amended it to, "There might be leeches, or worse."

"If there are any, we'll just pick them off," Rora retorted practically. Compared to everything else they had been through, squeezing off a few bloodsuckers—while disgusting—would be relatively easy to endure. Wading farther around the edge of the pool, she aimed for the mossy bank. Emerging, she set down her boots, then moved around the area, gathering more edible plants.

Her sister joined her, picking whatever Rora pointed out was safe to harvest. Hunger was a definite concern; berries and leaves didn't go far to fill their stomachs, but it was a very pleasant change from fish, more fish, and oh, look, another round of fish. Raw fish, at that. If she never had to eat another raw fish in her life, Rora would be very happy. The diet of the Shifting Plains was high in meats, but most of those were land animals, with only a few river fish now and again . . . and all of it was cooked, thank the Gods. They actually ate more birds than they did fish, though there weren't many avians on the Plains, either.

Once they had something of a feast, they divided up the edibles and ate them on the half-sandy, half-mossy bank of the pool. The air under the shade of the trees was a bit too chilly, but out in a patch of sunlight, it was comfortable. There was even more sunshine to enjoy if they were to climb out onto a couple of granite boulders that had fallen from the cliff behind them, landing halfway into the pool and just beyond the worst of the waterfall's spray, but the perch didn't look nearly as comfortable as the soft, thick moss.

Once the last of her slightly overripe berries had been eaten, chasing down the bitter taste of the leaves, Rora gave her sister a grin. "Time for us to wash out our clothes, I think."

Finishing her own mouthful, Mara nodded, swallowing. "Fine. Where's the soapweed you thought you saw?"

Narrowing her green eyes, Rora studied the far bank. Two blinks, and her vision converted. She had relaxed the food-finding hues and now concentrated on Seeing whatever would help them to clean their clothes. Small shrubs on the far side glowed a pale yellow. It wasn't much, but it should be enough to help get the sea salt and sweat out of the fabric layered on her body. *Speaking of which, they'll be easier to remove while they're still dry . . .*

Standing, Rora stripped off the doubled layers of her and her sister's *chamsas*. The knee-length, side-split tunics dropped to the moss, followed by the drawstring-gathered pair of *breikas*, then her undershorts. Neither of them was heavily endowed enough to require a *hara*, the fitted under-vest of the Plains, though they had originally brought some in their belongings. The summer heat of the southern Aian coastline had made both women tuck the garments into their packs when they had set sail; being dashed against the reefs of the Sun's Belt had subsequently parted them from those packs, leaving them literally with only the clothes on their backs.

"I'll fetch the weeds," Rora offered, "if you'll find a good rock to mash them with."

Mara nodded, and Rora waded into the water. With or

without clothes, with or without sunlight, it was a cool shock to her body. But the cliff above them faced north, which in this part of the world meant it faced the sun, and that meant it was slightly warmer than it otherwise might have been. Close to the midway point, she had to swim outright, but it didn't take much effort to reach the far side of the pool.

Since the soapweed grew closer to the cliff than to the distant shore, she aimed that way. Glancing at the waterfall, Rora admired the cascade of glinting white. It was noisy, wet, and colder by the frothing waters at the base of the wall, but it was also fascinating to watch.

Waterfalls were rare on the Shifting Plains. There were a few surviving fountains in the heart of the Plains, where the great capital of Aiar used to be, but mostly it was a ragged, oversized hole gouged in the ground, with a few surviving towers, basements, and half-crumbled walls resurrected into the one permanent city of her people. Rora found the sheeting, pounding water both powerful and beautiful; she drifted a little closer, squinting against the splashing spray.

An uneven shadow behind the water drew her attention. A bit of squinting—of normal sight, since she didn't know what to Look for, exactly—took only a few moments to resolve the truth. The uneven shadow was a fold in the rugged cliff face. Not just a fold, she realized, wading closer to the crumbled rocks on that side, but an opening. A potential cave.

A glance back at her sister showed Mara wading out to one of the rocks. Mindful of her chore, Rora returned her attention to the oddly shaped shrub that was supposed to be similar to soapweed. Back home, the lacy-leaved weed was planted at certain intervals along the streams and small rivers spiraling in from the edges of the Plains. Any Family of any Clan could borrow a certain amount of the weed each time their travels brought them within washing range. Following that rule of thumb, she picked less than one in twenty of the thumb-shaped leaves on each bush until she had a thick handful, then half waded, half swam back across the pool.

For only two sets of clothes, it was a bit more than the amount of soapweed she would have picked, but this cousin of the more familiar plant was unknown to her and weaker in its vision-glow. Soapweed was added to the cleanser made from rendered oils or fats and lye leached from clean wood-ash; it gentled the abrasiveness of hardsoap, softened the mass of the soap itself into a semiliquid form, and even moisturized the skin. Used on its own, it wasn't quite as effective at removing dirt, but at least it wasn't as harsh as hardsoap.

If this plant was related to soapweed and they could get a good, dirt-removing lather worked up, the two of them could even wash their hair. There were plenty of those little bushes on the other side of the pond.

It seemed to be a close relative, from the way the mashed leaves quickly made a greenish foam. And it did seem to get the dirt out of their clothes well enough. Mara scrubbed their clothes, able to add strength behind her muscles because of her abilities; Rora rinsed them under the pounding spray of the waterfall. Crossing the pond a second time, Rora fetched enough leaves to clean themselves as well, taking her turn at mashing the vegetation into a slippery paste.

She laughed when she applied the green goop to her scalp. "If this turns my hair funny colors . . ."

Mara chuckled. "You should have been born with black hair like mine, not that plain, plebeian brown."

Sticking out her tongue at her twin, Rora massaged the pulped leaves into her hair, picking out the occasional stringy bit of stem. It wasn't quite the same as actual soap, but it did alleviate some of the awful, greasy feel she had been forced to endure since the accident, and it did an even better job of detangling the knots that had formed over the last few weeks than the best softsoap from home. Her sister was a shapeshifter, of course; Mara could clean and untangle her hair simply by retracting and regrowing it. Since Rora couldn't do the same, her twin shapeshifted dull claws to paw at Rora's tangles, teasing them free under the slippery influence of the soapweed mush.

Sometimes Rora envied her twin such an incredibly useful ability, but the Gods had created each of them with different purposes in mind. Mara's was easy to tell: She was the most talented of the Shifterai and would one day be free to return and rule them as their queen. *Presuming, of course, that we find a safe place for me to hide, somewhere that I can be safe and secure. Or as my sister would say, free of the ambitions of mortal men . . . so that she can let go of her need to smother me protectively.* Rora eyed the little grotto they had found, ringed by cliff, bush, and tree. *This land is supposedly that place, if my power has guided me right . . . but I don't want to live in a wilderness forever.*

The Gods had *something* in mind regarding Rora Fen Ziel's existence, though what and why were still shrouded in mystery. Rora knew that any number of mages would have argued that her purpose was to serve *them*, given what she was, but she didn't entirely think that was so. It seemed too petty a reason for her existence, to be born simply to serve the ambitions of a single, greedy mage. She wasn't a Seer, but Rora was fairly certain the Gods weren't inclined to be petty-minded.

When her sister had teased out the worst of the tangles, they scrubbed their hides with the last of the mashed leaves and splashed into the pond to rinse off. The lather clung a little bit, so Rora headed for the waterfall. The spray stung, even at the edges; it fell a good twenty feet, far enough to pound hard into the pool, exposing the tops of the rocks lurking just below the surface of the water.

She hung back, glancing at her twin to see if Mara wanted to go first. Her twin's attention was focused to the left of the waterfall, at the line of shadow presaging the cliff. Rora tapped her shoulder and enunciated over the driving rush from the downpour, "It's some sort of cave! I want to go exploring it in a minute or so!"

Mara eyed it warily, wrinkling her nose. "*You* do that!" she shot back. "I'm thinking I'll go back and get my boots and anything else I can scavenge!"

"It is a good place to set up a temporary camp!" Rora admitted, letting her twin duck under the spray first. "Eventually, we'll need to check for signs of habitation, but we can always come back here to rest while we recuperate from our ordeal at sea."

Her sister didn't seem able to hear her, but that was alright. While Mara fetched her boots from the raft drawn up on the shore, Rora would explore the cave. Whatever the size of the cavern beyond the waterfall, the entrance would be too wet to use it as a shelter. Unless there was another opening somewhere else along the brush-choked cliff wall. The thought excited her, even though it was highly unlikely she'd find anything other than damp rock inside the granite cleft.

Back home, Rora had occupied some of her spare time with the exploration of the old vaults that had once lain far beneath the capital of Aiar, cellars and basements and workrooms that had been the storehouses for old books, bank ledgers, spell-scrolls, and the like. She had been accorded a place on the Councils of Clans and Families as a scribe, but without being a shapeshifter herself, her input had been limited. It was only through her explorations of musty old passages carved into the bedrock beneath the spell-gouged valley at the heart of the Shifting Plains that she had eventually uncovered a smidgen of information about what she was.

It had given her a higher status, a place of honor, if a dubiously regarded one. The Shifterai didn't have much to do with "real" magic in their daily lives. Only a few among the Clans were "normal" mages; those who were invariably went into the priesthood, serving the needs of their people as a whole with their admittedly modest power. Rora's abilities were even rarer and stranger. She was too strong to help the priesthood, too strange to be a temptation to a people who eschewed magic outside of religious ceremonies, and in the end too precious to greedy outsiders to risk staying among her kin.

By fleeing, she had protected her mother, father, and three brothers, plus their kinsmen, their Family, their Clan, and their people as a whole. But it had meant further endangering herself and her sister, and it had meant a long, uncertain, and probably permanent exile from the Plains. Dipping under the pounding spray, wincing at its strength, Rora rinsed the mashed leaves from her hair, thinking less about the old vaults she had been forced to leave behind and more about what her sister had been forced to leave behind.

She didn't *like* being exiled from all that she knew, but then Rora was more philosophical about it than her sister; she hadn't lost as much. Mara had known fairly early on that she would one day take on the responsibilities of a leader, either of a Family, or a Clan, or even the entire Shifterai nation. Giving that up for Rora's sake was a huge sacrifice; Mara never *said* it was a massive loss, but Rora knew it was one. Giving up being a mere scribe was nothing compared to giving up being a queen.

Twisting under the spray, making sure all sides of her body were pounded clean, Rora did her best to believe that her strange magics had indeed led them to a land where she would be safe, and where her sister would finally be free of having to protect her all the time. Sometimes Rora could look at Mara and *see* the shifting emotions swirling around her twin. She knew her sister resented their exile, but until something could be done about Rora's powers, neither of them would ever be able to return to the Shifting Plains.

If this was where they were meant to live. Rora wasn't entirely sure, herself. She had enjoyed visiting other lands, when they weren't being actively chased by someone. She liked this strange new land, with its semifamiliar plants and untapped possibilities. A little more in the way of companionship wouldn't be amiss—Mara was more of a pessimist than she was, and it would be nice to be around someone who could be a little more carefree and happy—and of course, some sort of civilized means for the two of them to make a living would not be refused, either.

Like the other children of the Plains, the twins had been raised to ride horses, tend herd animals, preserve food, cure leather, spin and weave fabric, and occasionally farm land. Both of them could be scribes, though Rora had the better head for writing, and Mara the better head for figures. They had many skills with which they could make a living in this new land. *If we can hide my power, or find some way to get rid of it.*

Extricating herself from the pounding spray, Rora slipped back into the deeper section of the pond. Her sister had pulled herself up onto one of the half-submerged boulders. Swimming that way, she reached her sister's side, clinging to the rock with her hands, while the rest of her body floated in the chilly water. The other good sunbathing rock still had bits of mashed leaves on it, so she stayed where she was, pausing just long enough to take a mouthful of water. They had slaked their thirst earlier, but a little more wouldn't hurt.

"Going to fetch your boots, you said?" Rora inquired lightly.

Mara nodded. "I'll fly out there, grab them, and come back, I think. And maybe see if there's anything tasty I can bring down. We'll have to dig a firepit, and something roasted would be heavenly. Here, dry yourself up here while I'm gone."

Nodding, Rora watched her twin shrink rapidly into the shape of a sparrow. The fist-sized bird launched itself from the rock. As was her sister's habit when launching from low places, she started out as a sparrow, but quickly grew into the body of a hawk once she was close to the tops of the trees. Mara had once explained it was just easier that way; moving a tiny mass upward was less exhausting than a bigger mass.

It was never smart to *stay* a small bird, of course, or any other sort of small animal. Shifterai had been killed by birds of prey and other large creatures when in their smaller forms. But her sister was smart, fast, and well able to take care of herself.

Temporarily left alone, Rora tipped her head back, trying to enjoy the warmth of the sun. The rock was rounded but gritty, cold in the damp spots Mara had left, but reasonably warm in the drier ones. Once in a while, a vigorous splash from the waterfall struck her in the shoulder, but so long as there wasn't a breath of wind, the sunlight was warming and drying her skin.

Her damp, darkened hair clung coldly to her skin, threatening to tangle; patiently, Rora picked her fingers through her locks, smoothing and airing the strands. Being without a comb was a petty thing to be mournful for, compared to the lives of the others that had been lost, but she and her sister had been rudely dumped into the sea by that storm and those reefs. At least they were alive, and finally on land . . . but that didn't stop her from wishing for something to brush out her hair.

A little while later, her sister winged down out of the air. No sooner had she landed on the next boulder over than Mara transformed back into her naked self, her hair and hide completely dry. Rora smiled at her, hiding her envy since her own locks were still damp, but Mara didn't give her time to speak.

"I've spotted someone on the beach. He'll probably find the raft in a few moments. Gather up some food and get yourself into that cave," Mara directed her twin. "Take your half of the clothes. I'll take mine, go back to the raft for my boots, and act like I'm the only one here. Until we know what the local people are like, and how dangerous they are to you, it's better if no one knows that you're here."

And so it begins again, the hiding, the skulking, the hoping, the praying . . . but hopefully no more Gods-be-damned chasing, Rora thought, nodding in agreement. Not that she wanted to skulk and hide, but she wasn't naïve. She *had* searched with magic-enhanced vision, striving to See a land where she and her sister could finally be safe and secure—and she had been led here by the strength of that vision—but caution was still the wisest course to follow. Slipping off the rock, she ignored the chill of the water lapping around her thighs, wading over to the mossy bank to fetch her share of their clothes.

"I don't know how long I'll be gone, making contact with the locals. I don't even know if I'll be able to communicate, since we certainly don't speak the local tongue; it's doubtful anyone here speaks Aian," Mara allowed, "but I'll do what I can to figure out what's going on. You should have enough food around here to keep yourself going until tomorrow, from the looks of things. I'll try to come back late tonight, or tomorrow morning, depending on how things go.

"Keep yourself out of sight, alright?" she asked. "We know nothing about this land or its people. Until I know just how dangerous the locals are, it's better for them to remain completely ignorant where you're concerned."

Resisting the urge to roll her eyes, Rora nodded. Her sister's overprotective attitude was necessary and useful, but complying with it was tedious. "I'll be fine. I *do* know how to take care of myself, Mara."

"Just make sure you do," Mara admonished her. Then offered, "I'll try to get my hands on something better to eat and bring it back with me."

Rora smiled at that. "Please do. Now, go—find this fellow you've seen, and try to communicate some peaceful intentions, alright?"

"Spoilsport," her twin teased. Hugging Rora briefly, Mara grabbed her socks and headed off downstream on foot to hide her shapeshifting ability. Rora wasn't the only one whose skills might be coveted, after all, just the greater prize to claim. "Remember, stay well out of sight until late tonight!"

Within moments, Rora was alone in the clearing.

Bundling up her clothes, the Aian maiden slung her boots around her neck by their laces and started picking her way around the edge of the pond, where she could find edible plants. Gathering those as she went, she made it to the far edge of the waterfall with a fistful of leaves and a clutch of roots. Part of the spray splashed over the opening; by keeping her body between it and the bundle of clothes, she managed to keep her things from getting any wetter.

Once inside the cleft in the granite wall, she pulled on the damp garments, leaning on the uneven surfaces for balance. She was reluctant to put her boots on over her socks, but at least they were wool. No longer able to bask in the direct light of the sun, hidden in a cave behind a damp cascade, she quickly began to feel cold.

Exercise will keep me warm . . . exercise, and exploring this place, Rora thought, turning to survey the back of the cave. It twisted into the darkness, reminding her that while she still had the knife slung on her belt, she didn't have any way to light a fire, let alone make a torch. *Alright, I know I've done this before . . . It was a long time ago, but . . . Eyesight, I* want *to See in complete darkness, as well as if I had a decent source of light!*

Her eyes twitched, strained—and the light from the mouth of the cave grew unbearably bright under the focus of her will. Facing away from the water-splattered opening, Rora peered into the shadows. The cavern indeed twisted into the depths of the hillside. Curious, she climbed over the rocks, expecting the cracked rock to terminate just around that corner.

It didn't. In fact, it smoothed out, mainly thanks to a long spill of chipped stones that looked like they had been poured from a higher level. Curious, Rora squeezed her feet into her boots, damp socks and all, laced them up, tucked the roots and leaves into her *chamsa* for safe keeping, and carefully scrambled up the incline.

The rough bits of stone ranged from as large as her fist to as small as dust, with plenty of sharp corners and rough edges. Her people didn't do much work in stone, but they did do some, mainly repair work for the wintering halls located at the heart of the Plains. This stuff looked like the rubble left after something had been carved in stone, only on a massive scale. Dozens of stonecutters would have had to work for days and weeks to accumulate this many leavings, surely.

Climbing to the top of the cleft in the rocks wasn't easy; she backslid several times and cut her palms once or twice, trying to find something stable enough to grip. But when she made it up to the top, she found the "floor" to be a heavy, long ribbon of compacted stone chips, filling the narrow cavern to within twelve feet of its ceiling. Stepping carefully along the surface in case it wasn't as well packed as it looked, she headed deeper into the cave, letting the muffled roar of the waterfall recede into the distance—and then dodged up against the wall, heart pounding in her chest at the sight of something coming her way!

It approached steadily, if slowly, swerving only to follow the natural twists of the granite corridor. Silently, a large, ironbound, wooden-planked bin floated up to Rora, and then past her. It swerved only enough to avoid her, but otherwise ignored her presence. It stopped over the sloping spill of stones, tilted, and let its load of granite chips, splinters, rocks, and blocks clatter and rattle down onto the pile she had just climbed.

If I had still been down there, she thought with wide-eyed wonder, *I could have been badly injured by all of that mess!*

Righting itself, the hovering cart reversed direction, heading back the way it came. It traveled faster as it did so, relieved of its heavy burden. Rora watched it approach her position, realization dawning.

Wait—if it came from a mason's workshop, then it's going back to the masons who loaded it, and that means to a point of civilization! Eyesight, is it a good thing for me to hop on this cart and ride it to its end?

The cart glowed green, a healthy hue. Rora moved quickly, for it had already drawn up next to her. Scrambling to match its steady pace, she grabbed the rim and hopped up, hauling herself awkwardly over the edge. The cart bobbed as she tumbled inside, making her fear that it was going to reverse course and dump its new load down onto the other stones, but it didn't. Smoothing out its steady flight, the hovering cart continued on its silent, merry way, ignoring its uninvited passenger. It traveled faster than it had arrived, though not quite as fast as it had moved when it was empty, reassuring her that the trip shouldn't take too long. Maybe.

Since the front and back of the cart were sloped, if deep, Rora found she was able to recline quite comfortably. Unsure how long the ride would take, she tried not to get *too* comfortable. Hopefully the loading process at the other end wouldn't be quite as mindlessly, magically automated as the dumping process had been.

Rora also hoped it wouldn't take so long that she'd miss meeting her sister out by the pool this evening. Hopping into this thing *was* an impulsive act, she had to admit, but she had learned to trust the instincts of her powers. Those instincts said the cart would take her to her future, hopefully a good one. She knew she was hoping for a lot, but her magic, such as it was, tended to smooth things in whatever direction she thought . . . which meant Rora had learned how to think carefully positive thoughts, just in case.

So this trip will *be smooth, swift, and trouble free . . . hopefully . . .*

THREE

Morganen studied the brown-haired woman in the cart wending its way through the darkness, illuminated by a special augmentation cast upon his favorite scrying mirror. She was well on her way to the underground labyrinth that his sixthborn brother had created. Wrapped as she was in antidetection energies—for whatever she was doing wasn't quite a spell, as he knew it—she had slipped through Rydan's detection wards without even a whisper of an alert. At some point, Morg might have to trip the wards himself, to draw his brother's attention to her . . . but not just yet.

First, his brother had to dream for a little bit.

Rydan had drunk the mixed juices that Morganen had poured for him. The black-haired mage had drained his cup dry, in fact, which pleased the youngest of his siblings. It hadn't been easy for Morganen, palming the potion he had made, pouring it into the one pitcher without anyone seeing the vial in his hand. And, of course, he hadn't been sure just how much of it Rydan would drink, so he had used quite a lot when tainting the pitcher, before topping up his brother's cup.

The rest of the fruit juice had gone into his own goblet, so as not to inflict the brew's effects on anyone else. Morganen hadn't drunk from it after that, but had instead ensured it was poured down the drain while helping the others clear the breakfast table. The youngest of the brothers didn't need to come under the influence of that particular enchanted drug. He knew who his Destined bride was. Until his fifth-, sixth-, and seventhborn brothers were happily wed, Morg couldn't claim her, couldn't invite her across the Veils separating her universe from his. Dreaming about a future with her would be too frustrating right now.

But for Rydan, dreaming about a loving, fulfilling future with a woman who would be perfect for him might be frustrating, but it also just might melt the brooding, stone-loving mage's heart. Morganen was convinced Rydan had one; he did seem to care about his other siblings, after all. Whatever his problems were, Rydan kept them to himself. Morg knew all about the underground maze of chambers, passages, and caverns, about the Fountain his brother had found and claimed, even that Rydan didn't actually use his designated tower on the outer wall of the palace compound for casting his magics, but instead used rooms built beneath the northern mountains. But Morg didn't know what was going on inside of Rydan's heart.

I don't think even Rydan knows that, Morg thought, shifting the focus of the mirror on his desk, looking for his brother in the northwestern wing of the castle. Rydan hadn't changed his wards recently, allowing his distanced view to slip inside the heavily curtained bedchamber . . . and find the bed empty. Not just empty of Rydan, but missing some of its bedding. Panning the mirror's view through the other rooms in the suite, Morg found no signs of his sibling. *How odd . . .*

It was possible Rydan had chosen another bedroom. Possible, but not likely. None of the others in that wing had the thick, double-hung curtains that allowed the night-dwelling mage to sleep through the day. On a hunch, Morg directed his mirror's focus down and northward, approaching from the south. Those wards, he discovered, were freshly set. The ones on the north end of the Isle hadn't been altered, but these ones, erected much closer to his brother's lair, had been freshly changed.

It took him time and patience to work his way through

them without breaking or damaging them, like a burglar picking a lock, trying to keep quiet so that the owner wouldn't notice his entry. Rydan would be unpleasantly upset if he discovered any of his brothers invading his privacy, which was why Morg was always extra careful when breaking into his sibling's territory. The sixthborn mage had a way of throwing his anger at others almost like a physical blow. He didn't get angry often, but when Rydan went into a rage, it was very apparent why he fit the bill for the brother Prophecy had nicknamed the Storm.

At last he slipped through, ghosting through Rydan's wards and leaving them with the impression his magic wasn't actually there. A bit of swooping through the corridors, a final warding carefully surmounted, and Morganen peered into the suite his brother had carved for himself. It wasn't completely dark down there; being deep inside a mountain meant the chamber would be pitch-black, an awkward thing if one woke and needed to go to the refreshing room.

Rydan had left a single lightglobe lit, rapped to one of its dimmest settings. Staring through the mirror, Morganen noted his brother's deeply relaxed state, face twisted to one side as he lay on his stomach, hugging his pillow. If he hadn't seen his brother doing that in the past, Morg might have thought the brew had taken effect, but it was still too soon. That particular potion was most effective after putting the drinker through a solid night's sleep, leaving him refreshed, relaxed, and vulnerable for the dreams that would come shortly before awakening.

It amused Morg to see his brother's lips were parted, allowing a little drool to leak out and stain his pillow cover. He'd never mention it to Rydan, of course; not only was the sixthborn the closest to Morganen in power, but he was also rather prickly at the best of times. But it was amusing to see the stoic, brooding mage was indeed quite normal. At least, once in a while.

Satisfied his brother would be put into the proper, receptive frame of mind with the extra-strong dose of potion, Morganen closed the link for now. It was time to return his attention to that other woman, the shapechanger, and see if she had met up with Trevan yet.

* * *

Not sure what to expect, save for cave, cave, and more cave, lulled into a semidoze by the smoothly, silently floating cart, Rora gradually became aware of two things: daylight and carvings. The daylight, she discovered when she rubbed at her eyes; she squinted against the uncomfortable brightness and cancelled their augmentation. Apparently, it came from the same sort of ceiling-mounted crystals that had survived in the lingering underground chambers of the Shifting City, or simply the City, as it was most often called. There was undoubtedly some sort of network of crystal shafts laced through the stony hills above her head, some way of refracting sunlight down into the mountain, the same as there was back home.

Of course, our suncrystals had originally been laced through the materials of the old capital's buildings, not piercing a small mountainside . . . and the basements of old Aiar were never ornamented quite like this. Sitting up in the cart, Rora peered all around her. There were a few places where rough stone still existed, but most of the walls and the arched ceilings of the passageways and caverns she floated past had been carved in painstaking detail.

There was a recurring theme of thin, graceful lines sharing their carved geometries with swirling, tangling plants, thin rectangles, ovals, triangles, stars, and trapezoids intertwined with elongated flowers and vines. Her hands wanted to reach out and caress the passing folds of stone. Between those sections were broad panels of realistic bas-relief landscapes. They looked like paintings set in elaborate frames, save for the fact they had been carved out of the almost monotonous speckled white of granite.

Here and there, darker striations of stone had been incorporated into the carvings. An image of a woman in a paneled gown looked almost lifelike, for the fluttering folds of her skirt had been limned in darker gray shadows, giving her carving added depth. A winter-bared forest loomed with dark, leafless intent; a tower blazed in white against a patch of heavily speckled black. Two lovers embraced in shadowy granite, obscuring some of the visible details but none of their intimate curves.

She almost didn't notice when the cart came to a halt, she was so busy staring at everything around her. It wasn't until she realized the carving of an underwater scene next to her was incomplete that she noticed the cart had stopped in front of it, instead of silently sweeping her past the view. A glance downward showed a wooden toolbox resting on the smooth-polished floor, laden with steel chisels and mallets of various shapes and sizes.

This was where all that stone-chip debris had been made. There was no sign of the mason, however, just a minor maze of archways to choose from, should she wish to explore. Hungry and thirsty, unsure how long she had been floating, or how far, Rora hauled herself out of the cart. It stayed where it had stopped, no doubt waiting for its owner to fill it and send it off once more. She knew she could probably retrace her path on foot, though she didn't know how she'd manage without any food or drink to sustain her.

As it was, the meager sustenance she had consumed for her lunch was letting her body know it had indeed been consumed, and now the inevitable result was approaching. Since this place seemed to be occupied at least part of the time, Rora closed her eyes and concentrated on Seeing what she needed. *A nice, civilized refreshing room within reasonable walking distance, with running water and all the best possible amenities . . .*

The likelihood of something truly civilized being both near and accessible wasn't high, but she had learned to Look for the best choice first. Opening her eyes, Rora Looked, and *Saw* one of the carved archways glowing with a golden haze: a will-o'-the-wisp had formed, responding to her will. Since she didn't have anything better to do and didn't want to do something uncivilized in a corner—it would be too much of an insult to whomever had gone to all the trouble of carving so much beauty—she padded that way, following the glow.

The cart had risen and fallen, according to whatever angle the passages had contained. Reclining inside the floating container, she hadn't seen if those angles had been due to slopes or stairs. Now she descended a gently undulating stairwell, traversed three large chambers, and mounted another set of steps, this one spiraling in a tight, one-way curve.

The steps were broad and shallow, the ceilings tall, and the space between the walls broad. There were ridges on either side that could serve as handrails, and carvings that decorated the horizontal and vertical surfaces of each step, as well as the inevitable murals. On the tightly spiraling one, the carved images on both the inner and outer walls portrayed an ongoing mountain stream, one so realistically carved despite its unpainted granite surface, she kept expecting leaves on the bushes lining the banks of the stream to flutter in a breeze. The steps themselves formed the turbulent water of the stream, though even the outlines of boulders diverging the permanently frozen waters were so shallowly carved, more an outline than anything else, they posed no impediment to her feet.

The will-o'-the-wisp brightened, letting her know she was getting close to her destination. The silence of her surroundings had her walking as softly as she could; a careless footfall echoed too loudly, too brashly, in such ornate surroundings. With only her own breath to add sound to the soft padding of her travel-worn boots, Rora felt as if the world was holding its breath around her. A silly notion; while Mother Earth *was* a Goddess, She was a representation of Shifterai reverence for their planet. The actual world under her feet didn't have any lungs with which to breathe.

At least it was a restful quiet. The lighting wasn't overly bright, the air was comfortably cool, and her clothing had finished drying somewhere along the way. Despite the pressures of nature, Rora was enjoying her tour of this strange underground maze. Until she reached a barrier impeding her progress.

For the first time since being forced to abandon that ship, Rora found herself confronted with a door. The will-o'-the-wisp vanished through its surface, carved to depict a night sky filled with unfamiliar, undoubtedly southern patterns of stars and the familiar sight of the two moons that circled their world. Unlike when she was on the ship, where she had been very careful to open and close doors by hand, Rora reached out with her mind and let her power open this door. No one was around to see her doing it that way, and thus no one would wonder *how* she opened a door without using her hand.

Back home, before being chased off the Plains, she had never touched a door, once she had discovered her mind could do it for her at the age of seven or so. It had caused some annoyance among not only her kin but among the other Families and Clans, generating a stern lecture from her parents about respecting others' privacy. Because of that lecture, Rora normally wouldn't barge through a strange door without knocking and waiting for permission, but her need for that refreshing room was too strong to ignore. It was often easier to beg for forgiveness afterward . . . even if it would be difficult to do so without actually speaking the local language, whatever that might be.

Nudging the door open with her mind, Rora poked her head through cautiously. The area beyond was a corridor, not a room. The decorations were a continuation of the night-sky theme on the ceiling coupled with the arching limbs of a forest to either side. The stars were tiny suncrystals, in fact, coupled with the larger crescents of Brother and Sister Moon, one at each end of the hall; together, they shed a dim but comfortable level of light.

Surprisingly, the geometry-and-vine framework found elsewhere wasn't visible here, but it wasn't a bad thing; the carvings reminded her of being outside. A couple of doors lined the hall to either side, but the will-o'-the-wisp formed by her intent hovered at a door at the end of the hallway. Padding quietly up the hall, she opened that door with a touch of her will, stepping into near darkness. Zipping to the left, the will-o'-the-wisp disappeared through another doorway with a brief, bright flash. Rora had a quick impression of a bed frame with tall, stone-carved posts and gauzy curtains, but that bright flash let her know her goal was finally at hand. Swinging that door open with a gesture, she stepped inside, letting the door close quietly behind her again.

Like the other room, it was dimly lit at best, though not by the suncrystals she had seen elsewhere. The familiar shape of a lightglobe sat on a loop of stone projecting out from the wall; beneath it dangled a strip of odd, nubbly fabric. It perched over a broad counter holding a sink and an odd, cork-plugged tap of some kind, with a lever on one side and a tray holding a sliver of soap on the other. The light also illuminated a broad bathing tub carved out of the granite surrounding her, surely large enough for four or five people to use; it had two cork-stuck spigots with levers, a sea sponge, and a small collection of mysterious jars and bottles along the far ledge.

Tucked into the corner was the stone-carved, wooden-seated object of her current, fervent desire. Using it, Rora readjusted her clothes in relief, then gingerly pulled on the cork of the sink spigot. Water flowed out of the pipe, warm and welcome to the touch. She made it even hotter with an experimental nudge of the lever to the left, and grinned. Instant hot water, no needing to wait half an hour while a pot boiled over a brazier.

Her sister might long for life on the Plains—well, technically, her twin preferred life in the City to running around on the Plains—but sinks with running water couldn't be hauled from grazing ground to grazing ground in the tent-dwelling life most of their people followed, and the pipes that did exist in the Shifting City were all cold-water ones. Her people had no mages beyond the ones in the priesthood who could enspell their plumbing, and the mage-priestesses had their hands full with more important magical tasks, such as keeping outsiders from invading the Plains. As a whole, the Shifterai could purchase Artifacts such as lightglobes to illuminate their domed tents and their winter homes in the City, but they couldn't enchant very many things for themselves.

Soaping her hands, she scrubbed them clean, drank several mouthfuls of the sweet water from the palm of her hand, and recorked the spigot—finding it very easy to stopper, despite the full flow of water that fell from it. Rora dried her fingers on the fabric dangling under the glowing sphere of the dimly lit lightglobe. The material, softer than it looked, absorbed the droplets from her skin faster than a smooth sheet would have. Pleased, Rora rubbed it again between her fingertips, enjoying the nubbly texture, then reopened the door, heading back out into the bedroom.

It was only then that she realized the room wasn't empty. Entering through the other door, her attention had been focused on finding the refreshing room. From this door, she emerged looking straight at the foot of the stone-framed bed. A dark coverlet draped over the end, rumpled by the splayed outline of a pair of legs. They led up to a rounded hint of a rump, a tapered torso, a plait of dark hair, and pale, bared shoulders and elbows wrapped around a pillow sheathed in white.

The owner of that body stirred as she stared, making her breath catch in her throat, afraid she was about to be caught invading the sleeper's privacy. It was a man, she realized, listening to the figure groaning softly, restlessly; the groan was deep, masculine, and a little odd-sounding. Like a cross between pleasure and pain. Concerned, Rora moved closer, stepping quietly. He groaned again, twisting partially onto his side, clutching at the thick-stuffed pillow in his arms.

Reaching the side of the bed, she could now see his face. Another of the head-sized, dimly glowing globes sat in a holder carved from the same stone that formed the floor-to-ceiling posts at the corners of his bed. This close to the source of light, she could tell his hair was about as black as her twin's. With those thick, dark lashes resting against his cheeks, she couldn't tell what color his eyes were, but she could see that his brows were pinched together. One corner of his mouth kept twitching up, as if he were trying to smile, while the other trembled, torn between a smile and a frown.

The dichotomy made her curious. *What sort of dream could he be having, if it both pleases and upsets him at the same time? I don't dare wake him even if it's a bad dream, being a stranger in his rooms, but he doesn't look all that happy to be dreaming.*

He pushed the pillow away, groaning again, then snatched it against his chest, burying his face in its softness. She watched him twist onto his back, rubbing the pillow as if it were someone's back, his movements growing softer, slower . . . He quieted, falling asleep again.

A few strands of his hair had pulled free in his restlessness, tangling over his brow, threatening to tickle his longish nose. Unlike the faces of Aiar, with their rounder heads and pointier chins, his face was a longish oval, ending in a stubborn-looking jaw. She felt an urge to touch his pale skin, accustomed to seeing the tanned complexions of Shifterai men, who spent most of their lives outside. It occurred to her that a man this pale had to spend a lot of time indoors and that all those carvings had to have taken a lot of time. This was probably the sculptor whose work she had admired.

He whimpered in his sleep, mumbling something. His hand fumbled over the pillow, as if shoving something away, but then caressed the plump rectangle. Unable to quell her curiosity, Rora focused her will. *Show me what he's feeling . . .*

Colors flared up out of his body. Some were darkened shadows: fear, frustration, uncertainty. Others were bright, pulsing, and glittering: longing, joy, need. The glittering disconcerted her. Rora was used to Seeing emotions about as readily as she saw edibility in plants, but the glittering effect was something she normally only associated with magic. Frowning softly, she focused her will on the glittering, trying to evoke how they were affecting the man restlessly sleeping before her.

From the flow of the energies, they were emanating from within him, as emotions normally should emerge, but they were also turning around and bending down, smothering him. That was where the fear and frustration came into play; those darker emotions tried to push the others away, to keep the false feelings from smothering him. A bit of internal questioning told her the effect came from his having absorbed something physically—a potion or a salve, rather than an amulet or an enchantment.

This meant the emotions were bound into his flesh; there was no way to escape the overwhelming ribbons of love, acceptance, and happiness throttling the man. Rora had Seen a number of things in her twenty years. She wasn't naïve, by any means. Too much happiness could choke a person, especially if it was forced upon him. As she had once explained to her twin, it was like eating an entire honeycomb; too much sweet in the diet could make one stomach-sick or worse, even if it was tasty at the time.

Someone had chosen to force-feed this man sweet emotions, and from the look of him, he wasn't digesting them very well.

Hands clinging to the pillow, he twisted his head, simultaneously grimacing and smiling in his sleep. A tuft of dark hair tangled over his face, nudged there by his writhing. That made his nose scrunch from the tickling of it. Impulsively,

Rora leaned over him, gingerly scooping the lock away from his skin. He moved again just as she did so, making his cheek collide with her palm. Her breath caught, as his eyes snapped open. The glittering glow of his emotions, still swirling and arcing around him, surged up into her—she felt nothing, but it visibly targeted her.

His hands released the pillow, shoving it aside, as she jerked back, startled and afraid of how this dark-eyed stranger might react. Those hands snagged her arms before she could fully retreat, pulling her onto the bed. Gasping again, Rora found herself hauled onto her back and half-smothered under the bedding being pressed into place by the sculptor's body. She had a moment in which to stare up at him, wide-eyed, wondering how angry he would be with her for invading his home—and then his head descended, his hair blotting out the faint light of the globe overhead, his lips smothering any protest she might have made, devouring her mouth in the very first kiss of her life.

Laughing—giggling—she ran ahead of him, ducking around corners, leaving him only a flash of an ankle, a wisp of flying hair. Forced to chase after her, Rydan pursued her through the halls of his underground home. Once quiet, the corridors now rang with her voice, echoing, distorting the words, but the tone remained the same. Teasing him. Beckoning him onward. Challenging him to catch her, and love her.

No, this isn't real!

But it felt real. She knew every nook and cranny, every stairwell and corridor. Eluding him, she lured him onward, compelling him to chase after her. He could feel his feet slapping the stones of the floor, as bare as hers, felt his hair flying about his face as he turned a corner, trying not to skid on the polished granite. And when he lost her for a moment in a dome-carved chamber with several archways, he could hear his own panting breath echoing off the walls.

A leg, bare and shapely, curved around the edge of one doorway. She unfurled an arm, beckoning him after her. A hint of shoulder and hip, and a bit more in the way of curves, let him know she was naked. Sharply aware of his own unclothed state, Rydan stalked after her, determined to catch her and hold her. He had held her before, could remember caressing and cupping those curves, lingering over each hollow and peak. The warm scent of her skin teased his memory now, spurring him forward.

Her limbs vanished just before he reached the archway, and when he turned the corner, she was already darting through another. Flashes of memory beset him: laughing together—*but laughter makes me panic*—cuddling before a roaring fire as they discussed their dreams and aspirations—*I* know *I've never felt that anyone else understood me*—sharing a meal eaten from each other's fingers—*I have never been that intimate with anyone in my life!*

Longing and loathing warred within him. He *remembered* being intimate with this woman, and being *happy* about it, deliriously so. *But I've never been delirious in my life . . . haven't I?*

It felt so real! He wanted to consume her laughter, to devour her teasing, to feel her deep inside of him, letting her grace replace the awkward, agonizing beast beneath his skin. To make love to her until she begged for surcease, because this teasing was deeply arousing to him.

He had to know if any of it *was* real. Rydan forced his limbs to race faster, to chase harder. If he could only *catch* her—irony of ironies; if this were a forest of trees instead of corridors of stone, he would think he was fulfilling his twin's Curse—if he could catch her, touch her, feel her, he'd know if she *was* real, if these feelings flooding him, drowning him, suffocating him were true. He was desperate to know if this sense of connection, this wholeness, this completion, actually existed.

Therein lay the dichotomy propelling him through the maze of his underground palace: The holes that existed in his life for so long—rubbed and torn and hollowed out of his soul by the torment of being forced to endure the tumultuous, uncomfortable company of others—somehow felt filled by this mystery woman, as if she and he had been made one. As if she had healed him. As if she knew him, understood him, and could soothe the painful beast that gnawed upon his nerves whenever he was around the others.

No one knew him that well. No one understood him. No

one could heal and soothe him; they usually just made the beast inside of him worse.

Why do I feel this way? He wanted to shout it, to make the walls echo with his demand, but he couldn't even mumble. All of his breath was saved for the chase. It didn't help that his heart was choking his throat with the painful thumping of hope, making it harder to breathe. Whipping around a corner, he flinched at the way his hair tangled in his face—and *she* was there, touching his face, jolting him out of reality, or maybe out of his dream; he couldn't tell anymore.

Reality, fantasy, whatever this was, she was *here* in front of him, above him, touching him with gentle, soothing concern. Her touch was as intoxicating to him as the touch of his Fountain, rushing through his nerves, singing to him. Luring him that last little bit more.

Hungry for truth, for release, Rydan grabbed her, hauling her onto his bed. He rolled on top of her, unable to spare the breath needed to curse the blankets and sheets tangling around his legs, separating them. Her mouth tasted as sweet as his heart said he remembered, parted in surprise at the suddenness of his kiss. She smelled of stone and soapweed, tasted of water and woman, and felt warm and willing beneath him as he pressed her into his bedding. Her fingers tangled in his hair, braided to keep it somewhat tidy as he slept, then pushed at his shoulders.

Rydan wasn't about to be deterred; she had teased him long enough. She was his wife, his woman, his love, and—having caught her—it was time to claim her. But he would slow down; he could feel her startlement, could tell how she wasn't quite ready, yet. Now that he had caught her, pinned her firmly to his bed so she couldn't flee, they had plenty of time. Licking her lower lip, he nipped it in his teeth and released it, then suckled his way down her throat, wanting, needing, to taste her collarbone, her breasts. Her clothes were in his way, he discovered.

It wasn't fair; here he lay, tangled in the bedding, yes, but naked all the same. Yet *she* still had on her clothing! He couldn't kiss her lower than her throat because her tunic was in the way, so he moved back up over her mouth, smothering the soft, uncertain, wordless noises she made. She whimpered, her hands clutching his shoulders. Rydan moaned, agreeing with her. Weight braced partly on her and partly on one elbow, he moved his other hand from her biceps to her breast, tracing his fingers over the smallish, cloth-covered curve.

The sharp intake of her breath through her nose pleased him. Circling the soft peak with his fingertips, he took advantage of her parted lips by licking them. He felt her shudder, but it was more than just on the surface; her shivers shook him to his bones. When he traced his tongue along her lower lip, she moaned; a slow glide of his tongue along her upper lip increased her volume, and he felt her chest expand, pressing her breast further into his touch. He felt a small nub hardening under his touch and shifted his hand so that he could rub the pads of his fingers against her nipple, stimulating it in slow, dragging circles.

That made her moan and arch again. Her fingers flexed on his shoulders, then slid around his neck. Experimentally, her tongue followed in the wake of his, licking his own lips. Pleased with her response, Rydan encouraged her with more tasting of his own. This felt tentative, new, delicious, yet somehow familiar. Like the difference between reality and a half-remembered dream . . . and he still couldn't tell which was reality and which was the dream . . .

If I am dreaming, a wistful corner of his soul whispered as he kissed her, as she reciprocated, *may I never wake up.*

Kora had never been touched like this before; the courting rituals for the Shifting Plains were very strict on what a courting male was allowed to do with a maiden of his choice. No kissing; no contact of mouths on mouths or mouths on skin. No touching of sexual body parts, clothed or otherwise. No touching of bared skin beyond the hands, wrists, throat, and face . . . and certainly no pinning a woman to a bed! Yet this foreign man was doing all of these things and more.

The punishment for a man forcing himself on a woman of the Plains could range from a heavy fine and public censure, all the way through to castration, branding, and banishment. It depended on the severity of his actions, how unwelcome those actions might be, and the ruling of the Family princess if the Family had one; a Clan princess if one was available; or, failing that, the judgment of the three eldest non-shifting females in the offended maiden's Family.

But . . . that was on the Plains, where the women of the Shifterai had a solid historical reason for establishing such a restricted method of courtship and such a severe system of punishment for transgressions. Other lands in Shattered Aiar were different, some of them greatly so, and this land was so far away, it wasn't even in the same hemisphere, let alone on the same continent.

What he was doing to her, aside from the initial shock . . . wasn't bad. Unfamiliar, yes, but not bad. At least, it didn't feel like a violation, and not really a forcing of himself upon *her*, per se. Whatever concoction gripped this man, Rora honestly didn't think he was aware of the difference between asleep and awake. She wanted to tell him—really, she did—but his mouth was sort of occupying hers, and that thing he did with his tongue felt so nice, if ticklish . . . Well, it was only polite to reciprocate when someone made a person feel really good.

And for all she knew, given the rumors of licentious, hedonistic foreign lands, this might just be the local way for two adults to say "hello." A *very*—if startling and unfamiliar—nice way of saying hello. He didn't let up in conveying his greeting, either; the hand teasing her left nipple shifted to her ribs, then her waist, rubbing her flesh through her clothes. He reached her hip, tugging impatiently on the folds of her *chamsa*, working the long hemline up with a relative minimum of fuss. The man kissing her did so with a distracting new trick: He licked her mouth until she returned the flicks with some of her own, and suckled her tongue.

Oh! That . . . My . . . ohhh, yessss . . . That soft suction somehow connected her tongue to her breasts, making her ache; to the hand on her hip, which seemed even more unnerving, and which coupled the twanging of her nerves to her womb, clenching her lower abdomen so sweetly, she moaned into his mouth. He groaned in agreement and kissed her harder, thrusting in his own tongue for her to suckle as well.

Good maidens don't do this! her conscience nagged sharply.

But I'm not on the Plains anymore, and not likely to return, am I? Oh . . . oh . . . must keep . . . keep control . . .

Good girl, bad girl, it didn't matter. The way he was devouring her mouth, teaching her what kissing was all about—his people must have widow-priestesses skilled in the art of lovemaking, too, to have taught him all of this! Rora didn't care if it was wrong by her people's standards; it felt too good to protest anymore. It was her fingers that unbuckled her belt, giving him better access to the drawstrings of her *breikas*, her hips that lifted into his caress of her lower abdomen, inviting more of the same.

When his fingers slipped not only into her underdrawers, but brushed the curls of her mound, Rora gasped, surprised by how sensitive her flesh was to such a light, almost ticklish touch. Craving more, she instinctively parted her thighs, earning an appreciative moan from the dark-haired man so determined to pleasure her. With a twist of his hand, he slipped his fingers lower, gliding them into her folds.

She wasn't ignorant of what lovemaking was about; she knew from the slick moisture that met and eased his touch that he had managed to bring her body to a definite state of readiness. Rora had just never felt it quite this way, aroused by the touch of someone other than herself. No one had told her that it was possible for a complete stranger to have her trembling and starving for something other than food. Only that, at the appropriate time, the suitor she chose to be her husband would teach her the full joys of their marriage-bed, joys which she had only explored on her own before now, in places only she had ever touched.

This . . . this was unnerving and exciting, all jumbled together. It was all she could to do keep control of herself, to lock down the power within her, which churned at his touch as if he were bringing her to a boil. Certainly he was making her very hot, and very wet.

From the way he groaned into her mouth, then ground his hardness into her thigh, rubbing his groin against her through the layers of fabric between them, he found her dampness exciting, too. His fingers slipped and slid, rippling into an intimate massage of her flesh. The palpitations were different than what she normally did; they were slower, more sensual, yet exciting in their own way.

Matching the steady rubbing of his fingers to the sucking and nipping of his lips, he added the curling of his tongue, connected her mouth to her loins. Rora cried out, the sound muffled by his mouth. Eyes snapping wide, Rora was deluged not only with a shiver of pleasure but the sight of his glitter-filled emotions swarming into her and drawing out her own. Not just drawing them out, either; the aura of his feelings pulled the glow of *hers* into him, where he seemed to absorb them like air into his lungs. Each time that happened, his own pulsed stronger, taking on more of the hues that were her emotions.

The startling Sight distracted her from his touch, but not for long. Apparently not content with a single muffled cry, he rubbed and gently pinched, coaxing more pleasure from her. Whimpers escaped Rora's throat; her hips bucked up into his, sinking back into her passion. He groaned and released her from his kiss, whispering words that she couldn't quite understand, though his tone was encouraging.

Within her body, energy rose. Not just sexual, but magical energy; somehow, he was tapping into what she carried. That was alarming, but it also felt too good to stop. All she could do was struggle to contain it, to keep her power from pouring into him and literally scorching the poor man with her passion.

The only safe outlet was in physical expression. A wordless groan escaped her throat, followed by another, and another. The pleasure coaxed by his talented fingers lifted her higher, harder, fuller than before; with each thrust of her hips, each rhythmic cry of her voice, he caressed a little faster, pressed his loins to her blanket-draped thigh a little harder. And then he licked the edge of her ear, tickling every single nerve into shimmering, excited life. A lightning bolt of sensation sparked straight through to her groin.

"Gods!" Rora shouted, feeling her body wrenching itself in a spasm stronger than any climax she had felt before. "Father Sky above! Ah, *Gods*!"

Her tormentor stilled, his body tensing over hers, his head flinching away from her ear. She didn't know if it was because she had shouted in his ear, or for some other reason; right now,

Rora was too involved in her own pleasure to care. Part of her still struggled to keep from burning down the bed, but the rest of her melted into sensation. Vaguely, she felt him yanking his hand free from her *breikas* with a hiss, wanted to protest his abrupt withdrawl that left her whole body chilled and needing more, but her orgasm still trembled through her flesh. Dragging her eyes open, having squeezed them shut at some point in her bliss, she glanced languidly around, searching for her unexpected lover.

He had scrambled away from her, rising up onto his knees, and was staring at her with a shocked look on his face. Confusion and doubt swirled around him in dark oranges and browns, twining with the deep red of rising anger and the pale green of disbelief. And still the magic infused within him continued to spill its sparkling veils of tenderness, longing, and desire. The ribbons of color swirled and tangled, reaching out to brush against her, turning inward to attack him.

She watched him clamp his palms over his ears, as if the emotion-storm swirling around him had developed voices inside his head. A groan escaped him, and it was her turn to be confused. Very confused.

"What in the Gods' Names is *happening* to me?" he demanded roughly, squinting at her as he spoke . . . in flawless, Shifterai-accented Aian.

Bewilderment made Rora push herself into a sitting position, even though her body was still feeling nicely lethargic from her release. "You . . . you speak my language?"

"No, the stupid *potion* is speaking your language—how did you get in here?" he demanded, his voice deep and harsh. "This whole area is warded and off-limits!"

"I, ah, didn't feel any wards," she admitted, carefully omitting the fact that she couldn't feel them, nor could they sense her, when she had her magical signature as tightly locked down as it still was.

"Why are you here?" the black-haired, bare-chested man snapped next, still wincing as his own emotions attacked him. The sickly yellow green of suspicion battled with a glittering, baby blue urge to apologize . . . and lost as brownish red irritation squeezed around both of them. "Who are you?—Did Morg send you down here?"

"I . . . don't know anyone by that name. I landed on the shore after weeks at sea, found a pool with some freshwater and a waterfall, and saw there was a cave behind it," she confessed, gesturing vaguely behind her. "When I explored it, there was this magical cart dumping gravel, and figuring it would take me to civilization, I just hopped into it and let it take me for a ride. And, um, well, when I reached somewhere near here, where the cart stopped, I went looking for a refreshing room.

"Then I saw you, and you were having some sort of bad dream—you looked like you'd been drugged," Rora added, not wanting to reveal *how* she knew, but knowing she had to help him. His emotions were still attacking him, after all, feeding on themselves like some sort of cannibalistic nest of snakes. "Did you eat or drink anything, before you went to sleep? Or maybe touch some Artifact?"

Concentration, colored a bluish gray, swirled up out of him, blanketing a third of the other aura-veils before giving way to a bright yellow in remembrance. "*Morganen*! He drugged my fruit juice—I'm going to *kill* him!"

Wrenching the blankets away from his lap, he scrambled out of the bed. That bared him from the hips down. Rora couldn't help gasping. She'd seen Shifterai men naked before, but they usually covered their genitals in a cloak of feathers or fur for modesty before divesting their clothes. Aside from a smallish patch of short black hair curling around the edges of his masculinity, providing dark contrast to pale skin, he was distinctly nude. More than that, he was distinctly aroused.

She quickly covered her mouth, but it was too late; he had heard the sound. Glaring at her, flaring with dull orange embarrassment, he snatched up the top blanket, wrapped it around his hips, backed up from the bed, then jabbed a finger at her. "Stay right there!"

Hurrying off before she could even think of a place to go—not that she knew many places in this strange land—he vanished through the refreshing room door.

FOUR

Gods, Gods, Gods! Rydan grimaced at his image in the mirror, still feeling torn inside. Anger and loathing warred with love and tenderness, battling for control of his body. Morg must have slipped him some sort of love potion in that double shot of juice. He had thought it tasted strange just because the two liquids had been mixed together, but no, his youngest idiot of a sibling had probably dumped some third liquid in with the other two, leaving Rydan a conflicted wreck.

Part of him wanted to lock and ward the refreshing room door, to hide in there until one of them rotted, or just run as far away from anyone and everyone as he could physically get. Part of him wanted to go back out there, apologize to that woman on his bed for his brusqueness, kiss her to prove his sincerity, and touch her liquid heat until the bone-deep shuddering of her body beneath his became the shuddering of his own, until she cried out his name—but she didn't even know his name! He certainly didn't know *hers.*

Did Morg set this up somehow? She said *she didn't know him, said she arrived here by the passages under the mountain . . . Oh, Sweet Kata.* Rydan stared at his reflection in the mirror over the sink, horrified by an awful realization. *If she's the fifth woman to come to the Isle . . . then she's Destined for my* twin, *not me! And I . . . and I forced myself on her . . .*

It was all muddled up, mixed into that damned, yearning-filled dream, but he had a vague recollection of her hands pushing on his shoulders, of her trying to get him off of her at the start of their kisses. The fact that she had ended up enjoying his touch didn't stop his stomach from turning in a doubled load of guilt and self-loathing. Gut clenching, Rydan aimed into the sink, overcome with nausea from having forced himself on his *brother's* future wife.

Morganen was just as much at fault—and he *would* pay—but right now, it was all Rydan could do to keep himself standing between each wrenching heave. There wasn't much in his stomach, at least, since he had been asleep. When the nausea passed, when there was nothing left to escape him but the tears on his cheeks and the mouthful of water he used to rinse the taste from his teeth, he grabbed the toweling cloth from its holder. It already felt damp, proof she had spoken true about needing to use a refreshing room. *His* refreshing room, where her energies would linger and contaminate his aether . . .

Blowing his nose, Rydan probed for those energies, wanting to cleanse them as quickly as possible. This was supposed to be his sanctuary, his relief from the problems and pesterings of others, the one place where no one could make his skin crawl and his moods swing . . . and . . . she wasn't there? Confusion welled up within him.

Washing and drying his hands, Rydan tried again, opening his mage-senses wider. There was no sign of her presence in the refreshing room, no hint of her in his bedroom—prompted by his power, the door swung wide on the heels of that alarmed thought, showing her still reclining on his bed. At least, as far as his eyes were concerned. To his inner senses, though, she didn't exist. It shouldn't be possible; he was very sensitive to magical energies radiated by others—excruciatingly sensitive, at times—but he could not sense her that way. Even a non-mage left *some* trace of his life force in the aether.

Is she . . . a construct? An illusion-woman, like the kind my twin was trying to make?

She glanced his way, biting her lower lip, and offered him a tentative smile. If she was a construct, she was the most complex illusion he had ever met, for he could have sworn he smelled her feminine musk upon his fingers before washing his hands. When her gaze dipped below his navel, accompanied by a blush, Rydan was reminded of the blanket wrapped awkwardly around his hips.

That reminded him in turn of having forgotten to bring a clean set of clothes to wear. Snapping his fingers, Rydan Summoned his previous clothes, piled on top of a stone-carved cabinet to one side. The moment they floated his way, her eyes widened, large enough that he could see their whites, despite the low level of illumination in the room. A silent command closed the door again, giving him a moment of privacy in which to use the facilities, cast a cleansing charm, and dress.

Emerging, Rydan found her still staring in his direction. This time, she wasn't half-sprawled on his bed, her legs stretched out in front of her and still splayed from having had his hand down her odd, gathered trousers. This time, she had donned her belt and had scooted back against the wall at the head of the bed. He could feel her nervousness now, her wary fear of him.

Emotions. He could sense emotions from her. Illusions and constructs didn't feel emotions; they only simulated them through gesture, word, and deed. Rydan had never once been fooled by enchantments or Artifacts in that way. Whoever this woman was, she *was* real . . . even if Kelly, who was an outworlder from a low-magic universe, radiated more power than she did. But whoever she was, this plain-faced, plain-clothed, unfamiliar woman radiated fear of him.

Gods . . . climax aside, she must be remembering how I forced myself on her . . .

Self-loathing churned his stomach a second time, though there was nothing left in it to try to make its way out again. At least between it and his guilt over having touched Trevan's Destined bride, his angst was killing the still-lingering urge to take her into his arms and proclaim some idiotic love for her. Fighting through the shame that clenched his teeth, fists, and guts, Rydan crossed to the nearest corner of the bed. She shrank back a little, so he stopped there and choked out the necessary words, not coming any closer.

"I am *sorry* that I . . . that I violated you. I can only say that I would *not* have touched you, had I been in my right mind," Rydan stated quietly but firmly, hating himself for this. He hated embarrassment of any kind, avoided shameful situations with a passion, and now had to endure this moment that he himself had created. At least in part. "I . . . I believe I was drugged by one of my brothers. I will personally hold him down for you to extract your penance upon. Come."

She didn't move from the bed, though she did blink at him. "Why would your brother drug you?"

"Because he is insane, obviously. Come." Lifting his hand, Rydan waited impatiently for her to take it. Her fear increased sharply, beating against his nerves like the wings of oversized, panicked butterflies. "I *am* in control of myself, woman. I will not harm you now."

"You're a mage," she murmured, still staring at him uneasily.

"Yes," Rydan agreed impatiently, wondering why that was such a surprise to her. He *had* mentioned wards earlier. "I am the second-most powerful mage on this island." Her fear increased, making him flinch physically; the wings were now robin-sized, and swelling to rival a hawk's. Something about his being a mage was making her afraid of him. That roused the beast under his skin. Struggling to keep from shuddering, Rydan tried to gentle his approach, though it was difficult, considering how irritated he still was. "You are in my private chambers. My inner sanctum, where *no one* is allowed to go.

"However you got in here, you must leave. Now. I will show you where the others dwell. The Gods may have dragged you here, but it is among *them* that you will find your Destiny."

Some of her fear receded, replaced by a puzzled quirk of her light brown brows. "You . . . don't want to keep me here?"

"No." Hadn't he made that obvious enough?

"You . . . *don't* want to touch me again?" the woman on his bed asked next. Her fear still lurked, but hesitancy and uncertainty had joined the itch she was sending under his skin.

"No! I told you, I was not myself! I don't like touching *anyone*," Rydan added gruffly. That had always made his inner turmoil worse. He gestured sharply. "Now get out of my bed, if you please. Yours awaits you upstairs." More confusion, this time the meandering creep of exploratory ants against his nerves. "Just get out of the damned bed!"

Her eyes widened. She slipped off his bed as he demanded, but didn't move from its side. "Your em—"

"Go!" Jabbing his finger at the door, Rydan made it fling open with a *crack* as stone met stone. Stone was insulative, cool, still. He had surrounded himself with it, crafting doors and hinges from it rather than going to his twin for help in working wood, when wooden doors would have led to uncomfortable questions about why he needed them, and where they would be hung.

Jumping a little at his sharp imperative, and more at the banging of the magically reinforced door, she hurried out ahead of him. Rydan followed, pausing only long enough to go back to the nightstand and grab his cryslet. Fitting it on his wrist, he pushed back the urge to chase after her, to pull her into his arms and soothe her fears. That was just the damned potion talking, not his true feelings, for which his youngest brother would dearly pay.

Directing her with curt orders as to which way to go, Rydan strode in her wake, plotting in between as to how, exactly, he would make Morganen suffer. Not just for the potion, nor for her violation—gentle or not, he had forced his attentions on her, thanks to the confusion he was suffering—but for the fact that he, Rydan, would have to go to his own twin and *confess* that he had *fingered* his brother's soon-to-be wife. Having placed a tracking charm on his twin a few years ago after Trevan had nearly died from a watersnake bite, Rydan was aware that his next-eldest brother was up in the palace right now, somewhere near the heart of it. That meant others would be nearby. He would have to lure his brother into a private meeting before confessing what he had done.

Self-loathing choked the back of his throat, making his orders more terse than before. She scuttled ahead of him, this nameless woman, fear wafting from her like a stench that stained the roof of his mouth, that dirtied his hands from fingernails to elbow points. Rydan hated himself for this as well as for the rest of it, but if he didn't make her loathe him, she wouldn't turn to his brother for comfort. He *had* given her a satisfactory climax, and he knew too well how a woman could mistake the blissful but temporary feelings of mere satisfied lust for actual love.

She was his brother's Destiny, not his own. No matter how wonderful she had smelled in his half-dreaming state, or how sweet the feel of her flesh under his fingers: She. Was. Trevan's.

Dammit.

Rora didn't like the look of his emotional aura, when she glanced behind her after the third stairwell they had climbed. It swirled in ever-darker colors, serrated and sharp, tangling around his body with intangible, invisible veils that throttled him, drained back into him. That took in her emotions, too.

Like a beast, she realized, *feeding on my emotions. Not yanking them out, not stealing them from within me, but definitely draining the runoff. It's as if he's a sinkhole, and anyone near him runs downhill—when he was in the refreshing room, my own aura didn't drain into him, but when he came within a few body lengths of me . . .*

Other than what she could See, she couldn't imagine what it felt like for him. *But I suppose it makes sense for him to live down here, if the others on this island he mentions live elsewhere. The farther away he can stay from people, the less likely their emotions will affect his own. Poor man.*

He choked, and she glanced back at him. Lit by the sun-crystals mounted in the ceiling of the current corridor, his eyes were colorlessly dark; they looked black, though she had never heard of such a thing. Right now, they were wide, his expression dubious. She faced forward again, picking up speed a little.

He's aware of my compassion? Mother Earth . . . I don't think he's fully *aware of it, but somehow I don't feel quite so afraid of him anymore, and if he was feeling* that *a little while ago, and now I'm feeling something different . . .*

Deciding she would *not* be afraid of him—because feeling her fear probably didn't feel good to him—Rora cleared her throat. She didn't know what to say for a moment, then remembered that they had never actually introduced themselves. Starting with that, she offered, "Um . . . my name is Rora. Rora Fen Ziel. What's your name?"

"Rydan of Nightfall. Turn left, and go up the stairs," he ordered curtly.

Obeying, Rora focused on his name. "Of Nightfall . . . that's an interesting way of putting it. I take it 'Nightfall' is the name of this island? Or is it the name of a city or a town, or maybe just the name of this lovely place, down here?"

"Island. Go through the trapdoor and through the next door, up the stairs."

"Ah. It must not be a very big island," Rora allowed. She was growing winded from climbing so many stairs after being stuck on a makeshift raft for two weeks. She had swum several times for exercise and for makeshift bathing, clinging to the raft, but it didn't use the same set of muscles. The trapdoor opened before she reached it, responding to a swell of magic from the mage following her. He didn't respond to her comment, just followed her through the opening, so she tried again. "We don't name ourselves after our locations, where I come from. We name ourselves after our parents. Fen is short for Fennon, my father, and Ziel is short for Ziella, my mother. I'm from the Shifting Plains—that's at the heart of Aiar, where the old capital used to be. Only it's now a hole in the ground, surrounded by lots of grasslands. Have you ever been to Aiar?"

"No."

Ha—so he does *speak . . . when given a question to answer.* She tried again, struggling to control or at least conceal her amusement from him. "Well, I suppose that's only fair; I've never been to Nightfall, before now. If you do not use their names as part of your own, what are the names of your parents?"

He didn't answer her. A glance behind showed his jaw set, his eyes narrowed. He knew she was trying to get to know him better and clearly didn't think it was a good idea. Given how he had apologized for pouncing on her, and how those ribbons of guilt were still strangling him emotionally, she was pretty sure she knew why.

"Look, I know you're upset about what happened back in

there, but I don't blame you; I mean, I could tell you were drugged, and really, no harm was done."

He grunted, and a door several steps above them swung open, but not as fast or as hard as the previous ones they had used. Taking the offered exit from the stairwell, she found another door opening, this one finally leading outside. It was at that point that Rora realized she was about to be introduced to several other people, *without* Mara at her side, watching over her. Slowing her footsteps, she stopped next to a gong set in a black-painted stand and stared at that open doorway.

"Go through the door," Rydan of Nightfall directed her. When she didn't move in that direction, he added with a trace of impatience, "That is why it opened, so you may use it. *Use* it."

"Um . . . I'd rather not meet anyone, actually. Couldn't I just . . . stay with you?" Rora found herself asking, even as the cautious corner of her mind shouted, *He's a mage! He's a mage, and if he touches you again, he'll realize what he didn't realize back when he was drugged and not in his right mind!*

The vile yellow green that welled up from his skin, spiraling outward before swirling back in again, spoke of self-disgust to her Sight. Violent self-disgust. It unnerved her. She watched a muscle twitch in his jaw before he growled his reply. "*No.* Your Destiny is out *there*. You will have *nothing* further to do with me!"

"Well . . . I'm kind of shy, and I'd really rather not meet anyone else," she cobbled together. "I'm terrible in large crowds. It's not a good idea to, um, just toss me out there. Truthfully."

"Go!" he ordered, pointing at the open door.

Rora shook her head. "No—I don't want to."

"I said, *go*!" The black-haired mage reached for her arm, his aura filled with red orange determination.

"Don't touch me!" Rora flinched back, bumping into the gong stand. He flinched, too, his aura turning bilious and olive with self-loathing. Realizing belatedly that he thought she was afraid of him because of what they'd done on his bed, Rora raised her hands between them. "No—it's not about *that*. I *told* you, I'm not upset by what you did back in your bed; I'm really not! Just . . . don't touch me."

Confusion seeped through his self-disgust. "Then why not, if it's not about that?"

Inspiration struck as she Watched the shifting colors of his aura. Hoping Father Sky would forgive her for the blatant lie, Rora said, "It's . . . well . . . I'm sort of emotionally sensitive. When I touch other people, I feel what they're feeling. And it's overwhelming. They're not *my* emotions, you see.

"That's why I don't like meeting new people," she added, improvising as she Saw his emotions change, picking up hues of startlement and hints of wonder. "Because they'll want to clasp hands with me, you see, or touch me, and then I get a surfeit of their curiosity or lewd interest or disdain or boredom—it's like being dashed in the face with a full goblet. Sometimes it's just harmless water, but other times it's like mud, or like wine. Even the pleasant emotions are like being given a whole spoonful of honey all at once, and it's . . . well, it's overpowering. So I don't like letting people touch me.

"At least, not under normal circumstances," Rora added, watching some of his self-guilt creep back. "When you touched me, downstairs . . . well, your touch felt good in and of itself, and I could tell that you thought that touching me felt good, and so it was *startling*, and not quite anything I'd ever felt before . . . but it was nice, in the end. Very, very nice," she finished awkwardly, feeling her cheeks heat, but not just in embarrassment at such an unmaidenly admission.

It was out of discomfort at *his* discomfort. *Something in my admitting I really enjoyed his touch discomfits him. How odd; I'd better backtrack a bit, in case his people are actually more like my own in matters of courtship.* The thought was a little disappointing, but she quickly pushed it aside.

"As I said, I know it was a one-time thing because of whatever you were suffering."

That relaxed him a little. Rora had the impression that he was worried about her wanting more of what he had done to her. It was a disappointment to realize it, but now that she realized how emotions troubled him, she could understand why. *Without caring between a couple, without the involvement of wonderful emotions to fill in all the leftover corners, sex is meaningless and empty. Very fun, but very meaningless*, she acknowledged, sighing silently.

Rydan studied her, no doubt gauging the emotions radiating from her. His mouth tightened, then he spoke. "You cannot stay. You belong with the others."

"Then would you at least go with me and keep them from touching me?" Rora asked, desperation giving her the idea. He drew in a breath to speak, but she cut him off. "Rydan, I don't *know* anyone here! I don't even know if they'd speak my language. *You* could introduce me to people, and . . . and intimidate them into keeping their distance around me. You're obviously good at that."

He snorted, a thin beam of humor-hued aquamarine seeping into his aura before quelling. Folding his arms across his black-clad chest, he deliberated her request. She didn't know what was going through his mind, and his emotions were too muddled and streaked for a moment to tell what he was feeling, but he did seem to be thinking about it. He finally sighed, resolve coloring his aura in a leathery hue. "Fine. But once I hand you off to my twin, you're *his* responsibility."

Guilt streaked through him at that, for whatever internal reason, but he lifted his chin at the open door, clearly ordering her to move. Glad she had his tacit protection—even if he didn't know the real reason why—Rora nodded and moved away from the gong stand. He wasn't Mara, but he would do as a protector. She had no idea what lay beyond that door, other than stone, sky, trees, and, somewhere out there, lots of people.

When she stepped through the doorway, she discovered what lay outside: a tall, stout stone walkway carved between crenellations, forming the ramparts of a broad wall encircling a large compound. Beyond the wall lay slopes forested in the same sort of trees and bushes she had seen earlier, and the same sort of granite peaks that she had seen from the shore. Inside the compound, gray white stone, blue gray tiles, and gleaming windowpanes formed the four-story wings of a building every bit as ornate as the few surviving structures from the Shattering of the Aian capital.

The nearest branch of the building, connected to the surrounding wall by a wooden drawbridge Rydan was telling her to take, half blocked her view of a broad blue dome in the distance, one with a sort of cap, an extra chamber with a conical roof and a large, gleaming, crystalline sphere perched on top. Then she could see no more, for she entered the building through a door that, yet again, swung open for her without having to be touched. Her first glimpse of the walls startled her, for it looked as if she had stepped into a snowstorm broken only by the age-darkened wood of several doorways and the clean-swept floor ahead of her.

"Keep moving," Rydan directed her gruffly when her progress slowed.

They walked a long distance, past a *Y*-shaped junction, and then entered a stairwell. Here, the walls were plain, but when they emerged a few levels down, the hall showed a slowly shifting scene of cattle grazing in a field. Again, she slowed, and again, she was verbally prodded along. This time, the reason for her distraction came from the way the cattle on the walls looked almost nothing like the cattle she was used to seeing. These—presumably the local type—had short, stubby horns, not the longer, more elegant kind seen on the Plains cattle.

They could hardly use those for making into drinking cups, she thought, bemused by the idea. *One pair of cups per bovine? Not to mention a lack of horn buttons, toggles, belt buckles, spoons, and all other manner of useful . . . My, this room is big!*

The walls in the broad, towering, octagonal chamber had been painted to resemble a snowstorm made of pink cherry blossoms swirling around gray-barked trees. Red velvet carpeted the floor, conjoining four hallways, each just like the one she had exited. Around the room, tiers of balconies marked each floor, and the great dome vaulted overhead. Long, sunset-hued banners half hid the main support columns.

There was a fifth length of carpet, Rora belatedly noticed. It was a little narrower than the others, and it angled toward one of the four sets of windows spaced between the hallways. In fact, it led to a simple, low dais of the sort Aitava of the Sixteen Shapes preferred whenever she was in the City, replete with a bench seat broad enough for two, and padded with aquamarine silk not that far from the hue of the Sun's Belt Sea after that nasty storm had passed. Above that bench hovered a magnificent, elegant, gleaming thing.

"Oh!" Her exclamation, while not loud, echoed through the chamber.

It's a crown, Rora thought as she stared, absently turning to walk that way. *A Gods-Blessed, incipient-kingdom crown! I've heard of this phenomenon—who in all of Shattered Aiar hasn't, as kingdom after kingdom drags itself out of our lingering ashes? But, I've never* seen *one until now.* The Shifterai Queen's own crown wasn't nearly as spectacular, but then it had been worn on the brows of female shapechangers for roughly a hundred and fifty years by now. This crown was brand-new and still floating within the divine glow of the Heavens.

The sight of rose pink wonder swirling around her body made her blink, returning her attention to the rest of the world before she could get close enough to touch it and perhaps offend the people of this land. Aware that she had diverted from her path, Rora glanced back over her shoulder in time to see Rydan stopping in front of a man with exotic, coppery blond hair. They had a similar build, but comparing the scowl on Rydan's face and his darker-hued, roiling emotions, versus the smile on the other man's face and his pastel feelings, they were as different as day and night.

Rora started in their direction, guessing it was time to meet the others in this strange, echoingly empty place. It was a palace, but she hadn't seen any servants. As she crossed from carpet to stone, angling their way, the two men exchanged quiet words. Then the redhead lifted his finger, glancing past his brother's shoulder to her, indicating she should wait.

Stopping, she saw him nod, and guessed they wanted a private moment alone, first. But it disturbed her to see Rydan's aura darkening and tightening around himself, binding him in increasingly sharp veils of loathing and shame. Thunder rumbled outside, though it still looked like a mostly clear day, confusing her. Wanting to help, yet not knowing if she should interrupt when she had clearly been gestured to stay out of the way, Rora waited impatiently for some sign of what to do.

The words choked in his throat. Rydan knew he had to say it, to confess his damnable sin, but didn't know how to tell his twin that . . . that . . . He let out a frustrated breath and said the first thing he could think of saying.

"I am going to *kill* Morganen." He struggled to keep his voice low, not to let his rage overtake him.

That made Trevan blink his green eyes. "Morg? Whatever for?"

Trevan glanced past his shoulder and raised his hand. Glancing back, Rydan saw the young woman halting, thankfully staying out of earshot. He turned back to his twin and confessed their sibling's crime. "He slipped me some sort of drug at breakfast. I . . . *dreamed.* And somehow, our lying, manipulative brother slipped her past my wards and into *my* bedroom—the hidden one! I thought I was *dreaming*, Trevan—and I couldn't control myself!"

Green eyes widened, flicking back and forth between Rydan and the woman behind him. "I don't understand . . ."

"I *touched* her!" Rydan hissed, heart pounding painfully in his chest. His face felt as if it was on fire, as if he had thrust it into one of Koranen's forge-fires. "Just . . . just my hand—my lips—but I *violated* your woman. I don't care what the Gods have Prophesied. I have had enough of his manipulations, and I am going to *kill* that son of a—a *shame* to his very own mother!"

Trevan's mouth dropped open, eyes flicking back and forth between his twin and the woman who was at the heart of Rydan's shame.

"He *deserves* to die . . . as do I," Rydan finished under his breath, legs threatening to shake, and so sick to his stomach at this confrontation, he could barely breathe.

"Whoa!" Trevan snapped, scowling and grabbing his twin by the shoulders. "Get that nonsense out of your head!"

Lifting his arms, Rydan knocked away his brother's grip. "Don't touch me—and didn't you hear what I *said*? I *violated* the sanctity of your bride!"

Grabbing his shoulders again, Trevan spun his twin around, jerking him to a stop so that he faced the concerned woman standing near the middle of the hall. Shame burned in his stomach again, warring with the sharp edge of his twin's bizarre amusement. That was, until Trev pointed firmly over his shoulder and muttered in his ear, making them burn from a different reason.

"*That* is the *second* woman to reach the Isle today, Brother. The first one, I encountered *hours* ago. Since I'm assuming you woke up only a short while ago, that means she is woman number *six* to grace us with her presence, and *not* woman number five. You did not violate my woman; *my* woman is down in the herb room getting some scratches treated by our Healer. *That* woman is *your* woman . . . and you cannot violate what is yours. At least, she doesn't *look* like she feels violated." Releasing Rydan's shoulders, Trevan planted a palm in the middle of his back and shoved, making his shocked younger twin stumble forward, toward the woman in question with the admonition, "Go get her, Rydan; she's *all* yours!"

Vaguely aware of being abandoned by his twin, of Trevan disappearing back into the eastern wing, Rydan stared at Rora. An uncommon, uncomfortable, unpleasant emotion now rolled up from his gut. It wasn't the choking, strangling, self-aimed loathing of earlier. No, this was something else. Terror. For a moment, his flushed face turned icy cold, washing over his body in a soul-chilling wave . . . Then anger boiled up through his veins.

Damn the Gods! How dare *They play with me—and* damn *Morganen, too!*

He couldn't strike out at her; *she* wasn't the source of his pain, though she was a fellow victim. And with Morg nowhere in sight—author of this fiasco that he was—Rydan had nowhere to release his pain and rage, save straight up into the sky.

"GODS!"

Thunder *BOOMED* overhead, shaking the windowpanes around them, making her wince and flinch from the paired flash of lightning, brighter even than the light of day.

A door banged open in the distance, and a strawberry blond whirlwind of fury yelled at him. "*Goddammit,* Rydan! I just ripped a huge *hole* in Saber's shirt! If you're going to play with *lightning*—" Kelly demanded, flinging her hand imperiously at one of the banks of windows filling in the spaces of the octagonal hall between the four wings of the palace "—take it *elsewhere*!"

Whirling in a ball of visible indignation, she stalked back the way she came. The door slammed shut, reverberating with less than a twentieth of the force of his sonic boom, but almost as much irritation. Pain stabbed through him as she left. Crying out, Rydan clamped his hands over his ears, curling over, trying to make it stop.

It was no use; this wasn't a physical pain. The only way he had ever found to stop himself from hurting this bad was to run away—but there was too much light in the donjon for him to shadow-race. Bolting forward, he aimed for the northern corridor, flinching away from the green-eyed woman who had forced him to leave his sanctuary. He could feel her sudden, sharply rising fear mingling with his twin's equally abrupt worry like a double stab in his back.

"Hey—don't leave me *alone*!"

Staggering, Rydan dropped to one knee, but the pain of landing on the age-worn stone didn't register under the bludgeoning panic that had struck. Desperate to escape, he lurched to his feet and ran, flinching away from his brother's concern, and abandoning her—Rora—to the others. Even if it meant the guilt formed by his broken promise to protect her chased him up the hall.

FIVE

It started with the furious woman on the balcony and the strange words she had hurled at Rydan. Irritated orange fire leaped down and slashed into the dark-bound mage. Rora stared in shock as the darkness ripped open from scalp to shoulder, pouring out crimson blood. She was so shocked, it made her blink off her Sight for a moment, expecting to see a real wound. But no, he had simply doubled over, hands clasped to his head. Then the colors raged back, deep indigoes, sickly greens, and that crimson wound that looked all too real, cutting across his head.

Then he moved, abandoning one corridor entrance for another, running—*running*—back the way they had come. *He's leaving me? Alone? In* this *place, without anyone else to help me?* "Hey!—Don't leave me *alone*!"

Rora Saw her panic rising, forming an ivory white horn that had stabbed into the dark-shrouded mage's back, wounding him a *second* time. This time, it was a stab wound turned gangrenous at its edges, though the blood it bled was fresher and redder than the dark crimson of the other wound. The impact, for all it was pure emotion, drove him painfully to one knee.

Choking in horror, Rora struggled to control her panic,

using her Sight to focus her will, reeling her fear back into her body. The black-haired mage regained his feet, sprinting as if demons, not mere feelings, spurred him away from her. Not that she could blame him, not if those wounds hurt as much as they looked like they hurt. Closing her eyes, she banished the ability to See emotions and focused on her breathing as the priestesses had taught her during puberty, calming her mind—and with it, her heart—as quickly as she could.

Her mother had sworn up one side and down the other that the Gods Themselves had kept Their Hands on Rora as a child, keeping her sweet, sunny, fearless, and even tempered. But when puberty had hit, whatever protections They had held upon the power within her had eased. After Rora had nearly torched their encampments half a dozen times, Fennon and Ziella had packed up both of their daughters and taken them to the City. As soon as her powers were measured, Mara had been apprenticed to Aitava, Queen of the Shifterai, as well as to many of her advisors who had come and gone. Rora had been handed off to the few priestesses who had magic, in the attempt to control whatever magic lay within her.

It hadn't worked, of course. While Mara had studied the stretching of flesh and bone, Rora had struggled to master her will. At first, they had thought she was just blocked; many young mages couldn't quite tap into their powers. But after extensive examination, it had been determined that the blockage *was* her magic . . . and that it was carefully and firmly containing what the priestesses could only describe as "the heart of a thousand mages squeezed into one." The only thing she *could* do was learn to control herself so that she didn't spark another pure-magic fire.

The discipline that helped control—or at least stabilize—her magic helped her now. Within moments, she was able to open her eyes, knowing she would See a much calmer aura—she squeaked, flinching back from the coppery blond man, greenish blue concern swirling around the arm reaching for her. "*Gods*! Don't touch me!"

He pulled his arm back, brow crinkling in a confused frown. "Why?"

"Don't you *dare* touch my sister!" To Rora's surprise, her own twin, Mara, charged into the huge chamber, scowling at the man, who glanced between the two of them in confusion. "*Back off* from her!"

Hands up, the redheaded man did as she demanded, giving the two sisters room for their reunion. But not a pleasant one. Shifting her scowl from him to Rora, Mara glared at her twin.

"*What* in all the Gods' Names are *you doing* here? I thought I *told* you to stay at the waterfall!"

Now *Rora* felt as if she was being struck by emotions, flinching back from her sister's righteous but overblown attack. Knowing she had to stop this madness before it could worsen, Rora drew in a deep breath, clenched her hands, and did what she rarely did, ever: She yelled back at her sister. *"Stop it!"*

Mara jerked her head back, as if she, too, had been struck. Struggling for breath, for control, Rora forced herself to speak in a calmer voice. A firm one, but calmer than her shout.

"We are being *disrespectful* to our hosts by shouting like a couple of . . . of Amazai *seagulls*! This is *not* the time or place to have this discussion."

Mara's jaw tightened. Catching Rora's wrist, she tugged her toward the same hallway Rydan had used. "Then we will *find* a place to have this discussion!"

"Shouldn't you introduce her, first?" a voice called down to them. Both twins stopped and tipped their heads back, peering up at the redhead Rora had seen only moments before. She had come back and now leaned her forearms on the stone balustrade so she could peer down at them.

Giving up, Mara complied. "This is my sister, Arora Fen Ziel of the Shifting Plains."

Rora, hearing the honorific, tried not to wrinkle her nose in visible distaste. She always felt like a fraud whenever someone called her that; as a Shifterai, it was only her due *if* she was a shapechanger, like her sister. The priestesses had bestowed the title on her, claiming that she was Favored by the Gods because of what she carried, but the title didn't feel like it belonged to her.

"You are all forbidden to touch her," Mara added. This time Rora had to conceal a wince as well, as her sister was sometimes just a little too blunt-spoken. Mara gestured between her and the woman on the balcony. "Arora, this is Kelly, incipient Queen of Nightfall."

Rora jerked her gaze back to her sister, affronted by the *lack* of a title—even if the woman wasn't Shifterai and neither expected nor understood what it meant—when her sister was so prickly proud about using her twin's empty, useless honorific. "*Ai*kelly!" she snapped, stressing the double honorific with a thump of her sister's arm. "Show some respect."

"She is an *incipient* queen," Mara retorted, flipping her hand at the bench off to the side, and its hovering, golden coronet.

"Then at the very least, that deserves an *A* . . . but she *will* be a queen," Rora stated under her breath, "and currently still outranks *you*." Tamping down her irritation, Rora looked up at the woman on the balcony and curtsied. She *was* civilized, even if she was very far from home. "It is an honor to meet you, *A*kelly of Nightfall."

That was to remind her sister that, incipient or not, the woman *was* going to be the ruler of this land, provided nothing happened to interfere. It might have been tactless to remind her sister of it, but unless they could figure out a way to fix Rora's problems, Amara, Princess of the Shifting Plains, would probably never become Aimara, Queen of the Shifterai. Pledged as she was to protect her twin from those who would kidnap and harm her, Mara had complained before that she had to stay with her sister, even when it meant having to leave the Plains and all her plans and expectations for the future far behind. This moment was no different.

If only Mara could learn to let go of what could *have been, and embrace what* can *be*, Rora thought wistfully, glancing at her sister again. *Then she wouldn't be quite so stress filled all the time.*

"Arora, this is Trevan of Nightfall," Mara introduced, gesturing at the redhead who had talked with that poor, beset man, Rydan. "He is the *mage*," she stressed in not quite subtle warning, "I had spotted on the beach. In fact, this is a whole *island* of mages."

"I beg to differ," the strawberry blond woman on the balcony interjected, a smile curling her lips. "I'm about as far from a mage as anyone can get." Her smile quirked higher on one side. "I rule this land through sheer charm, a hint of intimidation, and good common sense—why don't you bring her up here, so we can speak more comfortably?"

"If Your Majesty will forgive us," Mara countered, using the same smooth, polite tone of voice she would have used on a fellow princess, Rora noted, listening, "I really do need to speak with my sister first. Alone."

Hauling her sister under the balcony the incipient queen stood on, Mara strode up the hall. In tow, Rora put up with it only long enough to catch up to her twin's long-legged stride and free her wrist. "I *am* capable of walking on my own, you know!"

She kept her voice low, aware that the corridor might funnel their voices back to the two redheads in that large, domed hall.

"I am *very* upset with you. I *told* you to wait at the waterfall until I had studied this place!—We'll discuss this in here," she added, opening a door at random. The room inside was a little dizzying, as it was painted in the slowly rippling, blurring sort of image one would see if the viewer had submersed himself in a turbulent, rocky stream. Mara pushed her sister inside and shut the door. "Now, how in the name of Mother Earth did you get here so fast? Did someone find you? Did anyone touch you?"

"I explored the cave. There was a magical cart that had been sent to dump rock chips, and when I asked if it was a good idea to hop inside as soon it was empty, the answer was yes . . . so I *did*," Rora asserted, turning to face her sister at the midpoint of the chair-and-table-strewn room. From the placement of the chairs, she suspected it was meant to be a gaming room; card games were very popular in Aiar, and the chairs and tables seemed to be arranged for it. "I Saw an opportunity, and I *took* it . . . and I *will* not apologize for it."

"How am I supposed to *protect* you, if you run off like that?" Mara retorted. "And you didn't answer my question! Did anyone *touch* you?"

Rora could almost *feel* those fingers at the demand, rippling and working their undeniable spell between her thighs. Her face flushed at the memory, to the point where someone far less sharp-sighted than her sister would have noticed.

"Arora Fen Ziel, Princess of the People, *who touched you*?"

Defensively, Rora folded her arms across her chest and jutted out her chin. "I'm not going to tell you—you'll just blow it out of proportion."

"Blow it out of proportion? Dammit, Sister, only one—" Mara cut off, grimaced, and corrected herself. "Only *two* people on this land are *not* mages, from what Trevan said. Unless either of them was that redheaded pretender or a little boy I haven't even met yet—*anyone* touching you would have been a mage—how many *times* do we have to run?"

"He was drugged!" Rora found herself admitting defensively. She thought of the angst and suffering the poor, black-haired mage had undergone and gave her sister an annoyed look. "He said he thought he was dreaming, and since I was in his bedchamber—*don't* give me that look!" she protested as her sister's face went from irritated to taken aback. "I went searching for a refreshing room and didn't realize the bedroom was occupied until after I stepped out again!

"Since I was in his bedchamber, and . . ." She struggled to find a way to be tactful without lying, because her sister would call her all shades of irresponsible for having approached a dreaming stranger. "And I had to pass close to the bed. He thought I was someone else, in his drugged stupor, dragged me down, and . . ." *What do I tell her that won't make her reach for a gelding knife? The least damaging thing, I guess.* "And kissed me."

That got her a look of such shocked affrontery, her sister looked like she had bitten into an unripe fruit.

"You look like a sour-faced aunty," Rora pointed out dryly, once again wishing her twin would *let go* of life on the Shifting Plains.

That wrinkled Mara's nose even further. "And *you* look like you . . . like . . ."

"Like what?" Rora challenged her, hands slipping from their folded position.

"Like you *enjoyed* it!" Mara accused.

Planting her hands on her hips, Rora faced down her twin. "I *did*."

"Arora Fen Ziel," her sister started, and Rora cut her off.

"*Rora* Fen Ziel! I am *not* a princess of any people, not anymore!" she stated firmly. "Get it through your head, Sister: *We* are in *exile*. For as long as I live, I will be carrying this . . . *thing* around inside of me. And as long as I am carrying it," Rora reminded her twin, "every single mage around the world will be wanting to get their hands on it, *except here*!"

"You don't know that!" Mara scoffed.

"I *do* know it. I Saw it," Rora defended.

Disgusted, her twin flipped up her hands, then planted them on her own hips. "That's what you *say*, but you're no Seer. The Gods didn't bless you with Divine Foresight. They *Cursed* you with that *thing* you're carrying!"

Rora gritted her teeth. "I may not be a Seer . . . but I can still *See*. And I have *Seen* that our days of running end here, in this very place! Open your eyes, *Mara*. We are so far from the land of our birth, they don't even know the significance of *Ai* and *A*—so why bother using them? Why bother dragging around the dust and the grass of the Plains, when we *should* be learning how to move through these trees? *I* am not going to hide behind the walls of Shifterai customs. Not when I'm never going to return to Shifterai lands!"

Her sister flinched back, and Rora caught her wrist, trying to make her twin understand.

"*You* have to face the fact that, if you still want to protect *me*, that means *you* will never return to the Plains again." The words were too harsh even for the gentle tone she tried to use, but Rora needed to make her twin understand. "Face the truth and embrace it, Mara. As *I* have done."

Releasing her sister, she watched Mara's mouth pinch sullenly. "I am what I was born, Sister. A Princess of the People. I *should* have been Queen, were it not for you."

That hurt. It was just as much truth as her own statement, but it hurt all the same. Mastering herself, Rora offered her sister the only thing she could. "Then *leave* me. I *know* I will be safe here! No, I am not a Seer, but I *still See*."

"I gave my word!" Mara reminded her. "I gave up my birthright for you—try to show some gratitude!"

"Then lighten up your *attitude*!" Before she could say anything worse, Rora reined back her next retort, expelling what she could of her anger in a hard exhale. *If that man Rydan were here, he'd likely be bleeding in several places, just from the backlash of this mess.* Cutting her hands between them, Rora negated the rest of the argument. "On this point—at least until you can see *reason*—we will just have to agree to disagree.

"Don't think you can run my life," she added in warning, green eyes boring into gold. "You may protect my life . . . but you *aren't the one* living it."

Spinning on her heel, growling under her breath, Mara yanked open the door—and jumped back as a cat yowled. Rora jumped, too, startled by the apparition. It—he, for it was a ginger cat, with coppery-striped orange fur—sat on his haunches just long enough to reassure himself with a little grooming. Then he padded forward and rubbed up against her sister's leg, seeking reassurance and attention.

She watched her sister sigh and scoop the cat up, cuddling the big fluffball, who immediately purred. He even tried to groom Mara's cheek, so happy was the house cat to be cuddled. It was hard to stay angry when a clearly pampered pet was being so affectionate with a blatant stranger. Letting go of the rest of her irritation, Rora joined her sister at the door. She offered her fingers to the tom, who sniffed them daintily and permitted her to scratch behind his ears. He squirmed in Mara's grip, almost dropping out of her arms, then pushed upward, seeking more attention from Rora.

"Mother Earth, he's fat," Mara muttered, shifting her grip on him to get him into a more comfortable position. Rora was in a position to see those green eyes narrow a bit, as if the cat had somehow understood her comment, but he purred and nuzzled after a moment, burying his triangular face under the loose strands of Mara's long black hair as she stroked his fur. "Probably spoiled with tidbits from the table, as well as mice from the granary."

"Probably. Look, I'm sorry we yelled at each other. This whole chased-into-exile thing doesn't sit well with me, either," Rora offered. "But I am trying to make the best of things. All I ask is that you *let* me try to be happy, regardless of our circumstances. You *do* want me to be happy, don't you?"

"I want you to be *safe*, first and foremost," Mara countered. "*Then* you can be happy."

Rora, enjoying the soft fur under her fingers and the way the cat was easing both of them into a better mood, allowed herself a brief chuckle. "If I'm *happy*, then wouldn't it follow that I'm also safe?"

"Maybe," Mara begrudged her. The cat nuzzled her, twisting his head upside down to peer up at her, and she smiled. Involuntarily, but it was a smile nonetheless. "Fine . . . I'm sorry I yelled at you, too. It just . . . It seems like you don't take our predicament *seriously* enough."

"Oh, I take it seriously enough. I just don't want to be like *you*," Rora dared to tease, switching from scritching the kitty to tugging on one of her sister's locks, "and take it *too* seriously."

Mara wrinkled her nose and changed the subject. "Come. There's a set of rooms they've offered to me. If nothing else, we could at least rest before supper. At which, I intend to interrogate everyone available with a Truth Stone, in order to discern exactly what kind of a threat these people are." At Rora's bemused look, Mara amended, "Well, let's just say I came up with the possibility of my 'knowing' the secret location of some powerful Artifact that most mages want, and I'm going to be asking what everyone's intentions will be toward that possible source of power."

"That's a clever twist," Rora praised her sister. The cat's tail twitched; figuring he was annoyed by the lack of attention, she petted him again. "But where will you get a Truth Stone?"

"The redheaded man, Trevan, has promised to loan me one. He promised it *on* the Stone," she added, leading the way out of the gaming room.

Rora couldn't be absolutely sure, but she thought she saw a hint of a blush in her sister's cheeks . . . and remembered what she had asked the power within her, to show her a place where both she *and* her sister could lead happy, safe lives.

Now if she can only get the stick of Shifterai customs dislodged from her breikas, *and allow herself to* enjoy *non-Shifterai customs, here in non-Shifterai lands . . .*

Mara glanced back over her shoulder. "Are you sure this other man didn't notice anything?"

Rora shook her head. "If he did, he didn't say anything,

and probably mistook it for part of the dream. But I suppose if he's at supper, you can always just get him alone long enough to interrogate him with that Truth Stone."

"Make sure you point him out."

Rydan entered the Fountain Hall, winded from running so far and so fast, and staggered over to one of the support pillars. Slumping back against it, he let his trembling legs shift out from under the rest of him, sliding him down to the polished floor. This time, it had been worse. The beast had clawed him, stabbed him; it crushed his flesh, made him feel as if there should be blood on his palms from the pain of his wounds . . . but nothing stained his skin. Tightening his hands into fists, Rydan shuddered.

The Fountain Hall was his last refuge, his final sanctuary. No one could get into it from outside, and after having one of his elder brothers sent through the Fountainway to him from another continent by that brother's brand-new wife—their relationship had made him cringe during the short time it had taken Dominor and Serina to fix the problems between them—he had erected too many wardings and fail-safes for anything beyond a voice sent in message to reach him without his direct permission. There was no way anyone could pry him out of here, if Rydan chose to stay . . . though thirst and hunger might.

Right now, though, his pre-emptied stomach had twisted the remainder of itself into knots. Food wasn't on his mind. No, it had to be a pair of green eyes wide with surprise, of soft cheeks flushed with desire, that haunted him. Part of him—it had to be the drug, whatever Morg had slipped him—longed to see those eyes widen and those cheeks blush once more. His youngest brother had much to answer for, given what had just happened. Slipping him some sort of love-hallucinating drug, easing the woman through his wards so that she would reach him while he dreamed . . .

Violating her in my sleep . . .

Bracing his elbows on his knees, Rydan buried his face in his hands. His brother's voice echoed into his thoughts. *You did not violate my woman*; my *woman is down in the herb room getting some scratches treated by our Healer.* That *woman is* your *woman . . .* that *woman is* your *woman . . .*

You cannot violate what is yours . . . Go get her, Rydan; she's all *yours . . . cannot violate what is yours . . .*

But I violated her! Groaning, he tipped his head back, thumping it against the carved granite pillar bracing his back. *Destiny or not, no one should be forced like that—and I* violated *her right to choose!*

Eyes squeezed shut, he blocked out the play of lights that flickered through the vaulted hall, emanating from the silent, chaotic power of the singularity that formed the Fountain and the pipes and ribbons of energy that arced up and flowed out like the fronds of an anemone around the base of its collection pool. Most of them doubled back down into catch-basins in the floor that then drained through minute cracks in the mountain, spreading out to diffuse with distance, and infuse the countryside with various energies. Some poured into holes in the columns closest to the Fountain, while a few others rose up to the ceiling, where the energies vanished into funnels that drained to somewhere else.

It was comforting to be in the presence of that light and its power, for it soothed his damaged nerves, calming his inner beast. It was like how waves washing on a shore tricked listening ears into relaxing under the constant susurration of sound. In the presence of so much power, lesser concerns were masked and troubles eroded. Though the lights were sometimes peacefully hypnotic, right now he didn't need to look at something that roiled and shifted like his stomach still threatened to do.

Slowly, the pain inside of him eased. The stinging of his nerves settled down, prickling less and less under the magic that thrummed throughout the Hall. Resting against the cool, hard stone, Rydan let his anguish seep out of him. Stone was soothing, even if it was cold. It blocked pain, eased anxiety, replaced agony with relief. And what it could not absorb from his flesh, the Fountain bathed away with its scintillating light and silent vibrations.

Memory came back to him, unwelcome and unbidden. The taste of her mouth, the soft curves of her body . . . He pushed it away, not wanting to remember anything else his fingers had touched. But something lingered. Something familiar. Eyes closed, Rydan found himself straining to remember what it was. She had felt . . . like . . .

She felt like home, he realized, opening his eyelids, only to blink against the pulsing light of the singularity resting in the air several body lengths from him. *She felt like . . . like* this *place. Thrumming, yet soothing. Gods, I wanted to sink into her like I do the Fountain and just bathe in the feel of her . . .*

It was a stupid notion, of course. The sensations of *home* and *soothing* were clearly by-products of whatever Morganen had used to dose him. And he couldn't *bathe* in anyone. As for Morganen . . .

One too many betrayals, Little Brother. When I can stomach being among the others again, you will *pay*, Rydan decided grimly. He felt his anger stirring again, felt the twinges under his skin warning him against pursuing that particular line of thought while still hurting inside, and pushed it away. *I am surrounded by the solid comfort of stone and washed clean by a sea of pure energy . . .*

Not that he would ever be foolish enough to enter the Fountain while agitated. Mastery of a Fountain required self-mastery of the mages who attempted to claim it. They had to be powerful enough to handle the wild, strenuous energies without literally burning up from the inside out. They had to have enough self-discipline *not* to say or do anything that would cause the Fountain to react to the wrong thing. Serina and Dominor's relationship had come about as a side effect of trying to cure one such error, in fact.

Rydan hadn't had enough self-discipline, at first. Looking around the longish Hall, with its rows of widely spaced pillars and vaulted ceiling sections lit by geometrically carved suncrystals transmitting light from the quartz-studded peaks of the mountains, he remembered what had led to him finding this place. It was his sanctuary now, but it had taken time to make it that way.

When he and his brothers had been ordered into exile, Rydan had accepted it with relief. His beast had birthed itself at some undefined point in puberty, growing stronger alongside his magic and his body. By the time the Council of Mages on the Katani mainland had decided that the eight of them fulfilled the Seer Draganna's ancient, rhyming Prophecy, Rydan had been a nerve-wracked twenty-two.

Ten years' worth of dealing with the beast under his skin, exacerbated by the presence of others, had forced him to shun daylight hours, for that was when most of the others living in Corvis Castle had been awake, making him feel as if they were pressing in around him like a smothering blanket, even if they didn't come near. Being exiled to an island where contact with outsiders would be limited to supply ships once every two weeks had turned out to be a blessing in disguise.

Not that Saber didn't knock it in my head a time or two that I had to show *myself at least twice a day, to prove I was still alive . . . which was a good thing when that bastard Broger started sending his magical pets. If we had known at the time it was him, I would have done something about it. Ended the misery he was inflicting on everyone around him, including poor Alys. Of course,* he allowed wryly, *if I or Morg had smashed him into dust years ago, Alys would not have felt the need to flee her uncle's grip, which would have left Wolfer without his Destined bride.*

But before she came here, before Morg-the-Matchmaker dragged Kelly from her world to this one, to inflict her on Saber . . . I had finally started to heal *from the wounds of my damnable beast . . .*

Scrubbing his hands over his face, Rydan remembered the day Saber had decided he and his brothers should keep their magical efforts confined to the outer towers ringing the compound. There were eight of them, and they were detached from the main palace, if one didn't count the drawbridges connecting the palace wings to the ramparts of the compound wall. Rydan could still see his brother, honey blond hair gleaming with highlights that rivaled those of Trevan's copper blond locks, thanks to the glow of the setting sun. Saber had explained that they needed to start making things to sell to the twice-weekly ships that stopped by, so that they could gain more than just the bare pittances the Council was permitting to be sent their way; if anything exploded, burned, or melted as a result of their attempts at creating magical items for sale, it was better not to ruin their best source of shelter.

Each brother laid claim to one of the towers nearest the particular wing he had claimed for his living quarters. Technically, Rydan's palace wing was the northwest one, while his tower was due north, directly opposite the fork in the *Y*-shaped wing, but then they had all taken towers shifted partway to the right around the wall. Rydan knew from his brothers' grumblings that the towers had contained more or less the same things: old bunk beds, tables, benches, age-worn bits of armor, rusting spears, and brittle bows and arrows abandoned when the island's previous residents had fled more than two centuries ago.

Despite Evanor's complaints that his brothers never bothered to clean anything if they didn't have to, Rydan had systematically worked his way through each room in his own tower, removing refuse, storing what could be salvaged, and spell-scrubbing his way from the attic crawl space all the way down to the subbasement level. It was down there that he had found the trapdoor . . . or rather, it had found him. Picking up a scrap of dusty parchment to see if anything had been written on it, his knuckles had scraped the floor.

Runes had blazed at the contact, forming an elongated rectangle that lifted open after a moment, revealing the trapdoor that had lain hidden for so long. Warily, Rydan had gone through it, quickly finding himself descending into a half-hewn maze of corridors and steps. Symbols had lit on some of the walls, runes that brightened at his approach, then faded, luring him onward.

Luring him here.

SIX

When he had first seen the huge, shimmering ball of swirling, spilling energies hovering over the basin, and its array of pipes spouting colorful, filtered energies from that basin like narrow vines growing out in different directions, the younger Rydan hadn't known what to make of it. The pulsing energies had drawn him to within a few pillars of it, but a golden mist had snapped into place between two of those pillars, stopping him. From that mist, a woman's voice had spoken, strange and powerful, compelling yet echoing and distorted. He could still remember the riddle the unseen woman had given him.

To control within
Is to control without
But to control without
You must control within
You do not control within
You do not control without
Take yourself within
Or take yourself without
The power within
Is the power without

But the power without
Is without the within.

No matter how he had tried to approach the shimmering thing, Rydan couldn't reach it. The mist had risen up between each pair of pillars when he tried to approach, blocking him as firmly as if the swirling energies had been formed from stone. In fact, the angrier he had gotten, the farther away the walls had pushed him, forcing him to turn away from the Fountain, forcing him back to the opposite side.

That had given him his first clue. After the fourth time of increased frustration, to the point where he had struck the mists with his fists, Rydan had been shoved back several steps by reciprocal energies. It was then that he realized what the *within* part of control meant: He had to control *himself* in order to pass the mists of the pillars. That task hadn't been easy, though being separated for hours on end from his brothers did help while he explored this underground realm. At least, he was calmer and found it easier to control himself when he wasn't forced to spend excessive time with the others.

Focusing and practicing his magic had also helped get him closer, but only by so much. Together, the combination got him past the first riddle, but not the next, leaving him with one row of columns between himself and that scintillating sphere. The mist that stopped him had shifted to an opalescent silver, and the message of the voice changed.

You are what you are
You know what to be
Drink in your power
Fulfill Destiny.

And again, he was blocked. It wasn't until almost a month later, after retreating from the buzzing energies of a storm sweeping across the island, that the voice had spoken to him. He had heard a smile in her voice, and her words had puzzled him.

Getting closer
Getting warmer
But you're not your

Brother's charmer
You are what you are
You know what to be
Drink in your power
Fulfill Destiny.

Frustrated, he had pushed against the mist . . . and it had bowed under his touch. The barrier had merely bent a little. Up until that moment, it had been a solid wall for all that it looked like a translucent haze of glittering mist. It took him a few moments to realize the only thing different about him was the storm energy still singing along his nerves. Racing back up to the surface had proved futile, however; the storm had moved on, leaving him to wait impatiently a few more weeks for the next one.

Fully charged, hair and clothes crackling with static energy, Rydan remembered descending to this chamber, fully confident he would finally be able to touch that fascinating, glowing orb and its dripping energies. He had passed through the final row of pillars, only to be stopped by one of the fountaining pipes of amber-hued energy. The graceful curve bent away from its catch-basin and poured into a roughly body-length mist that splashed and faded as it curled across the floor.

Not that easy,
Not that quick
To get inside
To pass this trick
To tune yourself
To ring the bell
Who do you serve
Heaven, or Hell?

A Truth Stone had emerged from the mist, with that new challenge. The white marble disc looked exactly the same as the ones Rydan had seen his father, the late Count Saveno of Corvis, use when sitting in judgment on some petition or problem in their home county. Catching it as it dropped, Rydan had fumbled with it for a moment, then clutched it in his hand, thought of the riddle, and gave his answer. Heaven, of course. Uncertain what to do with it, he finally lobbed it back into the roiling amber mist.

Once the translucent cloud contracted abruptly around the Truth Stone, he had tried to get to the object of his curiosity, but the mist had shifted, blocking his path. Then something clattered to the ground. Rydan, crouching, found and picked up a scroll. The unseen woman spoke again, her words still echoing oddly in his ears, though this time without poetry in mind.

Study. Learn. But do not take it out of this Hall, or forfeit all. When you are ready, when you understand, by Stone you will be judged once again. Only when you have passed and bound your powers in an Oath of Service will I release this place to you, who are worthy and welcome. But do step up to the task. I did not know how long it would take for you to arrive, but you are most definitely needed, now that the time is near. Approach only when you have read and learned.

With that, the mist had boiled toward him, forcing him back in wide-eyed wariness before it could touch him, until he was behind the closest row of columns . . . and the silver curtain had come back. The scroll, upon examination, explained it all. The shimmering sphere was a Fountain, a source-point of incredible power. Its pipes and ribbons, like some exotic, thin-petalled flower, were filtered magical energies a hundred times more potent than what most mages could conjure and control. A Fountain was a rare resource that had to be guarded against evil intent and against a lack of self-control in the person guarding it.

Usually, that was a mage; those who were born powerful were built capable of handling and manipulating a great deal of energy. Sometimes, it was a Seer; they were not born with the ability to manipulate power, but they could act as a conduit for it, if that power was given a specific purpose before they touched it. That was what the pipes were for, of course; filtering and purposing magic. Even an unskilled Seer could perform magic with a Fountain. They didn't need skill, just the ability to hold and aim power.

That was how Seers could withstand the touch of the Gods in their lives; the Gods' will shaped what They poured into Their Servants, and the Seers did whatever that power directed them to do. In the case of a Fountain, a Seer could not only anticipate through Divine Foresight when a problem might occur and what it might be, they could also take the energies filtered by the artistic, fountainlike pipes, tap into the funnel-shaped basins that the energies of the pipes poured into, and direct those pre-purposed energies at a specific target. It was one of the few ways a Seer could cast magic, for he had no natural ability to draw upon his own power and shape a spell.

A mage, on the other hand, could use the energies raw and fresh from a Fountain, reshaping them to his or her will. But that took a lot of personal energy and self-control, since it was literally being shaped by word and will alone. Or they could do like a Seer did and direct the pre-filtered energies found beyond the basin. That took far less effort. In fact, it took very little personal power to use the correct pre-filtered energies for a particular task, yet whatever the intended task was would still be fully empowered. This was why it was imperative that a good-souled person be a Guardian. Putting so much readily available power, easily manipulated, into the hands of someone with evil intent was a Very Bad Idea.

But it only worked when even a mage of good intent was calm; the scroll was very clear on the consequences of a troubled mage touching the energy-waters of a Fountain.

For over two and a half years, Rydan had managed to balance his need to be untroubled versus his brothers' demands for *some* social interaction. His brothers had their own quirks and temperaments, their differences and their similarities. They were familiar, and he could adjust to their mood swings more or less as soon as they happened. For roughly three years since taking up the Guardianship of the Nightfall Fountain, Rydan had managed to use its powers without having to work very hard at being calm.

Then the woman Kelly had been dragged into their world. Fierce, determined, and scared to her back teeth at first about being trapped in a castle on an island on a world in another dimension with eight bachelor men and no magic of her own to counteract anything they might have done to her . . . if they hadn't been raised to be gentlemen. Their father and their mother, the gentle Lady Annia, had dented proper courtesies into their heads, but that didn't stop the freckled outworlder from being . . . vigorous, to put it politely.

After Rydan had spent a few months learning to endure Kelly's presence, Alys had arrived. Shy and hurting one moment, bold as brass the next, being around her was like being on a tree swing, never quite knowing what momentum the bowing of the branch overhead would add to the ride. He was careful to not upset her whenever he had to be around her, for that upset him, making the beast within him nauseated from her shifts in attitude.

Serina was somewhat better; the Arithmancer was comfortable to be around when she was working . . . until the magic she was calculating vexed her. Then she was like a pressurized pipe that had lost its containment spells and popped its cork, spewing energies everywhere. Uncomfortable, to say the least. Not to mention her physical nausea increased the discomfort of her presence, for him.

Mariel was probably the calmest of the women on the island, but she was a mother as well as a Healer, and her son got on her nerves. Gods—Mikor got on Rydan's nerves even more than on his mother's! All that energy to expend, with only a fraction of an adult's self-control, made Rydan's beast scratch and growl.

And now there were two more women on the island. One woman he hadn't met yet . . . and one woman he had. Intimately. Because his youngest brother had drugged his breakfast juice, he knew one of those women a little too well. Of course, Morg's complicity was something that Rydan had to prove beyond doubt, to be just and fair, before punishing Morg for his potential crime.

Suspicion alone wasn't reason enough to pound the smug little matchmaker into the earth. It might be satisfying to vent his anger, guilt, and shame in such a fashion. Viscerally satisfying, if disturbing at the same time. But he wasn't going to accuse his sibling of something Morg hadn't actually done, if it weren't true.

Pushing himself upright, Rydan crossed to the base of the Fountain. Whoever had carved the border designs for the original caverns, with their graceful intertwinings of arch vine and angle, had echoed the designs in pipes and spigots, forming a literal fountain of energies. Madam Mist, as he had eventually taken to calling the mist-borne voice, had actually drawn the Truth Stone from a hidden niche in the carved base of the pipe-strewn fountain. Since the arching not-waters of filtered energies flowed smoothly into little basins and pools that drained into the roots of the mountain, he simply had to duck beneath a couple of them to reach the niche.

She, whoever she had been, had also hidden a small, blown-crystal handbell in the same niche and a place for the scroll to rest, released to him when he had been ready to take the Oath of the Guardian. What little knowledge most mages held of Fountains led them to believe that all they had to do was bind the energies of a Fountain to their personal magical signature, and that was that; they would have access to immense power surpassed only by that of the Gods Themselves.

This, as the age-worn scroll had taught him, was far from the truth. A mage did not, and could not, bind such raw, chaotic power to his signature. It would be like a fly sitting on a horse and commanding it to move. A random tail swat would be enough to throw off the impertinent fly, if not squash it outright. No, the bell was specifically tuned and blessed to the underlying pulse of the power, the susurration, the *sound* of the Fountain, for all that it was silent to the unaugmented ear.

Music, it was said, was one of the most powerful yet non-magical Gifts of the Gods. The mage rang the Fountain-tuned bell and adjusted his magic to match *that*, rather than the other way around. An untuned mage *could* attempt to take over a Fountain, but the emanation was so distinct and difficult, it was a wonder that anyone had actually succeeded in taming the first of the Fountains untold ages ago.

Of course, the first Fountain had most likely not been warded, or its harmonics harnessed and amplified by the filters built into its catch basin, which would force a would-be Guardian to strive very hard to match himself to the modern Fountain. But, once matched, the mage could *change* the Fountain, making it resonate to his own energies, usually to the point where no one else would be able to use it unless and until the Guardian in question was dead. Or unless the Guardian wrapped a guest-mage in a shield of his own resonances, buffering the other mage from the Fountain while at the same time permitting that mage to act.

If Rydan hadn't already had practice in matching his power

to his fourthborn brother's magical singing by that point in his life, it would have been very difficult to match the bell. Most mages didn't think about the resonances of their powers; they just used them. As it was, he had passed between the smaller basins with time and effort. Three years had passed since he took on the Guardianship of this place, giving him plenty of practice at adjusting his personal shields enough to match the harmonics of the wards.

One of the copper-hued ribbons of energy, pouring from pipe to channel, ruffled and fluffed out into a mist. A familiar voice echoed into the chamber, startling Rydan. He knew the speaker, but he hadn't been expecting contact from her.

"Guardian of Nightfall, are you there?" The voice belonged to Sheren, one of the first fellow Guardians he had ever *met*, if that was the right term for someone whose face he had never actually seen.

Speaking through the Fountainway distorted one's voice, but he was used to it. Shifting toward the mist, he held up his hand, letting the energies trickle through his fingers, half blinding him in a metallic haze. *"I am here. What does the Guardian of Menomon want?"*

"I have some news you need to pass to Serina. I've been chatting with a couple of mages who have recently arrived from Shattered Aiar, and they've given me some rather good information about the aether on that continent. One of them, Zella, gave me coordinates for three still-functional Fountains, one of which is in her homeland of Amazai. That's one of the few regions that wasn't devastated and thrown back into savagery when the old Empire blew itself to pieces, so it'll make a good control subject for what has been considered mostly normal.

"Another arrival, Xenos, is working on reconstructing from memory an energy map of some of the lands he's visited in the interior, including a region close to what used to be the capital. The aether is finally beginning to lose its turbulence, according to him."

"So he says," Rydan cautioned the unseen woman. *"Have you been able to verify any of this?"*

"Don't worry; I used a Truth Wand on both of them—I really wish we weren't as isolated as we are. It would be nice to import some new Artifacts, but the Council members are

adamant about not exposing our location to outsiders, which they claim trade would do. They seem to think my Fountain is vulnerable, especially now that I'm getting on in years. As if," Sheren snorted. *"After so many years, this thing is as much attuned to me as I am to it!"*

The scroll had spoken of carefully choosing successors and "introducing" them to a Fountain a few times before attuning them to it so they could take over. Rydan lifted a brow at that, though the other Guardian wasn't able to see it. *"When* are *you going to pick and train a successor?"*

"When one shows him- or herself worthy, of course," Sheren snorted, her voice ruffling the coppery mist playing over his fingers and fogging his eyes. *"Xenos has the power and is a bit of a charmer, I'll admit—I'm not so old that I can't appreciate a handsome enough man—but he's not a native, and I'd rather a local mage took over. Same goes for that Zella woman. She's got the power, but she's a bit of a coastal fish. Her focus is still aimed at her homeland. Someone local would understand the needs of this city a lot better and be able to navigate the politics with greater success.*

"How about you, boy? You getting ready to retire yet?" she inquired.

Rydan chuckled. *"Not on your . . . "* His humor faded under the return of that one line in the Song of the Sons of Destiny. The thought of losing the Guardianship of Nightfall made him edgy. Sheren speaking of feeling old made him hesitant to use the phrase "not on your life"—at least, not tritely. *"Not unless there's a damned good reason. Be careful yourself, Sheren. Especially around foreign mages."*

"Oh, don't worry about me. Only two of 'em that came into the city have enough power to be potential candidates, and I'd much rather pick a local, as I've said. The third one, the blond, he's not strong enough to tap into anything. No, I've got four or five from among the locals I could choose if they had just a little more power. Anyway, we're getting off topic. I'm sending through some of the papers Zella and Xenos have drawn up and will be working with them to refine their calculations. I'll also try to get ahold of the Guardians Zella mentioned. Pass the scrolls on to Serina, will you? Thanks."

"I will." Withdrawing his hand from the mist, Rydan blinked

to clear his vision and waited. The wards were set up so that if he wasn't in the Fountain Hall, he would be alerted to an incoming call, and anything sent through the Fountainway would be caught in a net of energies. But since he was here, such spells were suspended. That meant he had to catch whatever came through.

It only took a few moments before a clutch of scrolls came sailing through. The odd paper Sheren's people used was visibly pulpy, oily to the touch, and tinted yellowish green, and the writing done with purple ink. Setting the scrolls on the floor, he touched the coppery ribbon with his fingers.

"I've received five scrolls."

"That's all of them, thanks. Have a good day!"

Ignoring the scrolls for the moment—he would leave them in Serina's workroom in the middle of the night, along with a note as to where they had originated—Rydan shifted back over to his original goal. A touch here, a press there, a twist and slide of a bit of seemingly solid-carved stone, and the panel opened. Pulling out the Truth Stone, Rydan closed the little niche and retreated. Once he was free of the Fountain, he flipped open the lid of the cryslet on his wrist. A tap of numbers summoned a connection between the Artifact on his wrist and the one he hoped his youngest brother wore.

Thankfully, Morganen was wearing it, for the mirror-reflection of Rydan's face flickered and shifted to an angled view of Morganen instead.

"Yes?"

"I need your assistance on an important project. Meet me in the gong chamber."

"But it's almost supper time," Morganen pointed out, his face framed by his light brown hair. It was the same shade as that woman Rora possessed. Rydan refrained from grimacing at his brother, reminded once more of Morg's potential complicity.

"This will only take a minute, if you cooperate."

"Fine. I'll be right there."

Closing the lid with a soft *snap* that terminated the connection, Rydan glanced idly at the Stone in his hand. Shifting his thumb showed a touch of palest gray marring the surface, but only a very pale gray. It wasn't so much a "project," as an interrogation session.

Overhead the suncrystals were beginning to shift a little in color, signaling that sunset had fallen. There was a quality to daylight that made it more difficult to shadow-walk past it than at night, even when there was plenty of artificial light. Once he was away from the Fountain Hall, which boasted too much light even in the darkest hours of the night, he should be able to shadow-walk the distance back to his tower in only a fraction of the time it had taken him to run all the way down here.

Despite Rydan's ability to shadow-walk for half of the distance, Morganen still managed to arrive ahead of him. Emerging from the stairwell leading up from the basement of his tower, Rydan entered the room at rampart level to find his youngest sibling already in the chamber. The younger mage, light brown hair tucked into a braid beneath a headband, gave him a welcoming smile. Like Rydan, he was clad in a layered pair of Katani-cut tunics and a pair of trousers. Unlike his sixthborn brother, who preferred wearing black, Morg was dressed in cheerful shades of light blue for his trousers and jacketlike overtunic, and a light yellow for his undershirt.

"What can I do for you this evening?" Morganen inquired politely. His aquamarine eyes were bright with good cheer and nothing else.

Rydan didn't buy his brother's innocence. He crossed to Morganen, stopping within an arm's length. It was a little closer than he normally liked to be, since proximity pressured his beast uncomfortably, but it was necessary for the moment. "Hold out your hand."

Morg quirked an eyebrow but complied, lifting his left hand, palm up.

Dropping the white disc into his brother's hand, Rydan held his gaze, not giving him any time to realize what was in his hand. "Did you, or did you not, put some sort of drug into my drink at breakfast?"

Glancing down at his hand, Morg looked up again at his brother. "How clever. You call me out here to help you . . . only it's to help you interrogate me. How very clever."

"Answer the question. Did you put some sort of potion into my breakfast juice?" Rydan pressed. "Yes? Or no?"

"Yes. For your own good." Flipping the Stone up, Morganen displayed both unblemished sides. "You have this asinine idea in your head that love is something to be avoided—"

"Did you slip that woman past all my wardings?" Rydan demanded next, cutting off his brother's words. At Morg's bemused look, he repeated himself. "The woman! Rora, with hair the same color as yours! You *had* to have slipped her past all of my wards. You're the only mage on this island who is strong enough."

Morg studied him, mouth tightening for a moment. He gripped the Stone again and spoke honestly. "Since you insist upon knowing the truth . . . I allowed her to slip past the wards around the island as a whole, so that she could arrive undetected. Any wards she encountered after she landed were her own problem to surmount. I did not assist."

Again, the Stone was clean. It was Rydan's turn to clench his jaw. He forced the words out. "So you had no idea that, after you drugged me, she managed to make her way into my most private quarters on her own?"

"Well, I knew she was wandering around under the mountain at one point, but no, I didn't know that," Morg admitted.

"So you did not see me in my bed, suffering the effects of your little *prank*," Rydan growled. Outside his tower, thunder rumbled in the distance. It didn't crack with the immediate force of his earlier strike, but it did give warning to his rising temper.

"No, I didn't see that part. Why don't you just get to the point, Rydan?" his youngest brother asked bluntly.

"Did you know what effects that drug would have on me?"

"Yes. You were supposed to dream about being *happy* for once. Happy in a relationship with a good woman," Morg admitted.

Rydan let the thunder growl again on his behalf. The light outside, coming through the curtains of the few windows in the room, dimmed quickly as his anger started forming literal clouds overhead. "Oh, I *did* dream about being happy, Brother. I dreamed about being happy with my *wife*. Very happy."

Grabbing the Truth Stone from his younger brother's hand, Rydan squeezed the marble disc between his own fingers as he continued. He wanted Morg to see the truth of his own words this time.

"I was so happy that, when I woke up, I thought it was just another part of all that dreaming . . . and being *eager* to continue *being* happy with my *wife* . . . I pulled her down onto my bed—*and I violated her*!"

Lightning *cracked* outside. Rydan flung the disc at his brother's chest. Stunned, Morganen caught it as it *thumped* and rebounded, though the sound of the enchanted marble denting the folds of his tunics was lost in the sound of the rising storm. Aqua eyes wide with alarm, face draining of all its color, Morganen slid his gaze down to the Truth Stone in his hand. The pure white stone, unblemished thanks to the truth of his sibling's words.

"Oh, Gods . . ." Morganen closed his eyes, looking like he was going to be sick.

Unable to stay in proximity to his agonized brother any longer, Rydan snatched up the Stone and backed away. Nerves twitching, he spoke when he was two body lengths away. "*That* is what your meddling led to, Brother. Because of *your* stupid act, I forced myself on the woman *you* thought was meant to be my bride!"

He refrained from mentioning the humiliation of having thought it was *Trevan's* Destined bride he had violated with his hands and his lips and refrained from clarifying that the violation had been just an act of hands and lips. As far as the sixthborn brother was concerned, Morg *deserved* to be sickened by the implication of what must have happened, never mind what actually did take place. Rydan watched as Morg covered his mouth with his palm, looking very much like he wanted to be ill right then and there.

"Next time you get the urge to meddle in my *affairs*, Morg," Rydan warned him pointedly, "Prophecy or no Prophecy . . . *don't*!"

Whirling, he stalked back down the stairs to the basement, letting his anger slam and lock the door behind him. The *bang* of the door was followed by another *crack* of thunder, adding emphasis to his words.

There was no way he was going to go to supper now. That woman would be there, which was bad enough, but so would Trevan. And his twin would not refrain from smirking at him, thinking that Rydan's situation was *amusing*. Morganen might even end up there, if he recovered from being appalled at what he had done. The pressure of so many people, and so many differing reactions, would be too excruciating right now.

SEVEN

When the copper-haired man came to take them to supper, his arrival coinciding with a musical ringing of bells in the distance, Rora was grateful that he didn't demand that she touch hands with him. Nor any other greeting touches of the sort common in other lands. And the way that he introduced her and her sister to the others was easy and painless, just a round of introductions with some pointing and some descriptives, before they were invited to pick a seat at the long, half-occupied table in the dining hall. No need to clasp forearms, just a general acknowledging nod to each person introduced.

Which meant she had to try to memorize all those names and faces. She tried to do so as her sister guided her to the place setting farthest from the rest. Naturally, Mara took the seat next to the lightest of the two blond brothers, Evanor, to act as a physical buffer. That forced the copper-haired Trevan to move around to one of the unclaimed sets of tableware on the far side, but he did so with an easy, unruffled smile.

As soon as he was seated, platters and bowls of food were passed their way. Apparently, it wasn't the custom in this household to wait until all were present. It wasn't the custom in Shifterai lands, either, unless there was a Family-wide feast planned. Grateful she didn't have to wait, Rora blinked and shifted her vision to see which dishes would taste best, and which might potentially upset her or her sister's palates.

In reading the scraps and bits of half-moldered records in the archives back at the Shifting City, Rora knew that some places were so foreign, they didn't keep and raise milk-producing animals, and so could not digest even the easiest of dairy foods, such as cheese. Her people raised and tended cattle, goats, sheep, and horses for their milk. Plains cheese was a sought-after commodity on the edge of Shifterai territory.

Rora was pleased to see cheese on two of the dishes passed their way, and discovered after an experimental nibble that both had been made from cow's milk. One was sharp and tart, the other smooth and lightly herbed. There was a pitcher of milk to go with it, as well as two pitchers of juices.

There was also an offer made by the mage with the dark brown hair to pour them each a mug of something called "stout," which after a quick inquiry was revealed as a fermented beverage made from several different kinds of grain. Rora had to refuse, pouring herself a mug of fresh-squeezed juice instead. Anything fermented, whether it was grain or milk based, made it difficult to keep control of the power locked within her. Mara, cautious and wary, declined as well, sticking instead to an offer of fresh milk.

Rora wondered where Rydan had gone, as she ate. *Probably back to his underground home. It would be far enough from the radiating emotions of the others to give him some relief, I think.*

There is something seriously wrong with the way emotions attack him. Not just the emotions of others, but his own as well. Negative emotions are clearly destructive, but it might be just as painful for him to suffer from positive emotions, too. Since they seem to be capable of causing physical pain and emotional injuries in a negative form, I'd imagine that too much joy would be exhausting, too much pleasure chafing, and too much happiness sickening for him to endure in large quantities. Like too much honey on the tongue, or how endlessly rubbing someone's back can irritate their skin after a while, even if it starts out as something soothing.

There must be a way to stop emotions from attacking him.

No one should have to suffer like that . . . The voice of her sister speaking dragged her attention back to the others. They were apparently discussing the plan to question the others about their intentions.

". . . I would ask the rest of you to prove your honesty as well," Mara stated firmly.

"Under Truth Stone? Isn't that a bit extreme?" That came from the curly-haired woman—the shorter curly-haired woman, since there were two at the table. Mariel, that was her name.

"Given our recent history," Rora answered before her twin could, "I don't think it is. Most of the mages we have met in recent months have . . . unfortunately proven themselves untrustworthy in the end."

"And now we come to a whole household of mages," Mara added dryly, then nodded slightly at the boy, Mikor, and the redheaded woman at the end of the table. "Minus only the two of you. You may refuse, of course, but if any of you do, I'm afraid my sister and I must leave. Regardless of how favorably the rest of you might answer."

"Then I'll be the first to answer, since it seems you're Destined to join us anyway," Kelly stated, her aquamarine gaze roving along the others to gauge their reactions. "We might as well set any possible fears to rest right now."

There was that word again, the word the man Rydan had used. "*Destined*?" Rora asked, arching her brow. "I keep hearing that word whenever someone on this island talks to me. What is all this talk of Destiny about, Akelly?"

Kelly's husband—Saber, that was his name—coughed slightly. "My, ah, seven brothers and I are the fulfillment of an ancient Katani Prophecy. Each of us is Destined to fall in love, with specific things happening as each does so. It's called the Curse of Eight, or the Song of the Sons of Destiny . . . depending on whom you ask."

The brother with the dark brown hair—Dominor, if she remembered right—joined the conversation. "There is a second Prophecy involved, by a different Seer. It is called the Curse of Nightfall, and it also seems linked to our presence here. When both Curses are lifted," he explained, gesturing with his hands, "the island will be capable of returning to its former glory as a center of trade and commerce. The sooner we all meet and marry our Destined brides, the sooner that day will come."

"And since we have less than a year and a day in which to make ourselves into a kingdom, we're eager to see our brides appear." That came from the auburn-haired brother, across the table and separated from Trevan by a seat. The young man shrugged. "So, ask us what you will. If the two of you are Destined for two among us, the sooner we can make you comfortable, the sooner the last two of us can find our own brides, completing the Prophecies."

Mara glanced at her sister, then looked at the copper-haired man across from her. "So *that's* what you meant. You expect me to be Destined for you."

He didn't look repentant at being caught. Rora was tempted to call up her ability to See emotions, but decided to let her energies rest. Too much use of her power exhausted her control over the power inside of her, and she didn't think burning down this palace would leave a good impression with their hosts . . . not to mention how it would clue them in to her little secret.

"The way things have been progressing? Yes," Trevan agreed, nodding slightly. "I'm next in line, and I met you first."

"That doesn't *guarantee* I'll find you worthy of *me*," Mara retorted. Under the cover of the table, Rora shifted to touch her sister's thigh, to remind her to not be quite so damnably arrogant, but Kelly's voice interrupted them.

"That doesn't guarantee that *he'll* find *you* worthy of him, either."

Ouch. I get the feeling these two women are going to butt heads like two shapechanged goats, if we don't distract them—bless you, Trevan! she thought as he did just that.

"Here, pass this down to Kelly," the redhead was saying, procuring a white marble disc.

When it reached her hands, the freckled woman eyed it warily. "What is this?"

"It's a Truth Stone," her husband, Saber, explained. "You hold it in your hand, or someone presses it to your flesh, and when you state a lie, the proof of it shows up on the surface."

"But if you state the truth," the fellow with the thick brown hair and even thicker muscles next to Saber added, "it will remain clean and white. The effect fades a few moments after you release the stone and display it to the others, resetting it so it can be used again. There are other kinds, of course: wands that light up, special tablets that rewrite a written lie into the truth, and so forth, but Truth Stones are the ones most commonly used."

"Ah. Hm." Gripping the disc, Kelly tested it. "My name is . . . John." Shifting the Stone in her grip, she eyed the black marks, quirking an eyebrow and smiling. "Wow—I like this thing! I know a bunch of people back home I could make *really* nervous with this. And now for the truth . . . my name is Kelly . . . yep! It stayed white. I *definitely* want one of these for myself," she added, grinning at the others before refocusing her attention on Mara and Rora. "Okay! I'm ready for your questions. Ask away!"

"Fine. If you had a chance to grab a huge source of power and use it, even though it wasn't rightfully yours," Mara asked, "*would* you?"

"What kind of power are we talking about, here?" Kelly asked. "Solar? Electrical? Thermal? *Hydroelectrical?* What I mean is, sunlight, lightning, heat, water . . . *what* kind of power?"

"Magical," Mara clarified, her tone edged with superiority, making Rora want to nudge her twin in the ribs. "What other kind is there? If you had a chance to grab and use a vast source of *magical* power—even if it wasn't yours to use—would you do it?"

"Why would I need to steal it?" Kelly asked, holding the disc. "If I needed magic for some reason, I'd simply go to someone who has it, like my husband or brothers-in-law, and ask one of them for their help. For that matter, *how* could I steal it?" she challenged, briefly displaying the unmarred surface of the Truth Stone. "I have no magic of my own, and unless something is pre-enchanted to respond to a physical touch or a simple verbal command, I can't even use it. So, *no*, I wouldn't try to steal it. Now, is that your only question?"

"No. If someone held the secret of *where* to find this vast source of power . . . would you try to get it from them? Even if you couldn't use it directly yourself?"

"Again, why would I need to?" the redheaded woman countered. "I don't *need* any extraneous sources of power, and I don't care what secrets you hold, so long as those secrets do not endanger this island or its people. Anything else?"

Rora was relieved to see the disc was still unblemished. Mara lifted her chin at the well-muscled man with the dark golden hair. "Your husband, next. Same questions: If you heard of a source of vast magical power, would you try to steal it? Would you try to get the secret of its location?"

"No, and no," the golden-haired mage stated. "I have enough magic of my own for most of my needs, and whatever more I may need, I can call upon my brothers."

Displaying the Truth Stone's untouched sides, he passed it to the even more muscular man beside him. Wolfer, she remembered, Saber's twin. His answer was short and to the point. "No, and no. Same reasons."

A flash of two white sides, and he passed it to his wife. She was the one with curls almost the same color as Saber's straight, dark gold hair, Rora saw. Mariel had light brown curls, but this one . . . Alys, that was it, had the lighter hair. The woman gripped the Stone, cleared her throat, and stated, "Um . . . no, I wouldn't steal it, and no, I don't need to know any secret about its location."

She uncurled her fingers and grinned, displaying the unblemished marble. Not as if she had been in doubt of her answer, but in relief that her faith in herself was proven true. Rora idly wondered how Rydan reacted to such innocence.

The Stone got passed to the dark-haired Dominor. "I have no need to steal any power. You may keep your secrets, provided they do not bring harm to this Isle."

His pale-haired wife took up the disc with her left hand, setting down the chalkboard she had been holding. She kept the fork in her right hand as she gripped the Truth Stone and spoke. "I have been the guardian of a vast magical power myself. I have protected its secret well, and I have used its energies for the greater good while I was its guardian.

"Though I am not that guardian anymore," Serina

continued, golden brown eyes shifting from Mara to Rora and back, "I have permission from its current protector to return to it and use it as I may, because my guardianship was true. So, no, I don't need to steal anything. And any secret I may learn about some other putative source of power will not affect my decision."

Mikor's name and face were easy to match, since he was the only child there. He took the Stone gingerly, glanced up at the two women flanking him, then nodded and gripped it. "Um . . . I don't even know if I'm gonna . . . *going to* grow up to be a mage, yet," he corrected himself at a nudge from his mother. "And stealing is wrong. There."

He hesitated, then passed the Stone to his mother, who displayed both sides. He grinned in relief, showing the gap in his teeth. Mariel gripped the disc herself. "I am a Healer. If I suddenly needed a vast supply of magical power, regardless of ownership, it would only happen because one of my patients was two breaths from death and that source was the closest thing I had to draw upon to help save my patient.

"Other than that, I wouldn't need it . . . and if you have a problem with my possibly needing outside power to save someone from the edge of death, then you'd better pray to all the Gods you've ever heard of that you never end up as my patient."

Rora respected her for that answer. In an emergency, if the Healer needed energy to save someone, she could and would give it; she had already done so for the priestesses back home. If necessary, Rora could demand that the other woman keep confidential where that extra energy came from. Most Healers followed a strict code of ethics that was similar from region to region. So far, this one seemed to be no different.

Evanor took up the Stone next. His answer was short and succinct, delivered in that smooth voice of his. "No, I wouldn't steal it, and no, I don't need to know about it."

He tossed the disc to Trevan, who eyed Rora's sister pointedly, making Rora wonder what had transpired between the two of them while she'd been busy traveling through all those caverns. "No, and no, as you already know. Kor?"

That was Koranen, to his right. The auburn-haired brother took the disc and gripped it. "No, and no, as all the others have said. Are you satisfied?"

"No."

Even Rora looked askance at her sister. Mara didn't retract her denial. Instead, she lifted her chin.

"There are *eight* brothers . . . yet I see only six of you here. Until the other two have answered—and yonder would-be queen swears on the Stone that these are *all* of the inhabitants of this island—I am not, and *will* not be, satisfied."

Rora resisted the urge to drop her face into her palm and groan. It was a near thing, but her sister did have a point. A paranoid one, but a point.

Thankfully, though the incipient queen of this place tightened her mouth for a moment, she didn't object. Instead, she pushed back the gathered sleeve of her dress and flipped up the creamy oval top of a largish gold-and-silver bracelet. She touched the base beneath the lid part and spoke.

"Rydan, would you please come to the dining hall? . . . I must insist that you come anyway, immediately. Thank you." Touching the bracelet again, she said, "Morganen, your presence is requested in the dining hall. Immediately, if you please?" Snapping the lid shut, she held up her hand. "Pass me the Stone, so I can swear that everyone in this room, plus the two that are coming, are all the inhabitants on the Isle."

It appeared to be some sort of communications Artifact. Rora wondered that all of them could afford to have such a thing, and wondered again at the level of power it would require to link them all together. *If they have that kind of power at their disposal . . . maybe they* wouldn't *need the power I hold within me after all?*

Feeling like her faith had been renewed, she nudged her sister, whispering in Mara's ear. "See? I *told* you this was the safest place for us. They use magic like it's as common as water, even the non-mages among them. They don't *need* any more of it, if they can waste it on giving a young boy his own bracelet like that."

Her sister gave her a brief, dirty look, but said nothing.

"I repeat, the only people living on this island are the people currently in this room, and the two men that I have just summoned here. No one else currently lives here, for all that we hope to change that." Kelly started to say more, then closed her mouth, glancing at one of the others. The man on

Mara's other side, Evanor, decided to fill the tense silence following her words with a bit of forced cheerfulness.

"Well, why don't we enjoy dessert while waiting for the other two to arrive?"

Dessert was a spell-cut, fruit-topped layer cake. Rora didn't know most of the fruits, but they all Looked safe to eat . . . and the green-colored slices were sweeter than the rest, while the red ones were deliciously tart, and the yellow and purple ones flavorful and complementary. Fruit and sweetened cream filled the spaces between layers, while the cake itself was seasoned lightly with spices. The whole dinner—beef and root vegetables in a wine sauce, some sort of cheese-egg pie, leafy greens of a sort similar to the ones she had found near the shore, only tossed with a sweetened mustard sauce and more cheese—was a far cry from raw fish and rainwater. She had eaten lightly to spare her stomach any sickness, but this cake was too good to resist.

Covertly, she eyed the platter supporting the remains of the cake. There were three slices left, and two people expected. Chasing down a few crumbs with her fork, she was wondering how to go about asking for it without sounding terribly greedy, when the door to the dining hall opened. The black-clad, black-haired, black-mooded Rydan stepped inside. Rora quickly blinked and shifted her Sight, wanting to know what sort of mood he was in.

Muddied brown green. He was disgruntled. A wisp of pale yellow threaded through it; she gauged that to mean he was also just a little hungry. The colors of emotions changed with the intensity and sub-flavors of whatever he was feeling, she noticed. Upon sweeping the table with his dark gaze and spotting her, the muddy hazel shade covering his skin darkened to a deeper brown with discomfort hinted around the edges with olive drab guilt. She could See his previous wounds, too, though they weren't bleeding anymore; instead, they sort of interrupted his aura like a mirage-ripple, bending the colors where they passed over the scars.

He was frowning, of course; she didn't expect anything less, or anything more. Not yet, at any rate. Glancing at Kelly, he moved toward her, stopped, and grunted, "What?"

Nice to know I'm not the only one he's brusque with. She

listened as the incipient queen handed him the Stone, and her sister asked her questions again.

"If you knew someone else had control of a vast amount of magical power, would you steal it away from them for your own use? If the location of that vast power was being kept secret by someone, would you try to wrest the secret of it from them?"

Annoyance threaded across his aura in a webwork of muddy orange. "I have more than enough powers and secrets of my own. I need *nothing* of you *or* yours."

His gaze flicked to Rora's face just for an instant, but it let her know he counted her among the things to be discarded. Except when he dropped the Stone back into his sister-in-law's hand, she eyed the slightly mottled surface askance. "Um, Rydan, would you care to explain *this*?"

Rora saw the flush of his embarrassment, dusty pink, streak out of him, then swirl back inward again, attacking with yellow-tipped tendrils of shame and discomfort. Prompted to speak, she offered quickly, "Perhaps, if you rephrased your answer in a way more specific to the, ah, questions asked . . . ?"

The look he shot her seemed to be a glower of disgust, but she knew better. Rora could See hints of minty relief in his aura as he snatched up the Truth Stone again. "I neither want your powers, nor have need to steal any secrets—does *that* satisfy you? Now, stay away from me! *Both* of you!"

Dropping the Artifact, he strode out the door—and nearly tripped over someone on the other side. His aura flared with anger, rage, disgust, shame . . . and satisfaction? Rora blinked, trying to see if that smug aquamarine color was real, but he didn't linger in the doorway. Dodging around whomever was in his way, he vanished from view.

The young man who entered in his place had light brown hair, medium blue clothes . . . and a guilt-choked, remorse-riddled aura that nearly smothered him visually. It was so heavy that Rora couldn't begin to imagine what he had done to loathe himself so much. His emotions didn't suck themselves back into his body as Rydan's did, but they did cling to him like a heavy fog, blurring his body. This one had to be the brother named Morganen, the last one unaccounted for.

It struck her a moment later *why* he was so guilty . . . and why Rydan had been so satisfied despite his ire. *The two men must have had a confrontation; it's the only thing that fits. Morganen must have actually drugged Rydan, to be so guilty, and Rydan must have confronted him about it, and about that silly bit about violating me, to have this one so remorseful—yes, he cannot even glance at me without suffocating in his shame.*

She would have to corner him and get the truth of the matter out of him. Not that she would have to go far, Rora realized as he shifted her way. Stopping across the table from her, he cleared his throat, unable to lift the weight of his guilt to look at her directly for very long.

"I am terribly . . . *terribly* sorry about what happened," he muttered, and she could See the emotions he was choking on as he spoke. "I *thought* it would help, but . . . it only made things a hundred times worse. It was entirely my fault—he wouldn't have done it, if it wasn't for what *I* did to him. Anything you want, anything in reparation," the youngest of the brothers pledged, "I will do."

Mara snagged her elbow, hissing in her twin's ear. "What in the Blessed Names of Sky and Earth is he talking about?"

Feeling her cheeks heat, since she knew very well what this Morganen was referring to, she muttered back, "*None* of your business."

"Everything you do *is* my business," Mara retorted. "If someone caused an offense, it is for me to judge the severity of it!"

"Not in this case—look, we have agreed to disagree on this subject, so *drop* it," Rora stated flatly, giving up on keeping her voice quiet. Looking up at the young man across from her, she addressed him and his guilt. "You and I will discuss your reparations for your part in this at a later point. Your queen has a request to make of you. I suggest you attend to her."

"Actually, *they* have the request, and I have the Truth Stone. Come here, Morg," Kelly ordered him, displaying the blemish-free marble disc in her hand, "and answer two simple questions: If you heard someone had control of a vast source of magical power, would you steal it from them for your own use? Or if they merely held the secret of its location, would you try to steal that secret?" she asked as he reached her end of the table.

Morganen took the stone, held it, and shook his head. "No, and no." Dropping it back into Kelly's hand, he bowed slightly to her; his aura was still strong with remorse but the colors were muted. "Now, if you'll excuse me, I'm not feeling very hungry right now."

Kelly's husband snagged Morganen by the wrist before his brother could leave. "It seems you have too much *free time* on your hands, Brother, if you are wasting it getting into trouble."

Rora could see Morganen wince a little, while his guilt flared a lot.

"You've been neglecting your sword work. In the salle, in a quarter of an hour. *Don't* be late," the eldest of the brothers ordered. From the way the youngest of them flinched, his aura darkening with depression and resignation, this was not a good thing . . . but not something he would protest, either.

Waiting for her sister to admit that this was a safe place to stay, Rora stared at her. Mara picked up her fork, prodding at the remains of her dessert, until her twin couldn't stand it anymore. Elbowing her sister, Rora gave Mara a pointed look. A heavy sigh escaped her dark-haired twin.

"I think it is time we retired and think carefully about your answers."

Of all the . . . !

"You *never* give an inch, do you?" Rora demanded, losing her patience with her twin. She shoved to her feet, glaring down at her sibling. "I *tell* you this is a safe place to be. I *tell* you that these people won't hurt you or me. You even ask them *yourself* under Truth Stone, and even *they* tell you!

"You know what? I give up. I *give up*," she enunciated through gritted teeth. "You can go do whatever you want! *I'm* going to stay here," Rora claimed, jerking her thumb at her chest, "and see what kind of life I can make for myself—go back to the Plains if you want, since that's *all* you ever talk about!" she ordered, part of her relieved finally to be able to *say* that, after more than a year's worth of putting up with her sister's overprotectiveness because it *had* been necessary at the time.

Part of her, however, was very glad Rydan was no longer in the room, for she could see her own resentment, a bitter orange yellow tinged in muddy green at the edges, being shed by her aura in waves; she could only imagine how painful that would feel when scraping against him.

Her sister shoved to her feet, towering over her by an inch. It annoyed her whenever Mara did that. Normally, they were the exact same height and build, but her sister subconsciously used her shapeshifting skills to loom over people she wanted to intimidate. This was the only time when Rora wished she, too, could shapeshift . . . or could cast some sort of spell to lock her sister into her proper shape. She certainly had the power for it, if she could ever learn how to tap into it.

"I gave my *word*," Mara ground out, her teeth bared. She flung out her hand, indicating their silent, seated witnesses. "And just because *these* people say they're trustworthy, it doesn't mean no one *else* will come to this place. I *remind* you, those were mages that were following us! How do we know they drowned at Sun's Belt? *We* didn't!"

"*Fine.* I concede you have a point," Rora allowed civilly, even if she had to bite out each word. "*You* can spend your days looking for outsiders all you want. *I'm* going to lead my own life—one that *isn't* joined at your hip, the last time I looked, so stop trying to tell me what to do! Until you remove the burrs from under your saddle, don't try to talk to me. I'm not the one keeping them there, and I'm not the one who refuses to admit when she's wrong, and *I'm* not going to let *you* keep galling me!"

Whirling away, she marched around the empty end of the table. It gave her enough time to realize the two of them had just had a fight in front of their hosts in this strange land. Gritting her teeth, Rora did what was right, stopping next to Saber and Akelly at the end of the table. She didn't know what Saber's rank was, and hadn't yet given him the *A* honorific out of hesitancy—in fact, she hadn't even addressed him by name, yet. Indeed, the only reason why she used the outlander title for Kelly was to ensure that when she spoke the other woman's name, her sister would hear her using the proper honorific.

"I apologize to all of you for forcing you to witness our

little spat. My only excuse is that my sister and I have had to endure each other's company for far too long, under very stressful circumstances. I'm certain we'll *both* try to behave in a more civilized manner, should you continue to let us stay here, in your graciousness."

"I'm sure we won't turn you out," Saber offered, glancing up at her before looking at his wife. "You're not the first pair to pick a fight within these walls."

"Your graciousness is appreciated," Mara offered. "I offer my apologies as well."

Rora could See from the brittle hues in Mara's aura that the apology had cost the proud shapeshifter. Ducking out the door, she hurried away from the dining hall, intending to get away from her sister. Since the great octagonal hall was just a short distance away, she went in that direction, knowing she had plenty of corridors in which to lose herself. Not that her sister couldn't track her by scent, but that involved shapeshifting, which Mara wouldn't do around witnesses if she could help it.

Turning left at the balcony, she took the next corridor, found a stairwell, and went down, as far down as the steps spiraled. Rora heard footsteps following her, and picked up her pace. "Leave me *alone*, Mara!"

"It's not . . . not her."

Slowing her steps as she reached the bottom, Rora turned in time to see the youngest of the brothers descending. Anguish still wreathed him, obscuring most of his figure. Dismissing her Sight with a double-blink, she backed up into the corridor at the bottom of the stairs, giving him room to finish his descent.

"What do you want?"

"To apologize again—to make amends. If I could go back in time and stop what I did, stop my brother . . . He didn't mean to hurt you—and he wouldn't! He's really very gentle . . . underneath his gruff surface," Morganen added quickly, his aquamarine gaze sincere but still troubled. "It's *my* fault he hurt you."

Definitely under a misunderstanding about what happened, Rora decided. She folded her arms across her chest, studying him. "What, exactly, did he tell you of what he did to me?"

The slender man flushed and couldn't quite meet her eyes. "That . . . that he grabbed you, pulled you onto his bed, and . . . violated you."

"He didn't go into any details?" she wanted to clarify. Dropping his gaze to the floor, he shook his head. Rora bit her lip to keep from smiling.

His contrition and guilt at merely *imagining* what had happened seemed to be a far worse punishment than letting him know the truth and making him pay in some other way. But on the other hand, she had Seen how heavy his emotions were in this matter, how they tried to strangle and choke him. Not quite to the extent of his brother, but badly enough that it invoked her compassion.

"Do you want to know what he did to me?"

He shook his head quickly, paling further.

"Well, I'm going to tell you anyway. He grabbed me, pulled me onto his bed underneath him . . . and he kissed me," Rora explained, her tone light. "I'd never been kissed before, and it was a bit startling. The unmarried maidens of my culture aren't to be kissed in any way until they're wed. And then he touched me. My breasts, my waist, my hip . . . and he put his fingers inside my *breikas*. Which is also something not permitted by my culture."

Morganen buried his face in his palms with a groan, clearly mortified.

Rora smirked; it wasn't entirely nice of her to feel this way, but she found herself enjoying his suffering. He *had* drugged his brother and deserved punishment for it, though she wouldn't let him stay too miserable. "Oh, yes, he put his hands at the crux of my thighs, and touched me *there*, too. While he was still kissing me. No one had ever done *that*, either. Well, aside from myself.

"I must say, I don't know if all men are that talented—since I've heard otherwise in the complaints of some married women—but from what I experienced, he's just as good at touching me as I am." When he lifted his head, fingers sliding down to cover only his mouth, she smirked at him. "And though it was unrequested, unexpected, and startling . . . I *enjoyed* it."

What she could see of his cheeks above his fingertips

turned bright red. As did his forehead and ears, bared by his headband and the way his light brown hair had been pulled back into a single braid, much like his brother's had been. Rora smirked at Morganen for a moment more, then deliberately dropped her smile.

"But you still *drugged* him. For that, you owe both of us," she warned him. She softened her tone a little, speaking more thoughtfully than firmly. "I suspect his not telling you what really happened, how that was *all* that happened before he woke up and realized what he was doing, was Rydan's way of punishing you. Whatever you could imagine would be far worse than the truth of the matter. Of course, that doesn't negate your debt to either of us, not in full.

"Had I *not* decided I enjoyed what he was doing to me, regardless of his own remorse about it afterward . . . well, the penalty for a man touching a maiden in such a manner is to have the offending body parts cut off."

She carefully did not mention how the shapeshifters among her people could regenerate missing limbs, if at a lengthy cost of time, awkwardness, and pain. Morganen's flinch let her know her point had been driven home. Allowing him a few moments to think about that, she continued.

"The fact that your brother agonized over what he did, even though I reassured him I was not offended, nor felt violated, did prove that he wouldn't have done what little he did of his own free will. Not without my permission. Which means the heaviest burden of guilt and shame in this matter lies on *your* shoulders."

"I know," the Nightfaller muttered, nodding. He still couldn't bring himself to look at her for more than a moment at a time, but her own confession seemed to have soothed his anguish a little. Squaring his shoulders, he lifted his head a little, if not his gaze. "As I said, I am truly sorry, and ready to . . . to suffer whatever punishment you have in mind."

"Even if I demanded that your hand be cut off, for delivering the drug in the first place?" Rora asked, wondering just how far his remorse went. He flinched, but swallowed and nodded. *Definitely remorseful, I'd say* . . . It was time to let him off the hook, just a little. "Well, it's your lucky day . . . because I'd say you've done an excellent job of punishing yourself, so far. I will not demand that either of you cut off your hands, nor let my sister demand it.

"As for restitution, that's another matter. You can start by answering all my questions, about this place, that Prophecy the others mentioned . . . and about your brother." At his startled look, his aqua eyes finally meeting her green ones fully, she gave him a wry smile. "If I'm supposed to be Destined for the man, I think it would be wise for me to be fully informed before I make any plans or decisions.

"Or rather, you can show me to a place where I may sleep tonight and come back to see me in the morning, to explain everything I wish to know . . . since part of your punishment, I believe, was a *sword lesson*?" Rora asked archly.

Morganen winced at her reminder. "Trust me, I won't get off lightly by it. If you'll follow me, I'll pick out a room for you. We've been putting each visitor in the same wing as the intended brother, but it won't matter where you sleep. He's moving his things out of his current bedroom, from what I can tell."

"That place under the mountain?" Rora asked, following him back up the stairs. She couldn't remember seeing many *things* in that spartan environment, other than the refreshing room amenities, the bed furnishings, and a few bits of stone-carved furniture.

"No, his rooms in the northwest wing. Which reminds me," he added, glancing at her over his shoulder. "How *did* you get past all of his protective wards?"

"Don't ask. *Truly*, do not ask," she repeated as he opened his mouth to speak. "It's none of your business, and it's going to stay that way . . . or I'll sic my sister on you."

She was fairly sure she heard him mutter, "How vicious," but let it pass. *Father Sky—Mara would be* proud *of being called that, so why should I protest? In fact, I think I'll pity that Trevan fellow, stuck as he is with some spurious Prophecy suggesting he should try to marry her. It will take an absolutely outstanding fellow to make my sister offer her hand across the flames . . .*

EIGHT

Rora sat at the dining table, playing her fork idly over her food. Information whirled through her head, distracting her from her breakfast. Morganen had stopped by about an hour before the bells for breakfast had rung, waking her from restless sleep. It had been good to finally be warm and dry and resting on a soft, feather-stuffed surface instead of that makeshift raft, but her dreams had been a strange jumble of everything that had happened.

Images of the open Plains had mixed with cavernous passages of stone. The dark brown, unsettling gaze of one of their most persistent pursuers, the mage Xenos they had met while traveling through the land of Verena, had shifted to the anguished aquamarine stare of Morganen. Memories of running *away* from mages had mingled awkwardly with images of running *toward* Rydan . . . who ran away from her, in a chain-like chase. Even now, she still felt unsettled.

Added to that were the things Morganen had told her. There was plenty about the history of this place, from the arrival of the eight brothers not quite four years ago, to the arrival of the first woman on the Isle, Kelly. A woman who apparently came from an entirely different universe. Rora could hardly believe it, but she knew it was too bizarre to be a lie.

Then there was some mess with Alys' uncle trying to kill the brothers before being killed in turn, a list of the troubles Dominor went through after being kidnapped and taken overseas, and Evanor apparently losing and then regaining his voice, just before they had broken away from the mainland formally by Ringing the Bell, the ancient rite that summoned the blessing of the Gods, and that hovering crown back in that eight-sided central chamber, which these people called a *donjon*, whatever that meant.

What whirled around the strongest in her mind were the verses of the two Prophecies that apparently concerned her and Rydan. Rora wasn't quite as skeptical as her twin, true, but she knew as well as anyone that Prophecies weren't always easy to discern from more random events, until after they had unfolded. Yet they did seem to have some relevance, at least in part.

The first one with the island's Curse can be explained, I think. "When dark is enlightened / And nothing's undone" *probably refers to what I think is his ignorance about how emotions affect him. Morg says no one knows why Rydan is so reclusive, grumpy, and obtuse, other than that he's decided to take the other Prophecy's verse about him seriously.* "Shun the day and rule the night / Your reign's end shall come at light / When dawn steals into your hall / Bride of Storm shall be your fall." *That would put me off the thought of allowing anyone into my presence, too, if I had to give up my independence and let my life fall to pieces, as that one seems to indicate.*

She pushed the remainder of her eggs into a small pile, then scooped them into her mouth, glancing covertly to her right. Rydan had deigned to come to the table to eat with the others, but didn't look happy about it. She herself had moved her place setting one chair down from her sister, not deigning to speak to Mara just yet, but Rydan had taken his all the way to the far end of the table. The emotion-scars weren't readily visible when she Looked at him, but he did look more sensitive than usual. Suspecting that his own emotions might make him all the more vulnerable, Rora focused on keeping her own muted and calm so she wouldn't be adding to his problem.

From what Morg said, I don't think anyone knows what

his problem is. Which means I'm the only one who can See it. I've never heard of mages being able to use their Sight in quite the same ways that I can, so I doubt anyone has ever Looked at his emotions. I don't even know if mages can. Maybe it's something that's unique to me. I do know that he needs my help. I may not have heard of anything like what he's going through, but I can imagine that being emotionally injured isn't good for him. And I won't be able to get him to trust me if I go anywhere near him around dawn, given the ominous-sounding last two lines in the larger Prophecy . . . but if he sleeps during the day, I'll be sleepy by the time he's awake in the evenings. That won't work very well.

The others were discussing what their plans for the day would be. There were chickens to feed, cattle to milk, land to clear, foundations to smooth . . . and some weird comment from their queen-to-be about "hiring an architect from the other realm." When she glanced their way, the lighter of the two redheaded men, Trevan, addressed her solicitously.

"So what are your plans for the day, Arora?"

"Sleeping," she decided. She *was* tired and explained why. "My sister could catch and eat food on our journey south, and digest it easier than I. All I've had to eat has been raw fish and rainwater, and I've lost a lot of weight and strength. If . . . if it's alright with everyone, I'd rather just spend my time over the next few days eating and sleeping. I *will* find something useful and productive to do to repay the cost of my presence."

A few of the others made noises about her being their guest, about no cost being involved, but she saw the redheaded woman at the left end of the table smiling slightly in satisfaction.

"I'm glad you want to make yourself useful," Kelly stated, "but it wouldn't be good to try to fit a square peg into a round hole. Why don't you tell us what you like to do and what you're good at doing, and then we can see if we have an immediate need for those talents, first?"

"Well . . . it would be in Aian and not the local language, but I'm very good at being a scribe. Especially note taking at meetings. I have a very fast hand, one that's still readable—if in Aian. I don't know the local language, obviously," she repeated wryly, shrugging. "But if you can all speak Aian, that might not be as much of a problem.

"Anyway, that's what I did before we had to leave the Plains; I sat in on the Councils of Princesses, Clans, and Families and took notes for everyone. I also organized the kingdom archives and kept track of various records. Crop rotations and quotas, trade agreements with the surrounding lands, which warbands were in what kingdom, and what they've bartered for and where they got it."

"Warbands?" Saber asked her, curious. Rora's sister answered him.

"The warriors of the Shifterai are famous in central Aiar. We make excellent hunters and trackers, whether it's escaped magical beasts, feral livestock, or groups of bandits. We also transport trade goods across the Plains for a modest fee. We don't like outsiders trying to cross our territory," Mara explained, "since they often don't understand the dangers inherent in a vast sea of grass, but we are nomadic three seasons out of the year, so it's not difficult for us to form chains of transportation from one side to the other."

"Why only three seasons out of the year?" Evanor asked.

Mara shrugged. "Winter is unpleasant. High winds, heavy snows, bitter cold. The best shelter we have is the City, so we use it. The Shifting City is our only permanent settlement," the shapeshifter added, warming as she always did to her favorite topic. "Built in the cratered ruins of the old capital and surrounded by farmland to grow the things we cannot hunt, barter, or gather, it shelters all the Clans and their Families each winter. It gives us a chance to socialize regularly, too, since we scatter across the Plains the rest of the year . . ."

Rora ignored the rest. Her sister could go on and on about the City for hours. There were times when she thought her sister loved the idea of ruling over the City even more than the thought of ruling the whole Plains, though neither was exactly feasible anymore. She peeled and ate one of the fruits that were available, spell-preserved and thus still fresh rather than the dried kind she was used to eating in the wintertime back home, glancing again at Rydan.

Their eyes met, his dark gaze locking with hers. He was looking at her, of his own volition, and for a moment, his aura looked as if it weren't quite as guilt-streaked as it had been earlier in the meal. Lowering the wedge of purple-fleshed fruit, she licked a ticklish drop of juice from her lower lip. His focus drifted down to her mouth, and she licked her lip again, staring at the swirl of colors rising and falling around him.

They shifted. Guilt speared up like a muddy green leaf . . . but a thin line of rich violet desire served as its central vein. *So he remembers all those kisses, too . . . Good.* She licked her lips a third time, top as well as bottom, recalling the warm taste of him, the way his tongue had touched hers, teaching it how to play in the ways of married men and women.

He broke away from her gaze, shoving his chair back from the table. Snagging one of the sweet-spiced rolls that had been served, he left the dining hall without a word. The purple vein, Rora noted, now had a streak of muddy brown self-disgust.

I'm going to have to do something about that, too, I think . . . which means cornering Morg again and asking him about the local courtship customs. I can't be sure if it's the local customs that prohibit such things, or if it's just Rydan himself who has such a big problem with it. Sorry, Mother, Father . . . but I'm not on the Plains anymore, and I really like the ways of men and women, now that I've had a taste of them. And I may just be his Prophesied mate.

Turning her attention back to her fruit, she bit into the wedge again. From the conversation of the others, it sounded like there *might* be something worth Mara's while here, since they were now discussing how they were going about the rebuilding of the old cove city somewhere to the west. That was good; if her sister could find a way to adapt to this place, to find a purpose worthy of holding her attention, then maybe Mara would stop longing for what she couldn't have and start living the life the Gods clearly wanted her to lead.

She couldn't shake the thought of being touched again by Rydan. Closing her eyes, she pressed her knees together, remembering the deft caress of his fingers. *Touch . . . oh, Gods . . . He can't touch me without learning what I am—and next time, he won't be drugged!*

Emotions swirling out of the others darkened, drawing her attention back to their conversation and the tension she could literally See thickening in the air. Apparently her sister was getting arrogant again. Rora already knew about Kelly's outworlder origins from Morganen, but now that the others were talking about it, Mara was acting less than impressed.

Stretching her leg sideways underneath the cover of the table, Rora kicked Mara in the side of her shin, delivering a silent, bruising reminder to be nice and get along with the others. Then she blinked away her empathic vision and asked her powers something she hadn't considered asking before.

Gods . . . can these people help *me with the mystery of my powers, of how to protect them, or maybe how to get rid of them—and especially of how to avoid being captured and worse by other mages? I know I can trust them with my problem . . . but can they* help *me with my problem, like we thought the Fortunai might be able to do?*

The glow that sprung up startled her. Each of the other people at the table, including her sister, glowed at least a little bit . . . but Dominor and his pale-haired wife glowed with an almost blinding, golden white light, Kelly glowed in a shade of bright aqua blue like her eyes . . . and Morganen *glowed*, if such a term could be applied, a deep indigo blue. It confused her.

What does that *mean?* There was a simple, or at least simplistic, way for her to tell. Concentrating, she thought, *Red for bad, green for good . . . in the context of my question, what does indigo mean?*

The young man glowed a bright emerald green for a moment, then resumed the intense blue of before. She returned her gaze to Dominor and Serina, who were the lightest and brightest of the quartet, and realized he was speaking. Blinking her vision free, she focused on his words, which were a brief recital of what Morganen had already told her about the thirdborn brother's recent adventure.

"It was ironic that my kidnappers in turn were captured by the opposing side," Dominor was explaining to her twin, "which was the kingdom of Natallia. That's how I ended up meeting my wife and was eventually able to come back home. But while I was in Natallia, I had access to an extensive library, filled with archaic and arcane information."

That was the best opening she could possibly have. "Then maybe you could help me," Rora stated, ignoring her sister's sharp glance. "In private, that is, both you and your wife," she added cagily, knowing Mara would *never* go for her revealing her secrets so publicly. Inspiration made her add, "Since you say the archive was where she was located, and all. There were a few old records that survived the Shattering, back at the City, and I hope you could fill in a few blanks for me."

"I suppose we could spare you a little bit of time," Serina allowed, shrugging. "So long as it doesn't take all morning."

"Hopefully, it shouldn't. Is there a place where we could go and talk?" Rora inquired, as the others took this as a signal that breakfast was over, rising from the table. "I'd hate to bore the others with talk of dusty, ancient history."

"Why don't we go to my workroom?" Serina asked, glancing at her husband.

"I think not. One look at your chalkboards, and you'll float off in a mathemagical daze," Dominor added, giving his wife a look that fell somewhere between exasperated and fond. "I suggest we retire to the palace library, in the south wing. It has old records of its own, if not as many as at Koral-tai."

"That sounds good," Rora agreed, rising from the table. She didn't know how the different shades of blue from Morganen and Kelly would affect the answers she sought, but these two had glowed bright and clear. They were her first and foremost chance at being answered, and she was going to take advantage of it.

It was time to figure out what her purpose for existing might be.

The library was on the same floor as the dining hall, though it was located in the opposite wing, down near the point where the hall split off into the two end wings boasted by each of the four main branches of the palace. It was a little dusty, but free of cobwebs, dampness, rodents, insects, and mildew, unlike many of the subbasements and dungeon cellars she had explored beneath the City. With the scent of parchment and paper filling her nose, helping to relax her nerves, Rora settled at one of the three tables dividing one half of the longish room from the other. Serina took the seat at the end of the table, while Dominor settled across from her, and the dark-haired man gestured for her to start.

"To begin with . . . if my sister knew I was going to tell you this, she'd kill you and take me off the island. She's been protecting this secret very fiercely for a long time . . . but she's forgotten that it's *my* secret, first and foremost. So I'll have your word, both of you, that if she asks, you'll only say we talked about dull, boring history subjects. Do you agree?"

"Of course," Serina agreed readily. "We're both capable of keeping a secret, when need be."

Her husband nodded, and Rora squared her shoulders. "Right. That vast source of magical power my sister talked about last night . . . is me."

Dominor blinked and arched one of his brows. "You?"

"Me," Rora confirmed. "I was born with it . . . and I have no idea why, or what I'm supposed to do with it. In fact, all I *can* do with it is contain it, hide it . . . and a few minor tricks I've come up with over the years. I have an ability to, well, to See with my mage-sight more than just magical radiation—I can ask questions, and when I concentrate, I can See the answers."

They exchanged quick looks, then Serina eyed her again. "You mean like a Seer? You ask the Gods, and They answer?"

Rora shook her head. "No. Nothing of the future . . . and not exactly of the Gods. More like . . . more like the universe itself. I can ask questions of what's happening right now—when we were shipwrecked, I asked the universe where the safest land for us was, secret and all, and it pointed me to here, to this very island. Well, it also pointed straight down, but while I'll admit drowning would have caused our enemies to stop chasing us permanently, it was a bit too abrupt a solution."

"So you came here?" Dominor prompted her.

"Yes, and after you proved yourselves trustworthy through the Truth Stone, this morning, I asked to See if any of you could help me solve my problem, the questions of why I'm this way, of what purpose the Gods had in mind for me . . . and the answer was the two of you," Rora told them.

Again, they exchanged a quick glance. Dominor spoke this time, returning his attention to the Shifterai woman. "You say you are a vast source of magical power, but when I Look at you with my own mage-sight, I See . . . nothing." He spread his hands and shrugged. "You have even less power than Kelly."

"One of the few things I *can* do is contain it," Rora reminded him. They both gave her skeptical looks. The simplest way to show them, she knew, was the same way her power had been discovered by greedy outlanders in the first place. Stretching out her left arm, she offered her hand to Serina. "Here. Touch me, and feel it for yourself."

Glancing at her husband, Serina lifted her hand, placing her fingers in Rora's. Her tawny eyes snapped wide, and her grip tightened almost painfully. Rora could feel the other woman's magic like a ticklish itch under her skin. She could only imagine what the pale-haired mage was feeling by comparison. One of the priestesses back home had likened it to trying to keep her hand flat on the head of a drum being beaten by the hooves of a running horse. The stronger the mage-priestess, the more they could endure it, but none of them had felt like touching her a second time, if they could avoid it.

With a sharp, indrawn breath, Serina snatched her hand away. She massaged it absently, staring at Rora's face, then blinked and turned to her husband. "Dom . . . you touch her. Tell me if I'm going insane, or if I'm really feeling what I think I'm feeling in her."

He gave her a bemused look, but stretched his hand across the table. Rora shifted hers to meet it. The moment their skin met, his blue eyes widened, then narrowed in abrupt thought. He withdrew his hand after a moment, shaking it as if to awaken it from numbness.

"Well?" Serina asked, pulling the long braid of her pale blond hair over her shoulder so that she could fiddle with the plaited end.

"It felt like . . . like being in the heart of the Fountain at Koral-tai all over again."

"That's what I thought," she agreed, tugging on her braid with an almost grim expression.

"You've felt this before? You know what's inside of me?" Rora asked them, looking from one to the other.

"Not exactly," Dominor hedged, giving her an apologetic look. "The only other thing I can compare it to *is* a thing.

Something we call a Fountain, or a Font. It's a singularity point, a weakness in the Veil between Life and the Dark . . ."

"Let me explain it, love," Serina told him, catching Rora's confusion. "I've put a lot more study into the phenomenon than you have. Do you know where magic comes from, Arora?"

"Mages?" Rora guessed. "And you can call me just Rora, if you like. I'm really not a princess, even if my sister could qualify, back home."

Serina shook her head. "Magic doesn't come from mages. It's part of everyone's life force. Everyone has at least a tiny bit of magic in them. It's sort of like the cycle of rain, too. Rain falls, runs across the land, gathers in lakes and streams, evaporates under the wind and sun, and goes up into the sky where it forms clouds and eventually falls again as rain, right?"

"Yes, I know all about that," Rora dismissed. "What has that to do with magic?"

"Magic radiates from animals—the more intelligent the animal, the more it radiates," Dominor explained, taking up the thread from his wife. "Humans, being fully self-aware, can actually use the magic we radiate. Unless we're containing and using it for a specific purpose, it flows into the plants around us, which absorb it, grow strong, and in turn feed us and keep us alive.

"This is why a lot of magic involves plant matter—herbs and such—because the magic can activate or enhance whatever effect the plant may have. Tea steeped from willow bark will ease a mild ache. A concentrate of that tea is three times as effective in dulling pain, but it affects the whole body. If you add in magic, it can be targeted to the head, to the back, to a stubbed toe, and it's ten times as effective."

"When you kill an animal for food, its life-magic is released," Serina told her. "Some of it goes into the local aether, and from there to the nearest plants. If a mage steals that energy, he becomes tainted by it, and it makes him more and more susceptible to corruption of the soul—it's negative energy, which attracts the whispers of the Netherhells, influencing the mage. It's easy power to grab, but it's wrong, evil."

"So that's why the priestesses insisted I be extra careful about thanking the Gods for the gift of the chicken's life, and praying that Mother Earth take its life force into Herself, rather than wasting it needlessly?" Rora asked.

"Something like that, I'm sure," Dominor agreed. "Each faith handles it a little differently, but each one releases it into the aether, rather than allowing it to be gathered."

"Some of it goes into the local plants, as I said earlier . . . but some of that energy goes into the Dark, the place between Life and the Afterlife," Serina continued. "It's dragged there by the soul of whatever has died. Whether it's a human that dies or the prey of some predator in the wild, that little bit of extra life-magic goes into the Dark. The soul goes on to the Afterlife, but the energy remains. Only it cannot *stay* there. It's a part of life, you see, not death . . . and so it *has* to come out somewhere.

"Those places where it comes out are tiny little pinprick holes in the Veil between Life and Death," Serina explained, lifting one hand from her braid so she could pinch her thumb and forefinger very close together. "This single spot, or singularity, is like a water pipe with a great reservoir behind it—the energy rushes out in such a volume from the sheer pressure of all that magic trying to escape. It's very powerful, and very difficult to control.

"Now, *normally*," she stressed, holding Rora's attention, "these Fonts, or Fountains, are located in a stable, specific place. They've been tamed by successive generations of Guardians and carefully protected, because they *are* massively magical. It takes a very powerful mage to endure the force of the magic, let alone bend it to their will . . . but when they do, all of that power is theirs to command."

"You're incredibly lucky," Dominor told her. "Not only to escape the clutches of whomever thought they could grab you and take control of it, but in coming here, where none of us cares about stealing it—actually, the real irony is that Rydan is himself the Guardian of a Fountain, somewhere in that underground labyrinth of his. I think I see now why the Gods chose to guide you here, though I'm still not quite sure why They pointed your sister at Trevan."

Serina whapped him in the arm for that, giving him a brief, dirty look before returning her attention to Rora. "Ignore him. As I said, *normally* Fonts are located in places. In fact, if you had asked Rydan, he would have stated that *all* Fonts are located in a place, not a person. But when I was the Guardian of the Koral-tai Font, I was doing some research on a problem related to that Font, and I ran across something that mentioned a Font being found inside of a living host . . . a scroll or something.

"I only glanced through it," she dismissed with a shake of her head, "since it wasn't all that pertinent to my problem. But I do remember there was more information to be read, things that I wasn't interested in, but which might pertain to your situation." She looked at her husband, tugging on her braid. "Mind if I go back to the Nunnery and ask the Mother Superior to snoop around in her book collection? I could also check on my other experiments with the aether and such at the same time, since I know Rydan won't tolerate me using his Font.

"Some of the other Guardians might also know something about this," she continued, returning to the original topic. "I know that Guardian Sheren has an extensive library of her own, some of it quite archaic, and Guardian Tipa'thia is in Mendhi, where language itself originated . . . I can contact Tipa'thia more easily from Natallia than Rydan can from here, though I'd have to go through Rydan to reach Sheren."

"*We'll* go, since I don't trust you to not wander off in a chalk-dust haze. But . . . we can't take her with us," Dominor stated, giving Rora a sidelong look.

"Why not?" Rora wanted to know. "Shouldn't I be there, too?"

"Well, for one reason, until someone gets around to mixing up another batch of Ultra Tongue for you and your sister to drink—it's a powerful translation potion," Dominor explained, "you wouldn't be able to converse with the nuns, let alone read ancient texts in archaic languages. For another reason . . . somehow, I don't think your sister would approve of you going anywhere without her."

"And for a third, going to Koral-tai involves traveling through the Fontway," Serina told her. "It's a path of pure magic that connects each Font and Fountain around the world. You're carrying a Font of your own inside of you, a singularity of immense power.

"There's a chance that nothing would happen, yes," Serina

allowed, "but there's *also* a chance of . . . of a vast explosion as the two power sources collide, or of the two points neutralizing each other . . . leaving us without a way back. You'd be cured of your problem, but we could lose both Fonts, and I still have a very important task connected to the Koral-tai Font that I have to finish at the right point in time, which won't be for several more months. I cannot in good conscience risk it."

"There is another reason," Dominor offered. "If you went with us, you would be *there*, instead of here. If it's your Destiny to be Rydan's bride, you should be here where he is . . . though I don't know why any sane woman would want someone as unreasonable and unsocial as he is."

You'd be unreasonable and unsociable, too, if the emotions of others attacked you like weapons, Rora thought, but refrained from actually saying it. He had a point, and she acknowledged it with a nod, though for a slightly different reason, inside. *If I stay here, I can get to work right away on telling him what his real problem with people is, and helping him to find a way to stop everyone's emotions from attacking him. If I went . . . who knows what more the poor man would have to suffer?*

"Your caution is wise," Rora agreed instead, nodding to Serina. "Anything you can find out about my situation, please let me know as soon as possible. It may just be a bit of research for you, but this has been my existence for my entire life. And if I *am* to become someone's Prophesied bride . . . I'd like to know if it's actually safe to . . . you know . . . touch that intimately. Especially given what I hold inside of me, and how the two of you reacted just now, just from clasping my hand. Can you imagine what it would be like to . . . *you* know . . . in the midst of such overwhelming power?"

Dominor coughed, face flushing as he struggled to clear his throat, while his wife tipped back her head, laughing hard and loud until she was red in the face, gasping for air. He gave up and chuckled, then snorted, snickered, and laughed heartily, throwing back his head while she collapsed onto one arm, the other pounding the tabletop with her palm. Their mirth was rather infectious, making Rora grin as well, though she didn't know *why* they found her comment so funny. Only when they wound down into snickering breaths did she have a chance to ask them about it.

"What was so funny about what I said?"

Serina, wiping at her eyes, managed a reply. "It's a private joke. Husband-wife thing. But thanks for the laugh; I think I really needed that."

"You're welcome. I'm just glad you'll be able to help me—I know you can't guarantee anything," she added as Dominor opened his mouth to speak, "but you've already explained so much that I've wondered about myself, and for that alone, I thank you."

A knock on the door presaged Morganen poking his head inside, interrupting them. "Sorry to disturb you, but I'm about to start brewing a batch of Ultra Tongue for Amara and Rora, here. I've also heard from the mainland," the youngest of the brothers added, entering the library, "and we'll be having our first resident arriving in roughly a week. His name is Marcas, he'll be bringing a friend, and together, they'll be running a ferrying service between here and the mainland, and doing a little net-fishing on the side.

"What that means in the short term is that *we* have to hustle to get city plans drawn up and a house or two built for them. Kelly wants you to use that pipe-tracing spell today."

Dominor nodded, glancing Rora's way. "We'll talk to Rydan tonight. Don't worry; we'll find out what you need to know."

That made Morg glance sharply between the three of them. "Excuse me, I thought matchmaking the lot of you was *my* prerogative? Even if I nearly messed it up."

Rora shook her head, slanting the other two a warning look to keep them quiet. "This is about something else. Dry-as-dust research. Now, if we're done, and since I'm not going to be of any help in building a house, I think I'll take myself back to bed. After all," she stated wryly, pushing to her feet and glancing Morganen's way, "if I'm supposed to chase down a man who sleeps during the day, I should probably adjust myself so that I am awake at night, yes?"

"Don't go to bed immediately," Morg warned her. "I'll have that potion ready in just a little bit. It'll help you speak and read any language you encounter." He paused, then flashed her a smile. "Well, almost any language. If it's so old no one speaks it anymore, Ultra Tongue has a hard time translating it, so it might not always be particularly useful for your dry-as-dust research needs."

"I'll keep that in mind. How much will I owe you for this potion?" Rora asked, curious. Then blushed. "Um . . . not that I have any coins to my name, but maybe I could work out a trade, taking over some of your chores, or something?"

"You could clean this palace for a whole year, and still not be able to afford the cost of half of the ingredients involved," Serina told her, drawing Rora's attention back to the Arithmancer. She flashed the younger woman a smile. "Luckily for everyone, I happen to have a ready supply of the most expensive component."

"What, you want me to do your chores, too?" Rora asked her warily. Thankfully, the pale-haired woman shook her head.

"Ultra Tongue is one of the perks of citizenship on Nightfall," Morganen reminded her. "Though if you feel the need to trade favor for favor . . . if you can find a way to civilize Rydan, we'll call the debt even."

"I'd say we'd be in *her* debt even after she drinks the brew, if she can manage such a monumental feat," Dominor joked, and got whapped again by his wife for his pains. Grinning, he captured Serina's hand, tugging her to her feet. "Go play with your chalkboards until lunchtime, wife. We'll help Rora after supper."

NINE

He ran from her. Dodging around corners, sprinting breathlessly up stairs, Rydan dashed from chamber to hall, from passage to room, trying to stay ahead of her, to stay out of her reach. Her laughter floated after him, haunting him, because now he knew what she sounded like. What she looked like.

Dammit, Morg—did you drug me again*?*

"Ryyyydaaann!" Her lilting voice echoed around him, making him dart through a doorway and sidestep, pressing his back to the cool stone of the wall. Heart racing, blood pounding, lungs heaving, Rydan tried to break out of the dream. He felt himself rising, *willed* himself to awaken . . . and she entered the room that was his refuge, peering into the far corners for him.

The dream took over, making him lunge forward, snatching her back against his chest. She shrieked and laughed, squirming, her light brown hair tickling his face before he had them twisted around, pinning her with her back to the wall and those green eyes, nothing and everything like his twin's, laughing up at him.

"Mm, Rydan," she murmured, and rose up on her toes, capturing his mouth with hers before he could evade her. Or maybe he didn't want to evade her. At least, not in the dream. His pulse leaped, his body leaned, and he crushed her to the wall, devouring her mouth. Her wrists struggled beneath his hands, and he managed to make himself release her, preparing to let her go—but she wrapped her arms around him fiercely when he tried, tilting her head back and baring her beautiful throat. "Oh, *Rydan*!"

Oh, Gods—he couldn't stop himself; she was too warm, too soft, too womanly, and far, far too willing. That alone was reassurance, for surely she wouldn't be so willing if this weren't a dream. Giving in with a groan, Rydan bit his way down her throat, making her shudder from the lightly applied sting of his teeth, then licked a path back up to her lips, listening to her hiss *yes, yes . . .*

This isn't real! That was his salvation, and his despair. *It isn't real, it isn't real, it isn't . . . Gods!* He rocked into her, dragging one hand down over her hip to hook behind her thigh, pulling it up, tilting her body into receiving the thrust of his. It felt so good, he buried his face in the soft silk of her hair, listening to her breathy, encouraging cries, feeling the tight clasp of her arms around his back. They were both still fully clothed, but it didn't matter; all he could do was drive against her, drive . . . drive . . . !

Groaning, Rydan awakened a bare second or so before he climaxed. He had tangled himself in the bedding, winding it around his ribs and one thigh, and had clutched the pillows to his chest. Shuddering into the mattress, he felt his body twitch and spasm, shuddering in hot, wet release. It was hard to breathe in the wake of such a powerful yet *empty* release, and he groaned a second time, this time in pillow-muffled misery.

First . . . your own brother drugs you . . . then you force yourself on an unsuspecting, beautiful woman . . . and now you waste yourself in another drugged dream about her . . . You are a pathetic, sick mess! Sick! Groaning again, in pain with the acknowledgment of his thoughts, Rydan thumped his head into the pillow half squashed under him. He wanted her—the evidence dampening his bedding was proof of it, no matter how much he wanted to deny it—but he didn't dare touch her, not with that Prophecy hanging over his head.

How long he lay there, anguished and sullen, didn't matter.

It was long enough to have the bedsheet cling to his belly for a moment when he finally deigned to roll over. Grimacing in disgust, Rydan fought free of the tangled bedding, then stood and tore off the sheets. Not that they needed much in the way of pulling; his restlessness had loosened the neatly folded corners he had established yesterday morning before his first day's sleep in this place.

A drugged sleep, for which Morganen still had to pay. Yesterday's vengeance had been a good start; he had led his youngest brat of a brother to believe that he had violated Rora in full. Morg had looked like he was two breaths away from being violently ill. There had been no trace of such a thing in the gong room when Rydan had passed through again, summoned to Kelly's side for that questioning last night, but it was possible his sibling had remembered to clean up the mess.

He didn't know what else he would do to Morg for a just punishment, just yet . . . but having been attacked by those dreams a second night, Rydan *would* find something appropriate. At least this time, *she* hadn't been here to be assaulted again. Gritting his teeth, he pushed thoughts of *her* aside and ran his hand over the quilted pad covering the down-stuffed mattress. A small but distinct damp spot, chilled by exposure to the air, told him the pad needed washing as well.

Tugging it free and wadding it up, Rydan turned to dump it and the sheets into the laundry hamper . . . and remembered that, though it was among the things he had brought down via mirror-Gate last night, it wasn't going to go away and be cleaned on its own anymore. He had decided to move all of his belongings from the northwest wing of the palace down to these chambers, to make them his permanent, heavily warded quarters, but their laundry was washed by Dominor, who was fussy about how garments were cleaned. Rydan wasn't about to let Dom into these rooms to collect his laundry, which left him the option of either hauling all of his laundry back up to the palace once or twice a week, or cleaning it himself.

Tossing the lot into a corner for the time being, he padded into the refreshing room. His pale reflection in the mirror over the sink showed the hints of shadows forming beneath his dark eyes. Turning away with a grunt, he moved to the bathing tub and pulled out the cork stoppering the spigot. A twist of the lever controlling the heat quickly filled the room with steam, though parts of the carvings decorating the walls of all these caverns were pierced with small holes leading to ducts that provided fresh air, even in the deepest levels underground. Sometimes, during a storm, the vent shafts whistled and wailed, but only when the direction of the wind was right.

It didn't take long to scrub himself clean nor to rinse off the softsoap residue. Feeling a little better, since a hot bath usually relaxed and calmed him, Rydan dried and dressed, then poked his head out into the star hall just beyond the bedroom door. It was a very clever design of his, for the patterns of the suncrystals, set to glow like stars in the otherwise unlit hall, brightened or darkened in patterns of Katani numerals, telling him what time it was and how close the sun had come to setting.

Breakfast was often just after dawn, even in winter, but supper always started at dusk. From the looks of the ceiling, he had more than an hour to kill . . . which meant he had time to do his own laundry. Grimacing, he withdrew long enough to bundle up his dirty clothes and the bedding, added a pot of softsoap suitable for laundering to the sheet-wrapped bundle, and left his suite. His goal was on one of the upper levels, but it had been designed much like a formal laundry. There were basins with ripple-carved, sloping sides perfect for scrubbing, whether it was by hand or by spell, and aging wooden racks placed in the path of some of the draftier passages and vents, suitable for gently drying everything.

Sometimes Rydan wondered why this place had been carved by whomever had come before. It was literally an underground palace, for there were corridors filled with bedchambers and refreshing rooms, grand halls for dining or dancing, even rooms with massive hearths and baking ovens that could have served as kitchens, replete with scullery alcoves. But aside from a few bits of stone or wooden furniture, the whole place echoed with abandonment and emptiness. It was all unfinished.

Of course, that's probably because of how the Isle was abandoned so precipitously, thanks to the Shattering, he acknowledged wryly, ascending the last stretch of curving steps. *There are so many things left unfinished in this place—like doors. Plenty of doorways, and holes carved into their stone frames for fastening hinges, but no doors beyond the ones I myself hung, and the few needed to hide all the entrances to this place.*

The wind was whistling slightly when he reached the laundry hall, bringing with it the faint but discernible dampness of an approaching storm. Or maybe it was a lingering aftereffect of waking up angry at his youngest brother for drugging him; sometimes he affected the weather without conscious thought, though he tried to keep it under deliberate control. It didn't matter how moist the air was; the breeze alone would be enough to dry everything by the time he needed to make his bed again.

Even if he had to wash his own laundry, Rydan decided he didn't mind. Hidden under the mountain range, away from the others, he didn't feel his beast feeding on their proximity, clawing and scrabbling beneath his skin. No dream of happiness could ever become a reality for him; the few times he had tried to court women back on the mainland, their mere proximity had irritated his beast . . . and the way they hadn't really loved him, just loved the thought of being in love, had rubbed his sensibilities raw. Or made him feel nauseated, if they thought he needed coddling to put him into a better mood.

If he didn't need sources of food and other supplies, if he didn't know the others needed his help and would come looking for him, demanding it, Rydan would have considered hiding here permanently. Those few times in the past when he tried to stay away for more than a day or two at a stretch, the loneliness had become unbearable, but it was a case of suffering the strain of being all alone, or the stress of being around others.

Now that there were more people living on the surface, riling his beast with their smothering presence, Rydan wondered not so idly if the loneliness would be the easier burden to bear.

Not long thereafter, he shadow-walked up to the surface, crossed into the palace, and strode toward the dining hall, ready for supper, which was his breakfast . . . only to be caught by two of his family, dark-haired and light, and equally determined to have access to his Fountain.

* * *

"No." He didn't have to think twice about the request. Serina frowned at him, Dominor scowled, and hovering in the background, *she* stared at him, equally bemused by his denial.

"But why not?" Serina asked him. "Why can't we use the Fountainway to get to Koral-tai, in the morning?"

"Because I said *no*." Rydan stared her down, not budging. Away from the peaceful tranquility of stone-wrapped space, his beast was particularly bothered today. Dominor drew in a breath to argue, and Rydan cut him off. "The next trade shipment to Koral-tai is in eight days. You may go then. *Only* then."

"Rydan, this is *important*," Dominor argued.

"I said no!"

The thought of them passing through his sanctuary, even if it was through a complicated system of mirror-Gates rigged to pass everything directly into and through the Fountainway between Nightfall and the heart of Natallia, made his skin crawl. After the upheavals of yesterday, just being in mere proximity to others was already wearing on his nerves. Adding their desire to disturb his peace and tranquility made him all the more stubbornly opposed.

"*Forget* it," Rydan growled, glaring at both of them before flicking his gaze to the woman hovering several lengths away, barely within hearing distance. "*All* of you! Leave me alone!"

Spinning on his heel, he strode away.

"*Dammit*, Rydan!" Dominor exclaimed. His frustration hit Rydan in the back, making him grunt from the impact, and *she* cried out.

"Stop it! Let him go!"

He didn't know why *she* would give him a reprieve, but he took it, dashing into the dimness of the nearest room, and from there, leaping from shadow to shade, escaping the pain. Rydan didn't stop until he was sealed behind the wards guarding his underground home, though he threw up an extra one, tracing the runes in burning energy on the surface of the trapdoor. Only then did he feel his beast calm down again, agitated by his elder brother's irritation.

Food could wait. Food would have to wait; he wasn't going up there again until everyone was safely and quiescently in their beds.

"Dammit!" Dominor growled, turning to face his wife and the woman who had requested their help. Anger and confusion swirled in veils of dark red and dust yellow around his body, tinged with streaks of worry. "He *always* does this. Only lately, he's been getting *worse*. Unreasonable little . . . !"

"*Stop* it!" Rora ordered again, hurrying forward so she could close the distance between them. She gave both of them chiding looks, though Serina's aura was more confused than upset. "Calm yourselves, both of you. Every time you get agitated, you make things *worse* for him!"

Dominor rounded on her, drawing in a breath to argue, but Serina touched his arm, cutting him off. Addressing Rora, she asked, "What do you mean, 'worse' for him?"

Rora glanced around her. They were alone for the moment, but she moved a little closer and whispered. "I told you how I could See things, remember? Well, I can use my Sight to See emotions . . . and his emotions—*all* emotions—they're attacking him. That's why he ran from here. Because *you*, Dominor, got mad at him, and it was like your emotional aura was a hammer, striking him in the back!"

The dark-brown-haired mage stared at her. He shook his head, skeptical. "That's *not* possible. Emotions cannot be seen—and they certainly cannot *attack* anybody. Words, yes," Dom allowed in a rough mutter, "but not emotions themselves! He fled because I yelled at him, and because he's being a stubborn, selfish ass, nothing more."

"They *can* be Seen. I See them like . . . like veils draped over your body, fluttering in a breeze . . . and they *can* be a weapon entirely of their own. I *know* what I See!" Rora argued, struggling to keep her volume under her breath.

Serina stepped in before their argument could progress. "All of this is moot," she reminded both of them. "The real problem is, so long as Rydan is the Guardian of that Fountain, we have no easy way to get to Koral-tai. At least, not for another eight days."

"Unless we can convince him otherwise," Dominor muttered.

From the shading of his aura, Rora could guess he was thinking along the lines of forceful persuasion. "*No.* You will not bully or badger him. We can *wait.* I've waited twenty long years to figure out what I am, and what to do about it, and I *can* wait eight more days. And *you* will keep yourself calm around him," she warned Dominor, "or you will keep your distance from him. Do I make myself clear?"

He eyed her for a long, tense moment, emotions flickering through his aura. The intensity of the darker colors subsided, slowly replaced by a growing beige mix of resignation and confusion. "Fine. But *if* you're right, then *you* have to do something about this . . . phenomenon you say is plaguing him. Which I highly doubt. The Gods made our thoughts the last bastion of privacy; every holy text I've heard about has guaranteed it."

"Our thoughts, maybe, but not our emotions," Rora countered, hands bracing on her hips. Today, she was clad in a green Katani dress, corseted and layered with extra skirts to ward off the winter chill in the air. "I know what I See . . . and I *will* do something about it. In my own time, and in my own way. *You're* not the one Prophesied to court him."

"And for it, I thank the Gods every single day," Dominor retorted.

His sarcasm was spoiled by an incompletely muffled snicker from his wife. Her golden eyes bright with amusement, she tugged on his arm, leading him away. "Come along, Dominor. Mariel promised she would make *pasta* tonight, just the way you liked it back at Koral-tai."

Letting out a shaky breath, Rora let them go on ahead of her. She didn't know if Rydan was coming back for supper, but she thought it was probable he wasn't. *If he's been getting worse of late, it's most likely because of the addition of so many more people and so many more volatile emotions. Even just the small gathering of the three of us looked like it was having an adverse effect on him . . .*

I have to figure out a way to block emotions, Rora decided, trailing after the other two as they entered the dining hall. *I know I can do it, even if I cannot do much with my magic. I can shield myself from anything and everything, making all of this power inside of me invisible to the inner eye. I can even make my life-signature vanish, if necessary . . . though the one time I tried to hide that hard, it felt like I nearly smothered to death. Surely there's some way for me to figure out how to wall off all those emotions?*

The memory of walling off everything, trapping herself in an impenetrable sphere in order to evade the seeking tendrils of that one mage's magic, the Verenai mage Xenos, made her consider something else. *Not to wall them off—that might trap him on the inside with his own emotions, and I could See without a doubt how they turned inward and attacked him. It's not just the feelings of others we have to take into consideration.*

The problem was, she didn't *know* magic very well. A few things here and there, but not nearly enough to know if there was some way of adapting a spell to the problem. Rydan was a real mage, a spellcaster. If she could present him with a spell that would alleviate his sensitivity, maybe he would feel better quickly enough to allow Dominor and Serina to go to that Koral-tai place a few days early.

Seeing the others filing into the dining hall, Rora figured that one of them probably knew of something that could be adapted and some way to adapt it. The problem was *how* to address the problem at hand. Her sister unwittingly provided the solution, seating herself between Rora and Evanor as she had every meal since their acceptance into this overgrown home.

"So, how goes the dry-as-dust researching?" Mara inquired, reaching for the nearest pitcher of juice and filling her and Rora's cups. "I haven't seen you since lunch. Were you hiding in the palace library?"

That's it! "Yes . . . yes, and I've hit a bit of a stumbling block. I ran across a reference to an old spell in one of the books," Rora lied. She didn't want to lie, but protecting herself from greedy power seekers had made it a necessity in her life. And this was for a good, unselfish cause, finding a way to secure Rydan some peace of heart and mind. "It was fragmented, the writing faded and the pages a bit torn, but it spoke of a special kind of . . . of one-way shield."

"A one-way shield?" Morganen asked, passing Trevan a large bowl of greens. He had taken the empty seat between the two male redheads, the copper-haired Trevan and his own auburn-haired twin, Koranen. "Did it say what kind?"

"I'm not sure. Something about . . . emotions." She resisted the urge to flick her gaze toward the doubtful Dominor. "It was couched in terms of auras and energies, but I think the spell was designed to let emotions *out* of the warding sphere, so that they wouldn't be trapped inside with the mage, but also to not let other emotions from outside sources work their way in. It was an intriguing idea, a one-way warding. But the book was very old, so I didn't know if any of you had heard of such a thing in this day and age."

"There are plenty of warding spells that allow energy to flow out, but not to flow in," Saber told her. "Most of them are standard combat spells, in fact—wardings against lightning coming in from opponents, but which allow the caster to fling their own bolts, for example. Most of them have a similar base, upon which the specifics are built."

"They also come as protective amulets," Trevan told her. "I've actually made a few, in fact, pendants, rings, brooches, bracelets . . . In *theory*, it should be possible to transcribe the pertinent runes for protection from lightning, in the example my brother used, to runes for protection from hatred, fear, despair . . . though it's not just the runes you'd have to worry about. It's the physical components. A ring of warding against lightning requires a different metal than a ring of protection from fire."

"Metal might not be the right answer," Mariel offered, countering his suggestion. The others glanced at the Healer in surprise, and she defended her position. "There are certain potions derived from plants that calm the heart and the mind, bringing clarity in the face of mental and emotional chaos. You could carve a ring from the heartwood of the *mandrakken* tree, for example; the sap is used as a calmative and is usually applied topically as a salve, since it's too bitter to swallow directly."

"That's not a bad idea, but it's not exactly the same thing," Mara pointed out. "There is a difference between blocking outside influences, and drugging someone into a stupor."

"But a combination of spell, rune, and plant could control the dose as needed, so that only when the patient was agitated would the sap be delivered to its target," Mariel argued back.

"Perhaps we're being *too* magical," Wolfer offered before Mara could retort. The gravelly voiced brother explained himself when the others glanced his way in their curiosity. "A well-disciplined mind is an untroubled mind. You don't *have* to rely on magic to calm your thoughts. In fact, if magic were the only cure, then the vast hordes of commoners who don't have enough power to even light a candle would all be foaming at the mouth from their unchecked, rampant feelings."

"He has a point," Kelly agreed. "Meditation has been practiced by some of the warriors of my world to ensure clarity of mind and heart, even in the chaos of combat. I myself practice some of these techniques—I don't always *succeed* in staying calm, but my temper would be a lot worse without it."

"Didn't Hope pass you some books on that, a few months back?" Morganen asked. "When she handed over all those other volumes on how your world is built?"

Kelly blinked thoughtfully. "I think so . . . I'll go through the bookshelves in our quarters tonight; if they're not there, then they got packed into the library somewhere. That is, if you'd like to read them, Arora?"

"I'd *love* to," Rora agreed, making her sister snort.

"Handing a new book to my twin is like handing her an entire iced cake to eat. If written words could be eaten like food, she'd be fatter than that cat I've seen wandering around," Mara joked.

"That cat is *not* fat," Trevan retorted, making Rora glance at his aura. His dignity seemed to have been pricked by her sister's comment a little harder than she would have expected for a stray jest. Squaring his shoulders, the copper-haired male gave Mara a lofty look. "He happens to be very fit, and very *muscular*, not *fat*."

"My apologies, then," Mara returned politely. Then asked, "Akelly tells me she thinks his name is just 'Cat.' Is that so, or does he have another one?"

Interesting. There's a little swirl of guilt in his aura, Rora observed. Trevan lifted his chin a little as he replied.

"*All* cats have a secret name, which they usually keep to

themselves." He glanced at the others . . . who were swirling with a tangled mess of amusement, Rora realized, bemused. "That's why they don't always come when we call them . . . because what we call them isn't always their real name."

Smirking, Morganen interceded on his brother's behalf. "Just keep calling him 'Cat,' Amara. I'm sure he'll answer to it, just for you."

Mara gave everyone else a skeptical, wary look as most of them grinned or chuckled under their breath, but she didn't look riled. Relieved that her twin was finally behaving herself—and that she both looked and Looked less stressed than yesterday—Rora served herself from the bowls and platters that had been passed her way. She stayed silent, letting the others at the table shift their talk to a comfortable, jumbled mix of what the boy, Mikor, had studied for his daily lessons, what Mara and Kelly had come up with for improvements to their city plans, and what the others had done to further clear and prepare the land down at the western shore.

The earlier conversation had given her a lot of food for thought, after all. *I think . . . I think I'd like to try the non-magical solution, first,* she decided. *Spells can be disrupted, and amulets taken away. But self-control cannot be so easily removed. At least, I can put it to him that way; if he doubts me, I can tell him to just adjust a spell from one of those lightning combat-wardings Saber spoke of to something that could pass for an emotion combat-warding and see how he feels.*

The pun in her thoughts made her smile to herself. *Heh . . . see how he* feels . . . She sobered after a moment. *The poor man . . . I'm surprised he's lasted this long without going mad from the impact of others' feelings all these years. Though being exiled for a few years with only his brothers to deal with may have helped, until women and romance and so many intense feelings came into the picture.*

I don't think I'll approach him tonight, though, Rora thought, spearing a bit of greens on her fork. *I'll give him time to calm down, and a good day's rest. Hopefully by then, I'll be on the same sleeping schedule as him—and if Kelly finds that book on the meditative practices of her world, I can read that to stay awake, tonight. I can only sleep so much in a single day, after all, so I'd better save it for tomorrow.*

TEN

"Gods!" Jerking awake—literally jerking, at the hips—Rydan strangled his pillow in his frustration as soon as his flesh stopped pulsing. In the next moment, he rolled over, flinging the pillow across the room. Fighting free of the bedding, he stumbled to his feet, whirling to glare at the damp spot on his bedding and the mess on his stomach. "Gods-be-*damned . . . ! Dramundic*!"

The sheets snapped and rustled, the stain vanishing instantly. Dominor hated anyone using the *mundic* cleaning spells on fabric, as he claimed it weakened the threads, reducing the lifespan of the material, but Rydan didn't care. He didn't use a similar charm on himself, since the spells irritated his skin, and that particular patch of skin was extra sensitive. But the bed needed cleaning, and he wasn't about to wash a second set of sheets with a laundry charm so soon after the last ones.

Glaring at the bed, he snarled and snapped his fingers, silently willing the tangled mess of blankets back into place. They slithered into position, each layer folding over at the sides and foot, tucking themselves into place. A second pulse of his will rapped the lightglobe on his bedpost into a brighter glow, allowing him to find and pick up the cryslet from his nightstand, half hidden behind a pair of books stacked on the corner.

Flipping open the lid, he jabbed the sequence of number runes that would contact the youngest of his siblings. It took a few moments before Morganen's face appeared on the mirrored surface covering the inside of the lid.

"Rydan! Good afternoon—you're up a bit early, aren't you?" Morg asked cheerfully.

Rydan let his lips curl up in a snarl. "You will tell me *exactly* how long this drug of yours is supposed to last . . . or by all the Gods of the world, I will *reach* through these mirrors," he threatened, letting his voice rise along with his ire, "*grab* you by the throat, and pull you *halfway through*!"

Aquamarine eyes blinked. The view jiggled a bit as Morganen adjusted his cryslet, or rather, the arm carrying it, then his face loomed larger as he leaned closer. "You mean, you're *still* having dreams?"

"Yes!"

"Extraordinary." Morg's eyes blinked thoughtfully—most of what could be seen from this close a view were just his eyes, forehead, and a bit of his nose—while his brother fumed, waiting for a reply. The youngest of the brothers focused on the sixthborn again. "I'm afraid I can't help you. The potion was designed to work for one night, and one night alone. Unless . . ."

"Unless. What?" Rydan demanded, enunciating each word.

Morganen pulled his head back, far enough to flash an impish grin at his brother. "If I told you *that*, Brother, you *would* try to pull me halfway through these mirrors. Since I have no inclination toward being sliced in two distance-separated halves, I shall have to decline your *charming* invitation."

"Dear Brother," Rydan stated as sweetly as he could, which meant speaking through teeth clenched in a parody of a grin. "I can see that you are in your workroom. That means you are currently standing upon a floor that is connected to Nightfall soil. I am the Guardian of Nightfall . . . and if I so choose, I could open up a *hole* under your feet! Tell me what you have done to me!"

"That's just it," Morg retorted. "I didn't do anything beyond the one night's dreaming. *You,* dear Brother, are dreaming about her of your own subconscious volition. Now, if you want to know how to make the dreaming *stop* . . ."

Rydan felt his beast itching with discomfort. Separated by corridors and stairwells and secret entrances, and his sibling *still* found a way to irritate him. Struggling with his temper, he narrowed his dark eyes in warning. *"How?"*

"Spend *time* with her." The advice was delivered flatly, bluntly, though a hint of humor still lurked in Morg's aquamarine eyes. "Either you'll get to know things about her that will make you dislike her and thus stop thinking about her even subconsciously in your dreams . . . or you'll get to know things that make you *like* her . . . and you'll stop disliking the fact that you're dreaming about her.

"Either way, this is a problem of your own making, and not of my brewing. I'll see you at supper."

The mirror darkened for a moment, then returned to reflecting Rydan's face. Snapping the lid shut, Rydan pinched the bridge of his nose, feeling the little pains shooting across his forehead that heralded a headache and threatened a migraine. Tossing the cryslet back onto the nightstand, he dropped onto his neatly made bed and draped an arm across his face. He could feel the evidence of his dreams slowly drying on his skin, chilled by the cool air of his underground home, but didn't bother trying to remove it just yet.

If Morg was to be believed, the stain of his arousal was there because it was *his* dream, not the result of some potion.

His dream . . . in which the woman, Rora, had been warm and willing, so willing . . . His loins throbbed, and his flesh thickened, recalling the sound and taste and feel of her in his dream. Soft curves, sweet voice, sultry skin—gritting his teeth, Rydan forced himself to remember the Curse.

According to the damned Song of Destiny, his *reign* would end at light, when dawn crept into his hall. Or rather, when Dawn crept into his hall. Each of the brothers had his own nickname, identifying them as the brothers in the Prophecy based upon some trait or other. His was obviously the Destiny of the Storm, with the way Rydan could and often did disrupt the weather. Sometimes the mage even wondered if his beast caused the weather to shift, not him, since it mostly only happened when he was upset.

So long as he avoided the woman in the mornings, so long as he kept her out of his halls, everything would be fine. But the other verses had come true, and that worried him. The only thing that Rydan *reigned* over, after all, just happened to be the most important resource on the whole of the island: the Fountain of Nightfall. He was its Guardian. It was his responsibility to make sure nothing and no one misused its vast power.

Before finding it, before painstakingly and stubbornly working his way far enough into Madam Mist's protections to learn what it was, Rydan had believed what the others believed. He preferred being awake at night, and thus could be said to "reign" over it. But after learning of the Fountain, after taking up its Guardianship, he had decided differently. He had no power over the night; he worked in it, stayed awake through it, even shadow-walked best in the midst of its embrace, but Rydan didn't rule it. He didn't *want* to rule it; that sort of hubris was for the Gods.

The Fountain was another matter. The Curse of Eight spoke of him losing control of the Fountain—he was sure of it. And yet . . . His mind whirled in thought. *The Curse of Nightfall. If the eight couplets of it match up with my eight brothers and their wives, as it seems to, the verse regarding* my *fate speaks of dark being enlightened and nothing being undone. Unless it refers to* her *. . . but she's fair, not dark. What could I enlighten her about, save to stay far away from me? And what has already been done, that could not be undone?*

Gods! Seers and Prophets—madmen, all!

At least in his turmoil, his burgeoning erection had faded. Needing another hot bath to clean off the residue of his dream, Rydan pushed himself out of bed, uttering an unhappy grunt. Mainly because his stomach had awakened and was cramping in complaint. If it was only midafternoon, according to his idiot of a brother, he still had a few more hours before he would get fed.

If he chose to join the others for supper. For supper last night, and for breakfast, he had chosen to dine late and eat early, taking food from the kitchens above. If he tried to go above and get something early, he would run the risk of encountering one of the others . . . and these days, his beast was too easily irritated by things he had been able to endure before.

It looked as if he would soon have little choice but to suffer loneliness in a self-imposed sort of exile, given how even the thought of enduring *company* was rapidly becoming unbearable.

Rora woke to a muffled pounding noise. It took her sleep-disoriented mind a moment to realize the noise came from a door, but not her bedchamber door. Wearing nothing but an old undergown for a sleeping tunic, she grabbed the top blanket as she left the bed, wrapping it around herself. The weather had taken an overcast turn, making the air distinctly chilly, despite it being late afternoon. The knocking continued as she passed into the front room of her suite, pausing now and again between raps.

Cracking open the door, Rora peered at the aqua-eyed man smiling back at her. "Morganen? What do you want?"

"Good news, of a sort. If I may come in?" he asked, gesturing at the narrow opening between them.

Conscious of her barely clad state, and the fact that, trustworthy or not, Morg *was* a mage, Rora shook her head. "I'm not dressed for visitors. What is the news?"

Morg glanced up and down the hall, then leaned in close to the door and whispered. "He's *dreaming* about you. Of his own volition. He thought it was a long-lasting drug, what I gave him. True, it opens the door to *potentially* dreaming about someone . . . but only if there's a connection already there. The potion itself cannot compel, past the first night's sleep, though I wouldn't tell him that part, if I were you."

Rora opened the door a little wider, just enough to frown pointedly at him. "I thought you had learned your lesson with the last bit of meddling you tried."

He had the grace to flush, but gave her a pointed look of his own. "It is *my* Destiny to matchmake my brothers. So I made a mistake. One mistake, which I have apologized profusely for, and still feel repentant about. That *doesn't* negate the rest of the good that I can and will do."

"Perhaps," she grudgingly allowed. "But I'll thank you

not to interfere." At the arch of his brow, Rora added, "There are things about your brother which none of you understand. Until I can find a way to fix those things, pressure from his family will only make them worse. Now, if you don't mind, I'm going back to bed. Good night . . . or good afternoon—whichever!"

Closing the door between them, Rora padded back to the broad, soft bed that was hers to enjoy. The last bed even half as nice had been at that inn they'd stayed at, waiting for a ship to carry them from the kingdom of Amaz to the Empire of Fortuna. Of course, the Amazai idea of a pillow—cylindrical and filled with grain husks—wasn't the same as these big, fluffy, down-filled things. True, they had matted down with age, but she preferred her pillows on the firm side of squishable. Resettling the blanket, Rora climbed back under the covers, seeking out the warm spot her body had made earlier.

Morganen had told her that she was most likely his brother's Destined bride. The biggest reason she could see as to why it was *her*, of all possible women, was that she could See why he was suffering, and thus so surly. *Well, that, and Mara and Rydan definitely wouldn't get along.* She smiled as she snuggled into the pillow. *Trevan and I are both naturally cheerful; Mara and Rydan . . . circumstances have made both of them surly. I suppose the Gods do have a sense of humor, pairing each of us with our opposite.*

At least surly can be cured—I'm not so sure about cheerful!

Dinner was a strange affair. Mara was more subdued than Rora could ever remember seeing her twin, while the icy dislike aimed Mara's way from the woman at the head of the table pinpointed the most likely source. Seated across the table from Mara, Trevan wasn't giving the black-haired woman a disdainful look like Kelly was, but he was sneaking the occasional puzzled glance at both Shifterai women. Unfortunately, Rora couldn't fix her sibling's problems this time around, or even wait to ask about them. She had her own to deal with, one of them being a certain overly brooding, self-isolating gentleman.

When Rydan didn't show by the end of the meal, Rora reached across the table, dragged the unused place setting away from his bemused twin, and corralled the serving bowls and platters of leftover food. Filling up the borrowed plate with whatever hadn't been eaten by the rest, she balanced the silverware in the middle, draped a napkin over the top, then poured juice into a deep mug snagged from the sideboard. Some of the others noticed what she was doing, and the one attempting to clear the table called her on it.

"Arora, what are you doing?" Evanor asked, giving her a puzzled look before picking up the now empty beef platter. "If you want more food later, you need only go down to the kitchens and fetch it. We won't make you starve, honest."

"It's not for me. It's for Rydan."

Wolfer snorted, waiting for Alys to finish the fruit-speckled muffins that had been passed around for dessert. He eyed Rora dubiously. "And how will you get it to him? You're no mage, let alone one powerful enough to breach his defenses."

"Wolfer's right," Dominor agreed, helping his wife stack dishes. "Rydan has wards all over his tower, reinforced by that Fountain of his. You'd need magical training above and beyond his to have a hope of getting in—raw power alone won't help you."

"I can be very persistent, when I want to be. Don't worry about *either* of us," Rora reassured Rydan's family. Mara pressed her lips together, but didn't object aloud; her expression spoke volumes on Keeping Certain Subjects Secret. Dom had come close to the truth in his little warning, but Mara didn't yet know how close he *was* to the truth. Keeping her own thoughts to herself, Rora simply added a final, "Good night, everyone."

Wishes of good night and good luck followed Rora out the door, which Saber politely held open for her, since her hands were full. Heading up the north corridor, she glanced behind her when she reached the stairwell at the junction between the two outer wings, but no one was following. Climbing, she continued all the way to the door onto the drawbridge linking the palace to the outer wall. A mere thought, and it swung open for her . . . much as it had for Rydan when he had brought her to the others.

They had that much in common. Crossing the drawbridge quickly, for it was open to the cold, damp night air, Rora wondered if her and Rydan's door-opening ability was a side effect of being a caretaker of one of these Fountain things, or if it was something else. Like, maybe it was a different way of approaching magic.

Like how Dominor refused to believe I can See emotions. I wonder . . . I wonder if the first-ever spells were a result of someone just thinking *about wanting to do something, like my wanting to See things. But I don't know how I do it*, she thought as the door into the northernmost of the outer towers swung open at her food-laden approach. *Only that I* can *do it. I don't know the first thing about translating it into an actual spell that others could use, mainly because I don't know how formal, official spells are created.*

Please show me the easiest path to Rydan's current location, she thought firmly as she entered the room she remembered before, the room with the gong in the black-painted stand, and blinked twice. A glowing ball of energy formed, a will-o'-the-wisp similar to the one that had led her to that underground refreshing room just a few days before. Lifting her chin and squaring her shoulders, Rora marched after the ball, *willing* herself to slip through any and all wards. *Preferably without a trace, since he'd probably try to lock me out if he knew of my approach in advance . . .*

The door the ball of light approached swung open, revealing the curve of a stairwell leading down into the base of the tower. It was the same one she had used before, so she descended readily, knowing the basement was four long flights down from here. Behind her, the door *thumped* shut again, and the tumblers in its lock *snicked* firmly into place. It was bad enough she was imposing herself on Rydan's understandable need for isolation; she wouldn't subject him to a chance of anyone else following her.

It wasn't until she was walking among suncrystal-lit corridors that she realized she had forgotten the book on meditation Kelly had found and loaned to her. Rora sighed and kept walking. It was bad enough that Rydan's food would be cold when it reached him. Worse, she was bringing it to him unannounced, unasked, and uninvited. But it was better to get this confrontation over and done while she had the courage to go through with it, than waiting and maybe losing her nerve.

Once she secured his understanding of the problem he suffered, *then* she could worry about helping him find a solution to it.

The will-o'-the-wisp led her in vaguely familiar directions at best. Of course, most of the corridors and halls she passed through looked familiar, thanks to the repeating motif of the carvings framing the vignettes cut in concise relief on the walls. But Rora was completely sure she was crossing unfamiliar territory when the ball of light took her through a vast dining hall lined with stone tables and benches.

The plate and mug were growing uncomfortably heavy by the time she heard noises echoing from somewhere up ahead. Of course, it still took her several minutes of following the glow before she got near the source of that commotion. First she had to go down a grand staircase to what looked like an underground grotto, save that the trees and bushes were carved from stone, and fountains and pools were utterly dry. Then from there, past a series of alcoves with benches broad enough to have served as beds, had they been covered in cushions instead of carved from bare stone. Then she crossed a bridge over what looked like a naturally carved chasm to a gallery of statues of men and women entwined in increasingly intimate poses.

Blushing, she hurried on, though the banging sounds she heard faded, the farther she got from the bridge area. Double-checking to make sure she was still following her will-o'-the-wisp, she ascended another stairwell . . . and found herself in a more than vaguely familiar hall. Her approach was from an unfamiliar angle, but the underwater landscapes were familiar, as was the slope-walled, rubble-filled, floating debris cart that she had ridden in before.

The box of tools had shifted to a new spot, as had the cart—and like the cart, the toolbox now floated. From the looks of the previous work spot, the carving looked like it was complete, leaving the black-haired sculptor free to work on another section of wall. Stripped to the waist and flexing an impressive set of defined muscles for such a lean body, Rydan was oblivious to her presence. In one hand was a silvery chisel; in the other, a gilded mallet, both of which he applied with quick, efficient skill.

Studying his work surface with intense concentration, he placed the tip of the chisel against the stone, rapped the butt of it with the mallet three ear-ringing times, knocking away three long slivers of stone, then tossed the chisel into the floating box and extracted another one, this one with a more wedge-shaped tip. Two sharp *bangs*, and he exchanged it for an oversized, awllike tool, which he rapped more gently, but many more times, detailing something in the speckled white granite in front of him.

Rora waited patiently until he paused to search for a new tool once that one was done. But it looked like he would just keep going if she didn't say something, so she did.

"Hello."

Rydan jerked around, eyes wide as he faced the intruder. He had been deep into his carving, yes, but he *should* have sensed her breaching the many layers of wards that lay between the surface and this place, long before she arrived. "How did you get down here? How did you get in here the *first* time?"

Ignoring his demands, Rora lifted the napkin-draped plate and the mug in her hands. "You missed supper, so I thought I would bring you some food." Glancing off to one side, where a trio of carved stone benches formed a curved semicircle, she tipped her head at them before moving that way. "Why don't you clean up a little and come eat? I'm sure that carving all these beautiful murals must make you very hungry."

He grabbed a rag from the toolbox and wiped his hands, then followed her to the benches. But not to eat. Looming over her as soon as she sat down, he addressed the problem of her presence. "You didn't answer my question. *How* did you get past all of my wards?"

Rora contemplated the black-eyed, black-haired mage towering over her. She hadn't summoned her emotion-Sight yet, wanting to be able to see his physical reactions clearly. From his expression alone, she could tell he wasn't going to give up on that particular subject. Lifting her chin, she gestured at the plate and mug she had settled on the bench beside her.

"Eat, and I will answer your question. At least, as best I can."

"Answer my question—in full—and I'll *consider* eating," Rydan countered, deepening his voice in the hopes of intimidating her.

She didn't intimidate easily. Instead, her chin lifted higher. "I bartered first!"

Rydan would have chosen to argue the moment, save that his stomach rumbled. Audibly. Giving in with a dark look, he snagged the plate and mug, dropping onto the bench set at an angle to hers. Eyeing the mug, he sniffed at the amber liquid within it. "Apple juice?"

"It's too early in your morning for stout. My father always said that a man needed his wits in the morning, not his wine," she countered.

"Ever since that boy came to the Isle, they've taken away my 'evening' drink, since it's breakfast for the rest," Rydan groused, though he sipped from the mug anyway. "There, see? I am drinking. Now, explain."

She twisted her hands together in her lap, searching for the right place to start. Someone—probably Evanor—had left a pair of green, *chamsa*-style dresses and a pair of darker green hose outside her door at some point between Morganen's visit and her waking up in time for dinner, allowing her to change into brand-new clothes. The hems and cuffs had been stitched in a pattern of diamonds within ovals set on either side of a sinuous wave, and she found herself tracing the couched thread between the ovals with her thumb.

Rydan muttered something that made his food steam and smell good, before picking up his fork and spearing one of the vegetables. "I am eating. Speak."

"I sort of . . . exaggerated, the other day," Rora stated, deciding that was the best way to go about explaining how she came to be in his underground palace. "I claimed that the emotions of others bother me, at a touch. This isn't exactly true."

He eyed her, chewing his mouthful of food, then swallowed. "What has that to do with you being down here, annoying me?"

"I have some abilities. They're not the normal sort. I don't *feel* others' emotions . . . but I can *See* them. Like mages can see magic if they squint right," she explained, glancing at him.

He was prodding the mashed roots with his fork, with more of his attention on her than on his breakfast. "My other abilities make it . . . awkward, I suppose you could say, if others touch me. But I'm not the one being affected by others' emotions.

"You are."

Rydan studied her a long moment, weighing her claim—and trying not to think of the lips she absently licked. It didn't quite work, but he forced both of them back onto the topic at hand with a grunt. "Nonsense—and *again*, how does that connect to you getting in here?"

"It's connected, because I can See things that no one else can . . . and I can also make myself *unseen*."

Starting to snort at the idea, Rydan paused. Shooting her a quick look, he activated his mage-Sight. Just as before, he Saw nothing. Not even the slightest glimmer of life-magic. She possessed all the energy of a weathered stick of wood, according to his mage-sense. Picking up the knife she had provided, he cut into the slices of beef on the plate resting on his thighs.

"So you've turned yourself 'invisible' to wardings. Why?"

She rolled her eyes, struggling to keep her impatience low-key. "Because we've been chased for over a year by mages who want to know how I can do what I can do. Or were you not paying attention to that part?"

"I wasn't told much about you. And I don't want to know much about you."

"Even if I say I know what's wrong with you?" Rora asked, and watched him stiffen a little. It hit her that her phrasing could have been less demeaning, and she quickly cleared her throat. "That is to say, I can See exactly what is troubling you—"

"Yes. You're *bothering* me, invading my privacy."

"I *meant*, the emotions that are attacking you!" Pulling back from her vehemence, Rora took a moment to calm herself, then *wished* her Sight into existence, double-blinking. Focusing on him, she told him what she Saw. "Right now, you're feeling resentful, wary, disgruntled, and skeptical."

"Anyone could tell that much," he scoffed before eating a slice of beef.

"But you're also feeling curious, hopeful, and scared,

inside. Scared that I'm right, a little bit . . . but also scared that I'm wrong," Rora revealed. "And you're more scared that I'm wrong—when you ran, that first day, you flinched from the bluntness of Akelly's rage, and then staggered under the stabbing attack of my fear. I owe you an apology for that, but I hadn't realized before then just how badly strong emotions can affect you. But that's why you run, rather than stay around the others."

The beef he swallowed sat awkwardly in his stomach. Part of it was fear that she was right, and part of it was fear that she *could* read his emotions . . . including his fear right now. But worse than that was the hope that gnawed at his guts. Because this plain, foreign woman was right. He *had* felt as if she'd stabbed him in the back, that time. Or rather, it felt as if she had stabbed his beast, which had in turn clawed at *him*.

A beast that was always riled and irritated by . . . emotions. Picking up his mug to give himself time to think, Rydan studied her over the brim. When he set it down again, he had a question to counter her theory. "What you say may or may not be so . . . but that doesn't explain why I feel"—he groped for a word, and finally settled on—"*injured* by being around others when they are *happy*."

She cast around for a way to explain it to him, and thought of the fluffy cat she and her sister had met. "When you pet a cat . . . they sit in your lap and purr for a good, long time. But after a while, they get irritated, jump down, and walk away. Even the gentlest of caresses can rub your skin raw, if you receive too much of it. When you are with your kin, and they're being happy . . . eventually, it rubs you the wrong way—even your own emotions can do that to you, feeding back on themselves. Either you get really, really happy, to the point of feeling giddy . . . or really, really sad, or really, really angry. Don't you?"

She was wrong on that count . . . sort of. "I *used* to. Not anymore."

Rora considered his words and realized why his aura seemed confident . . . and yet slightly clouded, as if he wasn't being completely honest with himself. "It's because you retreat from the others and try to keep your emotions in check, don't you?" she pointed out gently. "I think you've figured out that if you avoid the others, you avoid becoming raw and wounded . . . but there are more and more of them to irritate you with each passing day, and so you can tolerate less and less contact."

How can she know what I've been thinking? Rydan wondered warily. Then shook it off as a foolish idea. *No. The Gods made our thoughts private. We wear our emotions on our faces even when we do not speak or act upon them, but our thoughts remain private. That's one of the covenants between God and Man. My thoughts are safe in my head . . . but emotions are in the heart, not in the head . . . and the Gods have given Man no guarantees where their hearts are concerned.*

"If this . . . emotional sensitivity is my problem, then what is the solution?" he challenged her. "Surely, if you See the problem, you can fix it?"

"I don't know if I *can* fix it—but Seeing it, being aware of it, is the first and most important step," Rora hurried to reassure him the moment his black brows pinched together in a frown, doubt swirling around him in a dirty brown cloud. "I'm not a mage. Not a traditional sort, at any rate. The priestesses back home tried to teach me how to use my magic, but I couldn't master it. But I *can* See what you're feeling and how your own emotions get pulled back into you, as if they were water, and you were the drain hole of a sink. And I can see how others' emotions are pulled to you as well.

"If we can find a way to stop them from coming *in*, without bottling up your emotions as they're going *out* . . . I think that'll stop the irritation and pain," she offered. "And I think you should practice a lot more on how to keep your own emotions even and calm for the most part. It's not just the feelings of outsiders that are troubling you. Especially since a lot of what I See irritating you is self-inflicted—you don't have any control over the way it comes back into you, and so it tangles around you, choking you, the stronger your feelings are."

"And how do we go about that?" Rydan queried skeptically. "Cut out my heart, so I cannot feel at all?"

His skepticism annoyed her, and not just because she could See it binding him in brownish yellow streamers. "That's nothing but nonsense, Rydan. Cutting out your emotions would make you *dead*, even if you still walked and breathed.

Our feelings are too precious to deny; they give us compassion and help us to understand others, and they help keep us from feeling lonely."

Rydan paused in cutting up the next slice of beef, giving her a dark look. The ribbons of brownish yellow shifted to veils of dark red. "My emotions, from what you are telling me, are *forcing* me to be lonely, rather than endure the irritation of another's presence. Like *your* presence!"

"*Stop* it," Rora ordered. "You're making yourself angry. Stop complaining about the problem at hand, and start searching for a solution—because you're not going to *find* a solution if you're too busy snarling about it. Now, what I propose is that we work on you learning how to control your own emotions and how to control the impact of my own. Just the two of us, for now."

"And what if your emotions rub me raw? Do you think I will *like* being irritated repeatedly by you?" he challenged. "Wouldn't that make everything worse?"

"I am staying mostly calm right now, aren't I?" she countered. "The calmer my emotions are, the less they radiate from me, and the less they rub up against you. It's your own emotions right now that are causing you the most grief. And I have had years of practice in keeping myself calm and my state of mind lighthearted and cheerful. You can endure being petted for longer than being slapped, before that kind of touch becomes too irritating to handle . . . and that gives us time to work on your worst problem, the way your own emotions turn back on you and attack you."

Considering her words in silence, Rydan ate more of the meal she had brought him. Thankfully, she stayed silent, too. A thought crossed his mind as he drank from the mug, and he set it down again, staring at her. "Are you Seeing my emotions right now?"

"Yes." She saw no reason to prevaricate. "And I do appreciate the fact that you're giving my ideas some serious thought."

Rydan gave her a sharp, wary look. "You can read my *thoughts*?"

"What? No! Of course not," Rora denied. "Don't be silly. You were just . . . you know, wrapped in a veil of gray blue seriousness just now. I See emotions like veils and ribbons, vines and mists. The colors vary from moment to moment, but each one comes attached with a sort of *knowing*, an instant, instinctive interpretation of its meaning. And what I interpreted said that you were giving my suggestions due and solemn consideration. Whether it's a positive or a negative consideration . . . well, it doesn't look like you've quite decided just yet, from what I can tell. But you *are* considering it."

ELEVEN

Staring at her for a long, carefully non-thoughtful moment, Rydan picked up his fork and started eating again. Rora stayed quiet, bracing her palms on the edge of the bench while he ate, her gaze alternating between him and the scenes he had carved. Now that she had told him what she Saw . . . he could *feel* it. He could feel *her* emotions, the source that irritated the beast under his skin.

Rydan had to admit she was right. What he felt from her was no different than what he had felt from the others all this time; the only thing that had changed was his awareness of it. Like an unidentified noise in the distance, it had long irritated him without him being able to pinpoint the source of the sound.

But now that he knew, it felt like his beast was saying, *Ah—curiosity. That's the dripping of water from an improperly corked tap.* Or her next and more elusive emotion, which took him a few moments to track down, since it only flickered into existence when she glanced his way. *Is that . . . admiration? Like wind in the trees, the faint rustling of leaves? She admires me?*

No, that wasn't quite it. Frowning, Rydan tried to pinpoint it, but failed. It frustrated him.

"What are you thinking?"

He blinked at her. "What?"

"You're thinking something, and it's not making you happy," Rora told him. "I can See it wrapping down around you—that's what I'm going to do, at first, I think. Point out whenever your own emotions are affecting you adversely, because I can See it happening. So what were you thinking, just now?"

Setting down his fork, Rydan rubbed at his forehead. "I was wondering what *you* were thinking. When you look at me, my beast . . . this *thing* inside of me that makes me sensitive to feelings, I call it my beast," he explained at her silent confusion. "It feels whatever you're feeling, but I couldn't figure out what it was, other than . . ."

"Other than?" Rora prompted when he fell silent, his aura darkening slightly in disgruntlement. "You're puzzled by it. What do you think it is?"

"Admiration. Though you have *nothing* to admire in me," he added gruffly, cutting into the last bit of beef on his plate. "I don't even know why you're trying to help me . . . unless you think it's that damned Prophecy."

"Temper," Rora cautioned him. "Keep your mind calm. And I'm *helping* you because not only can I See the problem, I cannot bear to see anyone wounded so literally by their feelings. As for any Prophecy . . . I do not deny that Morganen told me about your verse."

Rydan snorted. "Meddler. He should stick to his own affairs."

"Matchmaking *is* his affair, or so this Prophecy claims. Personally, I feel sorry for him," Rora added in an aside.

"*Sorry* for him?" he demanded, scowling at her. The pointed arch of one of her light brown brows reminded him to curb his temper. Breathing deeply, Rydan struggled to let it go and addressed her point somewhat more calmly. "Rora, I remind you that he *drugged* me, and in doing so, caused me to violate you!"

Leaning on her hands, Rora waited until he calmed down and ate a little more before speaking. "Among my people . . . rape is the most serious of crimes, second only to murder. It's the underlying cause of all our many highly restrictive courting practices, because for almost two full generations, that's all my ancestresses knew, right after the Shattering of Aiar—and I don't tell you this to make you feel even more guilty, so stop feeling that way and *listen* to me.

"I'm telling you this because even among my people, with *that* for our history, we still share the same saying that I've heard expressed in several other kingdoms across Aiar: *You cannot rape the willing*."

Lifting his head, Rydan blinked at her. It wasn't just her words that shocked him, matched as they were to the pinkness of her cheeks. It was that feeling again, the feeling that wasn't quite admiration. He stared until the corners of her mouth curled up, and a bit of smugness added itself to her feelings as she continued.

"Now, I will admit I was *startled*, since such things are discouraged in our courting practices . . . but unlike my sister, I don't cling to those practices quite so tightly. And once past the initial shock of being, well, dragged into your bed so literally . . . Rydan, I *enjoyed* it."

She blushed hard as she said it, feeling her whole face heat with the admission, but Rora said it anyway. It wasn't maidenly of her, and her sister would have a fit if she ever heard about it, but Rora didn't care. Not when she could See his golden peach incredulity giving way to an almost purplish cross between pride and pleasure, engendered by the flattery implicit in her words.

"As I said . . . it's near impossible to violate the willing."

For a moment, Rydan blushed, too. But her willingness wasn't the only factor, and the other problem reared in his mind. It spoiled his pleasure over her delight in him, souring it in his mouth. "Do not think I *want* to succumb to some stupid Prophecy," he warned her, frowning once again. "The only thing I reign over, I *will not* relinquish."

His disclaimer stung, but Rora struggled to squash her disappointment as quickly as possible. "Who said I would demand such a thing of you? I don't even know what you 'reign' over, and I don't really care. The only thing that motivates me is making sure you'll no longer be injured by anyone you interact with. No one should have to suffer what you've been forced to endure, and that's all there is to it."

"But the Prophecy has been coming true," Rydan argued. "Brother by brother. If I fall for you, I lose control of what I guard."

"What, the Fountain?" Rora asked, and was subjected to a hard, dark stare. She hesitated for a moment, before deciding in a rush of faith to trust him. Trust had to begin somewhere between them, and if she could show him she trusted him, then maybe he would be more inclined to trust her. "Dominor and Serina told me about it. That's why they wanted to go to Koral-tai, because of what I am."

His puzzlement pinched his brow and wrapped him in confused yellowish green tendrils. "What you are?"

"Yes. I didn't even really know what I was, until I consulted with them. My sister and I thought we should go to Fortuna in the hopes that someone there would know how to help us, only the ship we were on was chased south into the Sun's Belt Reefs, and for the same reason I was chased off the Plains, my sister in protective tow."

"And what would that be?" Rydan inquired mock-lightly, setting his empty plate aside and picking up his mug for a drink.

"According to your kin . . . I'm a Fountain. Or a Font. Whatever you want to call it."

Rydan didn't quite choke, though it was a near thing. Controlling himself, he waited until the urge to spit the juice back into his mug faded, then swallowed carefully and set his drink back onto the bench. "Impossible. Fountains are places, *not* people."

"Serina says it's not impossible," Rora countered. "Just very, very rare. And she and Dominor both agree that I feel just like one of these Fountain things."

"Feel?" he challenged her, arching a skeptical brow.

In response, Rora lifted her hand. "Touch me and feel it for yourself. Feel what caused several mages to attack and kill some of my kin, just to get their hands on me, and what my sister would die to prevent you from feeling."

That only made him more skeptical. "And you offer this *feeling* to me freely? Aren't you afraid I'd covet the kind of power you say you hold within you?"

Rora grinned. "You swore upon a Truth Stone that you

wouldn't steal it. So I'm perfectly safe letting you touch me. Go ahead, touch me."

Skeptical even in the face of the amused confidence radiating against his inner beast, like sun shining on a cat, Rydan extended his own hand. Their fingers met . . . and warmth engulfed his nerves, thrumming straight up his arm to buzz at the base of his skull. It was very much like, and yet not quite like, the sensation he had felt that first time he had finally touched and claimed his own Fountain. The difference was hard to pinpoint, and it made his skin tingle almost as if it was his beast being affected—like petting a cat for too long, as she had said.

It wasn't quite irritating, but it was stimulating . . . and only now did Rydan recall with clarity the impression of *home* he'd received while under the influence of Morganen's drug. She felt like *home* because she Felt like his Fountain. The one place . . . where he had learned to *block out* his emotions.

Jerking his hand back, Rydan swore. "Jinga's Sacred Ass!"

Guessing that was the name of either a local hero or a local god, Rora didn't take offense. "I told you that you'd feel it. I am an actual, living Fountain, according to Serina."

"Not *that*," Rydan dismissed, flexing and shaking his fingers absently. Unlike his Fountain, which he had painstakingly attuned himself to, there was no sacred bell to help him adjust to *her* vibrations. "I just realized the only place I ever feel *peaceful* is when I enter my Fountain . . . after having locked out my emotions, so they cannot trouble my mind—the Gods-be-damned solution to my problems has been there this entire time! All I have to do is what I've done every time I enter the Fountain!"

That made her stare at him, taken aback by the implied suggestion. "Rydan, you can't lock out your emotions."

"Why not?" he challenged her. "If it works for the heart of pure magic, it should be able to work in the face of all my family members!"

"Because to cut out all of your feelings is to cut out everything that makes life worth living," she argued.

"*What* in my life is worth the pain and agony I must endure every time I interact with another person?" he retorted. "Pray tell me, *what*?"

For a moment, she was at a loss to come up with one single thing that wouldn't cause him irritation in the end. Frustration bubbled up within her, along with despair—and then a wild idea struck. It lunged her off her bench and made her hands clasp his face, holding it still so she could mash her mouth to his. He grunted in surprise, swaying back from the impact of her kiss and catching her elbows for balance.

It was an awkward kiss, untutored, a little rough, but undeniably a kiss. Power thrummed from her to him through her hands and her lips, making Rydan feel light-headed. Or maybe that was her fault; it had been a long time since he had allowed a woman to kiss him. Not that he had *allowed* this . . . but . . . her lips wriggled a little, no longer quite so mashed against his. A moment later, her tongue brushed his lips, and *that* felt good.

Instinct made him pull her closer, made him tilt his head within her grip and show her how to match and mate their mouths in sensual nips. Bent over at an awkward angle, she wobbled when he nudged her head to one side, so Rydan pulled her down onto his lap. For once in his adult life, his beast wasn't grumbling, wasn't snarling and snapping and clawing at his insides.

The energies thrumming through his nerves, roused by her touch, had caged the creature in his hard-won Guardian's discipline . . . and yet, he *did* still feel her emotions. He wasn't completely melded with the power inside of her, though, as he was with his own Fountain. Instead of being able to touch it directly, it helped keep him from drowning inside of her energies. He felt her enjoyment, her delight, but they didn't smother him; they wrapped him in a light embrace that warmed him from skin to bone and back again. It was almost as if he was falling into her kiss, now that she was following his lead, learning quickly whatever he enjoyed most in the meeting of their lips.

Falling . . . Prophecy!

One moment, Rora was on his lap, in his arms, having the breath kissed out of her, feelings stirring within her that seemed to prove *why* her people forbade the playing of lips among unmarried couples. The next, her rump hit the floor, making her grunt from the unexpected impact. Bewildered by the loss of their kiss as much as by her sudden unseating, Rora blinked and looked up at him, one hand on her mouth, the other bracing herself upright.

Rydan, now on his feet, moved away from her, hands tugging through his hair and emotions swirling in chaotic streamers around his body. She couldn't sort anything out, other than that he *had* enjoyed their kiss, but was now conflicted about it. Staring up at him, she asked, "Why did you stop?"

Tensing, struggling with his roiling confusion, Rydan gave her a dark look. This was all *her* fault, for sneaking in here, for being close enough for him to grab the other day, for grabbing him now and *kissing* him. Alright, some of it *was* his own fault. It was his own damn fault he was attracted to her, and definitely his fault that he had given in to his desire for her, even if only for a few fleeting moments . . . but he wouldn't have had his self-control imperiled if she hadn't thrown herself at him.

When he didn't answer for several seconds, she curled her legs under her, pushing to her feet. He backed up quickly, out of the semicircle of benches. Rora kept pace with him.

"Stay back," Rydan ordered her. "Don't even try to use your feminine wiles on me again!"

Rora, dusting off her new clothes, paused long enough to gape at him. His scowl and his aura were sincere, but his accusation . . . ! Straightening, unable to stop herself, she tipped back her head and laughed heartily, unable to believe him despite his visible conviction. She laughed so hard, she wound up staggering back onto the bench behind her, dropping abruptly to its surface as her arms clutched at her sides.

Through eyes streaming with tears, she could see her mirth pouring out of her like gilded yellow sunshine, soaking into him, banishing his rising anger and doubt. That sobered her a little, enough to wipe at her cheeks with the edges of her hands and struggle for breath. Panting, Rora finally sniffed to clear her nose—for her tears of laughter were clogging it—and grinned at him.

"*Thank* you. I have *never* in my whole life been accused of having 'feminine wiles,'" she repeated drolly, beginning to chuckle again. "My sister has always had far more wiles than me."

He gave her a dark look and folded his arms across his chest.

Leaning forward, elbows on her knees, Rora gave him a frank look of her own. "Aren't you a little old to be pouting?"

"I am *not* pouting—pouting is for *children*," he half growled.

Rora tapped the side of her face, next to one eye. "The Sight doesn't lie. You were pouting, just a moment ago. Though now, you're irritated. And *earlier*," she stressed, "you were *enjoying* our kiss. I Saw it quite clearly, so don't bother trying to deny it.

"Now, what I *propose*," she stated, sitting up and clasping her hands in her green-clad lap, "is that we spend our time conversing. Not just arguing, but sharing jokes, childhood stories, sad and happy memories, talk about our fears and our dreams . . . and I will gauge whether each of the emotions being raised on both sides is affecting you, or not, and by how much. The first step to solving a problem is awareness of the problem. Once you're aware of it, the second step is to study it to find its vulnerabilities, and thus find a solution for it. Agreed?"

Uncomfortable with her clarity, Rydan tightened his arms across his chest. The thought of her being able to See his emotions made him feel vulnerable, unarmored, exposed. Worse, she was right about him enjoying their abrupt kiss. He groped for a way to regain control of the situation. "What if I don't agree? What if I tell you to get out of here?"

Copying his pose, though she remained seated on the bench, Rora folded her own arms across her chest. "Do you really think you can make me leave, if I don't want to go? I am here to *help* you. I know you loathe your 'beast,' as you call it. I may not know just yet how to defeat it, but I'm willing to help you figure it out. You're *not* alone in this, Rydan."

You're not *alone in this . . . not alone . . .* He flinched at her words, but only a little. How many times had he *felt* alone, thanks to the irritability of his beast, forcing him into a self-imposed exile? Loneliness was as much his enemy as the beast, yet until now, he hadn't had any other choice that he could live with. It was only a slim hope she was offering . . . but it *was* hope.

Still, it wasn't easy for him to ask for help. Asking for help meant enduring the presence of another person. Yet . . . this was the longest he had spent in anyone's company, when that person had provoked within him so many different emotions, without making him feel as though his nerves were being shredded by her presence. Unnerved, yes; she unnerved the hell out of him. But not injured.

Resettling his arms, he lifted his chin slightly, struggling to control the defensive belligerence within him, in case she Saw it. "Fine. But we will *not* kiss again, and you will *not* try to make me fall in love with you."

"Rydan, I don't know *how* to make a man fall in love with me," Rora informed him dryly, hands resting on her hips. "That has always been my sister's province, with her exotic hair and eyes, and her alluringly high status among our people. *She* knows how to flirt with men. I've always been left in her shadow. In fact, of all five suitors I've ever had, every last one of them ended up moving on to try to court *her* instead."

He quirked his brow skeptically. "*That* annoying little . . . ?"

At a warning glare from Rora, he wisely didn't finish his sentence. "My sister has been under a lot of stress. She is like a fish tossed up onto the shore, flopping around and gasping for breath, thinking of nothing but slipping back into her liquid home. She is *also* a lot like you, prone to irritability at the least little offense." Giving him a superior look, she added, "If I can put up with *her*, I can put up with *you*. Now, what is your favorite color? Black?"

"Green, actually." At her briefly surprised look, he realized her efforts at trying to be calm and friendly really did make her more tolerable to be around.

If she was right about her effect on him . . . then she was possibly right about his own affect on himself. Sighing, Rydan let go of some of his belligerence. He even found himself confessing the real reason why under the carefully lightened weight of her curiosity. He would try to resist her feminine wiles—for she had them, despite her sincere protestations—but he would try to stop being such a pain in both their backsides, in the hopes that it really would stop aggravating his beast.

"I wear black to annoy Dominor. It is a very difficult color to clean without having it fade, or stain anything else that may be washed at the same time with it . . . and I look intimidating in it."

Amusement threatened to rise within her again. Struggling it back down before her radiant aquamarine mirth could reach him and be sensed, Rora managed a sober, sincere nod. "Yes, you do. But I'm not going to let that stop me from helping you."

"Pity."

This time, it was his aura that streaked with hints of aquamarine. Giving in, Rora grinned at him, pleased he was relaxing in her presence. "So, want to know what my favorite color is?"

He gave her a skeptical look. When her enthusiasm didn't waver, Rydan sighed. "Fine. What is your favorite color?"

"Wood."

Rydan stared at her. "Wood? You mean, brown?"

Rora shook her head. "No. I don't like brown, but I *do* like wood. I like the different shades, and the patterns of the different grains. Well, I should say, it's my favorite color to *look* at."

He looked around himself, his aura dubious. "I don't exactly have any wood down here to look at. You'll have to suffer."

"Don't get me wrong; stone is nice, too. As for other colors, I like to *wear* green, since it matches my eyes, but it's otherwise only so interesting, and no more."

A bemused, brief laugh escaped him. "You are a *very* strange woman, Rora Fen Ziel of the Shifting Plains."

She smiled back at him, Seeing more than just what he was saying. "Thank you!"

"You're welcome. Maybe. Shouldn't you be going back up above, to your bed?" he asked.

"Oh, no. I've been sleeping as much as possible during the last two days, so I could stay wide-awake at night and come down here to help you," Rora countered, giving him an ingenuous smile.

Rydan wasn't fooled. Throwing up his hands, he turned away from her, moving back toward his latest mural. "Stay and converse, or go and sleep, as you wish. I have work to finish."

Getting up from the bench, Rora followed him. "Did you carve all of these things, everywhere?"

"No. The frame carvings were here to begin with, and a few of the images in their centers. Most of the rest, though, those are my work," he admitted, gesturing at the walls.

"They're beautiful." Lifting her hand to the partially completed mural, yet another underwater scene, Rora caressed the stone. This one was of kelp forests and oyster beds that seemed laid out neatly enough to have been orchards and farms, had they been on the surface. Most of the carvings were polished, while a few details had been left rough for textural contrast. From the sheer smoothness of the polished parts, she suspected he had used his magic. "They're also very sensual, filled with motion and depth, dimension and texture—a blind man would enjoy touching this, and could probably even figure out what you've carved.

"You definitely have a gift for this. Do you sell your carvings?" she asked him, glancing over her shoulder. "I've seen carvings almost as fine as these on the civic buildings in the cities of Amazai."

"No." His reply was flat, closed. "They are . . . I use carving to release my stress. Most of the time, I don't even think; I just carve." Studying the image he had been working on before her arrival, Rydan lifted his own hand, skimming his fingers over the curves and angles he had carved. Her appreciation and admiration, almost a tangible pressure against his beast, though not too unbearable, prompted him to add in a murmur, "Whatever comes free from my chisels is almost like the will of the Gods. Sometimes . . . I don't even know what I've carved until I step back for a drink or a rest . . ."

"Then I shall watch you with my Sight to See what you're doing to calm yourself, when you carve," Rora promised him. "The more different ways we can look at your problem, the more different possibilities we may find providing us paths to a solution."

At his sharp look, she offered him a smile and backed away from the wall.

"I'll just sit and watch for a while. Then I'll ask you

questions, annoy and bother you until you *need* to carve," she teased, reaching the nearest bench and reseating herself, "and then Look while you carve yourself back into a calmer frame of mind." She fluttered her hand at him, too. "Go on . . ."

Simultaneously annoyed, bemused, and uncertain as to whether to throw her out or let her stay, Rydan finally gave up and reached for his tools. He could always throw her out later . . . if he could risk putting his hands on her, that was. Setting chisel to stone, he tried his best to forget the taste of her lips and how she had gone from badly mashing to almost mastering the art of the kiss, all in a matter of minutes.

After spending a couple hours alternating between blissful silence and being pestered into conversation interspersed with comments about his emotional state, Rydan abandoned his carving and took his uninvited companion farther into the maze of tunnels. The trip was intended for him to make his weekly check on an ongoing transformation spell carved literally into the rock at the very edge of the underground maze, where the granite gave way to a boundary of marble before becoming limestone. It was there that his longest-running piece of magic was still going.

That vein of marble had a predominantly white base, but it also had inclusions, brown and gray ribbons crisscrossing the stone, making it impure and thus improper for what he had in mind. Having found it about eight or nine months into his stay on the island while exploring the underground maze of corridors and chambers, Rydan had taken another month to research a spell for removing the inclusions and purifying the quality of the stone—this was the research that had led him into specializing in stone-wrought spells, in fact. Marble in particular could be used for constructing various Artifacts, though inclusions often caused problems. Pure white marble was an absolute requirement for Truth Stones, being very hard to find, and very slow to purify magically.

He didn't even know how big the vein was, but the runes he had carved into the surface and periodically refreshed with power were still transforming the stone. Once it was pure, he could make a fortune carving out discs and enchanting them into Truth Stones and other marble-based Artifacts. However, once it started, the purification spell could not be stopped. Not without having to carve all the way to the impure sections and restart the magic all over again.

The spellbook he had referenced spoke of mining-attuned mages spending one month purifying rock and five months carving and processing it. Given how they had been cast permanently into exile, Rydan had initially figured he had plenty of time to make a very large, purified vein. After about three years of nonstop transmutation, he had no idea just how large the vein was, but he did know the process was finally beginning to slow down.

He also knew that his family, busy with clearing the land by the cove, had neglected making lots of new Artifacts for sale, not just to the traders who came from the mainland, but to the nuns in Natallia. Truth Stones were easy to make, once a mage had a decent supply of purified marble . . . and a source of readily available power, such as a Fountain. If the vein was slowing down, he would be able to craft Stones by the handful each day. Some methods required special ingredients or timing, and the Stones created lasted decades, but the method he used could be crafted at any time, though it shortened the lifespan of the truth spell to just a handful of years. But the method was cheap and the price correspondingly affordable.

To Rora's openly radiated amusement, he chose a version of one of his floating ore carts to ride in, rather than spend all their time walking to and from the distant passage where the marble could be accessed. Actually, the cart more resembled a broad, legless armchair than a lidless, slope-sided chest. The seat was broad enough for him to have brought his toolbox along for the ride, but with her along, they had to leave it behind, sitting hip-to-hip and shoulder-to-shoulder as the contraption floated rapidly along, protected by cushioning spells to keep them from bumping into anything.

Since they had to share the seat—for Rora refused to be left behind—she tucked her arm around his waist and nestled her head on his shoulder. That forced him to wrap his own arm around her for balance . . . but her emotional presence remained tolerably calm.

It was her physical presence that disconcerted him. Not just the bone-thrumming magic he could feel, either. Rora was warm, feminine, and soft in certain places that felt a little too nice when pressed against him, even when sitting innocuously side by side. She smelled nice, too, freshly bathed with a hint of flowers. As much as his body enjoyed her proximity, her closeness troubled him. He could not forget the verse affixed to him in the Seer's Curse.

Shun the Day and rule the night
Your reign's end shall come at light
When Dawn steals into your hall
Bride of Storm shall be your fall

If by being the brother responsible for keeping an eye on things while his siblings slept, he supposed he *had* ruled the night, in the sense of maintaining safety and thus order . . . but he didn't *reign* over anything other than the Fountain. And though the woman *cuddled* against him had twice stolen into his underground halls, she had done so first in the afternoon, and then in the evening. Not at dawn. Yet.

She nuzzled him. Her head shifted, rubbing her cheek against his shoulder, and she sighed. "This is nice . . ."

The twisting tunnel they were floating through echoed her words, emphasizing the hiss at the end. Rydan could definitely feel a base level of contentment and happiness in her, but he wasn't sure why. "What is nice? Floating instead of walking?"

"Touching someone. Ever since we realized I was being uncovered by bumping into mages, I've had to be extra careful about not touching anyone other than my sister. You can't tell a mage just by looking at her or him," Rora added, her emotions dulling a little with unhappiness.

That made him twist his head, eyeing her askance. "Yes, you can."

Rora lifted her head, peering up at him. Since they were traveling through areas without suncrystals, the floating seat had lightglobes, two of which were mounted on tallish spikes rising up from the backrest. The one behind him haloed his midnight hair in bluish highlights, almost distracting her from her reply. Shaking it off, she gave him a bemused look. "No, I can't. I've tried."

"You can See emotions just by willing it, yet you cannot tell what a mage looks like with your Sight?" Rydan challenged, skeptical.

"No. It's all . . . fuzzy. Everything glows," she tried to explain. "Sort of like looking through a fog of light. I can Look to see if something specific is magical, but only a single, specific thing, and it does take time for me to focus my Sight. If I try to search a crowd of people, everything goes fuzzy, so I don't bother."

Rydan frowned at that. Squinting, he focused on Seeing her power—and winced violently away from her, squeezing his eyes shut. The floating chair rocked with his movement, slowing for a moment as it stabilized before picking up speed again. Rora's concern washed over him, prickling his beast a bit, though not quite in an irritating way.

"What's wrong?"

Rubbing at his eyes, mind racing as he recuperated from what he had Seen, Rydan waited for the stinging of his inner senses to fade before facing her again. Just to look, however, not Look. "I tried to Look at you with mage-Sight, just now . . . and you blinded me. I think I know why."

"You do? I did?"

"When I'm not touching you, I See nothing. No magic. But touching you, I'm inside your defenses, rather than blocked out by them," he explained under the light weight of her curiosity. "When you Look for magic in a specific thing, I think you're excluding yourself as well as most everything else . . . but when you're Looking for mages in general, you are blinded by your own radiance."

Rora wrinkled her nose at that. "Great. I was told by the priestesses that, if I couldn't discern magical from nonmagical, that would make it even tougher for me to learn how to *be* a mage. If I even can," she muttered, settling her cheek back onto his shoulder. "They did determine that I'm keeping the Fountain thing inside of me under strict control—they said that part of the power within me is containing all the rest of it," she added as she Saw a wisp of curiosity emanating from him, "and that it's two different types of power. Like how a willow basket can hold a cooking bowl. One is made from woven wood, while the other is made from baked clay, even though both are containers . . . but one is watertight, and the other is not. One is heavy, and the other is not."

"*If* you are a repository for a Fountain singularity," Rydan offered grudgingly, considering the possibility, "then if the power within you could be removed and anchored in place like a normal Fountain is . . . you could turn out to be a very powerful mage. You must be one, to have withstood it all along, let alone controlled it. But you would need training, if and when it is removed."

"Well, with so many mages in one spot, surely one of you could give me some instruction," Rora pointed out logically, hope rising within her. "Anyway, that's why Serina and Dominor wanted to go to that Natallia place. Serina says she's heard of this happening before, in some old records. I wouldn't mind going myself, now that I've had some of that Ultra Tongue stuff," she added, "but Serina said it probably isn't a wise idea to throw two rival sources of immense power together without checking the old records first."

"If you went, you would also not be able to help me with my beast," Rydan stated, trying not to think of why that thought irritated him a little. The way she tightened her arm around his waist a little appeased him.

"I'm not planning on going. While I *am* something of an expert at sifting through moldering books and scrolls, the power I hold scares me more than enough. The thought of rubbing it up against something its equal . . . Well, I'm staying right here, and you'll just have to put up with me." Tilting her cheek on his shoulder, she smiled up at him. "Not very irritating after all, am I?"

Rydan grunted, rather than risk a comment on that. They were near the end of the tunnel, and he had to slow the floating chair. Not that they would crash into the wall, but the magic-cushioned bump would jolt them. He didn't need to dismount, either; a curling of his hand, a flexing of his will, and the chair rotated as it drifted to a stop, allowing him to study the sigils painted on the otherwise pristine marble surface.

They were very faint, almost completely gone, but the

smallish lightglobes embedded in the front of the chair's armrests illuminated them enough for Rydan to gauge it was only a matter of months now, if not mere weeks. Extending his hands so that they brushed the stone, Rydan tapped into the Fountain in the distance . . . and stopped immediately. The energy within the woman pressed to his side had risen in rapid response, interfering with his control.

Sliding off the chair, he removed himself from her touch and tried again. Power flowed smoothly from him into the marble face, making the translucent surface glow beneath his palms. That made the sigils bonded to the surface flare a golden yellow, making the white light of the glowing marble seem bluish by contrast. If he could push enough power into the last bit of the spell, maybe he could finish the job within the next turning of Brother Moon, though it was difficult for him to access the Fountain's power this far from its source.

TWELVE

Rora waited patiently as Rydan worked, idly looking around. The marble zone stretched out to either side of the faint marks he was charging, most of it glowing now in response to his efforts. That allowed her to see where the marble section began and ended. Brownish blue bands marked the transition between speckled granite, pure white marble, and dull gray limestone for about four or five body lengths. It also made her curious, because the divisions only held true for the left-hand wall.

"Rydan . . . if that's marble, and that speckled stuff is granite, back where we came from, and that grayish stuff up ahead is limestone . . ." Rora asked him when he finished, sliding his hands free of the left-hand wall, "then what is *that*?"

Rydan craned his head to look where she was gesturing, behind the floating chair. The right-hand wall should have been mottled white; his stone-cleansing spell worked in one direction only, forward, and so he had picked the left-side wall to work on first, with the right half of the vein held in reserve. Instead, it was a mottled mass of brown and blue, with almost no white visible . . . except for the part directly across from the sigils he had wrought from the impurities in the deposit. A fist-sized spot of white existed there.

Twisting the chair around with his hands, he shone the lightglobes directly on the surface. For a moment, the white spot glowed brighter. Then, so slowly that his eyes felt like they were playing tricks on him, the spot grew larger. Rydan quickly held up his hand, spanning the diameter with his fingers. And Felt the power in the wall.

Blinking, he stared at the wall, then quickly double rapped the lightglobes off, leaving them in near darkness. Rora gasped from the sudden loss of light, but the tunnel wasn't completely dark. Behind them, the sigil-charged wall still glowed, if faintly . . . and the spot ahead of them glowed strongly, widening visibly. Lifting his hand to the faint, blue white circle, Rydan found his fingers had to widen farther than before to span the spot from edge to edge . . . and within ten heartbeats, his hand had to shift again to keep the thumb and the littlest finger covering the edge of that glow.

"All you did was . . . was just pour power into those marks?" Rora asked him in a near whisper. "And it's cleansing the stone that fast?"

"Yes." Rydan paused, then turned to look at her. With the fading glow of the wall behind her, she was little more than a silhouette. Acting on impulse, he spun the chair back around. "Put your hands on the wall, like I did. Picture . . . picture the smoothest, finest, purest white marble you could ever imagine—like milk skimmed of its cream, it is so smooth and pure—and pour that, and your power, into the stone."

Rora eyed Rydan's shadowy figure askance. "You want me to *what*? Rydan, every time I've tried to release what I hold, I *burn* things!"

"This is stone; you will not harm it. *I* will not let you harm it," he reassured her, touching her cloth-draped knee. "Trust me. Think of pure white marble, the white of clouds, the white of snow, flawlessly smooth and translucently clean, and pour your power through my sigil."

"If this tunnel collapses—"

"*Concentrate*," he ordered her. "Flawless, fine-grained, smooth . . ."

"Flawless . . . fine-grained . . . smooth," she repeated, trying to fix that image in her mind. What little the priestesses had been able to teach her had included the fact that it was the mind and the will as much as anything that shaped a true spell. She had never been able to cast a true spell . . . but this wasn't a spell, exactly. This was just a charging of what was already there. "Flawless, fine-grained, smooth . . . like milk and clouds and snow . . ."

Leaning forward, she pressed her hands to the wall and opened herself to its depths, clinging firmly to the thought of the wall glowing, not burning.

The wall brightened rapidly, making her squeeze her eyes shut within a few heartbeats. But it remained cool under her palms. Nothing burned, nothing scorched, and nothing collapsed. When the light was too bright, even with tightly closed lids, she closed her mental doors on the energy, slowing it to a trickle before cutting it off. The light faded much more slowly. It took almost a hundred heartbeats before she felt it was safe enough to open her eyes.

When she did, the tunnel was brightly lit, as if illuminated by a summer sun. Not just the walls; the slightly curved floor and the arch of the ceiling glowed, too. The only darkness to be seen was an arm's length of what looked like black marble ringing the boundaries of granite on one side and limestone on the other. Above, below, ahead, and behind, all of it was pure white, without even a hint of the marks that had been there before.

"*I* did all of that?" she asked Rydan hesitantly, a giddy disbelief welling up inside of her.

Rydan grabbed her by the ribs, hauling her off the floating chair and into his embrace, shifting away from the chair so he could spin her around, feeling her rising, astonished delight. "Yes, you did!"

Shocked by the bright blue happiness swirling around him as much as by being whirled around, Rora laughed. "I did, didn't I? I did magic! Well . . . it was *your* spell . . . but I did magic—*real* magic!" Flinging out her arms, she let him whirl her around again, off her feet. "I did magic!"

Giddy himself, astounded by the implications—that the vein ringed the whole of Nightfall Isle, for it to have come back upon itself like that, since the spell only worked in one direction, deeper into the marble—Rydan found his head reeling with a double dose of joy. Yet touching her as he was, forced by her literally vibrant flesh to temper his reactions as if in the presence of a Fountain, he didn't find their commingled feelings to be a raw irritation on his nerves. Exhilarating, not irritating.

Instead, he set her down with her back to the still-glowing wall and kissed her. It seemed the best outlet for his—their—overwhelming joy, and it *was* the best outlet. Caught by surprise, she clutched at his black tunic. At first, he thought it was to catch her balance, and pressed her body into the wall with his own, before realizing she was doing her awkward best to return everything he did. A single, singular realization wound its way through the last of his thoughts: *She wants this she wants this she wants this . . .*

He pressed her more firmly into the wall, starting at their mouths and enjoying the softness of her breasts. When his hips nudged hers, she squeaked into his mouth. That made him pause and start to draw back; unlike their last time, body-to-body, he was fully in control . . . if one could call this head-spinning desire fully controllable.

Feeling him retreat a little, Rora opened her eyes. Purplish red lust poured out of him, swirling around her so strongly she could almost feel it, but threads of dull yellow doubt were beginning to creep into his aura. Hands trembling with uncertainty—the kind where she had never done this sort of thing before—she slid her fingers from his ribs to his hips, and then around to his backside. A tug pulled his lower body back into place against hers.

Rydan sucked in a sharp, startled breath. Physically, she felt delicious, a treat he hadn't enjoyed for far too long. Emotionally . . . she was too unsure, too nervous. Too rushed, for all that she was enjoying their interlude. Struggling against the weight of both of their emotions, Rydan concentrated firmly on the thrum of her magic. For all she had nearly blinded both of them, it still pulsed strongly within her. Slowly he cleared his head with his hard-won discipline.

Though she wanted more kisses, Rora could See him struggling within his aura, pushing his emotions outward. Relaxing her grip on his bottom—though she did so with a little reluctance since it seemed like a very nice bottom—she focused on her breathing, calming herself as well. The glow had almost gone out in the walls around them, and she could barely see him physically, though his emotions still glowed, thanks to her Sight.

Knowing their lust was fading, she rose up on her toes and found his mouth with hers. Not for a heated kiss, just a soft one. A nice one. He returned it with a gentle press of his own lips . . . and someone's stomach rumbled. Rora giggled at the unexpected sound, then wrapped her arms around his ribs, hugging him affectionately. Hesitating only a moment, Rydan returned her embrace, then reached through the darkness at his side until his hand bumped into the side of the floating chair. She heard him fumble a moment more, then a soft glow sprung up from the nearest lightglobe, making both of them flinch from the sudden illumination. His stomach rumbled again, and she caught the way one corner of his mouth quirked up, matching the rose pink curl of amused embarrassment winding ribbonlike around him.

"Come. It's time to go." Shifting her around to the chair, he helped her up onto the seat, then settled himself beside her. This time, when she wrapped her arm around his waist and laid her head on his shoulder, his own arm was already in place. Only two worries bothered him as she asked him questions about the process of turning purified marble into Truth Stones: his emotional control in her presence, and his ongoing concern over the potential threat she posed to his Guardianship.

With a train of five ore carts enchanted to follow, they went back to the marble tunnel. Carving out blocks of translucent white stone didn't take long, though once heavily laden, the progress of the carts slowed considerably for the trip back. That gave them plenty of time to talk, mostly of Rora volunteering information about life on the Shifting Plains, the groups of kin-families that made up the larger tribe-Families, their associated Clans, their various territories and how they survived on such a seemingly empty landscape as the vast grasslands surrounding the old capital, living in tents spring through autumn and houses only in winter.

It was very different from Rydan's childhood. He had

grown up in his family's castle, nestled in a region of Katan that consisted mostly of forested hills and farm-choked valleys. The only times he had camped in a tent were when his father had taken him and his brothers on hunts and the occasional long-distance journey. Yet there were similarities, from playing games of tag and hide-and-seek, to reminisces of boys putting bugs down girls' tunics in both cultures. Of course, he had been the boy, and she had been the girl, though they had been a quarter of a world apart.

She told him about her people's worship of Father Sky and Mother Earth, and how rainstorms were the Father's way of courting and caressing the Mother. Rora blushed when she confessed her people believed in the occasional, passionate tempest between married couples, though it was strictly a thing of privacy, and that one carefully pretended that one did *not* hear certain noises emanating from within the walls of a particular *geome*, the domed tents her people used. That was also when she confessed she had the bad habit of unconsciously willing doors to open for her, though since her exile, she had tried to be careful about not doing that where anyone could see it.

Rydan confessed his own habit of not touching doors had stemmed from his youthful habit of carrying large piles of books to his room for hoarding and reading. That led to her enthusiastically talking about all the books she, too, had read. The Shifterai *could* read and write, but it wasn't easy to lug books all over the place when one lived as a nomad for three-quarters of the year. Some of the older books each of them had read overlapped, mainly thanks to her rummaging through the surviving cellars of the capital of Aiar and his scrounging among the shelves of the palace here at Nightfall.

When they reached the suite of chambers containing his newly claimed bedchamber, Rydan let her settle in the cushioned chair in his study so she could read her way through one of his earliest lesson books on magic. As far as he was concerned, the sooner she started reading the theory of magic, the better off she would be, even if his brother and sister-in-law found no safe way of extracting the Fountain embedded in her flesh. Not that Rora objected; in fact, she told him one of the things she missed most in her exile was being able to read. That made him glad he had heeded his instincts and packed even his oldest books among the belongings he and his siblings had been permitted to bring with them into exile.

It also freed him to work on shaping the large chunks of marble into many smallish discs in his main workroom, which was just through an archway off to one side of the book-lined room. Occasionally, she would call out a question, and he would come to the archway and give her an answer before going back to the tedious but necessary steps of preparing the stone for future enchantment. It was easiest to work on one step at a time, so that he could get into an efficient rhythm—Koranen had taught him that trick, when Rydan had occasionally helped his next-youngest sibling with the manufacturing and enchanting of lightglobes.

In fact, he got so into the rhythm of first cutting, then shaping, then polishing each chunk of stone, it wasn't until he was almost halfway through the stacks of rough-hewn discs that he realized it had been a while since she had last asked him any questions. Concern nagging at his conscience, Rydan abandoned his work, dusting off his hands as he walked to the archway. In the light of the globes, he could see her light brown hair at the top of the well-padded chair, tilted to one side.

Moving farther into the study, he came around to the side and caught sight of her face. One cheek was pressed into the upper wings of the padded chair, and the book had sprawled in her green-clad lap, no longer supported by her hands. Approaching the chair, Rydan studied her slack face, thinking about what had just happened. Not that she had fallen asleep . . . but that he had just spent more continuous time in her company in one night than he had spent with his family in almost four years.

And his beast, aside from a few irksome twitchings now and again, hadn't really complained.

Dropping into a crouch, Rydan eyed the young woman asleep in his chair. She was twenty, just five years younger than him, yet she had lived more of life than him. She was annoyingly persistent, yet had been pleasant company when he had allowed her to stay. And though her kisses were as unpolished as rough-cut stone, they held the promise of the finest, highest polish in her enthusiasm to learn. She also wasn't all that pretty while sleeping, he acknowledged, but when she was awake, this Shifterai woman was fascinating to behold. Like the glow of pure magic illuminating and transforming ordinary stone, she lit up from within whenever she spoke, enchanting him into ignoring his dislike for regular company.

"What are you doing to me?" Rydan murmured, quietly enough that she didn't wake. "More important . . . what are you *going* to do to me?"

There were still the verses of the Prophecies to consider. Not just the Song of the Sons, but the Curse of Nightfall had to be considered, too. Saber had encountered it in the library, in the white-bound tomes that contained the history of the old Duchy of Nightfall, and had offered it to Rydan to read, as a way of enticing his black-haired sibling into conversing about the books' contents. The last volume had been filled in by the scribe whose job it had been to follow around and record the words of the last Duchess, who had been a Seer of some renown. Rydan had been quick to realize the Curse of Nightfall was related to the Curse of Eight.

When doomed is delighted
And royalty has reigned
When cautious is bold
And wildness is chained
When dominance submits
And submitted is free
When sound has been silenced
And alone now is three
When swiftness is slowed
And bound to please one
When dark is enlightened
And nothing's undone
When passion has burned
And quenches its thirst
When returned is match-made
Thus ends this Curse!

It was quite obvious. Saber's verse in the Song of the Sons spoke of a Disaster, which could be translated as a doom.

Wildness being chained referred to Wolfer's verse, and dominance . . . well, that was Dominor. Sound was definitely the musically inclined Evanor. He wasn't so sure about his twin, Trevan's, link to the fifth couplet, unless one counted the *bound to please one* part the ending of Trev's pre-exile, hedonistic roamings, but the bit about dark being enlightened, that was clearly him. No denying the last two verses, either, about burning and quenching for Koranen, and matchmaking for Morganen.

But the part about being enlightened, yet nothing being undone, he didn't understand. *Unless* . . . Rydan, studying Rora's expressionless face, wondered. *Unless . . . it's my ignorance about my beast being roused by emotions? I never really associated emotions with my discomfort, before now. Mainly because I was irritated by any excess of emotion, even the positive ones, the kinds one wouldn't think should be a problem.*

It makes sense, though . . . I wonder—if she *can See emotions, I wonder if I could See them, too? If I could* See *what I'm fighting* . . . He smiled wryly and shifted out of his crouch. Sliding his arms behind her back and under her knees, Rydan scooped her out of the chair.

She mumbled and slouched the other way, curling her head against his chest. She even roused enough to squirm and loop her arms around his neck before quieting again. The buzz of all that tightly sealed power was still there inside of her, tickling his flesh, yet it seemed more quiescent now that she was sleeping. *I'd ask you to help me figure out how to See what I need to fight, lady . . . but right now, you aren't feeling anything but the contentment of sleep.*

That's really why I've preferred being awake at night, isn't it? he acknowledged, carrying her from his study. Polishing the rest of the incipient Truth Stones could wait for a while. *Not just because fewer people were around to annoy me with their mere presence, but because only dreams can stir emotions in someone who sleeps, and only an hour or two of sleep belong to dreams.*

His bedroom wasn't far, and years of carving—even if spell-assisted—had given his arms plenty of strength to hold her. *This isn't quite creeping into my hall at dawn, and it isn't quite dawn, but both Prophecies are coming inexorably true . . . which means I should prepare against losing my "reign" over the Fountain. Just because Fate weaves the overall tapestry doesn't mean we cannot embroider our own Destinies over whatever was originally designed for us.*

Reaching his bedchamber, Rydan carried her to his bed. But when he laid her down, her arms clung to his shoulders. She stirred sleepily, radiating protest, and he found himself almost overbalanced onto her from the strength of her grip, braced off the bed only by the strength of a quickly planted arm.

The woman needed something to cling to, but he wasn't about to join her in a bed until she was fully awake and completely willing. Snagging his favorite down-stuffed pillow with his free arm, Rydan wormed it up between them. After all the many years he had slept with it, the pillow smelled just like him. Rora sighed and snuggled her face into it, breathing deeply. That eased her grip around his neck, if only so she could clutch at his pillow, too. In fact, as soon as he was free, she rolled over, emitting a humming sigh and snuggling up to the mangled rectangle with a smile that definitely radiated pleasure.

Forcing himself to back away, to stop basking in that happy, contented glow, Rydan retreated to his workroom and the stacks of marble still awaiting him. Before he could pick up the first of the roughly shaped blanks, one of his wardings chimed. The sound was limited to his ears alone, but it was clear that someone was trying to contact him through the Fountainway.

Shadow-walking to the Hall, Rydan noted which of the coppery-hued energy ribbons was ruffled. It was the one that flowed almost due north. Guardian Sheren, then. Striding over the channels, Rydan dipped his fingers into the misting stream. *"Guardian Sheren. What are you doing up so late?"*

"Ah, good, Guardian Rydan. And I'm not up so late. I'm up so early. Damned arthritis is giving me fits, but then, given my so-called climate, it's an overly common complaint. And at my age, there's only so much the Healers can do for you. Anyway, remember those maps of Fountains in Shattered Aiar I had you pass to Serina?"

"Yes. She received them the other morning," Rydan confirmed.

"Well, I've managed to contact two of the Guardians in question, and they're willing to pass along their own, more direct observations of the local aether for her research. Seems this Zella woman actually does know them personally," Guardian Sheren informed him. *"However, they're not overly keen on continuing communications with non-Guardian mages, and I do believe you said Serina has stepped down from her Fountain?"*

"Yes, but she still has her integrity," Rydan pointed out. *"Her stepping down was a voluntary act, so that she could join her husband. My brother."*

"Perhaps . . . but what about this brother of yours?" the unseen Guardian challenged him. *"Is he trustworthy? Is he Guardian material? I'm not so old that I can't remember a time when my head could be swayed by a pretty face and a pretty word."*

Rydan stifled the urge to state that Dominor was arrogant, power hungry, and other things, the sorts of things that no longer applied to his brother. In the months since coming back from Natallia and bringing his wife to stay among them, Dom had changed. Mellowed, almost. Choosing his words carefully, putting aside his old feelings on the matter, Rydan gave her the truth. *"As he used to be, he was . . . unpolished in certain facets of his life. Having a wife has polished him. Tempered him, too.* If *I ever had to give up my Fountain to someone, I suppose I would consider him for a candidate. He's strong enough. Though I'd be far more likely to hand it over to Serina directly. She's done it before."*

"True. And we've both worked with her; she understands the job. Anyway, I just thought I'd pass along the good news. I won't have anything for a few more days, probably, but didn't want to surprise either of you. The sooner we can quell the disturbances in the aether, the happier I'll be. If we can restore the ability to Portal between continents, the damned Council won't have any excuses left not *to trade with other realms."*

"Why bother with the Council?" Rydan countered, thinking of the Mother Superior of Koral-tai, who had taken over

the Guardianship of Serina's old Fountain. *"You're a Guardian. It is your prerogative to import and export items through the Fontway, if you so desire. I'm already trading goods with the Guardian who replaced Serina, Guardian Naima. It wouldn't take that much more to open up trade with you."*

Sheren's chuckles sounded odd, echoing as they did through the communication mist. *"Of course, of course. And what then would stop me from turning around and reselling my 'purchases' to my fellow citizens, is that it? A clever idea! I'll give it some thought. But now I must go. A few minutes bathing in the singularity energies usually relieves enough of my arthritis to let me rest, and I'm feeling sleepy again."*

"Watch your back," Rydan cautioned her, glad the nature of the Fountain and his self-defense against it helped block out emotional overtones. He was fond of the occasionally crotchety woman, and she sounded particularly tired this time around. *"You haven't got a replacement yet, so don't let anything happen to yourself."*

"I've been a Guardian longer than you've been alive, young man. Trust me, I still have a few tricks up my sleeves, fitted though they may be."

The mist stopped rippling before it reached his fingers. Rydan extracted his hand, thinking about Rora's comment on why Dominor and Serina wanted to travel through the Fountainway ahead of the scheduled trade with Guardian Naima, the Mother Superior of the mountaintop nunnery, Koral-tai. Perhaps he should let them go ahead of schedule anyway. If there was information on what Rora was, and what could be done about her condition, they should examine it to help her.

Wanting nothing more than to go back to bed, Rora climbed the last set of stairs to her suite of rooms in the palace. Rydan had awakened her, made her eat a plateful of food—which had contributed to her sleepiness—and then kicked her out of his domain with the command to go reassure her sister that she was alright. Right now, Rora didn't care about checking in with Mara. All she wanted was a bed to call her own, since Rydan wasn't going to let her share his while he occupied it. At least, not yet.

At her door waited a fluffball of orange cream fur. The air was damp and cold this morning, with clouds threatening to rain outside, and it looked like the humidity had gotten to the cat's fur. It was too much effort to stoop and stroke it smooth again, though. Nudging her door open, she didn't care whether or not the cat followed her inside. Turning to close it, though, she jumped, startled by the sudden appearance of Trevan; she hadn't heard his approach.

"Oh!"

"Hello," he greeted her. "I was wondering if I could have a word with you about Shifterai courtship practices?"

Rora blinked at him, disconcerted by the topic, then held the door wide, letting him enter. "I suppose so, though I'm still awfully tired . . . Not that there's much to know, really. I take it you want to know for my sister's sake?"

"Who else? Just give me the basics, and I'll come back later if I have any questions," the redhead bargained. "I take it kissing isn't a part of the culture, but what else do I have to watch out for?"

Explaining Shifterai courtships wasn't quite that easy. In fact, it would probably be easier to dump Shifterai customs and just do things the outlander way. But he looked determined to try, and she knew her prickly twin would feel better about being Destined for him if he made an effort to respect her background. Resigning herself to staying awake for a little while more, she gestured at the fireplace and the chairs flanking it. "Light a fire to get us warm, Trevan, and I'll try to tell you what you'll need to know. If you'll tell me what *I* need to know, too."

He grinned and headed for the hearth. "Agreed."

THIRTEEN

When he joined the others that evening, Rydan discovered he couldn't send Dominor and Serina through the Fountainway; at least, not immediately. Kelly had returned from an afternoon visit to the other universe laden with outworlder drawings for building designs, which had to be sorted through, accepted or rejected based on various amenities or flaws, and compared with sketched ideas of their own. That meant all of them had to work together to figure out how to integrate what they knew of magical construction techniques with the needs of building that first house for the incoming sailor, Marcas, whose boat would hopefully net them more settlers as well as more fish.

It was all suddenly very real; they *were* going to build a city, and they *had* to build homes for people to occupy. The debate went on for a while, but eventually they had a modification that fit in with the proposed designs. Pipes filled with cool water running through the stone walls for each house would reduce the heat of the warmer seasons, while pipes filled with warm water under the floors would heat each home in the winter. The profligate use of water was a good thing, in this instance, since it would allow them to increase the production of the island's salt and algae blocks as the Permanent

Magic of the desalination plant converted ocean water to drinkable water.

There was a brief altercation between Amara and the others at supper—one that he actually managed to withstand, despite the volatile emotions Rora's twin emanated. And he endured the surprise all of them suffered when Amara defended Trevan against the rest over one of Dominor's quips. It was a relief for Rydan that he did survive it, blocking with the same inner reflexes he used around the Fountain. It hadn't occurred to him that he could use the same discipline to ward against excess emotions as well as excess magic, but then he hadn't known that his problem was with emotions and not the others themselves.

Given how raw his beast had been rubbed in the months since his siblings had started encountering and collecting wives, normally, he would have been forced to flee. But thanks to Rora, he didn't have to escape just to save his sanity. Grateful, Rydan silently took his cue from Rora and ignored her sibling's outburst.

Once everything settled back down again, Rydan was assigned the task of aligning the pipes below street level, now that one of his brothers' spells had traced them along the surface. The pipes had been crafted from stone, after all. It meant he couldn't spend time on the Truth Stones, but he could and did take Rora with him. Or rather, she insisted on following, though she fell asleep at some point after their midnight supper, bundled up in a quilt in the bed of the horseless cart Rydan had driven down to the bare-scraped land now surrounding the western cove.

But that was forgivable, since it gave him plenty of uninterrupted time to carve runes and paint sigils onto the cobblestones and foundation slabs of the old city, following the glowing marks the pipe-tracing spell had left. There were four main processing tanks at the desalination plant; only one of them was working currently; that one's pipes were traced in blue; the others were marked in gray, purple, and green. In order to get water to the northern side of the bay, he had to reroute some of the blue pipes, most of which headed up toward the palace perched in the pass between the two mountain ranges.

When the sky behind the mountains began to lighten, he roused Rora from her slumber, explained in simple terms what he wanted her to do, and guided her carefully into pouring her vast power into the master symbol he had created, one that had been tied into all the magical marks he had made. He had used the Nightfall Fountain to speed his work, and it would maintain the pipeways, but his family wanted the pipes to be functional in a single night, and that required a large surge of energy. Having Rora participate spared his Fountain from being weakened, while giving her the chance to use her power.

Her face, illuminated by the multihued light glowing from the brightly charged runes scattered across the landscape, displayed her delighted grin in an eerie underglow. He had to coax her into tapering back her magic, but in the span of less than a hundred heartbeats, she had done what would have taken him half an hour, had he been forced to draw on his own Fountain at that distance. Once again, she fell asleep on the ride back, though this time it was while she was cuddled against his side, clinging more to him than to the quilt in the chilly dawn air.

Rora yawned several times through the task of helping him prepare breakfast; she was now on the chore roster posted outside the dining hall, paired with Rydan, whose most frequent task was preparing the morning meal for everyone. When it was served and she had seated herself next to her sister, across the table from Rydan, who had deigned this time to sit next to his own twin, she found herself falling asleep again, still not quite used to a nocturnal life. Rydan nudged her with his foot under the table, waking her up before she could smear her chin in the jam daubed on her egg-dipped toast. Giving him a bleary smile, she ate what she could, struggling to stay awake as the others discussed the day ahead.

When the others started moving away from the table, she stood, yawned, and moved away, too. Rounding the table, she headed for the door. Tired as she was, she did her best out of habit to avoid brushing against anyone. Unfortunately, Morganen, chatting with his eldest sibling, turned and stepped away from Saber just as she reached the doorway, bumping into her.

They *oofed,* he caught her hands in his—and power *flared*

between them. It streamed out of her body in pulsing waves of golden white and poured into him, drawn from her body to his. The thrumming of her magic increased in the same way it used to when accidentally scorching something, before she had gained control of her powers, but Morganen *didn't* burn: He *swallowed* her power, like water sucked through a reed. With each gulping wave, she grew more and more dizzy, while the expression on his face shifted from startled to wide-eyed, almost giddy—

"NO!" Tearing his hands free, Morganen stumbled back, out of the room. He thumped into the far wall, hands fisted, eyes wide, nothing odd visible about him other than his almost frightened tension and a few fluffing strands of hair escaping from his braid.

"*What* did you just do to my sister?" Mara demanded, hurrying up as Rora swayed, then staggered back.

Rydan got there first, catching and steadying her. The thrumming of her power wasn't as intense as before. At least, it didn't seem that way, though the buzz against his nerves was regaining some of its strength.

Rora held up her hand, grateful for Rydan's support as she reassured her twin. "I'm alright. Just a little disoriented."

"What did he do?" Mara demanded anyway. "What was that light? And you—stop touching her!"

Pushing away from Rydan, Rora headed through the door, toward Morganen. His eyes widened further, and he scrambled sideways along the wall, almost scuttling like a crab. "Stay away from me!"

"But . . ."

"Stay away!" the youngest of the brothers insisted, his voice cracking. "Don't touch me!"

That was a twist. Rora glanced behind her, meeting the puzzled look on her twin's face. "I didn't . . ." Turning back to face him, she stayed where she was, but asked, "Did I hurt you? What did I do?"

Morganen licked his lips. He opened his mouth, then squeezed his eyes shut, throwing up his hands. "Just—*don't touch me.* Don't *ever* touch me!"

He glared at her, and when she didn't move any closer, he whirled on his heel, stalking into the donjon.

"Morg?" Koranen asked from the doorway, poking his head through. "Are you alright?"

"I have work to do!" His tone was curt, almost angry, as he strode out of view.

The others exchanged puzzled looks. Mara touched her sister again. "What did he do to you?"

"I don't know . . . but I'm *fine*. I was just a little dizzy for a moment, but I'm feeling better already," Rora firmly reassured her sister. Mara tended to be a bit overprotective whenever she bumped into someone, though in the past they'd had good reason to worry. This time, Rora didn't worry about herself. "Actually, I'm more concerned about whatever I may have done to *him*."

"What *did* you do to him?" Koranen asked.

"That's just it; I don't know," Rora shrugged helplessly. "I'm just glad I didn't hurt him . . . I think . . ."

Rydan had his suspicions, but he didn't voice them.

"What I want to know is, *how* you did whatever it was that you did," Saber stated. "You didn't say you were a mage, but that looked like magic to me."

Serina drew in a breath, but subsided when she glanced at Rora, leaving the choice of what to say up to the Shifterai woman. Guessing it was time to confess to everyone, Rora squared her shoulders. "According to your Arithmancer, here . . . I am a living Fountain."

"Arora—" Mara protested.

"They have a right to know! I *am* a living Fountain, and I *think* he drew energy from me . . . but I'm not sure," she hedged. "I've spent most of my life containing my power, rather than using it, so I'm not sure what actually happened just now. But . . . that's why Mara and I fled the Plains. Because there are mages out there who *aren't* as ethical as the lot of you are."

Wolfer snorted, his voice floating through the doorway of the dining hall. "Not just ethical; we're also highly empowered. When you've always had plenty, you rarely crave more. Except for Dominor."

There was a sound like a hand whapping the back of someone's head, though Rora couldn't see anything from her current angle. "Were you not paying attention last night, when the lady's sister lectured us about not assigning such shallow character profiles?"

Rora smiled at the sound of Dom's scold, since her sister had gone off on one of her protective rants last night over a comment Dominor himself had made about Trevan. That Mara had defended him last night spoke volumes about Trevan's standing in her sister's eyes. Rora smothered a yawn behind her hand, then said, "Please pardon me. As interesting as all of this has been, I'm awfully tired now. Good night—or rather, good day."

"I'll walk you to your quarters," Rydan murmured, slipping between Rora and her sister so that the dark-haired woman couldn't pester her twin any further. A narrow-eyed look from him stifled the impending smiles on his brothers' faces. Satisfied they would stay silent, he guided Rora up the hall with an arm lightly tucked around her waist. When her arm slipped under his, looping around his ribs, he thought he felt a pulse of humor, but at least no one snickered aloud. It was bad enough he was Destined to fall; he would not tolerate being mocked for it.

"You're doing a lot better, emotion wise," Rora observed sleepily as they reached the *Y*-junction and turned left. "Not as . . . aaaahh, pardon me"—she yawned—"not as sensitive to an attack. I *will* be more awake tomorrow night. Just need to get used to your hours, is all."

A part of Rydan felt an odd twinge, an impulse to alter his hours so she didn't have to stay up all night. He squashed it flat. "I guard the night, so that my brothers don't have to take turns doing it."

"That makes sense," Rora murmured, head drooping against his shoulder. She was tired, but being next to him, being touched by him, was waking her up again. They reached the door to her suite; Rydan opened it for her. Taking advantage of his distraction, Rora slid her arms around his chest in a hug. That made him still for a moment, then he straightened. Another pause, and he hesitantly enfolded her in his own arms. Happy that he was returning her embrace, Rora sighed and leaned into him, half burying her face in the curve of his throat.

"No falling asleep," Rydan warned the woman in his arms after a few moments. Holding her wasn't the main problem;

it was the *contentment* she radiated, clinging to him. "Come on, wake up."

That made Rora chuckle and nuzzle his throat, brushing her cheek over the soft black wool of his outer tunic. "When I'm supposed to be going to sleep? Besides, you're comfortable."

"I could say the same for you," Rydan found himself confessing. That caused her to lift her head from his shoulder. He took advantage of her momentary alertness, gently removing her arms. "But I will not rush this . . . whatever this is. Go to bed—*alone*—and sleep well. I'll see you in the afternoon."

"Sleep well, yourself," Rora returned, lifting onto her toes so she could plant a kiss on his cheek.

He turned his head a little at the last moment so that her lips landed on the corner of his mouth. It was half-instinctive, half-deliberate, and undeniably nice. For a moment, he studied her, dark eyes gleaming. Then he darted in and claimed her mouth for a deeper, better kiss. Releasing her after only a few moments, he stepped back, gave her a little bow, and headed farther up the corridor, toward the last stairwell in the wing. He heard her sigh and close the door, and smiled to himself. Rydan didn't have to see her to feel her wistfulness at his departure.

He felt wistful, too, but thinking about staying with her led to thoughts of that damnable Prophecy, and his slated fall. That led in turn to thoughts of being match-made with her, and that led his thoughts back to Morganen. Once he reached the rampart wall, he detoured to the east, passing through Trevan's tower in order to reach the door to Morganen's. From there, it was simply a matter of descending the curving steps to the bottommost chamber, where he knew his youngest sibling preferred to work.

Pacing, agitated, Morganen was muttering to himself as he flipped through the pages of a tome balanced in one hand. He glanced up briefly at Rydan's approach before returning his aquamarine gaze to the book. "Go away, Rydan."

"No."

Morganen stopped pacing long enough to arch a skeptical brow at his brother. He shook his head and resumed pacing and flicking through the pages. "Go *away*. I'm not in the mood to deal with you."

"No. You will tell me what happened back there," Rydan countered. When Morg kept pacing, Rydan snagged his brother's elbow.

The voluntary touch made Morganen stumble, having to swing around to catch his balance. It also made Morg stare at him in puzzlement. In the past, Rydan had avoided all forms of physical contact. But right now, the black-haired brother needed to know what was going on.

Two things struck the sixthborn brother's senses. For the first, Morganen was suffering from a strange tumble of guilt, euphoria, and self-disgust, threaded with hints of fear. For the second . . . he thrummed with power. Not quite to the level that Rora radiated, but Rydan knew immediately what that golden, pulsing light had been.

Somehow, his brother had drained part of Rora's hidden magic—stolen it, rather, for Rora hadn't consented to its transfer, let alone realized what had happened.

"Thief!" he hissed. Switching his grip, Rydan grabbed Morganen beneath his jaw and lifted the thinner mage onto his toes. Anger riled the beast within him. "Give it *back*!"

The book thumped to the floor as Morg scrabbled to pry Rydan's fingers from his neck. "Can't!"

"Kata's Ass, you *can't*!" Rydan growled, thrusting his brother back. Unable to check his momentum, Morganen tripped to the ground, smacking his shoulders and cracking his head into the cabinet doors beneath his main worktable. Rydan advanced, jabbing his finger between them; his hair fluffed and crackled, roused by the static energy of his magic-backed anger. "You will give it back *now*!"

Hand rubbing gingerly at the back of his head, Morganen glared back. "If you turn this into a magical fight, Brother, I don't know if I'll be able to *control* what I'm carrying! And I *cannot* give it back to her!"

"Why not?" Rydan demanded, glaring at his sibling. It was a struggle to rein in his emotions, to muzzle his inner beast. After barely two days' respite from the creature, it was hard not to be affected by it, now that it had been aroused once more. "Tell me!"

"Because that would mean *touching* her again!" Morganen snapped, shoving to his feet. He swayed and clutched at the table behind him, grimacing, then touched the back of his head again. "Look, I *didn't* know that would happen, when we touched—and you'll note I tore myself away as soon as I could! But *do not* ask me to go near her again. Gods—what kind of a mage do you think I am?!"

"I don't know," Rydan returned darkly. "I *thought* I knew . . . but I don't. Do I?"

"Well, I am *not* a blood mage, whatever you may be thinking," Morganen told him firmly, sullenly. "There are two kinds of mages in this world—"

"—Good ones, and evil ones," Rydan interrupted. "I know my ethics lessons, the same as you."

"Wrong! There are two kinds of mages in the world," Morg repeated, touching the skin beneath his jaw, where Rydan had grabbed him. "They are givers and takers. Givers give their own excess life force to create magic. It comes from within them, and mostly only from within them . . . and yes, they're predominantly the good ones. Takers usually have very little internal magic to give, but they can *take* magic from the aether around them, shaping and guiding it with what magic they do have.

"*That* is what makes taking the life-energy released by a death so tempting to a taker-style mage," he lectured. "They can take it from the aether, and from the air, from plants and bugs and little animals . . . and even from people. *Without* having to kill anyone. They use whatever power they have, plus whatever they can grab and control, to augment their magical efforts . . . but temptation is always there. I realized what I was when I was young, when I 'took' energy from *you*, and noticed how it made you tired, as if you were falling ill.

"You didn't know what I had done—Jinga's Sweet Ass, *I* didn't even know what I had done," Morg confessed in the face of Rydan's scowl. "Not until I made the connection between touching you, my sudden boost in power, and the corresponding drop of yours. *You* just thought you had eaten something that made you tired and dizzy that day, and slept it off. *I* had a hard time controlling my sudden surge in power—that was the day I levitated all the horses in the stables, in case you were wondering when exactly it happened," he added, wrinkling his nose. "I was *supposed* to be practicing my levitation charm on one of the new colts and somehow ended up levitating all of them.

"Since then, I've read as much about it as I could find. I've tried very hard to avoid taking energy from anything other than the aether itself—I haven't even killed any of the damned chickens during our entire exile," Morganen reminded his brother. "I've even traded fishing duties with you and the others, taking on the worst of your chores just to avoid that kind of temptation. And when I have touched our brothers, I have been very careful about *not* pulling energy from any of you."

"But you sucked it from Rora!" Rydan accused, feeling his beast growling under his skin.

"I didn't!" Morg protested. "The moment we touched, her power *shoved* itself upon me!"

"Liar."

Snapping his fingers, Morg held out his hand. A wand made from rune-carved copper and tipped with crystal flung itself off one of the shelves, smacking into his palm. He held out the shaft to Rydan. His elder brother took the Artifact, activated it, and touched the glowing crystal to the back of Morg's hand.

"I swear to you, when Arora and I accidentally touched, her power *pushed* itself into me!"

The glow stayed bright and clear. Rydan narrowed his black gaze. "And did you *draw* upon that power, after it started pushing its way into you?"

Morganen flushed at that. He started to withdraw his hand, but Rydan caught his wrist, holding crystal and flesh together. "Fine! *Yes.* It was overwhelming, heady—like drinking too much fine wine. But when I realized what was happening, I knew it was wrong, and I *stopped* it. By removing myself. If I go back to her, it may happen again, because I don't know *why* it happened. I just know that I am buzzing with more power than I've handled in my entire life, and I am *trying* to find a safe and useful way of discharging it."

The glow remained steady, proving Morganen spoke the truth. Shutting off the Truth Wand, Rydan tossed it onto the table behind his brother. He held Morg's wrist for a moment more in silent warning, black eyes boring into aqua blue, before releasing his sibling. "What kind of use?"

"I don't know. But I do know I have a lot of energy at my command, and it feels like I need to use it up soon, or it'll start leaking out my ears, or something," he muttered. "I was thinking of something to do with the city we're trying to build—something to level and repair the streets, maybe even shift them into the new patterns Amara's been plotting. I should have enough power for at least some of that." Stooping, Morg picked up his fallen book, taking the time to smooth out the pages. "If you're done harassing me, I have *work* to do."

"Just make sure you *do* stay away from her," Rydan ordered, before turning toward the door. He whirled back, scowling at his eighthborn sibling as his beast rumbled, emotionally irritated. "And stop gloating! The only thing I *reign* over, O Matchmaker, is that Fountain I guard. Do you *want* to see the Prophecy tear it from my hands?"

"Saber thought that fulfilling his own verse would bring about the destruction of Katan," Morganen dared to remind him. "Obviously, it didn't. If you'd stop fretting over what *could* be and just be ready for what *will* be, you might find things are less unpleasant than you imagine."

Unable to deny that his brother had a point, Rydan bit back a grunt and stalked out of the workroom. It was late, he was tired, and his beast was irritated by Morganen's smug satisfaction. His brother hadn't shown it on his face, but it was there, radiating from him. At least now he knew what roused his beast, and he might even be able to control it most of the time, provided he wasn't sorely provoked again.

Somehow, Morganen managed to straighten and align the streets of the incipient city without alarming the others. Rydan didn't really care. So long as Morg didn't try to practice death-magic—which wasn't his way anyway—or touch Rora again—which was possible, but hopefully not probable—or tap into the Nightfall Fountain, as far as Rydan was concerned, his youngest brother could play with all the aether energy he wanted.

He did tell Rora what had happened with his youngest brother, though. It was only right that she know, though he waited until they were traveling on his floating chair toward the marble vein, where the coarse grains of the granite in that area would make it easier to extract quartz. Koranen wanted that quartz and a few other minerals for grinding into the base material for faience, which could be molded and fired much like clay. They needed lots of roof tiles, but the island lacked clay deposits.

They had plenty of wood, but Kelly wanted something more practical than wooden shingles, which would dry out too quickly in the sunny heat of the island's summers. That could turn the impending city into a potential fire hazard. Kor had suggested faience instead, since it was easy to make both watertight and attractive to look at.

The sand on the beach was as much limestone as it was quartz; the granite at the edges of the deposit was coarse grained, easier to separate out the inclusions from the base quartz. There might even be gemstones lurking somewhere in the bedrock under the island, so the task of mining and refining what they needed could have a twofold bonus. At least, it wouldn't hurt to look for other resources, not to mention mining stone was as easy as gathering sand, for the sixthborn brother.

Rora, listening to Rydan's comments about what Morganen had said, shrugged. "I have no idea what happened, myself. If he says my power pushed its way into him, then it may indeed have. Of course, if he should have a need for it in the future and asks next time, I don't think I'd mind sharing it."

"I'd rather you didn't," Rydan stated flatly. At her puzzled look, he remembered how little she knew about magic. Morganen's explanation was simple enough to incorporate into his explanation. "There are those who use only the power the Gods granted them. Others can draw upon outside sources of power. They take magic, more than they give it. Those who are good draw that taken magic only from the air around them—every living animal, humans included, sheds life-energy, which is like unrefined magic. It goes into the aether, where these mages can take it from. Those who are evil *steal* the life-energy magic from living creatures. Usually by sacrificing the life of the creature and snatching up all of their life-energy when it's released by death.

"Morganen does not want to be tempted into that kind of

death-based magic, or blood-magic, as it is sometimes called," Rydan told her, "mostly because theft and murder both corrupt the soul. You must avoid him and refrain from tempting him," he instructed her. "If both of you avoid each other, neither of you will court such trouble."

"Alright," she agreed. "I can understand and respect that. But what about you? You've been touching me. If touching is what allows a mage to 'steal' my energy . . . well, it would explain why I was pursued by those other mages. But I don't want to stop touching *you*."

"I'm not a taker. I have more than enough power on my own, and the Fountain to add to that." Rydan realized suddenly that Morganen hadn't said how strong *he* was. Just that most mages who took from the aether were weak and thus usually in search of more power. *How strong is my brother? Is his power nothing more than a herding together of many stray energies under the crook of a single shepherd's staff? Does that make* me *the most powerful in the family?*

"But you take the power of the Fountain and use it . . . Doesn't that make you a taker of sorts?" Rora asked, curious.

Blinking away his thoughts, Rydan considered her words. "You're right. I *do* 'take' from the Fountain, though it's more like the Fountain *gives* it, since there's no way to stop it from pouring out its energies—wait, how do *you* stop your own Fountain from radiating its power? You can't suppress it forever . . . can you?"

"Oh, no, the priestesses taught me that much. Each night, when I'm getting ready to sleep, I push it down into the earth beneath me. They called it 'grounding' the energies and said that every time I do that, it makes the land healthier and the plants greener for miles around. Aitava—our Queen—would take me with her whenever she did a circuit of the farm holdings ringing the City, so that I could contribute to the harvests during the handful of years I spent apprenticing at her Court. I've actually spent more time in her personal retinue than my sister has, for all I wasn't apprenticed to her. Sometimes I forget," Rora added with a shrug, "or am too tired to remember, but usually the pressure doesn't bother me too much, so long as I clear it out at least once every few days."

"What does it feel like when it does bother you?" Rydan asked, curious.

"Like a humming in my bones—you know the kind, where you almost clench your teeth together and hum, until they sort of buzz in tune with your humming?" she asked. "It's like that. Only much more annoying, because it's all over, not just at my teeth. It wasn't that way when I was very young, just since I reached puberty. But I want to get back to the other problem.

"I may be wrong, because I don't know magic like you do, but . . . it seems to me that magic is as much *will* as it is *power*," Rora offered, gesturing with one hand. "If you don't have the power internally, but you do have the will, you can still gather up the power from other sources, not just your own. And you would be motivated to do so, if you don't have a lot of power at hand. But if you *do* have the power, or at least enough of it for whatever you want to do, then why would you *need* to go looking for sources outside of yourself? Maybe that's the biggest difference between givers and takers . . . or am I wrong, and that doesn't make any sense?"

Rydan studied the woman at his side, then sighed. "No, I don't think you're wrong. For someone with no training, you do seem to have an understanding of magic."

"Most of that, I suspect, is simply because I've had most of my life to observe myself and wonder about this thing I'm carrying around inside," she said. "It's only natural I can't look at it from the same point of view as a more formally trained mage, because I can't tap into my magic like a formally trained mage can."

They rode in silence for a few minutes. Pondering her situation, Rydan finally asked, "Rora . . . if they can extract the Fountain from you, but it takes away your ability to do magic as well . . . what will you do?"

She considered that for a moment, then shrugged. "The same as I've always done, I suppose. Offer my scribal services, dig through old records, endure paper cuts happily as I read through dusty books and ancient scrolls that would make other people's eyes cross. Or if there's no need for that, I can always teach reading and writing. I could even play herder girl. I am Shifterai, you know."

"Strange, I thought you were a *toska* fruit," he teased her lightly. "So, it wouldn't bother you to lose your magic?"

"No, not really. Except I'll have to start opening doors all the time, not just when others might be watching. *That* would be rather annoying," she admitted, wrinkling her nose in mock distaste.

Rydan found himself chuckling at that. Even more surprising, she leaned into him, cuddling close.

"I like it when you laugh. You Look like a flower in bloom, with all those happy colors streaming out of you. And your voice . . . I like how deep it is."

"Very few men like being compared to a flower, woman," he groused, though it was more to tease her than to actually protest the comparison. "And Wolfer's voice is deeper than mine . . . though not by much. If you retained at least some of your own magic, what then?"

"Then I suppose I should learn how to use it, if I can," she answered pragmatically. "Otherwise, I'll continue as I have. Find a way to make myself useful, help you calm your 'beast' . . . and sneak in a few more kisses here and there. You don't mind me practicing my kissing technique with you, do you?"

Irritation flared through him, roused not by the thought of her practicing her kisses on him, but by the implication that she was preparing herself for someone else. Rydan wasn't ready to surrender to the more ominous aspects of his Destiny, but he acknowledged he wasn't able to let her go, either. But she was giving him a concerned look, no doubt Seeing his jealousy. Cupping her jaw in his hand, he angled their mouths together, giving her a lesson in the proper mating of lips and tongues.

Damned if he did; damned if he didn't . . . At least he was mostly enjoying her company in the process. Given the vagaries of his beast up until now, that was no small accomplishment in itself.

FOURTEEN

"And so the roof should be finished by tonight. Morg's been putting the color-changing paint into framed sections of the walls to make moving paintings. The effect is quite—ow! Quite *nice*," Dominor added, gritting his teeth and striking back, trying to land a blow that would repay, bruise for bruise, his annoyance at letting Rydan through his guard. "You should come see it when it's finished."

"I have to, anyway," Rydan grunted, absorbing some of the blow on his shield before bashing the spell-enforced steel into his brother's shoulder. "Kelly wants a garden—*wall*—!"

"Ha! Missed!" Dominor said, twisting away from Rydan's practice sword, only to grunt as Morganen *thwacked* him in the back. Dominor rounded on him with a glare that was visible through the grille of his helm. "Hey! We're not fighting *you*, you know."

"Doesn't matter!" Morg panted back, fending off a thrust from Evanor. "You should be prepared for anything, Dominor."

The four of them were taking their turn in the palace salle, practicing against each other after breakfast. Sometimes they practiced after supper, whenever it was convenient, but Evanor had scheduled an hour for the four of them this morning. The youngest of the brothers grinned and whacked at the thirdborn again.

"Pookrah-pile-on-Dominor!"

"*Tyuroh*! Don't even try it," Dom ordered, shoving Morganen back a few steps with the quick-snapped spell.

"Hey, no fair," Morganen argued, only to have to fight off both Rydan and Evanor. "We're not supposed to be using magic in here."

"*Dead*," Rydan chided his sibling, stabbing Morganen's breastplate. The sword didn't puncture the metal, though it could have, had it been a real weapon and had Rydan used all of his strength. As it was, the blade was nothing more than a piece of pot metal enchanted to leave nothing but bruises. Some mages never bothered to learn how to protect themselves from a physical attack, but even the most powerful of spellcast defenses could be exhausted and overwhelmed if enough bodies were thrown at a spellcaster. "Your left-hand guard is sloppy."

Morg stuck out his tongue, the tip of it almost reaching the grid of bars protecting his face.

"I could always rearrange it so you spar with Saber," Evanor pointed out, lightly smacking the flat of his blade against the back of Morg's helm. He pointed with his other hand at the hourglass resting on a shelf above the armor rack in the corner. "Two more minutes, and we're done with this."

"Dom, regarding your request," Rydan stated, catching his brother's attention. Dominor faced him. "You may go to Koral-tai after the house is done. You don't have to wait until the scheduled trade."

"Thank you. I'll let Seri"—he flung up his shield, blocking Rydan's blow with a *clang*—"na know. And you'll have to try harder than *that* to get past my—"

"*Pookrah-pile!*" Morganen and Evanor both shouted, whacking at their thirdborn brother while he was distracted, toppling him in a clamor of indignant protests and banging metal.

Their high spirits rubbed at Rydan's beast. It was a minor irritation, not enough to prevent him from grinning and joining in the roughhousing. Seven days ago, if he had come here to practice instead of skipping a sparring session, he would have fled, his beast rubbed raw and thus sensitive to such teasings . . . but seven days ago, Rora had come to him and convinced him that he wasn't slowly going insane. That there was a way to control what he had suffered until now.

He couldn't tolerate his family for an entire day's worth of interaction yet, but he was getting there.

"This looks nothing like the Font at Koral-tai," Serina said a few days later, peering at the vaulted arches of the long, broad hall, arches supported by columns carved out of the granite bedrock surrounding them. The house was now finished, and just in time, for the sailor Marcas and his friend had apparently arrived on the island that afternoon, plus some woman who had come for a visit. Rydan was forced to hold to his word, allowing the Arithmancer and his thirdborn brother access to the fastest way to return to Koral-tai, and Serina was clearly ready to take advantage of it.

"I'll admit I didn't get a good look at it, the one time I was in here," Dominor added. "I thought there were channels in the floor, but those are merely carvings outlining where the catch-basin pipes run, before being absorbed into the mountain—and I don't remember those streams reaching up to the ceiling."

"You were naked and distracted at the time," Rydan reminded his brother dryly. "And I was yelling at you, with good reason."

"Well, you'll just have to suffer my presence this time around," Dom chided his younger sibling. "Mariel says morning sickness gets worse with mirror-Gating. Even on the best of aether days, Koral-tai is too far away to Gate there, the Portals aren't even an option at the moment, and I'm not letting my wife wander off without me to watch over her. If nothing else, I can keep an eye out for vomit in the Fountainway."

"Don't be vulgar, dear, or my stomach might think it's a good idea." The tall, pale-haired Arithmancer touched some of the markings carved onto the pillars as she passed them. "No, this room is just . . . wrong. At least, compared to Koral-tai. For one thing, it's far too bright. For another, the room isn't balanced right. Mathemagically, the Fountain should be in the center of the chamber, not at one end. Of course, if I had a chalkboard on hand and could run some simulations on what these ancient sigils and rune-patterns were for . . ."

"You are *not* dissecting my Fountain," Rydan told her curtly. "You are *only* here to pass through to Koral-tai."

Sighing roughly, Serina eyed the pillars wistfully. "I can't wait until we can re-invoke the Convocation of the Gods. With that kind of political influence, I could get a lot more cooperation out of the mages in the areas where the worst damage from the Shattering struck."

"Re-invoke the *what*?" Rydan asked, eyeing her askance.

Dominor grimaced. "Sorry—I guess we forgot to tell you. Kelly's decided to invoke all of the Gods and Goddesses as our Patron Deities, rather than attempt to evoke a Patron of our own."

"That's insane!" the sixthborn brother scoffed.

"No, it makes sense," Serina argued. "With barely more than a dozen people on the island, we don't have enough faith amassed to create a brand-new deity, but by providing a home for the Gods to reconvene the Convocation, we don't *have* to have a massive amount of faith built up to supply Them with the strength to act on our behalf."

"If it worked for the whole of Aiar, bolstering the power of half a hundred local Gods and Goddesses into a massively powerful nation, it'll work for an even smaller island," Rora agreed.

"That's something else we get to look up, when we get to Koral-tai," Dom told his brother, nudging his wife away from the pillar she was covertly trying to study. "So if we could get on with it . . . ?"

Sighing, Serina allowed herself to be guided away from the rune-carved columns. Dominor gave his wife a one-handed hug in consolation; the other hand balanced the strap of the pack slung over his shoulder, holding changes of clothing for both of them, and no doubt a few of Serina's ever-present slates. Rora brought up the rear—until copper gold mist spewed into existence in front of her, blocking her approach. A voice rippled the fog barrier, issuing from its depths.

"She may pass, but she may not
Keep her safe, or keep her not."

Rydan spun on his heel, taken aback by the sudden appearance of the sparkling fog. "Madam Mist?"

"Who?" Dominor asked.

"It's a sort of protective spell," he dismissed, waving off his brother. He addressed the magic directly. "Madam Mist, who do you . . . ?"

"Keep her back, to keep her out
Life is lost, when life flows out."

Shifting to the side, Serina peered at Rora, then at the fog. It had spread itself between two of the pillars, forming a visual barrier to the younger woman's progress. "Oh . . . I get it! *I* can enter, but *she*—the other 'she' referenced—cannot! How clever; it's some sort of enchantment, obviously, but where . . . ?" Eyeing the columns to either side, Serina tipped her head back, following the rib of one of the arches until she was facing another pillar. From there, she moved toward the Fountain. "Mine at least *looks* like a Fountain, even if it's a Font. This one looks like a fancy-tied bow, the kind made from many strings."

"Serina," Rydan warned her.

"I'm just tracing the power. I won't touch anything . . . ah! How interesting," the Arithmancer stated, and pointed at two of the pipes spewing their ribbons of energy. "These ones here are where the energy originates. A stasis flow, which is the amber one, and a communications stream, the copper one. The latter goes into this catch-basin, yes, but some of it is diverged at the basin, flowing it up and through this decoration here," Serina continued, pointing at the floor as she followed her previous path back to the source, "which looks like it's several sigils layered one over the other. And . . . it . . . is triggered by . . . temporal runes?"

Straightening Serina gave the mist an intrigued look.

"Amazing. Whatever this thing is, I think it may have been set in place by a Seer working in close conjunction with a highly educated mage. Some of the runes are Fortunai, if I'm not mistaken, while others look to be Katani, and I know at least one of those sigils appears to be Draconan in origin. Of course, if the island was abandoned at the Shattering of Aiar, and I've heard no rumors of hermits living in permanent exile in this place," she mused thoughtfully, "then it's likely the last Guardian was before the Shattering, which means before we lost the great, cross-continental transportation Portals.

"There's definitely something deliberately different about this Font. I *must* study it!"

Rydan gritted his teeth. It was bad enough Serina had insisted on seeing his Fountain in person, wheedling it out of him, but he would not tolerate her lingering in his sanctum. Luckily Dominor got to her first. Catching her by the shoulders, he gave his wife a gentle shake.

"Set it aside, Serina. *That* is the Font we're supposed to be studying, remember?" He pointed in Rora's direction over his wife's shoulder. The younger woman was stuck behind the curtain of translucent mist, but her outline could still be seen.

Serina tugged on her braided hair, pouting. "*Fine.* Spoil my fun. I'll focus on Rora, I promise. But this apparition only seems to emphasize my belief that it would be dangerous for her energies to combine with those of a second singularity point. And I *will* study this Font someday."

"That day is not now," Rydan told her. A gesture, a pulse of his power, and several of the ribbonlike energies flowed out of their graceful arcs, bending down to almost touch the floor near the base of the Fountain before curving back up again, continuing on to their original drain spouts. Stepping around the Fountain and its petal-like pipes and energy streams, he played his fingers through a different copper-hued stream, one that led off to the unseen east. When he spoke, his voice echoed oddly through the hall . . . much like the female voice that was Madam Mist. *"Guardian Naima, are you there?"*

"I am here, Guardian Rydan. Are they ready to cross?"

"Yes."

"Then I am ready to receive."

Extracting his hand, Rydan held up his arms, swirling his fingers in a binding motion. The deformed ribbons of filtered energy knotted themselves together. Energies blended, stretched, striped, and abruptly swirled. They formed a colorful vortex that glowed white at its center, which seemed to bend in an eye-dizzying way up toward the softly glowing sphere, marking the boundary of the Fountain's source-point.

A curt gesture waved Dominor and Serina toward the oval tunnel he had created. First Serina, then Dominor stepped into the vortex. Each vanished with a gleaming *whoosh* of light and sound. A moment later, the ribbon Rydan had touched shifted and roiled.

"They're both here, and they're quite safe. Here—they can speak for themselves," Guardian Naima's voice reassured him. Rydan extracted his fingers from the misting magic so that he could unbind the energies used to create the Fountainway tunnel.

Serina spoke first. *"Wow—I thought for certain I'd feel nauseated to pieces, traveling through the Fontway. But no, I feel perfectly fine! Not a speck of morning sickness. Hey, it might be it's because of the Permanent Magic I'm currently working on; our baby was conceived in the heart of this Font, after all."*

"Focus, woman." Dominor's voice came through, chiding his wife as Rydan sent the streams of energies back into their normal arcs. *"We'll grab a few texts tonight and get a head start. Serina thinks she can remember the general section of the Archives wherein she glanced through the information on Fountains being carried around by living hosts, so we'll start there. With luck, we'll be back in time for the party."*

"Party?" Rora asked. She was still blocked from getting physically close to the Fountain by the wall of mist that had sprung into being, but it didn't block the sounds the others were making. "What party is that?"

"Rora wishes to know 'what party,' as do I," Rydan relayed, fingers brushing through the rippling ribbon of communication magic once again.

"It's your citizenship party. Kelly's decided that citizenship takes a declared intent to stay and settle on the Isle, an oath of citizenship, and a ten-day minimum waiting period. Amara has already stated her intent to stay, so there's just Rora's declaration, and two more days of waiting. Kelly's planning a party to welcome you to the family."

"My sister has agreed to stay?" Rora inquired dubiously. "To become a citizen, of her own free will? Mother Earth, what have I been missing by staying up all night?"

"I will set the wards to alert me instantly, should you find

anything worth sharing. Go and start your task," Rydan directed his brother and sister-in-law. *"And . . . good night."*

"Civility from my brother? Has the Third Moon resurrected itself?" Dominor's voice quipped, only to be followed by a reverberating, *"Ow!"*

"Thank you, Serina," Rydan offered politely, trying not to smirk.

"Actually, that was me. I will not tolerate blasphemy in my presence, even if it involves someone else's Patron Deities," Guardian Naima stated quellingly. *"Good night, Guardian Rydan."*

"Good night, Guardian Naima."

Extracting his hand, Rydan checked the Fountain to make sure it had been returned to normal. Serina was right; it did look like a fancifully tied ribbon. Or perhaps the blossoming flower that Rora had compared his emotions to, when she had Seen him during a moment of amusement two days ago. Satisfied it was safe, he retreated from the pipes and ribbons. Stepping around the mist-blocked pillars, Rydan rejoined Rora, who gave the wall of mist a last look before turning to join him in walking away.

"I do hope they can find the right information. I've waited all my life to find out what I am, and I know I can wait at least a few more days with patience, but I don't know if I could wait a few more *years*," she said.

"My brother is tenacious when he wants something. Serina will hunt down anything that interests her with equal fervor," he told her. "Together, they will succeed. There is no other conclusion."

"If you say so," Rora agreed. "So, what now? The house has been built, work on the rest of the city won't be quite as urgent, and we have to wait for Dom and Serina to uncover something useful. What shall we do while we wait?"

Catching her elbow, Rydan swung her around to face him. Deliberately, he took a half step forward, bumping their torsos together; they had stopped just within the last set of pillars lining the Fountain Hall, not far from the corridor that led to his underground quarters. Black-clad chest to green-covered breasts, he let himself radiate his desire for her, waiting for her to See it and hopefully act upon it.

Rora looked at him, waiting for him to do something. When nothing happened, she cleared her throat. "Yes?"

"Aren't you Looking at me?" he asked her.

"What? Oh, no, I wasn't. Sorry." Double-blinking, she concentrated, shifting her vision. Yellow annoyance tinged the edges of his aura, but the veils of his emotions quickly flushed with purplish red desire and violet blue longing. They formed tendrils that brushed her face, particularly her mouth, which was where he was gazing. Blinking it away again, Rora quirked her eyebrow. "You would like to kiss me?"

He slipped his hands around the back of her waist, pulling her even closer. "Yes. I would."

"Patience is a virtue, Guardian."

Rora yelped, startled. Rydan loosened his grip a little, twisting to face the source of Madam Mist's abrupt, echoing voice. Copper gold fog had risen between the two nearest pillars. The mist almost brushed his elbow, it was that close.

"What?" There was no face, no body in the roiling of the sound-disturbed mist, but Rydan *felt* her disapproval. Expecting a rhyme from the fog, he blinked as she continued in plain speech.

"I have invested too much effort to allow a moment of untimely lust to cloud your good judgment. Patience," Madam Mist repeated, *"is a virtue."*

Frowning, Rydan drew in a breath to argue, but the mist faded quickly, leaving him with nothing but empty air.

"How did it . . . she . . . know what we were going to do?" Rora asked him, confused.

Rydan shook his head. He didn't know what was going on, other than that he apparently wasn't supposed to kiss her. The disappointment that ran through him left a sour taste in his mouth and irritated his beast. Struggling to master his mood, he let go of Rora. Frowning at the now empty air, she tucked her arms around his elbow, then stuck out her tongue.

"I'm not giving him up! Do you hear me?" she asked loudly enough for her voice to echo through the Hall. "I really like him, and he likes me. Whatever you are, you have no say in that! Only *we* do . . . right?" she asked, glancing up at him as she lowered her voice.

He didn't answer for a moment. The emotion her words

stirred made his beast ache, but in an unfamiliar way. Rydan set aside his confusion as her confidence faltered. Pressing a soft, brief kiss to her lips, he rested his forehead against hers. "Yes. I like you."

Her smile was eclipsed by the rush of warmth his words stirred. Rydan closed his eyes, basking in the feeling. Leaning in closer, he touched his mouth to hers again, wanting to return some of those feelings.

"I said, patience is a virtue . . ."

Irritated, Rydan flipped his hand up in a rude gesture. He kissed Rora a little longer, but his conscience nagged at him. Madam Mist was right; he shouldn't let his emotions and needs overcome his common sense. Ending the kiss, he exhaled roughly, resting his brow once more against hers. His forehead tingled from the contained force of her magic.

Rora cupped his cheek, knowing he could feel her silent sympathy and her own frustration. Covering her hand with his, he pressed it to his face, then shifted enough to give her palm a kiss before stepping back. He kept ahold of her hand, but put some mind-clearing distance between them.

"We need something to occupy our time while we wait for Dominor and Serina to figure out what we can do with you. Something *platonic*," he added, resigned but not happy about it.

"Well, there's always enchanting more buildings," Rora offered. "Though that runs the risk of waking the newcomers who apparently arrived earlier today. But it's after supper, so it's probably too late to visit anyone, and that means it's too late to be force-growing stone frames."

Tipping his head back, Rydan studied the suncrystals. "It *is* getting late," he agreed, gauging the time by the brightness of the crystals embedded in the ceiling. "But we can work inside sound-dampening wards. Come. We'll shadow-walk to the harbor. Working on the city will be a productive distraction, and more useful than carving mindless pictures into stone."

"But I like your pictures," Rora said, earning her a bemused look. "I don't think they're mindless at all. They're very expressive and lyrical—they make me want to visit the places you've carved."

"They're not real places, Rora," he told her. "They're just from my imagination."

"But that's not true. Down in the river passage?" she offered in example. "The carvings on the lower gallery walls look like the port city of Alasia, in Amazai. It has three domed towers that are very distinctive, viewed from the harbor, and the perspetive is from the harbor. I remember seeing it as we left Aiar, the day we set sail for Fortuna.

"And the upper balcony, I'd swear that was a view of the village of Five Springs in the kingdom of the Mornai. I haven't seen it from the cliff overlooking the river valley for almost a decade, but there do seem to be enough streams meandering through the image to match up with what I can remember. We kept passing those sections on our way out to the marble vein and back, so I have had more than a few chances to study the murals," Rora reminded him.

"Perhaps they have a superficial resemblance, but not the others," Rydan argued. "At least one of those cities is underwater. If *that* is a real place, you would think that someone would have heard of it by now, for it would take a great deal of magic to sustain, and who knows how they'd sow and harvest crops, underwater. You should remember that one, since that's where you found me, the second time you visited me. And there are images of war, of women and children being hunted by guardsmen on horseback, of unspeakable evils being done in horrible places . . . *which I carved*."

Mindful of his rising agitation, Rydan took a moment to breathe deeply and calm his beast. They were still within the Fountain Hall, after all. He shook his head.

"For those latter ones alone, I pray to the Gods they're not real. Such torments should not exist. That *I* should carve them disturbs me."

"I may strive to be perennially cheerful, but I am aware that evil does exist. And it is not *evil* to record that such things happen. It is only evil to *do* them," she stated with conviction. "*You* do not actually do those things, therefore you are not evil."

"Then why do I carve them?" Rydan asked her, frustrated.

"Why do judges have court scribes who write out the details

from a case of murder or rape? Why record such evils?" she challenged him softly. "It's so that we do not forget, so that we remain vigilant for the signs of such things in the future. You are probably the most heavily affected by the evils and agonies of the world, because of your sensitivity. Something inside of you wants to make sure that no one else forgets—that's all."

Rora wrapped her arms around him, hugging him as he bowed his head. A stray thought flitted through his head. Rydan almost kept it to himself, since it was partly an uncomfortable thought, but the woman in his arms deserved to hear it. "You . . . seem to understand me better than my own twin. Or at least tolerate me more."

That made her chuckle and squeeze him. "In some ways, you understand me better than my twin does. Or at least believe in me more. But never doubt that Trevan loves you. As do the rest of your brothers. They do more than just 'tolerate' you."

"I exasperate them," he pointed out. "Even you cannot deny that."

Twisting a little, she peered up at him with a mock-innocent look. "True, but isn't that what family is for?"

Caught off guard, Rydan laughed. Hugging her close, he kissed the top of her head. Then, mindful of Madam Mist's interference, he shifted from hugging her to merely holding her hand. "Come. We have plenty of work to do while we wait for news from Koral-tai."

"You mean, while I can still work what passes for my version of magic," Rora amended wryly.

"Madam Mist wishes us to work, rather than to play. I would like to know *why*," he muttered, glaring at the pillars and the spaces between them, "but until then, we should fill our time with work . . . unless you wish to tell us, Madam?"

The air remained quiescent. If Madam Mist knew, or had known, she wasn't sharing it right now. He owed her, though; the mysterious voice *had* guided him into being the Guardian of the Nightfall Fountain. If she wanted him to remain in ignorance for now, he would. Sighing roughly, Rydan led Rora out of the Hall.

FIFTEEN

Rydan was very uncomfortable at the party. For once, it had little to do with his beast. By applying the same inner discipline that granted him the calm control of a Guardian, he was able to endure and even enjoy the company of his family and the newcomers to the Isle at the plaza he and Rora had created during the night.

Though he *was* just as taken aback as the others by Kelly's declaration that their Patron Deity would be *all* the Gods in Heaven—which meant somehow figuring out a way to resurrect the Convocation, the earthly meeting of all Gods and Goddesses, formerly held once every four years to discuss face-to-face with Their worshippers any inter-kingdom or widespread spiritual concerns the world might have—that wasn't the source of his discomfort, either.

It was Rora, and that damned order by the mysterious Madam Mist not to kiss her anymore. Not until further notice, at least, and that was the crux of his problem. Rydan was aware it was merely the result of being denied the right to hold her, to kiss her and touch her that made the thought of doing those things all the more alluring. Before being denied, he had been able to keep his head mostly clear. Now, though, it was hard to concentrate on the conversations of others when he could see her lips moving out of the corner of his eye and could remember how those lips felt against his own.

He was so distracted by trying not to notice her too much that he almost missed his twin's innuendo-laced inquiry, hearing it with only half of his attention.

"I'm rather surprised by you," Trevan stated as their next-eldest brother started setting up for a bit of music. Rydan grunted, pretending he was paying attention, though he was more interested in watching Rora chat animatedly with the professional wench, Cari, about something. Trevan continued. "I never knew you had so much industry in you. All these building frames, erected in just a couple of nights? When it took you two nights to help get the first house set up?"

"The first test of new spells always goes slowly," Rydan replied absently.

"Yes, but to erect so many, so soon . . ."

Rydan shifted in his seat. The word *erect* made him feel uncomfortable. Glancing at his twin, he flushed when he realized Trevan hadn't missed his discomfort, or its source. Deciding he would rather do the baiting than be the baited, he replied, "It's amazing what you can do with time on your hands and plenty of motivation."

"Motivation?" Trevan challenged him skeptically, dropping his green gaze to his brother's lap. "Or frustration?"

"Motivation . . . frustration . . . same difference," Rydan dismissed, giving his twin a quelling look. "How 'motivated' have *you* been lately?"

That made his brother grimace. "More than I'd care to admit. Though I am making progress."

"Better you than me," Rydan told him, thinking about his verse of the Prophecy.

"You'll have to face your fears at some point," Trevan retorted, lifting his chin in Rora's direction. Clapping a hand to his twin's shoulder, Trevan squeezed it briefly, then released. He was usually mindful of Rydan's distaste for physical touch, though he had done so anyway, this time. "Don't fight Destiny too hard, Brother. You'll have a lot more fun if you give in, believe me."

"Fun is the least of my concerns." Rydan muttered, but

Trevan was already moving away. Sighing, the sixthborn of the brothers resumed his current obsession: Rora-watching.

Even with her back to him, Rora Felt him looking her way again. After so many days of Seeing emotions, of trying to *Feel* emotions like Rydan did, she was finally getting the knack of it. Perhaps it wasn't wise, exposing herself to the same forces that had caused Rydan to retreat into himself, but so far, the only emotions she could sense were his. That was how she wanted it, of course, and she worked on her magic, focusing it to stay that way with her will. He was important to her, both as a friend and more than a friend.

The touch of his attention felt like a warm, gentle hand on her back. Reaching behind her, she groped for his hand. His fingers met hers, gripping for a moment, a gentle squeeze of physical contact, before he released her. The wench, Cari, noticed their brief touch. She smiled at the younger woman, her teeth looking extra white in her naturally tanned face.

"You *do* know I came here with the impression I'd be offering my services, right?" she murmured to Rora. "Not that I'm going to, given how you're all tied up or celibate for one reason or another, men and women both, but that is the original reason I came here."

"Yes, I know," Rora agreed. She hadn't known until the morning after the woman's arrival who—or rather, what—their visitor was, when a chance comment at breakfast had enlightened her, but she did know now. Cari was a *professional* wench, sort of a secular version of the priestesses found on the Shifting Plains. "I'm, um, sorry you came all this way only to not have any fun."

Cari shrugged. "Her Majesty is still paying me for consultation on the idea of a Wenching Guild, so either way, I'm not losing my income. And it's rather relaxing not to have any pressure to tease and please. If no one needs me, then I don't have to feel the need to 'perform.' Not to mention it's very flattering to be *respected* for my profession. I'm appreciated on the mainland, but not necessarily respected. It's different. I like it."

"Nightfall is special," Rora agreed, glancing at the others. "I Saw it from far away and led my sister straight here, in the belief this would be a good place to go. I'm glad I did. The possibilities of this place are exciting to think about."

Cari chuckled at that. "You sound like your sister."

Rora grinned. "I'll take that as a compliment. Mara and I don't always get along, but we do love each other dearly. And I'm happy that she's finally happy. I wasn't sure if she'd ever give in and agree to settle here permanently, but it's a far better place for her than back home would have been. Here, she isn't judged constantly by *what* she can do, but by *who* she is. Or rather, by who she chooses to be."

"I think I know what you mean," Cari murmured, her tone thoughtful. "And I thank you for it."

"What?" Rora asked.

"You have helped me make up my mind," the professional wench told her. "I've had a little hesitation on moving here, because I won't have clients for a while, and there's that fifty percent of my income to pay in taxes for the first few years of citizenship—even if it does go toward covering the cost of housing rent, and Ultra Tongue, and scrying bracelets—but you're right. Here, I can be judged on *who* I am, as you say, not just on what I can do. And I have the respect of the Sovereign, which means the respect of the government. I *will* move here and open a guild."

"I'm glad," Rora said honestly. "If you want to know more about Shifterai priestesses and their, um, holy version of wenching, as an alternative approach to the whole matter, just ask. I spent a lot of time with them, for all I was expected to remain a maiden, since I wasn't really interested in taking holy vows."

"Now, that's another reason to come back here," Cari agreed, chuckling. "I have never heard of wenching being part of a holy calling before. Orovalis City has become too small for me, now that I know the world holds so much more potential. When I come back—since we're sailing back to the mainland tomorrow so I can start looking for suitable guild member candidates, and the boys can start contacting people they know to come and be settlers—if you're willing to answer my questions about Shifterai practices, I'll answer any questions you have about Katani ones . . . though I probably know a lot more than you do, if you're still a maiden. Agreed?"

Blushing, Rora nodded. "Agreed."

"Now, if you'll excuse me," Cari said, rising from her seat, "I think I'll go listen to the singing, since it's the closest I'll get to any romancing on this trip."

For a moment, Rora wasn't sure if she had Felt a touch of wistfulness from the other woman, but she shook it off. She didn't want to be sensitive to other people's feelings, just Rydan's. Glancing behind her, she saw he had left his seat and moved over to converse with his eldest brother about something. Rora studied him for a few minutes, watching the graceful, economic gesturing of his hands whenever he made a point and remembering how those fingers felt against her flesh.

Squirming in her seat, she finally rose from the table, moving closer to the music so she could enjoy it, too. That meant leaving the shelter of the covered walkway, but though it was cold out, there was no threat of rain at the moment.

Rydan and she had altered one of her sister's city plans just a little. Instead of a block of houses and shops, the two of them had erected a large square, a plaza bordered around the edges by a broad double walkway sheltered by a faience-tiled roof. The covered area held more than enough room to shelter a large dining table and several benches. It could have hosted twelve or more such tables, end to end, down one side of the square, with streets plotted around the edges and a platform in the center of the courtyard.

Rydan had suggested the platform be an octagon, since that was already a recurring theme on the Isle. Rora had in turn suggested that it be aesthetic as well as functional; her idea was a series of abstract, symmetrical fountain basins fanning out to either side, cupping the back of the stone dais as a sort of backdrop for ceremonial functions. And there had been a ceremony earlier, before the feast.

Idly fingering the polished metal of the cryslet thing they had given her—something for communicating over long distances, though she would have to get Rydan to explain the use of it to her again, later on—Rora decided the splashing of the fountain detracted a little bit from Evanor's performance. Not enough to really complain about, but it had caused a problem when listening to all those oaths they had made earlier to be good, law-abiding, hardworking citizens in this new land. Had there been an actual crowd, their words would have been lost completely, between the splashing of the water and the murmurs of the witnesses. She would have to ask Rydan how to reduce the noise of the fountain.

The music was good, and she caught sight of her sister learning to dance in the local way. Rora glanced behind her, seeking Rydan's dark-clad figure. He was still in a conversation with his eldest brother, though Saber was doing most of the talking and gesturing now. In the illumination cast by the lightglobes brought down from the palace and set in stone sconces, aided by the flickering flames of two small bonfires lit by Koranen to add heat to the night as well as their warm glow, she thought Rydan looked a lot more comfortable than he had in the first few days of their acquaintance.

Not that she'd call what they had now a mere acquaintance, though they weren't entirely courting at the moment, either. It annoyed her that the mist-woman said they couldn't court directly. Rora hated feeling annoyed. Still, there was nothing against her watching him or drifting back his way, since the music was now quite lively and loud, what with young Mikor drumming and Mariel singing along with her blond husband.

She didn't get too close to him; Saber had Rydan's ear, and didn't look to be giving it up anytime soon. From the shaping motions of his hands, he was talking about the columns and arches the two of them had raised overnight. Rydan had done most of the work, in her opinion; *he* had drawn the various runes and guiding marks, spending hours getting everything just right. She had done her best to help. Mostly, that had consisted of sketching the lines of walls and the squares and rectangles of where the columns were to grow, since she didn't know enough about sigil crafting or rune scribing to do the actual spells.

Once the marks had been laid in place, he had joined his power to hers, guiding the flow of her Fountain into the bedrock of the island, raising up the arches in smooth granite arcs broken only by the occasional niche or spur where a beam for an upper floor, a roof joist, or a window ledge would rest. They had done good work; once the others filled in the walls and windows with wood and glass, laying the upper floors and tiling the roofs, they would have a good fifty or more buildings ready to inhabit. Rora didn't deny that she could deliver more power to the raising of all those columns than Rydan could, but it was his magical marks that had guided and shaped her energy.

Or, to put it into Plains terms: she was the strong, sturdy horse pulling the loaded wagon, but he was the driver, harnessing her in place and guiding her efforts with the reins and traces. *One of these days, I'm going to learn real magic*, she thought, half-wistful, half-determined to succeed. *Presuming I can keep some of my powers if and when this Fountain thing gets extracted, of course.*

If and when would have to wait until Dominor and Serina had found the information they needed. It would also have to wait, because the music had ended at a plea from Evanor to take a quick break. Rora could now see her sister standing over by one of the two fires lit on the courtyard's cobblestones. Or rather, moving backward, away from Rydan's twin.

It was that backward movement that caught her attention. She knew that backward sidling; she had seen it before, though never from her sister. The redheaded mage didn't stay put as he properly should, however. He followed her, touching her, concern and confusion visible in his posture. Realization dawned. Rora quickly moved that way as her sister tried to retreat a second and a third time, only to be thwarted again by Trevan's concern.

"—*Yes*, something is wrong!" Mara replied tersely. Her voice was loud enough to catch the attention of the others as she added, *"Stay put!"*

Just as I thought . . . and poor Trevan doesn't have a clue, Rora decided, closing the last few yards between them. She *had* told Trevan some of the courting customs of the Shifting Plains several days ago, but it seemed her sister's attempted actions were too subtle for the outlander to catch. Catching him by the elbow, Rora dragged the redhead back from her twin. "Why don't you come stand over here?"

He frowned at her, rubbing at his limb as soon as she let go. Normally, she wouldn't touch a mage so carelessly, but Trevan was as trustworthy as the rest of his kin. At least he was in the right place now, positioned across the fire from her twin.

Rydan's voice startled Rora. Normally he didn't speak so loudly, and normally, his baritone didn't hold a hint of irritated jealousy, but his tone was both peeved and loud enough for the others to hear. "Why did you touch *him*?"

Giving him a reassuring smile, Rora stepped back from Trevan. She was acutely aware of the others watching, of their confusion, but she wouldn't have done anything different. "Because he was being rather dense about it . . . though I suspect he finally has a clue."

"A clue about what?" Kelly asked, bemused.

"When the kingdom of Shifterai was formed," Rora explained, tucking her arm around Rydan's ribs and choosing to ignore his perturbed mood in favor of a more physical reassurance, "it was agreed that the men could take the form of anything that walked on the earth, swam through the water, or flew through the air. It was the *women*, however, who controlled the fourth element, fire. We are the guardians of hearth and flame, you see."

Trevan's confused look shifted to one of dawning remembrance as she spoke, reminding him of the things they had discussed a few days ago, while at the same time enlightening the others.

"It was therefore decided that should any man want the honor of claiming a woman as his wife," she continued, sneaking a glance at the silently listening man at her side, "he would have to brave those flames in order to do so. But *only* if the woman herself asked him to. Thus every maiden—raised or adopted onto the Shifting Plains—is trained to avoid holding out her hand to a man when she stands across a fire from him. Not unless she wishes to offer herself as his wife."

Mara blushed, since she was clearly facing Trevan from across the flames of the low-burning bonfire. Rora couldn't see Trevan's expression, but he hadn't moved, yet. Which was a good sign.

Rora continued her explanation. "She may hold out her hand to the side, or walk around to face him directly . . . but if she offers her hand to him through the flames of a fire, it is her way of accepting him, of him being judged worthy of her. He need not *accept* the invitation, of course," she teased lightly, since it was obvious to her normal senses, never mind the extra ones, that Trevan wasn't about to refuse her twin, "but that is the custom where we're from.

"And if he does, if he leaps, or steps, or even crawls across the dangerous flames to her, catching her offered hand in front of several witnesses . . . they are wed."

Mara lifted her hand, offering it to Trevan. The man at Rora's side tensed. With only a little hesitation, Trevan backed up for a bit of starting room, then ran forward and leaped hard; his boots cleared the flames by a hand-span. Landing, he caught Mara's outstretched hand; the two were yanked together under the force of his momentum. Rora freed her arm from Rydan's waist, applauding the couple as Trevan used their spin to pull Mara into a close embrace. It was a well-done leap . . . and a very nice kiss, from what she could tell.

That was when Rydan left her side. Glancing at his retreating back, Rora Looked at his emotions. Envy was the strongest of the veils wrapping around him, threatening to tighten around his frame. Wistfulness edged the envy like a border trim, and wariness wrapped around him like a cord.

With her sister's Shifterai-style marriage explained and properly witnessed, Rora was now free to leave them to their happiness. Rydan was her bigger concern. With as little hesitation as Trevan had shown, just long enough to make sure her departure would pass unnoticed, Rora followed him. She caught up to him at the edge of the covered walkway.

Rydan knew she was following him and leaned against one of the pillars they had raised, waiting for her to reach him. Feeling that she was about to wrap her arm around him, Rydan almost moved away—he ached to hold her but wasn't supposed to do anything about that ache. But he couldn't deny her the right to tuck herself against his side. Not when he felt like she belonged there. That was his problem.

He was falling for her, even if he didn't want to admit it. That meant his verse of the Prophecy was nearly upon them, and he had no idea what would happen. The only consolation he had was her presence at his side, even if she precipitated the crisis somehow.

"Any news from Koral-tai?" Rora asked him. Tucked against his side, she could feel his emotions souring a little from frustration as he shook his head. Leaning her head against his shoulder, she added, "They did recruit—what was it Serina reported last night? Twelve, fifteen nuns to help them search the Archives? That should speed things up a bit."

"*After* Serina gave them Ultra Tongue, which meant *I* had to send that stinking fruit through for her," he complained.

The *myjii* fruit came from the Moonlands, Serina's former home, and it had several peculiar properties. The lumpy, fist-sized fruit reeked like a manure pile mixed with rotting meat before it was opened, but it contained six almond-sized seeds, which, when dried and powdered, formed the vital ingredient required to activate Ultra Tongue's extensive translation abilities.

"Yes, it stank, but let's hope that wind charm you used to freshen the caverns has done its job," Rora soothed him, wrapping her other arm around him for a squeeze.

That pressed her breasts against him. Rydan stifled a groan. He was doing his best not to get aroused by her. To be a gentleman instead, to heed Madam Mist's warnings and not stay in close contact with her, but it was difficult when she was so soft, so warm and willing. Confining himself to a single kiss—one delivered to her light brown hair rather than a more tempting expanse of flesh—he removed her arms.

Knowing why he was removing her touch, Rora sighed and permitted it. At least he didn't deny her the interlacing of their fingers. It was a small thing, but a comforting one.

It made her think of his emotions, and of her own. "Rydan . . . I know this is going to be a very strange question, but . . . how do you feel about me?"

Though his face was half in shadow and somewhat concealed by the aura of his emotions, his skin was pale enough that she could see one of his eyebrows rise. "I would think that obvious."

"Yes, I can See how you *feel* when you think of me and even Feel a little of it, myself. I guess I mean, what do you *think* of me?" Rora corrected impatiently.

"I think that you are . . . unexpected," Rydan admitted, trying to choose his words carefully. Feeling her puzzlement, he tried again. "I didn't expect you, when I contemplated my

Destined bride. Not that I knew what to expect, but not *you*. You're . . . warm. Caring."

Over in the center of the plaza, Evanor had started playing again, recapturing the attention of the others. That left the two of them alone in the shadows of the columns. It was cold, the air damp from the waters of the cove, but Rora didn't feel like moving closer to the two fires. Not when she could move closer to him.

"And I'm not supposed to touch you," Rydan muttered, pulling back from her when she swayed forward. "You are a threat to my Guardianship. Prophecy suggests it, and Madam Mist's interference suggests it. I don't know how, but you are. Or you will be. Even if you might not want to be, you will be. I should not allow you to distract me."

"Not when you have a duty to protect your Fountain," Rora quietly agreed. She wanted to lean into him, to smell the warm male scent that permeated his dark clothes, but that would be a temptation for both of them. Reluctantly, she stepped back, though she couldn't bring herself to let go of his hands. "Shall we get back to raising more building frames while we wait?"

"Yes. I feel *motivated* to do something exhausting," he muttered wryly.

"Motivated, or frustrated?" Rora quipped, leading him into the darkness beyond the plaza.

Rydan snorted. "Right now, is there a difference?"

Rora pressed her hand to her abdomen as they jolted back to their feet; she had to make sure her stomach had been dragged along with the rest of her body. That shadow-walking trick of Rydan's was fast and fascinating, but also a bit nauseating. She didn't have a chance to pause and rest, however; Rydan pulled her after him, hurrying along the broad tunnel that led from the outside to the Fountain Hall.

Given it was after midnight, the suncrystals embedded in the ceiling had lost most of their illuminating power, but the closer they got to the Fountain Hall, the stronger their glow remained. There wasn't enough shadow at this point to continue jolting breathlessly across long distances, never mind in the still brightly lit Hall itself. Knowing she wasn't supposed to get close, Rora didn't mind it when Rydan released her fingers at the halfway point to the pipe-and-ribbon base of the Fountain. It actually gave her a chance to let her stomach settle while he crossed to one of the spouts pouring a ruffled stream of copper-hued energies.

"Guardian Naima?" Rydan asked as soon as he had thrust his fingers into the mistlike flow. His voice, amplified by the Fountain's energies, echoed through the chamber. *"You called?"*

"Serina, actually. Is, um . . . is Rora nearby?" his sister-in-law asked.

"Yes. I think she can get a little closer to hear you bett—"

"NO!"

Rydan and Rora both winced from Serina's reverberating shout. He gave the communication stream a dubious look. *"No? What do you mean, no?"*

"That's what we've found out," her voice stated at a calmer, less ear-taxing volume. *"There's a whole mix of good and bad news that we've uncovered, this morning. The first of the good news, she* is *a Living Font. All the descriptions listed match. So they really do exist, though it looks like they come along only once every three hundred years or so.*

"There is *a way to extract the singularity from a living host—oh, and it's always* been *a 'her,'"* the Arithmancer related. *"Speculation by the ancients suggests that this is because women are associated with childbearing and thus have a higher quotient of life-energy, though of course the females in question also have to have an extremely high level of magical energy . . . Yes, Dominor, I know I'm digressing!*

"Anyway . . . the ancient scroll one of the nuns found suggests that if we just wait until she dies, wherever she does so, that *is where the Font will separate itself from her body. The bad news about that, however, is if she is killed violently . . . the Font will explode, and it'll look like a Portal explosion from the Shattering of Aiar, if I read the descriptions right."*

"We have to wait for her to die?" Rydan asked, unsettled by that thought. *"And we have to protect her from being destroyed by anything other than natural old age, even if it's just an accident?"*

"I think the violent death refers to murder. Besides, the text states that the Font can be extracted without permanently killing her—yes, Dom, I'll tell them that. He wants to add that it can be extracted while still leaving Rora with the normal powers of a mage. The bad news . . . well, there are two parts to it, and part of it is good news, so I'll start with that. The second bit of good news is that we found information regarding the Convocation of the Gods and how it was created."

Rydan frowned at that tidbit. *"What has* that *to do with Rora being a Fountain?"*

"Well, the bad news is that if one Font touches another directly, as in physically sharing space and making contact . . . that *is what opens the Gateway to Heaven and the realm of the Gods,"* Serina stated soberly. *"If that Fountain is still in a living host at the time . . . it literally rips the host open, destroying her."*

Rora sucked in a sharp breath, horrified at how close she had come to death. She suddenly had a much greater appreciation for Madam Mist's interference, even if the bodiless woman had banned her from intimacy with Rydan. Wrapping her hands around her green-clad chest, she shivered. "Trust me, I'm *definitely* not going anywhere near that Fountain."

"Don't worry, she'll stay away from it," Rydan promised Serina.

"Good. There's more. In order to remove the Fountain, the first step is to assign the living host a Guardian . . . which for reasons of indelicacy is supposed to be a man."

Both of them blinked, Rydan twisting to look back at Rora. His pale cheeks reddened with the implication. *"Then why would Madam Mist forbid . . . ?"*

"Forbid what?"

He blushed harder, having forgotten his hand was still bathed in copper-hued magic. *"Madam Mist forbade intimacy between us."*

Serina's answer echoed back to them after a short pause. *"Dom and I suspect it's because you're already a Guardian. If you're tied into two Fonts at the same time, there is a chance that the strength of the interacting forces could combine and rip you apart. I haven't had an opportunity to actually run the calculations for defining how big that chance is, though.*

"The other possibility is that you could actually wind up with enough magic at your command to threaten the Gods Themselves. Sort of like when a rogue mage gets hold of a Fountain. Either way, it's not a good idea. Rora will either have to take someone else for her lover, or you'll have to give up your current Guardianship."

Rydan extracted his hand from the ribbon of energy, disturbed by that idea. He glanced at Rora again; he could sense her anxiety and her concern, but he wanted to see her with his eyes. On the one hand, he didn't want to abandon his Fountain—not that there were many choices for a replacement—but on the other hand, he admitted to himself the thought of her going to another man was intolerable.

Serina's voice recaptured his attention. *"Now for the rest of the good news. If we can safely extract Rora's singularity, we can use a special levitation spell to move it into* your *Font, and open the Gateway to Heaven in a controlled, nonlethal manner,"* she continued. *"Using the same spell, we can also separate the two singularities when the Convocation is over. In between Convocations, the Font can be used much like any other Font, though a basin of some sort will have to be designed and built to contain, filter, and apportion out the relevant energies radiating from the singularity.*

"The last and biggest problem, however, is a bad one," Serina relayed. *"I'm afraid the scroll is so old, it lost some of its preservation runes. Unfortunately, the section detailing* how *to safely remove a Fountain from its living host was the victim. When I opened it originally, I only read enough to know it dealt with something that wasn't really what I was pursuing, though I knew I'd want to read it later. I didn't unscroll it far enough to realize part of it was falling apart. And the nun who found and opened the scroll for a more thorough perusal didn't realize that until it was too late. A full hand-span of the parchment cracked and disintegrated to useless dust when she unrolled it."*

Rora dropped her face into her palms, groaning. If it wasn't one problem, it was another. They knew *part* of how to free her from the curse of her existence, but not the most important part.

On the northern side of the Fountain, one of the other

copper-hued streams of magic ruffled and misted, disturbed by another woman's voice. *"Guardian Rydan, are you there?"*

"The only good news," Serina continued, oblivious to the incoming communication, *"is that the start of the scroll lists the scribe's name and '. . . 17 of 93, to be delivered unto the High Priest of Koral Monastery, in the Name of Tallan, Patron of Natall.' Since Natua became the Patron Deity of Natallia approximately fourteen hundred years ago, this means that it's a very old scroll if it references a different God and a different kingdom name . . . but it also means that it's possible that some of the oldest archives out there may have an intact copy of their own.*

"There's a storm brewing across the border in Guchere, and it's mucking with the aether, but I'm going to try to relay a request in the direction of Mendhi and Guardian Tipa'thia as soon as I can. If anyone would still have a copy—or even a remake of a copy—it would be the Great Library of Mendham."

"Scroll? Copy?" the voice from the other ribbon asked, ruffling its surface. *"I think I'm getting an echo, here. Guardian Rydan, am I interrupting something?"*

"Hold that thought, Serina," Rydan told his sister-in-law. Removing his hand from that stream, he moved around the base of the Fountain, ducking under some of the ribbons of energy arcing their way into catch-basins scattered around the floor. Touching the other one, he spoke again. *"Guardian Sheren, you wished to speak with me?"*

"Yes, Guardian Rydan—I apologize if I'm interrupting anything, but I finally got additional names of Guardians farther down the Fountainway, from the two Guardians named by that woman I told you about, the newly arrived mage, Zella. I have a stack of papers recording the fluctuations in the aether on the southeastern corner, the middle-east coast, and part of the northern mountains of Aiar I can send through, if you're willing to pass them on to Serina."

"I am," Rydan said. *"She's back in Natallia, so I'll just relay them straight to her. You're up rather late, aren't you?"*

"Rydan, is that Guardian Sheren?" Serina asked. *"Doesn't she have a large library of her own, wherever she is? Ask her if she has the, uh . . . Scroll of Living Glory."*

"Yeah, I'm up late. Or really early. I ate something last night that seems to be disagreeing with me. I guessed you'd be bright-eyed at this ungodly hour, so thought I'd get the work done I was going to put off until tomorrow, or rather, later today."

Rydan sighed. *"Guardian Sheren, Serina wants to know if you have a copy of the Scroll of Living Glory in your Archives."*

"The what of what? Do you know just how many scrolls my library holds? You'll have to give me a lot more than just a title, young man," the Guardian of Menomon chided him.

"It's a scroll covering the origin and creation of Fountains and the opening of the Gateway to Heaven," Rydan relayed.

"No . . . doesn't ring a bell. But I do have thousands of the things. If you like, I'll rouse my apprentices and go on a search for it. If the scroll has a title, we should be able to find it fairly quickly."

"Yes, please do that—and be very careful with it," Rydan added. *"The copy Serina was referencing lost its preservation spell and disintegrated at the part we were most interested in reading."*

"No worries; each one of these scrolls has a minimum of three copies of different ages, if not more, which is why *I have thousands of them. Menomon has been using scroll- and book-copying for centuries to train our young mages in rune-crafting, since it's good, safe practice for them. And it's tedious and time consuming, so it keeps them out of trouble,"* Sheren added, a dash of humor coming through despite the Fountain-based warping of her tone. *"It makes a great punishment for mischief makers, if nothing else."*

"We would deeply appreciate an intact copy, if you can find one," Rydan told her. *"Is there anything I can do for you in return?"*

"I would be eternally grateful if you could send a very large jar of honey my way. The largest one you can spare. The only sweeteners we have around here are barley water and fruit juice."

"I'll see what can be done," Rydan promised. *"I'll contact you as soon as I have some to spare."*

"And I'll contact you . . . ooh, a little dizzy, there. I'll call

you back as soon as I have any information on this Scroll of Living Glory."

"Guardian Sheren, are you alright?" Rydan asked her, frowning. There was something in the undercurrents of her voice, something that wasn't being said, but his beast couldn't pin it down.

"Oh, I'll be fine. Just sweating a little and a bit dizzy. I'll be alright."

"Sweating and dizziness . . . Guardian Sheren, are you having heart problems?" he asked, concerned. *"Does your arm feel weak? Are you having trouble breathing?"*

"No, it's not heart problems. I did train as a Healer, before ending up as the Guardian of this place. It's just something I ate that's disagreeing with me. I've taken something for it. I just have to wait for the cure to take effect, that's all. Anyway, I'm sending the papers through now . . ."

In a matter of moments, a bundle of the yellowish green sheets Sheren's people used flashed into existence, floating within the pulsing sphere enveloping the Fountain singularity. A moment of concentration, a touch of the sphere, and Rydan sent it on its way. *"Received, and forwarded."*

"Received!" Serina's voice stated from the other flow. *"Ooh, this is lovely . . . Yes, I know I have to focus on other things right now, dear, but can't I have a moment to mathemagically drool?"*

Sheren spoke at the same time, addressing Rydan. *"Remember, the biggest jar of honey you can spare. We'll talk later. I think I need to lie down for a bit."*

"Later, Guardian Sheren," he agreed. Extracting his hand, Rydan moved back to the other pipe and dipped his fingers into its flow. *"Guardian Sheren says she'll go looking for it. If she does have a copy of the scroll, she says it is likely it has been recopied at some point, and we'd be able to get our hands on a less fragile version."*

"Excellent! In the meantime, Dominor will transcribe what parts are still readable from the scroll we found, so we'll at least be able to make some progress on Rora's problem while we wait for results. I'll compose a query for Guardian Tipa'thia to ask the Great Library for information."

Another voice interrupted her, echoing loudly through the hall.

"Tell no one of the girl
Not of hide nor of head
The war to control her
Would render you dead!"

It came from the copper-flecked black that spewed into existence in the gaps between the four pillars encircling Rora. Centered in the midst of all four source-points, trapped by them, Rora cried out and clapped her hands to her ears, hunching over from the loudness of the voice. Rydan abandoned his conversation with Serina, concerned for her.

"Madam Mist, let her go!"

"You must protect her . . ."

It was merely a whisper, this last warning from Madam Mist. The wall of roiling black and copper faded. Rydan pushed through the lingering resistance, catching and holding Rora as she straightened. "Are you alright?"

"Just my ears hurt, and my heart startled," she said, slowly relaxing from her wince. Pressing a hand over her sternum, she opened her mouth to ask what that was about, only to be interrupted.

"*Alright, I'm off to go ask Mendhi. I'll talk to you later, Guardian Rydan*," Serina stated, voice echoing behind them.

Rydan abandoned Rora at that, hurrying back to the pipe. Thrusting his hand into the energies, he ordered, *"Serina, stop!"*

"What? Why?"

"*Tell* no one, *by hint or implication or outright saying so, of Rora's existence*," he ordered his sister-in-law. "*Say only that we are looking for a way to re-invoke the Convocation of the Gods, and if anyone asks you directly if we have a living host . . .* lie. *Madam Mist just predicted that if anyone else finds out about her, a war to 'control' her will break out."*

"That's because whoever can re-invoke the Convocation will have immense political power. I did consider that, you know," Serina told him. "*We cannot avoid talking about an attempt to resurrect the Convocation, not if we're going to*

actually attempt it. But I won't mention her, and I will lie if I have to. All we have to do is say that we have a fragment of the Scroll of Living Glory that says something about the creation of the Convocation and that we're determined to track down its origins for the full text of how to go about it. I can even play up Kelly's insistence on all *the Gods and Goddesses granting her the right to declare Nightfall an independent kingdom, to back her subsequent decision to find a way to make all of Them our Patrons.*

"I do know how to hedge neatly around the truth, if need be. As my husband can attest—ouch! I am *going to get back at you for that. Just remember, I know where you sleep at night!"* Serina added tartly, making Rydan briefly wonder what his brother had done to her out there at Koral-tai. He didn't worry too much about Dom's safety; despite the diluting effects of the Fountain energies carrying their voices, he could sense Serina wasn't truly annoyed with her husband.

He resumed their conversation once he was sure Serina's side comments to Dominor had subsided. *"Good. I'll do the same with Guardian Sheren, play up the Convocation and our ignorance of how it's created, and just say that the damaged copy we have mentions that it can be re-created."*

"Dom says you'd better brief the others at breakfast," Serina relayed. *"And if you could send through my slateboards from my workroom, I'd appreciate it. Oh, and a few more changes of clothes would be appreciated. Winter here is a* lot *colder than winter on Nightfall, and we've been layering everything we brought to keep ourselves warm, even with warming charms. I don't know how long we'll have to wait for a response from the Great Library, and I don't want to exhaust our powers, when wearing a few more layers would do the job just as well."*

"Understood. I'll take care of that shortly," Rydan agreed.

"Dom and I will also be staying here a bit longer. Probably for the length of my pregnancy, in fact. I've discovered that bathing in the energies of the Koral-tai Font seems to be helping quell my midday nausea and restore my health. Mother Naima suggests it's probably because our incipient solution to the Natallian problem was conceived in this

particular Font, so lingering near its specific energies help soothe the baby's growth. Not to mention, having access to a Font once again is speeding along my aether studies," Serina concluded.

"I'll get back to you before breakfast, our time," Rydan promised.

"I may not be available by then, but I should be up and around late tomorrow. If nothing else, you can send our clothes in a chest and I'll let it hit my catch-wards. Thank you, Guardian Rydan."

"You're welcome, Serina."

Extracting his hand, Rydan looked up at his Fountain, at the shimmering sphere of energies that marked the outer horizon of the singularity's strongest radiations. The thought of Rora accidentally making contact with that sphere, never mind deliberately doing so, turned his blood cold and his stomach sour. Abandoning the Fountain for now, he rejoined Rora.

"If I show you where Dominor and Serina sleep, can you pack changes of clothing for them? You wouldn't know which of her chalkboards to select, or how to shrink them."

"I can do that." She nodded. Rora gave the surrounding columns a wary glance, but nothing impeded her and Rydan as they headed back toward the entrance to the Hall. "A question . . ."

"What?" he asked, taking her hand as they walked. It felt good to touch her, but he knew he would feel a lot better once the Fountain thrumming against his fingers had been safely extracted from her body.

"If I am to be protected, if I need a Guardian . . . I would rather it be you, of course. I like you. A lot." Rora blushed as she admitted it, but forged on. "My question is, if Serina needs a Font to do her work, why don't you hand the Guardianship of yours to her? Surely you trust her? She seems trustworthy enough—she certainly hasn't coveted *me*, and I'm as unattached Guardian-wise as a Fountain can get, at the moment."

He considered her suggestion carefully. "The idea . . . does have some merit. I do trust her. She Guarded Koral-tai well, and she is committed to living on Nightfall, aside from the completion of her current project. But you heard her, just now.

I don't think handing the Nightfall Fountain to her would be good for the child she carries. Each Fountain has its own specific resonance, which must be matched by any mage seeking to become its Guardian. Her child is tied to the resonances of Koral-tai, not Nightfall."

"Well, what about the others? If a strong mage is necessary, your brothers all claim that Morganen is the strongest among you," Rora said. "What about Morg?"

Rydan shook his head. He remembered Morganen's word on that matter all too well. "He says it would be too great a temptation—when he touched you, Rora, he drained power out of you. Actually, he says your power pushed itself on him, but the end result is the same thing . . . and it's a frightening thing to contemplate, because he *didn't* attune himself to you, first. It is safer to wait until Serina has her child. She will give birth a handful of months before our year and a day is up. Once the child is born, completing that particular task, she can take up the Guardianship of Nightfall, probably a month or two later, to give her time to recover from childbirth.

"I guess you and I will have to be patient until then." Guiding her down the steps that led in the direction of the palace, Rydan caught her wrinkling her nose in distaste. "How long until the baby is born, do you know?" she inquired. "She looked like she might be starting to show, but then she's so thin, any little bump would show, baby or belly."

"I believe Serina is three months along, maybe a little more."

"So in about six more months, give or take. Babies aren't always punctual. What about Dominor?" she asked next. "If not Morg or Serina, what about him? He's mentioned he's quite strong as a mage. I noticed Trevan flinched from my touch at the party, but when Dominor took my hand that day in the library, when he and Serina agreed to help me, he didn't seem bothered by my energies. So what about him?"

It was Rydan's turn to wrinkle his nose. "And have him gloating about being the next Guardian? I'd rather wait six months."

"I could always keep you too occupied to pay any attention to your brother," Rora offered daringly. She blushed at his sharp, calculating look, but didn't lower her gaze. "What, because I'm a maiden, I'm not supposed to *want* to share pleasure with a loved one?"

Share pleasure with a loved one . . . with a loved *one . . .*

Rydan had never felt his beast purr, until now. Tugging her sideways, he crowded Rora into the corridor wall. *To hell with Madam Mist and patience, just for a moment . . .*

Threading his fingers into her light brown locks, he tipped her face up just enough to meet the descent of his. Their lips met and parted, touched and tasted. Rydan took his time; if they had to wait until the child was born and Serina was well enough to take up the Nightfall Guardianship, he didn't want to rush anything. She was certainly worth savoring.

They had already kissed before. Rora remembered most of what he had taught her of delicately nipping teeth, of thrusting tongues and suckling lips. Guessing that her words about sharing pleasure with him had invited this moment, she decided to be even more daring, and slid her palms over his chest. He made an intriguing noise when she cupped his pectoral muscles, so she did it again, and was kissed harder for her reward.

Wanting to know what other noises he might make, Rora slid one hand down to his stomach. Turning her wrist, she slipped her fingers down over his groin, caressing the bulge of hardening flesh. A rough sound escaped him, and he pinned her to the wall with his body, trapping her hand between them with a grind of his hips.

When her fingers squeezed and rubbed him experimentally, Rydan shuddered with pleasure, then groaned with regret. This was going too fast, too far. He wanted her, yes—her touch made his thighs ache from withholding the urge to thrust. But this wasn't the time, and it definitely wasn't the place. His mind flashed to that evening, less than a dozen days ago, when he had woken from his drugged dreams, her body pulsing beneath his with sexual and magical energy. Hers still thrummed with power, endangering him, but his was the one that pulsed with need now.

Breathing hard, Rydan shifted his hands to the wall on either side of her head. It was hard—he was hard—but he pushed himself away from her. There was a flaw in his plan to remove himself from temptation. She clung to him, one hand still on his manhood, exploring it with a kneading touch that was driving him wild, the other arm wrapping around his ribs, keeping her soft breasts pressed into his chest, and their mouths within mating distance. Tearing his lips from hers only encouraged her to press kisses to the vulnerable skin of his throat.

"Rora . . . we can't . . . cannot . . ."

She took advantage of the way he wasn't pressing her into the wall anymore, and searched under the hem of his tunic with both hands for the lacings to his trousers. Thankfully it only took a moment to tug the knotted bow loose and another to slide her finger under the crisscrossed strings to loosen them. Rydan groaned again, straightening away from the wall. He managed to catch and hold one of her hands, but she slipped the other one inside his trousers.

The moment he grabbed her forearm was the moment she grasped his shaft. One of his knees buckled, forcing him to let go of her and brace his hands against the wall again just to keep himself from falling down; the feel of her fingers wrapping around his flesh in a tentative stroke was too much to resist. Covering her hand with his own, trapping it under the fabric of his pants, Rydan struggled to focus through the pleasure of her touch. Every kiss she pressed to his neck shot pleasure straight through to his groin and back, connecting the two points and scattering his wits.

"Rora . . . mustn't . . . If your power rises . . ."

"It's not," she pointed out, leaning back just enough to give him a reassuring smile. She flexed her fingers against his shaft, rubbing what she could under the pressure of his palm. "I figured it out. It's roused itself a little, but then I'm only aroused a little. You're the one who is enjoying this the most. You're not carrying your Fountain directly, like I am, so *you* can enjoy my touch. It's only when you arouse *me* that we could start to get into trouble . . . so I can still please you like this."

Gritting his teeth, Rydan grabbed her wrist and pulled her hand out of his trousers. A tight sound escaped his throat, an involuntary whimper, but he did it: He removed her touch. Swallowing hard, he managed to speak. "My pleasure . . . lies in *your* pleasure. If you feel none, it's no good—*don't.*"

The remonstration came when she shifted her other hand toward his hips. Forcing himself away from her, Rydan moved a few awkward steps away and steeled himself against her disappointment, desire, and curiosity. Hands on his hips, as much to keep from touching himself as to keep his loosened trousers from slipping down, he waited for the throbbing to fade. Feeling the question forming within her, pricked by her emotions, he shook his head in negation, though he didn't turn back to face her.

"No. I *feel* your need, Rora. To not . . . to not *answer* it makes my own pleasure hollow. I would be using you, even if you wanted it. I didn't like being used by women for their own pleasure, before our exile. I will not do that to you."

From the stiffening of his posture, Rora knew he felt the emotion his words triggered in her. He felt it so much, she watched him stagger to the side, slump against the wall, and twist to thump his forehead against it. Which wasn't a bad thing, as it replaced her rush of admiration and even love with a more lighthearted amusement . . . and a touch of feminine satisfaction. Rora had seen her sister reducing would-be suitors to gestures of frustration; it was nice in a twisted sort of way to see that she could do it, too.

There was one point she wanted to make clear to him. "I hope you realize I'm *not* trying to tease you and leave you unfulfilled. I honestly do want to give you pleasure."

Thunk. Thunk. "I know . . . Believe me, I *know*."

The pain in his head—bedrock was uncomfortably unyielding—helped counteract some of the fire in his loins. Doing it one more time, he winced at the ache, then tied his trouser lacings. Pushing away from the wall, he didn't look back at her; he was still hard, but at least he could walk somewhat normally again. It didn't help that he could still feel her admiration lurking in the vicinity of his beast.

Focusing his mind on less pleasurable things, he gestured for her to follow. "Come. We still have work to do."

SIXTEEN

Rora waited patiently for Rydan to finish reading the scroll they had received through the Fountainway, exchanged for two sacks of clothes and a thick stack of slate-boards. Studying the Fountain, source of her biggest obstacle to a physical relationship with him, she wondered where all those ribbons of energy went, other than the immediately obvious answer, into channels that burrowed into the mountain around them. Some went up into the ceiling, making her wonder if their purpose was to keep the mountain from falling on them, but she didn't feel claustrophobic in the Fountain Hall, so it wasn't an actual concern. It was too open, too tall, and too brightly lit in the vast hall to feel that way.

Her gaze skimmed over the arcing streams of energy, taking in their hues: pale blue, deep green, amber gold, silvery gray, vibrant pink—a whole palette as varied as the many shades she could See in others' emotions . . . or the colors she saw when Looking for edible food, or for a safe place to stay, or a dozen other tasks. *I'm my own filter,* Rora realized. *I do by will what that basin thing is designed to do by rune and spell . . .*

It made her wonder if she, too, could communicate across vast distances, or perhaps even open a Fountainway vortex, like the one Rydan had just used to toss the clothes and slates to

Serina and Dominor. Then again, considering the warning Serina had given them about not letting anything make her Fountain literally rip open within her, Rora didn't think trying to access her Fountainway was a good idea. That was assuming she even had a clue of how to go about it, which she didn't, never mind whether or not she could. The report that she needed someone else to be her Fountain's Guardian suggested otherwise.

Bored, she glanced at the copper-hued streams. Opening an actual Fountainway might be dangerous, but surely she could at least communicate with her fellow Fountains? Or rather, their Guardians, since the Fountain was a pathway for voices.

The coppery ribbon Serina had used was smooth and tranquil, now that it wasn't being ruffled by the absent woman's voice. Rora tried to imagine what it would feel like to open up a stream of coppery communication magic. She didn't feel any changes within her and wondered if it was because the stream was smooth. Sometimes she sensed magic best when it was in action, not when it was quiescent.

A glance off to the right located the stream that Guardian Sheren had used. It wasn't smooth; at least, not as smooth as the flow Serina had spoken through. Neither was it as ruffled and disturbed as it had been when the unseen woman had been speaking through it. Knowing she couldn't get close enough to investigate, Rora edged closer to Rydan.

He was just inside the innermost section of carved columns. She almost expected Madam Mist to show up and stop her again, but the wall of coppery-hued magic didn't show. *Maybe because I know better now than to try to touch that other Fountain*, Rora thought, eyeing the singularity and its sphere warily. Touching Rydan's elbow, she earned a sharp warning look, but didn't back up.

Lifting her chin at the pipe in question, she asked, "Is that one supposed to be doing that?"

Rydan focused on the line of her gaze, but didn't see what she meant.

Rora frowned in confusion. "That's odd. It stopped."

"What did?"

"That ribbon over there, the one Sheren used . . . it was rumpled. Just a little bit, but now it's smooth again. Is it supposed to do that?" she asked him.

"Only if someone is trying to communicate. But if they were, they would have spoken," Rydan dismissed.

"What about listening?" Rora asked, eyes still on the smooth-pouring energies. "Sheren said she could almost hear Serina, even though you weren't actually touching her stream and speaking to her directly."

"Sheren would have no reason to just . . . shh," he whispered, barely hissing the admonition. The stream wasn't entirely smooth. Narrowing his dark eyes, he studied it, pondering the anomaly. Passing the half-read scroll to Rora, he strode over to the stream and stuck his hand into the flow. *"Guardian Sheren, are you trying to contact me?"*

For a long moment, there was nothing in response. He withdrew his hand, staring at the coppery mist reorganizing itself into a smooth ribbon. Just as he thought about turning away, it ruffled and projected a distorted voice.

"Ah, yes . . . Guardian. That thing we were talking about earlier . . ."

His beast tensed. Something was wrong, though he didn't know what. Touching the flow of energies, Rydan asked, *"The scroll? Do you have it?"*

"Yes, that's it. I have it right here, but I'm worried it might be a bit fragile. If you could open up your wards a little before I pass it through, that might help ensure its safe arrival."

That wasn't Guardian Sheren. The voice sounded like her voice, but not the words she said. She *never* failed to acknowledge him by both his title and his name at the start of every conversation they had. And she would *not* have gotten her hands on such a rare scroll so quickly, not when it would have required rousing everyone in the middle of the night.

As far as he'd been able to gauge over the past few years, wherever Menomon was, it shared roughly the same north-south segment of the world as Nightfall, within an hour of Nightfall's own sunrises and sunsets. There was no need for Sheren to rouse her assistants to search her archives, nor was there enough time for it to have been copied. He certainly hadn't demanded that the Scroll of Living Glory be copied and handed over immediately.

Something was seriously wrong here.

"I'm in the middle of something, but I should be free in

half an hour or so. Please try not to interrupt, or it'll take longer." A slash of his hand through the streaming mist coalesced and solidified it, turning it glasslike. "There, now they can't eavesdrop, whoever they are." Hurrying off to the right, Rydan stuck his hand into the communication stream that flowed off in the direction of Koral-tai. *"Serina, are you still there? I have a serious problem."*

"I'll get her, Guardian Rydan."

"Thank you, Guardian Naima."

Rydan looked up at his Fountain while he waited, wondering what had happened to Guardian Sheren. *She'd spoken of heartburn, of dizziness . . . sweating . . . poison! Did someone poison her?* he worried. *She said she was trained as a Healer, but did she think to check for poison, or did she just treat herself for some sort of stomach reflux?*

"Here I am, Guardian Rydan! My, you're being rather chatty tonight. Hanging around with Rora seems to be loosening up your tongue, according to your brother," Serina teased him.

"I think someone has poisoned Guardian Sheren and taken over her Fountain," Rydan stated without preamble.

"You . . . what?" Serina's voice, though distorted, lost its teasing in an instant, turning sober. *"Are you sure?"*

"Guardians always address each other by title and name, but we rarely tell outsiders what those other names are. She—or he, as they seem to be using a voice-altering spell—didn't know exactly what I had asked her to do, to fetch the scroll. She pretended to have it in her hands right there and then . . . and wants me to lower my wards in order to send it across, because it's 'too fragile' and might be damaged . . . when I asked her for a fresh copy."

"That's definitely not the same person, and certainly not someone who knows how Fountainway wardings work. At least, most of the ones I know are set up to catch even the most fragile item and contain it securely . . . Gauge your Fountain's energy level and resonance—I'll presume you froze the communication stream from her Fountain?"

"Of course. I may not know as much about Fountains as you do, but I do know how to guard my own," Rydan said. Removing his fingers from the stream, he caught one of the pipes and pulled himself up onto the rim of the Fountain basin.

Stretching up, he touched the singularity's horizon. He stayed that way for several moments, then flung out his other hand, diverting the flow of the coppery ribbon so that it looped up to touch his free hand. Removing his touch from the Fountain, he addressed his sister-in-law *"It doesn't seem to be diminished in power, but the tone* might *be slightly off. I can't tell yet."*

"Keep monitoring it at intervals," Serina warned him. *"If there is no sign of a power drop, then Guardian Sheren and her wards aren't dead, yet. But there were warnings in the Archives about rare mages who had an ability to mimic another mage's signature, given enough time to study and attempt to match it."*

"If I enter the Fountain directly, I should be able to block her out," Rydan offered. *"At least long enough for us to come up with a way to counterattack."*

"If you do that, whoever this is might turn against one of the other Fonts, which might not be able to stave off an attack. You and I, at least, can combine our two Fonts, but in order to hold their attention, you're going to have to let your Fountain's defenses look like they're weakening. At least until you're sure they're trying to take over. Right now, we only have a suspicion."

Rydan grimaced, but knew she was right. Jumping down, he let the ribbon follow his hand back into its rightful arc. *"What if it is an actual attack? Guardian Sheren wouldn't hand over her Guardianship without warning the rest of us, so that we knew the new Guardian had passed the proper character tests. What do we do, if it's a hostile takeover?"*

"I need to talk to Guardian Naima about that. I've done joint-Font work with Guardian Kelezam, but she hasn't the experience for it. Hold on, and keep monitoring the power and resonance of your Font."

"Hurry up; I put her off for a few minutes, but she'll be expecting some sort of reply." Removing his hand, Rydan eyed the glimmering sphere at the center of the Fountain, then paced, arms folded across his chest. He would give it a count to one hundred, then check again to see how quickly the Fountain was being taken over. If it *wasn't* being attacked, he'd give up his favorite pillow, but his instincts were convinced of it.

"Rydan . . . I think it's softening," Rora warned him quietly, pointing at the north-facing ribbon. It no longer looked like solid, copper-speckled glass, though its surface was still smooth.

"Jinga's Ass . . ." Crossing to the softening magic, he pressed his finger into it. *"I said to stay* out *of the energies, Guardian Sheren, or you'll risk a nasty backlash from my experiment. I'll be ready to receive the scroll in about half an hour,* if *you do not interfere. It will take longer if you do."* Removing his thumb, he cast a stronger spell on the stream. *"Stanastabula!"*

It hardened visibly. A glance at Rora showed her chewing on her lips with worry, her gaze on the hardened flow. He wanted to give her some sort of reassurance, but there was nothing he could say. Except that this challenge to his Guardianship didn't seem to be her fault. He didn't know where the city of Menomon was located, and from Sheren's comments about the city's isolationist attitude, he doubted Rora knew, either.

Rora kept her eye on the solidified stream. She could have opened the partially copied Scroll of Living Glory and read it through, but she didn't trust whoever it was on the other side of the Fountainway not to try again. Without having to be told, she knew Rydan had enough to worry about, without having to keep an eye on any more eavesdropping; she couldn't help him directly, but she could at least watch the crystalized ribbon for him.

The eastern stream ruffled and echoed. *"This is Guardian Naima to all Guardians in connection with this Font. I am handing my Guardianship back to Guardian Serina for the time being. Please cooperate with her as you have done before. Communication and Fontway accesses will be suspended during the transfer."*

Rydan watched as the energies in the copper mist shimmered and rang. The tone was distorted, unduplicatable, but he knew Serina had just rung the sanctified bell that had been forged and blessed to resonate at the same distinct frequency as the Koral-tai Fountain, allowing her to attune her powers in harmony. When he had taken over the Fountain, he hadn't had to warn anyone; the Fountain had been locked under Madam Mist's protection, its Fountainways and communication streams cut off from the rest of the singularities within range.

Under her tutelage, he had reestablished those connections, though some of those he had contacted had required Madam Mist's repeated reassurances that his Guardianship was legitimate before he was accepted. At least Serina was a previously known entity and was undertaking her Guardianship with Naima's consent; no one would question her right to be a Guardian, only her reason for doing so. It took a few moments before Serina's voice came back, but not as long for the two women to transfer the energies as it had taken Rydan to attune himself the hard way, with no one to assist him.

"This is Guardian Serina; I have resumed control of this Font. Thank you for your patience. Resuming normal functioning now . . . Guardian Rydan," she continued after a brief pause, no doubt to single out his communication stream once more, *"what is the condition of your Fountain?"*

Turning, he climbed up high enough to touch the shell of energies. A frown pinched his brow. Leaping back down, Rydan thrust his hand into the copper fog. *"It feels like the sub-harmonics are changing. It's still faint, but it is clearer than before. If this is an attack . . . what do I do?"*

"I haven't warded off an open attack before, since it's rare that someone unscrupulous gets ahold of a Fountain, but I have read past accounts of it happening, and I have shared power with other Font Guardians. What you and I will do is work together to construct a containment warding that should prevent whoever this is from making either a brutal thrust or an abrupt drain. But since she has the power of a Fountain at her command, that thrust is *going to be brutal, if and when she chooses to attack. Which she'll have to do. Her goal will be to take over your Fountain, and to be able to do that completely, she will have to kill you.*

"I've sent Dominor to fetch a book with the spell we'll use. It has to be cast in tandem from within both Fonts, to be able to use both sets of energies as a bulwark. Don't worry, he'll coordinate our efforts as soon as you've studied a copy of it. With any luck, we'll be able to get it established before that attack comes, which will leave me free to cast offensive magics through you."

"I do know more than a few combat spells, myself," Rydan reminded her.

"Yes, but your job will be to hold the containment spell stable, as the first line of defense. Yours is the first point of attack, after all."

"What if this person continues to try to match resonances?" he asked. *"Attacking by stealth instead of assault? She managed to soften the first stop-spell I placed on the north communication line. If she can do that, she can take over the bulwark, given enough time."*

"That's not good. If she continues to infiltrate, and we can't stop her, then we'll need additional help. Fetch your brothers."

He grimaced, thinking of his brothers' energies infusing this hall. *"I would rather not."*

"This isn't the time to play Keep out of My Room, Guardian Rydan," Serina chided him, her voice stern despite the distortions. *"Actually, having them on hand for secondary sources of attack would be a good idea—no, no . . . brilliant! Moons, I could kiss myself sometimes,"* she added in a bizarre aside. *"As soon as Dom gets back, I'll send him across to you. Mother Naima can copy the spell and direct our containment efforts.* You *will step down as Guardian and let Dominor step up in your place."*

"I will not!" Rydan protested. *"Nightfall is* mine *to Guard—"*

"Rora *is yours to Guard,"* she countered. *"Remember how you had to reconnect the Fontway, the first time we made contact? You'll have to do that with her Fountain, once you've established Guardianship of her. No arguing! In doing so, we'll have a second pathway to attack this person. And—not the least bit coincidentally—it will fulfill your Destiny, in both the Curse of Eight and the Curse of Nightfall.*

"I can't wait for this to be over so I can check and see how this affects my mathemagical projections. This is exciting—Naima, get me more chalkboards!" Serina ordered on the other end of the Fountainway. *"I need to record what is happening, so I can see how it affects the aether and my Portal restoration project . . ."*

Rydan covered his face with his free hand for a moment.

For all that he was getting the knack of staving off others' emotions, the impact of Serina's enthusiasm for her mathemagical project was like being hit with a pillow repeatedly. A glance up at the curving of the singularity's event horizon showed the rippling, opalescent patterns were beginning to shift, indicative that its resonances were changing. Not by much, but he was too familiar with the usual cascading hues not to notice even a slight deviation.

"I'll have to send Rora. I don't dare leave the Fountain unwatched." Pulling his hand from the mist, he faced her. "Use the cryslet to call and wake the others. You will have to meet them in the gong room of my tower and lead them down here as a group. I still don't know how you can do it, but you're the only way they can get past the wards on this place.

"Hand me back that scroll before you go," he added, holding out his hand for the forgotten scroll in her grasp. "I'll study it some more while you're fetching them."

"Everyone?" Rora asked, passing it over. "Even the boy?"

"No, not Mikor. Or his mother, or Evanor. Alys and Wolfer don't have the right kind of power to help, either. Fetch Morganen, Koranen, Saber, and Trevan," he instructed her. "Kelly has no magic, and your sister would only be of use in a physical fight, but the others are strong enough in combat magic to be of use. We used to be able to call out to Evanor and he'd hear us, but he hasn't reestablished those spells—we use the cryslets now." He paused, studying her soberly. "Rora . . . if you don't want this, if you don't want *me* to do this . . ."

Is taking Rydan as my Fountain's Guardian the right thing to do? Rora asked herself silently. She winced at the brilliant white halo that formed around him in reply. Blinking it off, she nodded. "I do. This is why I came here. *You* are why I came here, even if I didn't know it—keep an eye on that ribbon thing while I'm gone," she added, pointing at the frozen energy. "If it thaws, they'll be able to eavesdrop again."

Nodding, he glanced at it to make sure it was still solid, then moved to climb back up among the pipes, intending to check the Fountain again.

Rora turned to retrace her path back to the surface, then winced and swung around again. "Um . . . Rydan?"

"Yes?"

She lifted her left wrist, which bore her cryslet. "Which button on this thing is the one that makes the mirror display the names and numbers for everyone, again?"

"The center button closest to the hinge, the one with the mathemagic rune for 'number,'" he reminded her.

"Right." Flicking open the lid, she grimaced at the gilded symbols on the creamy little discs embedded in the silver base, then poked gingerly at the proper button. The reflection in the small oval mirror darkened to black, then filled itself with a list of names, each one followed by five digits.

Aiming for the door out of the Hall, she poked at the set of numbers attached to Morganen's name, waited for something to happen, then smacked her forehead and hit the symbol thingy to make the connection go through. Artifacts were not all that common on the Plains, aside from lightglobes, the occasional Truth Stone, and bluesteel, none of which were like this thing on her wrist. Rora picked up her pace as she waited for the cryslet call to be answered; the sooner she got to the tower, the sooner she could lead the others back down here.

The couple must first perform any form of sanctified marriage, Rydan reminded himself, skimming over the contents of the scroll for the fifth or sixth time, while at the same time keeping an eye on the slowly shifting hues of his Fountain. He didn't have to touch it to sense the presence of another seeping into it now, or even look at it, but watching the color change gave him something to do as he waited.

Then the Guardian must attune himself to the Fountain, make her sing, and match his own singing to hers. The actual text contains enough innuendos to suggest that "singing" is based in sexual pleasure . . . Hurry, Rora . . . He was also waiting for Dominor, but he wouldn't release the Fountain to Dom without her presence. *Then . . . the two are conjoined, and when the pair have conjoined and are "singing" together . . . basically, when they're tumbling about the bed like love-struck teenagers,* he translated, *then the Guardian opens his magic to the Fountain, the Fountain opens her magic to the Guardian . . . If their energies have aligned themselves properly—because if they don't, the pair will literally explode; what a comforting thought—their energies should merge, mesh, and stabilize.*

After that, the Guardian needs only touch the Living Fountain to be able to access and direct her energies . . . though the more flesh-on-flesh contact there is, the more power can be accessed, and the more control the Guardian will have . . . That sphere is turning a little too blue for my comfort. At least the stream leading to the Fountain of Menomon is still solidified, but Kata knows how long that'll last. Dammit, where is Domin—

"Guardian Rydan, prepare for my husband's arrival."

Clasping the scroll to his chest, Rydan freed his hand and touched the eastern ribbon. *"I am ready."*

Unlike the first time Dominor had traveled through the Fountainway from Koral-tai to Nightfall, this time Rydan was on hand to catch him, right him, and set him on his feet, without setting off the wards or jangling the alarms. Dusting off his dark blue garments, Dominor gave his younger brother a nod of gratitude, glancing behind himself to make sure the vortex was reabsorbing into the singularity's horizon. "Brother."

"Brother," Rydan acknowledged. He wished this wasn't necessary, but it seemed the distant Threefold God, Fate, was insisting on making his own verse in the Curse of the Sons of Destiny come true.

"The Fountainway at this end doesn't feel quite like it did, the last time I went through. Serina calculates that if it gets past the one-third mark, it will become too difficult to switch Guardianships. I suggest we get this taken care of as quickly as possible," Dominor stated, glancing at the sphere behind him. His businesslike air softened for a moment. "I am sorry I have to 'invade' your sanctum like this. I will hand it back, once Rora's Fountain has been extracted and she no longer needs Guarding.

"All I ask is that I be allowed to cross over and rejoin my wife at that time. She really is faring a lot better, now that she can bask in the energies at Koral-tai."

"Both Fountains will still need Guarding at that point. Rora will have the power to guard one, but not the knowledge,"

Rydan reminded his brother, his tone wry. "Once Serina is done with her project in Natallia, she can come be the Guardian here, in your place. She'll still need access to a Fountain if she is to continue her Portal project."

"And I'll be happy to hand it over to her—you have my sympathy," Dom added. "I read the scroll. I've already had one taste of sex-magic in the heart of a Fountain. I don't envy you in the least for the task that lies ahead. But to get to that task, you have to let go of this one." He poked his thumb over his shoulder at the graceful tangle of pipes and ribbons and the shimmering globe at its center. "Shall we?"

Rydan rolled up the scroll and held it out to his brother. "Take this and set it on the floor beyond the first row of columns. Then face me and prepare yourself for the Guardian's Challenge."

Nodding, Dominor took the scroll and strode away from the Fountain. At the prescribed distance, he laid the scroll on the floor, then straightened and faced his brother, who had turned to fetch the Truth Stone from its hidden niche. "I am ready."

"Are you?" Straightening, Rydan lobbed the Stone at his older sibling. Dominor caught it, arching one of his dark brows. "Control is *everything* to a Guardian. You are about to take charge of a level of power you cannot yet comprehend. Yes, you have stepped into the heart of a Fountain, someone *else's* Fountain . . . and though you knew it not, her power sheltered yours from the full effect of the maelstrom.

"There must be calmness within your center, if you expect there to be calmness in the heart of your Fountain. You must set aside strong emotions and besetting sins. *Your* greatest sins have been your pride and your arrogance," Rydan stated, challenging his brother. "Are you still prideful? Are you still arrogant? Or have you learned what self-control is? Answer carefully, for you will be judged on your words as well as the truth in them."

Dominor looked down at the white disc in his hand. He stared at it for several heartbeats, then clenched his fingers around it and looked up again. "I have been proud, and I have been arrogant. But my wife taught me the meaning *and* value of humility. I am not the center of arrogance that I once was.

My wife has taught me that I am not the pinnacle of intelligence or power. I am prouder of her accomplishments than I am of my own, and I support her fully. I do not give up one iota of what I am. I am still a powerful, educated mage. I still strive to better myself. But I do not delude myself anymore.

"I *am* what I am . . . and I accept what I am not." Displaying the stone, he showed how its surfaces were marred only by the faintest outlining in gray.

In lesser lighting than the Fountain Hall possessed, it might have passed unnoticed, but Rydan could see it clearly even with the body length between them. "I'm sure you try."

Dominor blinked, scowled at the Stone, and blushed. "I can do better than that."

Rydan chuckled. "Relax, Brother. I know you have learned your place in the universe. Your answer is acceptable enough. Now . . . as soon as the color has faded . . . there. Grasp the Stone and answer truthfully: Whom do you serve, Heaven or Hell?"

That earned him a snort. "Heaven, of course."

A display of the disc showed it was perfectly white this time. Dominor quickly mastered his relief, though not before the corner of Rydan's mouth had turned up in humor. Glancing up at the air between the columns, Rydan asked, "Madam Mist . . . do *you* have any objections?"

Copper gold mist formed above Dominor's head, forming a patch of fog no bigger than a dinner plate.

"No."

The single word was distorted only in tone; her meaning was perfectly clear. As was the way the mist faded rapidly, leaving the air clear. Satisfied, Rydan gestured for Dominor to step forward. He glanced off to the side, making sure the communication stream to the north was still crystallized. "Come. It is time for you to attune yourself with the bell. I haven't done this part before with anyone else, but you should be able to master it."

"Thank you for the vote of confidence," Dom quipped back. "I *am* older than you and more learned."

"Possibly." Taking back the Truth Stone, Rydan returned it to its niche behind the panel at the base of the Fountain, then extracted the bell. Careful to not ring it just yet, he flicked his hand, wrapping himself and his brother in a sound-deadening shield, then layered a magic-deadening one inside of it as well. "This is no ordinary bell. It was forged within the heart of this Fountain, shaped by the resonances of its singularity. Though it has a physical sound, you must listen for the *magic* within its tone and bring your own energies into alignment with it.

"Though it is purely internal, this will be the hardest task you have ever done—it is like trying to draw an image reflected in a mirror, without looking directly at the pen or the paper. And this is what you must do each and every time you wish to touch this particular Fountain, to the point where it is reflex. But first, you will practice," Rydan said, passing over the handbell. "You will practice matching resonances with the bell, and I will test you and help you to match resonances with me. Unlike what I had to do, matching the Fountain almost entirely on my own, I will lift you up into the heart of the energies and help align you to them. But it will go more quickly if we practice first."

Dominor looked at the bell in his hands, then up through the faint glimmering border of the double shields, at the increasingly blue-tinted sphere of the Fountain. "Do we have the time for this?"

"We will, if you stop dawdling. Ring it, and match your energies," Rydan ordered his sibling. He glanced at the sphere, too, and folded his arms across his chest. "You'll only have five tries at most to get it right, before we have to go up there."

"Sorry I'm late!" Koranen apologized breathlessly, hurrying into the gong chamber.

"What took you so long?" Saber demanded, scowling at his seventhborn brother.

"I finished forging these yesterday, but forgot to bring them to supper. This one . . . is yours, Amara," the redhead stated, handing a package to the black-haired twin after a brief check of its label, "and this one is yours, Arora."

"What are they?" Mara asked, eyeing the package dubiously.

From the look of Rora's sister, she had donned the first

things she could find, which were the buttery-hued *breikas* the Nightfallers had given her and the faded linen *chamsa* Rora had worn for her on their way to the island. Mara's hair was also mussed, as was Trevan's. Rora suspected her sister and brother-in-law had been otherwise occupied when she had called them. Then again, she hadn't exactly *seen* either of them since the night of their wedding-leap, but that was only to be expected in the newly wedded, regardless of culture.

"These are protection sigils, each forged with your names—you hang them on your bedposts, so they'll protect you from fire and such at night. All of my brothers have them, and their wives, too," he explained. "Rydan will eventually get around to forging other protections, too, though I can understand why he's been distracted of late."

Rora blushed at the implied compliment.

"You *could* have waited until morning," Trevan chided his sibling.

"Well, I didn't want to forget them! Besides, maybe this mage trying to take over our brother's Fountain thing will try to use a fire-spell," Kor pointed out defensively. "This way, the ladies will have the sigils with them, and be extra protected."

"You're only making me want to go and get my own," Kelly muttered. Like Mara had done with Trevan, Kelly had risen with her husband and accompanied him here. "But now that we're all here, let's not delay any longer, shall we? Arora, if you'll take the lead?"

"Please, it's just Rora," she demurred, leading the way to the stairwell door. "Unlike my sister, I'm not a princess."

"Yes, but you *are* a dawn," Kelly quipped. At Rora's blank look, she explained. "Your name? In the Song of the Sons of Destiny, the verse goes: *When Dawn creeps into your hall.* Isn't that what your name means?"

"No," Rora denied, shaking her head. "It doesn't mean dawn at all. *Rora* means 'small blue thread-runner flower,' of a kind we toss onto brazier fires when burning dried dung, to sweeten the smoke. There's nothing dawnlike about me."

"Except that you're usually full of disgustingly cheerful energy when you wake up," Mara pointed out, following behind Trevan a few bodies back.

"Yes, but by preference, I'd rather sleep in each morning."

"That's true," her sister conceded.

"Then . . . did you creep into our brother's mysterious hall in the morning, at any point?" Saber asked her.

"No—the two times I crept anywhere, it was late afternoon, or early evening. All other times, he knew I was coming. And again, it was inevitably much later in the day." Rora frowned thoughtfully. "If I don't have any connection to mornings and Rydan . . . how can I be the right woman in this Prophecy?"

Kelly's chuckle rang off the stones of the curving stairwell. "I don't think you have anything to worry about, because that's not the dawn to which I was referring. The sound of your name, with your title attached, *A*rora . . . Where *I* come from, in one of our oldest and most scholarly languages, *aurora* is the word for dawn."

"Ah. Then there's no problem." Leading them down into the basement chamber, she walked straight to the trapdoor. Like the doors, it opened at her approach, allowing her to lead them straight into the ground. "Watch your heads."

"Rora, how is it that you can duplicate Rydan's little door-opening trick?" Morganen inquired. "Not even I have been able to figure out how he does it."

She shrugged. "I honestly don't know. I just look at them, and if I want to go through them, they open for me."

"Given how my brother could do it before we came here, I doubt it has anything to do with that Fountain you carry," Trevan admitted. "He didn't do it as often as he does it now, but he didn't have to open doors if he didn't feel like it."

"He spoiled a couple of my favorite pranks that way," Koranen muttered.

"What, buckets of water perched over partially open doors?" Kelly inquired, glancing back at him.

Kor flashed her a grin, his teeth gleaming white in the soft light radiating from the suncrystals embedded in the ceiling. "How did you guess?"

About to say something regarding her own pranks as a child, Rora quickly looked ahead. Something was happening . . . something . . . coming—instinct made her raise her hands, stiffening her arms and firming her will. The others stopped when she did, exchanging puzzled looks. There was no sound, no light, nothing to warn her other than pure instinct, not until it *struck* her energies, skidding her back a few feet.

Something had indeed happened, and it was happening to the spells warding the tunnels around them. Instinct was all she had to go on, and instinct wasn't enough. Not when the wave of energy contracted around her shields. "Everyone—touch me! Quickly!"

"Don't argue!" Morganen ordered the others, pushing his twin and Trevan forward. "Touch her, now!"

Rora felt hands on her, Saber's and Kelly's, then Mara and Trevan, Koranen, all crowding in close so they could place a hand on her shoulder, her hip, her back . . . her shields buckled, contracted . . . held. As abruptly as it had come, the energy eased, leaving her staggering. Someone caught her by the shoulder, steadying her.

"Thanks—you can let go, now," she added, turning to face the others. Her green eyes sought Morganen, who alone had not touched her. He stood back from the others by more than a body length, which would have placed him outside her protections, but at her curious look, he shook his head, silencing her inquiry.

"What was that?" Kelly asked, freckled face a little pale. "Did someone attack us? The Fountain!"

"The Fountain is fine," Morganen reassured her quickly. "I suspect we just witnessed its Guardianship being transferred from Rydan to Dominor. All of the protective spells our paranoid, night-loving brother laid into these passages over the years just tried to squash us like a collection of bugs during the changeover—mainly because I think Rora, here, was matching herself to Rydan's protections, making herself invisible, and by extension, the rest of us. But Dominor's magic was just different enough that she couldn't adapt in time, so when it changed over to his control, those protections 'saw' us for a moment."

"That sounds logical," Saber agreed, nodding. "In which case, we'd have a little more time as the infiltrator will also have to adjust to Dom's resonances . . . but not that much more time. Shall we hurry?"

"This way," Rora told them. She led the way at a jog, wishing she knew what spell Rydan used for his shadow-walk thing.

SEVENTEEN

Hollow . . . I feel rather hollow, and empty. It was a strange feeling, after nearly four years of being filled. Of being part of something far greater than himself. His beast grumbled a little at the odd sensation, but otherwise didn't protest as much as he might have thought. He felt light-headed, relieved of a burden, yet disconnected from the world because of it.

Instinct told him it would now be difficult to shadow-walk. The spell had worked best because it was tied to Nightfall and its Fountain, just as he knew he could have called upon the land itself to defend him. He didn't feel weak, thankfully; none of his own magic was gone. It was simply that he no longer had a vast reservoir to call upon, only what he himself could carry.

A glance up at the figure in the heart of the Fountain showed Dominor's lips moving, though Rydan couldn't hear any of his brother's chanting. The opalescent hues were no longer increasingly blue, but instead leaned more toward green. When Rydan had held the Guardianship, the primary flickers had held golden highlights. Dom had a different energy to him.

The thought of the thwarted invasion prodded him into glancing over at the northern communication ribbon, the one that should have led to Guardian Sheren's Fountain. It was no longer crystallized and no longer smooth. His spell had been weakened, perhaps even broken, by his brother's commandeering of the singularity's energies.

Crossing to it, he dipped his hand into the energies—and froze, the moment his fingers touched the edge of the mist. He couldn't even grimace at having forgotten the anti-tampering wards that were no longer under his control. It made him think of Rora, how blithely she had walked through these underground halls without being trapped like this.

Stupid . . . I will not be held like this! This is simply another locked door! His hand moved as his thoughts shaped themselves, applying pressure. Breathing deeply, he dipped his palm into the mist.

"My experiment is almost complete, Guardian Sheren. Please do not interfere, or attempt to distract me from what is happening by trying to eavesdrop. Your ruffling of the energies is causing enough turbulence to create a delay."

"Apologies, Guardian," the unseen woman replied.

Rydan wished he could tell for certain if that woman was Sheren or not. She *sounded* like the right person, distortion effects included, which made his suspicions seem like a betrayal of their business relationship, but it wasn't as if he could stick a Truth Stone into . . . *Wait. Why can't I?*

Shifting away from the ribbonlike energies, he crouched and opened the secret panel at the base of the Fountain. It reacted sluggishly, as if its physical pressure points were trying to guard themselves against a non-Guardian accessing the niche, but it did open after a moment. Pulling out the Truth Stone, he carried it over to the stream. *"A quick question."*

"Yes?"

"Guardian Sheren, I thought I requested a copy of the scroll in question. Are you going to be sending me the original instead?" he asked, dipping the Stone into the copper energy.

"Yes . . . you seemed to be a bit eager to receive it, so I thought, why not send you the original, rather than a copy? It's right here, ready to go through, though it's quite fragile, as I said—that's a valid reason to send the original, rather than try to copy it."

He didn't have to pull the Stone out to see it turning black between roiling clumps of mist.

"Well, I just performed a major piece of magic; the aether needs to settle and readjust before I can accept anything incoming. If it is as fragile as you said."

"Oh, yes; you'll need to lower your wards to receive it. Unless you'd prefer to wait until I made a less fragile copy?"

"Waiting for a copy might be the better idea," Rydan stated, stalling for time. *"From the looks of the local aether, the post-experiment disturbances will continue for at least another hour or two, if not longer. In the meantime, please stay off the communication line. My experiment isn't going quite as I'd like it to, and I'd really hate to accidentally hurt you."*

That was certainly the truth. Hurting this impostor was going to be quite deliberate on his part, if Rydan had anything to say about it. He kept his words as truthful as possible; if *he* had thought of using a Truth Stone to gauge the impostor's sincerity, it was possible the impostor was doing the exact same thing—a slender chance, but still possible.

"I'll stay off the line, then. You'll hear from me within a couple hours, though."

The Truth Stone changed to gray, a half-truth. If whoever it was preferred infiltration to brute-strength attacks, Rydan had just bought himself and his family a little more time. If they didn't take much longer to arrive, that was.

To his relief, they arrived not more than a moment or two after the communication stream settled into a smooth, uninterrupted flow. Their echoing voices preceded the actual sight of them entering the Fountain Hall. The group was composed of the brothers he had requested, plus Mara and Kelly, but he didn't mind. Kelly, he figured, was there out of sheer curiosity and a need to know what was going on in regards to her adopted homeland.

Mara . . . well, her protectiveness toward her twin was already well established. He suspected she would confront him about his intentions regarding her sister at some point, but he wasn't deterred. Anything she asked him, he would be able to answer. No, the one thing that made him pause was that this . . . joining . . . was being forced by circumstance.

Glancing up at his magic-wrapped brother, Rydan wondered if his family could succeed by channeling their powers through the Nightfall singularity, rather than require a marriage of necessity just to be able to attack unexpectedly.

"Nice place you have," Kelly observed, joining him by the first row of columns.

Her aquamarine eyes swept the room, taking in more than just the spectacle of the Fountain—she even looked up at the arched sections of the ceiling. Rydan, sensitive to the emotions of his brothers, realized that Kelly made herself calm when addressing him. It was probably instinctive, but since she had figured out how to approach him even before he had learned what riled his beast, he respected her for it. "Thank you."

"Could use some color, though. Remind me to ask you what all of those pipes do, when we're not so busy," she added in an aside.

"They channel energies filtered from the singularity. Most of it keeps this island healthy," Rydan explained briefly, before looking up at Dominor again. "I would *like* to do this without risking Rora. He looks like he's done establishing the bulwark spell Serina wanted to erect. The green of the event horizon is Dominor; the blue is our mystery attacker."

"And the pinks, yellows, and purples?" Kelly asked him.

"The energies of the Fountain. With some blues and greens."

"Guard . . . er, Rydan, this is Guardian Serina. Are you still there?"

The others jumped, not expecting the sudden, distorted echo. Rydan crossed to the eastern pipe, touching the vibrating mist. *"This is Rydan."*

"We won't be able to contain the intrusion for long. At the current slow rate of infiltration, my calculations suggest we have maybe two hours before Dominor's influence on the Font will be overwhelmed. An outright attack might slow down whoever it is, but we daren't trigger one until Rora's Font is ready."

"I've convinced the person to give us a couple of hours, and to stop eavesdropping," Rydan told her, peering at the other copper flow. It was still smooth and tranquil, as far as he

could tell. *"I would rather we all attacked through the Nightfall Fountain, rather than risk using Rora like that. We don't know how casting magic through her Fountain will affect her."*

"And I would rather not have that much energy coursing through my husband, thank you," Serina retorted sharply. *"If we divide our attacks between the three Fonts, there is* less *risk for all involved, not more. Yes, some risk will be gained for her, but much of it lessened for him."*

"What about your child?" Rydan reminded her.

"My knowledge and experience with the Font is more valuable. And while Dominor has to be inside his Font to guard it fully, I do not have to be, so the risk is minimized."

A hand tugged on his sleeve, carefully avoiding his shoulder. He knew who it was even before Rora's green eyes met his dark gaze. Without his own Fountain filling him from within, he could feel her just beyond his skin; without a second source of energy to both buffer him and cause dissonance, the energy within her came across clear and clean. Potent, but no longer quite so dangerous. Even if he was no longer a potential convergence zone for two Fountains, it was probably still a good thing that she hadn't touched him directly, in gaining his attention.

"Rydan, it's all right. Or rather, it *will* be all right," Rora murmured as soon as he faced her. "The Gods wouldn't have led me here only to endanger me."

"Guardian Serina, give me a moment." Extracting his hand, he turned to face Rora. "Let us hope your faith is not misplaced—what is that?" Rydan asked, noticing she had something in her other hand. When she lifted the reddish, forged sigil into view, he winced.

"What's wrong?" Rora asked him. "Koranen made it for me. He says it'll protect me in my sleep from fire. Is it . . . is this some sort of courting gift I shouldn't have accepted?"

Rydan grimaced. "No, it's fine. Just a gift, nothing more. But I forgot to make a set for you and your sister—I make ones that guard you from attack as you sleep," he explained, keeping his voice low. "Magical or physical. Each of the other ladies has one, as do my siblings, but I've been distracted since your arrival.

"I should have made one for your sister for her wedding gift and one for you, if we're going to be forced into this." His beast grumbled, feeling her disappointment. Rydan realized his words were being taken the wrong way. Uncomfortably aware of his family's curiosity, he leaned in close enough to whisper in her ear. "I would rather you came to me of your own free will."

Rora blinked and Looked at him, gauging his sincerity. Not just sincerity, she Saw, but regret as well, curling around him like a drying, faded leaf, ready to crumble with brown-tinged disappointment at its edge. Trying not to hesitate, she lifted her hand to his chest, resting it over his heart while she murmured into his own ear, "Rydan . . . I *do* come to you of my own free will."

He looked sharply at her. She smiled a little, but mindful of the protective closeness of his emotional aura, self-conscious in the presence of his kin, she let him Feel her emotions. Focusing all of her attention on him, she rubbed her thumb against his black-clad chest. Rydan trapped her hand under his, holding it still as threads of hope crept around him.

"You . . . you want me?" he asked her, breathing the words as much with incredulity as to keep it private from his family.

Her smile widened. "I'm glad I was chased off the Plains. I can't be glad for the deaths of my kin, or of those sailors lost to the reefs, but I *am* glad I met you. Almost fourteen months of running from trouble—and who knows, maybe we're now fourteen thousand miles from home—for all of that, I *wouldn't* change a thing."

There was more to her revelation, something that his beast felt lurking beneath her words. Something his beast had only sensed when aimed at others, of late. Rydan stared at her, unsure of his senses. Heart thudding under the palm pressed to his sternum, he leaned in cautiously, carefully, and breathed, "You . . . *love* me?"

"Can't you feel it?" she dared to tease him, shifting close enough to brush their bodies together.

"Yes, but I doubt my sen—"

"—Rydan, I don't mean to interrupt, but whatever you're doing, would you please hurry it up?" Kelly called out.

Her abrupt demand made him jump back, startled. Whirling, upset by the interruption, he glared at the redheaded woman. Rora touched him on the arm again, her calm proximity soothing his agitated beast. Letting go of his defensive irritation with a heavy sigh, Rydan touched the mist.

"Do what you must, Guardian Serina. As soon as we are wed, Rora and I will retire to fulfill her Guardianship requirements. We will join you when we can. Whether or not we are successful, I leave Saber in charge of coordinating our strategies."

"Understood. If you need a myjii *fruit for a sanctified wedding ceremony . . ."* she started to offer.

Remembering the stench of the last one he had sent to her, Rydan wrinkled his nose. "No, *thank you. The Shifterai way will suffice. I leave you in Saber's hands."*

Pulling free of the mist, he turned to find Saber moving up to join him.

"I take it I just stick my hand in that stuff to talk?" his eldest brother asked, nodding at the coppery stream. "It doesn't seem to work like a scrying mirror."

"Yes, you have to touch it, and no, it's not like a mirror. It will cloud your vision," Rydan warned him. "The stronger the mage, the more you can see, but only of what lies in this room, not what lies at the other end. Watch *that* one, to the north," he added, pointing at the one leading to Menomon. "Whoever has stolen the Fountain of Menomon from Guardian Sheren seems to want to eavesdrop on our conversations . . . which suggests they are very skilled, to eavesdrop and infiltrate at the same time."

"I'll keep an eye on it," Kelly promised, shifting that way. "If I see so much as a flutter, I'll let you know. Of course, whoever it is could have an accomplice to do their eavesdropping, like we have accomplices for watching."

Saber favored his wife with a smile. "I like the way you think."

"Then let's get to it," Morganen told the others. At some point, he had picked up the scroll Rydan had left on the ground and had unrolled it partway, reading some of the transcribed text. "I believe Rydan suggested the Shifterai way of marriage. So long as it's touching Mother Earth, it will probably be considered sanctified. Koranen, a ground fire, if you please?"

"It would help if I had something to burn," Kor said, moving to a clear spot between four of the columns. "I can ignite the granite itself, but it would be too hot for anyone else to get close enough to leap. Not to mention it would ruin the lovely polish of this floor."

"Not on your life," Rydan warned his next-youngest sibling. He tugged at the knot of his belt, only to be startled by the sight of Rora's sister pulling her travel-worn tunic-dress over her head. Beneath it, she appeared to be covered in soft, sleek, cream-hued feathers from shoulders to waist, as if she wore a vest made from eiderdown.

"Here, use this. It's Shifterai, so it might call the attention of our Gods that much more." She gave Rora a wry smile. "It's only fitting if we're to burn the last of our bridges with both of us marrying here."

"Wait—let me get into position," Rora added as Koranen reached for the wadded cloth. Abandoning Rydan, she hurried to the far side of the auburn-haired mage, then turned to face the Fountain, and him. "Ready."

Koranen lobbed the cloth onto the floor. "Are you ready, Brother?"

"Remember, Rydan, wait until I lift my hand. If you move before then, it negates everything," Rora cautioned him. He gave her a nod, then looked at Koranen.

Holding out his hands, Kor frowned for a moment at the crumpled linen. The edges smouldered, then caught fire, burning with a crisp yet dusty scent that prickled at the nose. Nodding, the Pyromancer stepped back, lowering his hands. "It's burning on its own now."

Eyes on Rydan, Rora squared her shoulders and lifted her arm, palm turned up in marital offering. The black-clad mage waited two full heartbeats, then moved. He didn't run, as his twin had done. This wasn't an ember-filled bonfire, radiating its heat to the night. He didn't need to make a dramatic, flame-clearing leap.

As it was, stepping deliberately over the burning dress was a bigger threat, for the flames licked at his boots and trousers in passing. Not that they could harm him; his boots were leather and his pants were wool, neither of which burned well. But he did feel the heat. Clasping Rora's fingers as soon as he could, Rydan tugged the two of them together.

The moment their lips brushed together, her sister shouted, "Witnessed!"

"Enough of that, you two," Trevan teased the two of them. "Take it elsewhere, Brother. And do try to remember all the techniques I taught you."

"Make love to your own woman," Rydan retorted, shifting his grip to Rora's waist. "Not mine."

"Then get to it," Saber told them bluntly. Before his brother or newest sister-in-law could do more than blush, he turned back to the others. "Trevan, trace the energy paths to the north; see if there's more than that communications flow that connects to this other Fountain. I want other ways of reaching them. Koranen, put out the fire and help Kelly keep an eye on that northern line. Freeze it if it so much as twitches, and if they try to attack through it, figure out a way to fry them.

"Morganen, if you could find us a mirror, it would be helpful if you could guide it along the path of the flows and maybe scry the location of this other Fountain. Until we can actually See what our target is, we'll be casting blind. Even if there are too many wardings to cast through the mirror on the other side, I want to see who this infiltrator is, and which directions our counterattacks are striking."

Intent on leading Rora out of the Hall, Rydan pointed in the direction of the back wall. "I keep a mirror behind that panel there, the one carved with the interlocking rectangles."

"Here, the scroll," Morg returned, tossing it at the couple. Rora caught it. Morganen grinned at her, then looked at his brother. "Purpose and quality?"

"It's charmed against incoming scryings, but otherwise has no set purpose. Old, but excellent quality, no inclusions and only two minor flaws in the lower right corner."

"Depending on the distance, that just might do," the youngest brother replied, heading for the wall behind the Fountain. "Especially if I can tie it into that communication flow for added focus . . . maybe a thin thread, something too small to disturb the stream. I'll only need it to direct the scrying after all, not empower it."

"Try to find the other Fountain without tapping into it first," Saber ordered him. "The less our opponent knows of our actions, the greater our advantage."

Exiting the Fountain Hall, Rydan led Rora off to the side, taking the path that led to his quarters. His quarters, not Dominor's. As far as he was concerned, his thirdborn sibling could take the Fountainway back to Koral-tai each night to sleep with his wife. *Unless . . . unless Rora wants to live in a suite with windows . . . But we can't have her exposed to outsiders, at least not until we can get our hands on a complete version of that scroll. The reasons for not telling anyone in Mendhi that we have a living host will still be valid even after I've made myself her Guardian.*

Rora unrolled the parchment in her hands and frowned in concentration over the writing. It wasn't easy for her to read such an archaic script while moving through the dim lighting of the suncrystals they passed. Her eyes twitched every time she had to refocus them, the language was so old and her reading light so poor. The language used, metaphors and subtleties, didn't help her perusal much, either.

When they reached the starlit corridor leading to his bedroom, she had to abandon her study of the scroll for a few moments. Letting him rap the lightglobes into brightness, Rora unrolled the scroll and tilted it toward the nearest of the spheres, skimming to try to find the right spot without getting sidetracked by other bits of information. As much as she wanted to know more about herself, what she was and what it meant, she was aware of the passing of time.

"Rydan, did you read this?"

"Yes." Adjusting the light over his pillows, he came back to her. "I am to give you pleasure until you 'sing.' I presume that means an orgasm," he added dryly. "Then I am to match myself to you, until I 'sing,' too."

"Which part is that?"

Tilting the parchment in her hands, he shifted it up until he found the reference. "There."

Rora read the indicated passage, read it a second time to be sure, and wrinkled her nose. "You'd think the ancients would be a lot more straightforward in saying 'give each other pleasure until you achieve a mutual orgasm while focusing your power and attention on each other.' Even on the sexually restricted Plains, we're at least slightly more direct in our language than this grass-hidden dung."

Taking the scroll and the sigil from her, Rydan retreated to the nightstand, dropping them on the polished stone top. Coming back and catching her hands, he said, "Giving you pleasure will not be a problem. I gave it to you before, and I know you can give it to me. What I want . . . what I *need* to know is . . . do you love me?"

She blushed at his forwardness, avoiding his gaze. "You're an empath, Rydan. I *know* you can Feel it."

"I doubt my senses. I need the words—*why* are you uncomfortable with them?" Rydan asked, sensing her reluctance. Tucking his finger under her chin, he lifted her face until she met his gaze. "Why not just say it?"

"It isn't something you *say*, on the Plains. It's something you *show*," she explained, doing her best to keep her eyes locked with his despite her embarrassment. "We're a people of action, not of words."

"You aren't on the Plains anymore. In Katan, we *said* it. Not always sincerely," he admitted, remembering the women who had sought him out with sweet words, but wanted only their own pleasure. "But *some* of us say it with meaning and intent. At least, *I* do."

"Well, you're not in Katan anymore."

"Please."

It seemed silly; just a bunch of words, devoid of meaning. But he wanted to hear them. He wanted to *believe* in them. Taking a deep breath, she let it out, let go of her tension, and reminded herself of how she felt about him. A second deep breath was all it took for her to See her emotions rising up and reaching out. They wrapped around him, warm and tender like the hues of red and pink clouds at sunset.

"I love you, Rydan. You are the first person to want *me*. Not my power, not my political connection to my sister . . . *me*. You are bright and intelligent, you have a strong sense of right from wrong, you are funny when you let yourself be, and you are tender, warm, and caring, despite all of the suffering you have endured because of your sensitivities."

Reaching up, she cupped his cheeks in her hands, adding

touch to her arsenal of conviction. Yes, he would feel the thrumming of her Fountain, but she knew he would also feel her emotions that much more strongly. Rora could feel the slight rasp of stubble on his jaw and rubbed one of her thumbs over the corner of his lips, enjoying the contrast between soft and coarse skin. He twisted his head a little, mouth pursing in a reflexive, instinctive kiss, which made her smile. That was one of the things a Shifterai man did to show love for his wife, even if he didn't know it.

"Rydan, I used my powers to guide my sister and me to a land where we could finally be safe, where we could happily live out our lives. I *didn't* specify that either of us should also find love here. But we have. My twin has found your twin, and I have found you. Now, you have my words: I love you. Do you love me?"

There was no denying the warmth of her feelings; she made his beast feel as if it were basking in its very first ray of sunshine. "Yes. I love you." Clasping her hands under his, Rydan removed them from his face. "Would you prefer me to show you?"

"Yes, please."

Her polite request made him smile, since it contrasted with the excitement that spiked through her feelings. Aware of the press of time, Rydan led her by her hands toward his bed. Being alone with her in here reminded him of how they had first met; then, her presence in his bed had been all wrong. Now, it was finally going to be right.

Stopping beside the bed, he released her hands so that he could remove his belt. Not wanting to fall behind, Rora unbuckled her own belt. Her heart beat a little faster as she crossed her arms and plucked at her mint green *chamsa*, pulling the outer layer of wool over her head at the same time he removed his own black tunic.

She smiled when they tossed the garments to the side at the same time, like mirrored images of each other, and received a smile in return. That warmed her from the inside out. Just because this was her first time didn't mean she couldn't have fun. Admittedly, it was a first time under the added pressure of having to attune him to the magic she carried, and do so quickly enough to return them to the others to help defend the other Fountain. But this was Rydan; she had come to trust him as she trusted no one else, save for maybe her sister, and she didn't love her sister the same way that she loved this wonderful man.

Her emotions spiked again, wrapping around him like a heady, silken caress. Rydan swayed under the touch of her feelings. Distracted, he fell behind as she sat on the edge of his bed in order to remove her boots. In this room, next to this bed, it was clear to him why he couldn't quite believe his senses, despite her deep, radiant affection for him. He had forced himself upon her—however much she may have enjoyed it at the time—then snarled at her, thrown her out of his quarters, yelled at her, ran from her, growled at her, brooded around her . . .

Seeing a thread of darkness creeping back into his feelings, a deep reddish brown of remorse, Rora caught Rydan's hand and tugged him onto the bed. "Take off your boots. I want to see if your toes are as cute as I remember."

It was such an inane yet amusing request, it broke his cycle of self-recrimination. Rydan did as she bid, tossing his footwear next to hers. It was a domestic sight, really; his boots cuddling up to hers, with the calf of one draped across the toe of another. Peeling off his socks, he tossed those aside, too. Another time, he might have discarded his clothes into a laundry bin, but once they achieved rapport, they would have to dress and return to the Fountain Hall to help the others.

Light brown hair swung into his field of view. Rora leaned over his knees, peering at his feet. "Definitely cute. Now I want to see your ankles and your calves. Care to indulge me?"

"And my knees?" Rydan asked, bemused by her request. He rose from the bed, turning to face her, and found her gaze not on his knees, but on his thighs . . . and higher. Pulling his undertunic off, he cast it aside, then tugged at the laces on his trousers, pale hands contrasting against the dark material.

Despite the press of time, he took his time, framing his groin with the caressing of his fingers. The light self-touches weren't all that arousing, though they were pleasant enough. It was the way her gaze avidly followed each move. How he could feel her curiosity and interest mounting within her, spiraling upward with desire. That was what made his body tight with need, muscles tensing and manhood thickening. Once his trousers had been loosened, he unknotted the ties to his undertrousers as well, then skimmed his fingers just beneath both waistbands.

But he only teased, lowering the fabric by maybe a thumb length at most, enough to bare his hip bones. Sliding his hands free, he held them out to her. "Stand up," Rydan coaxed her. "I want to see more of you."

Breath in her throat, Rora took his hands and let him pull her to her feet. Her body swayed toward his, almost brushing against him. She could feel the heat of his skin through her linen undertunic despite the chill in the air; the contrast in warmth and coolness made her wish for a moment they were in her quarters, up in the palace. Licking her lips, she glanced around, then asked, "Is there a . . . fire place down here?"

"We're too deep in the mountain for it." Glancing to the side at a sigil carved on the wall over his bed, he commanded, *"Reshauf, lal nuf."*

The carving began glowing faintly, with a reddish peach hue. Within moments, Rora could feel the warmth it radiated. "That produces a lot of heat, doesn't it?"

"Only to start with, until the room reaches a certain temperature. Then it fades in and out, keeping up the warmth." He shrugged and watched her gaze dip to the flexing of the muscles in his shoulders and chest. "I normally only use it after a bath, to keep warm while I dry. Otherwise, I'm used to the cold down here."

"Well, I'm not. And I appreciate it," Rora said. With the carving on the wall radiating its heat, she was growing warm in her wool *breikas* and linen underdress. Pulling the pale green garment over her head, she bared her upper half without hesitation, though she did blush a little.

Rydan dropped his gaze to her stomach, taut against the drawstrings of her gathered trousers, then raised it to her breasts. They weren't large, but they were pert, peaks tight despite the warmth now invading his room. Their room, rather. It reminded him of his earlier thoughts. "I would keep the radiant sigil going, if you wanted to live down here, or I could move back up into the palace . . . but until we can extract your Fountain, I'd rather keep you away from any newcomers to the isle."

She nodded. "I agree. As would my sister. And we should stick to our nighttime hours, for the time being. But, um . . . would you always want to be awake at night, and live underground?"

Almost responding without thought, Rydan caught himself and carefully considered her words. "I hid during the day to avoid the pain of interacting with my family. I still feel too much, at times. Until I can completely control this sensitivity I have, I prefer the quiet of the night. And someone still needs to stay awake at night to keep an eye on the Isle. We may not have many enemies, but so far, when we've rid ourselves of one, another one takes their place within a few months."

"When we extract my Fountain, we can set aside some of its magic to watch for enemies, and rotate the island's protections among your family," Rora offered. "You need to start interacting more. And I need to start finding something to do with myself, besides tagging along with you. Even if it's just feeding those chickens I keep hearing about. Are they really that vicious?"

Rydan chuckled and wrapped his arms around her. "You can ask Mariel to show you her 'war wounds' from when she practiced her Healing techniques on some of them."

Enjoying the feel of her breasts pressed into the muscles of his chest, Rora snuggled into his embrace. The sensation of flesh on flesh was too intriguing to remain content with just a hug, though. Leaning back, she looked up at him. "So, what shall we do next? Fondle and caress? I know the basics of how all this works—Shifterai maidens are raised to be chaste, not ignorant—but I'm not sure what the proper order of everything should be."

That made him laugh. Only she would be so interested in ridding herself of her innocence. Hugging her close, Rydan pressed a kiss to her hair. "We do this in almost any order we like."

"Alright. I, um, understand that being completely naked helps, though," she offered into his shoulder . . . and slid her hands down his back. Fingers dipping into his clothes, she hooked the waistbands and pushed them down a bit. They didn't fall to the floor, though; something kept them from dropping. She suspected it was the lump pressing into her abdomen—either that, or the closeness of their bodies kept the layers of fabric in place.

Rydan could feel his undertrousers tugging at his arousal. Releasing her, he moved back a little and freed himself, letting the material drop to the floor. A glance at her face showed her eyes wide as she stared at his masculinity, but there wasn't a trace of shyness in her emotions. Avid curiosity, yes, but no fear or embarrassment. Emboldened by her interest, he pulled on the lacings of her *breikas* until the garment drooped halfway down her hips.

Glancing down, Rora smiled. A wriggle, and they fell, tangling around her ankles just like his trousers had done. She realized a moment later what she had done. "Rydan . . ."

"Yes?" Distracted by the sight of her curves, he tried to focus on her words despite the lovely way she inhaled before speaking.

"How do we untangle our feet without tripping or looking like left-footed fools?"

EIGHTEEN

Rydan laughed and moved his legs, shaking his feet free of the crumpled black folds. "Like that, of course."

"For you, perhaps, but my *breikas* are tied at the ankle, and I am now trapped," she pointed out, giving him a wry, amused look. "How can I escape while looking graceful?"

"With my help." Scooping her up before she could protest, Rydan swung her onto his bed. Her trousers trailed after her like a half-shed snakeskin. Settling her with her head on his favorite pillow, Rydan bent over her ankles, turning the cuffs so he could find the drawstrings. Once her feet were free of the fabric, he cupped them, sliding his palms up to her knees. One of his palms bumped over the knotted thong of a contraceptive amulet. Rydan decided it might be good to have children someday, but not until her Fountain was safely extracted and the Convocation of the Gods arranged.

She sat up when he reached her thighs. What he was doing to her, how he was touching her, felt too good not to reciprocate. Trailing her fingers over his arms and shoulders, Rora did her best to copy the way he smoothed his hand over her uplifted thighs; first he teased their outsides, then he coaxed his way to their insides, parting her legs a little.

There was only one drawback to her echoing his moves:

Rydan squirmed when her fingers brushed the soft inner skin of his biceps, up near his armpits, abdomen tightening visibly. Her eyes widened in realization. His narrowed in warning. For a moment, she contemplated tickling him anyway, but chose discretion over valor. Later, they would have time for such play, but not right now.

Instead, she shifted forward, crossing her legs so that she could reach not only his chest but his mouth as well. Their lips met, their tongues tangled, and their bodies brushed against each other. Rydan climbed onto the bed, pushing her back and down until he lay half over her, their legs side-by-side. Her flesh thrummed beneath his, her Fountain vibrating softly in time with the fluttering of her desire, like the rumbling purr of a contented cat. He wanted to purr in return, though that was more a trick of his twin's. She made him feel this way, ensnaring all of his senses, until it seemed like nothing else existed in his universe but for her.

Mindful of his task, Rydan focused on her body. Ending their kiss with a reluctant murmur on her part, he nuzzled her throat and praised her shoulders with the brushing of his lips. Swirling his tongue over her collarbone, he sucked on the hollow above it, then kissed her flesh down to the valley between her breasts. She didn't lie still; her hands feathered through his hair, caressing his scalp and tugging lightly on the soft black strands, pleasing him with the sensual touch.

Her quick intake of breath accompanied a spike in her lust as he nuzzled first one, then the other curve. Eyes closed, Rydan immersed himself in his other senses. The subtle, almost spicy-sweet scent of her skin, the warmth of her flesh, slightly chilled at each tip, the crinkled peak of each nipple beneath his lips. Each gasp and soft, quavering moan spurred him onward, making him rub his groin into the bedding beside her hip.

Opening his jaw as widely as he could, Rydan sucked her right breast into his mouth, swirling his tongue around and over her areola. Her fingers convulsed in his hair, accompanying a harder throb of power and desire. The temptation to indulge both of them was too much; Rydan suckled stronger, licked faster, even gently scraped his teeth against her flesh. Every little thing that gave her more pleasure, he did even more, until her back was bowing up from the bed, pressing herself into him, feeding both of their hunger.

"Rydan!" It was too much, yet utterly not enough. Fumbling, Rora found his hand and dragged it down, pushing it roughly between her thighs. "Please . . . touch me. Like . . . like before."

He shuddered at the memory. Switching to her other breast, he swirled his tongue over it, matching the pattern by tracing it with his fingertips on her inner thigh. Rora spread her knees wantonly. A shift of his hand allowed his touch to feather over the crinkly hair of her mound. Rora moaned and clutched at his arm, encouraging him.

The moment his finger slipped between her netherlips, two sensations struck him hard. She was very, very slick . . . and her power spiked, vibrating not just his inner senses, but his bones, hard enough to rattle his teeth. Forcing himself to hold still, to calm her with inaction—though her desire ebbed only a little—Rydan breathed through his nose, trying to relax into her power. That was the key to matching resonances, to let go of his sense of *self* and embrace the overwhelming sense of *other.*

But this wasn't just her Fountain; this was *her.* Magic and host were inextricably entwined. To relax, he licked her breast, returning his attention to her physical pleasure. Sucking on the skin at the base of her breast, he circled his fingertips lightly through her wetness, brushing against the peak hidden in her folds.

Divine. Rora instinctively circled her hips in counterpoint. She had heard from fellow Shifterai women who, upon marriage, had discovered they had to teach their husbands their favorite way to be touched like this. But Rydan didn't have to be taught. Somehow, he knew within an experimental stroke or two exactly what she liked . . . which made Rora laugh.

Of course he knows how to touch me—he's reading my feelings . . . and, oh, Father Sky, You taught him everything he needs to know . . . Her laughter faded into a moan. Working her hips, Rora clutched at his head with both hands, pulling his mouth back up to her nipple. The two spots were vying for her increasingly distracted attention, turning her delirious with delight. *I never knew breasts could feel this good—ah, Gods! Ah!*

Rydan savored her cries. He had caught both peaks, one in his lips, the other between his fingers, and tugged on them. Brilliant delight gave way to blinding joy; the thrumming of her body increased, and now he could *hear* it inside his mind, a sweet song that lured him in with open arms.

His own flesh ached for release. Muscles shivering with the effort not to climax along with her, Rydan braced his elbow and twisted onto his side, removing the temptation to thrust into the bedcovers. Gentling his touch, he continued circling his fingers through her folds, working his way down to her opening. The upward flexing of her hips was an encouraging sign, as was her emotional hunger when he probed gently inside.

Being needed like this made his chest hurt, if in a good way. This wasn't like the empty encounters of his pre-exile days; he could feel her love for him, her desire to reciprocate beneath her delirium. Allowing himself only a few gentle thrusts, Rydan removed his hand. He didn't have the chance to do more than lift it to his lips, however; Rora hungrily pushed him over, rolling him to his back . . . where he slid abruptly, awkwardly to the floor with a thump, a grunt . . . and an uncontrollable chuckle that rose into full-blown laughter.

"Oh! Oh, Rydan—I'm so sorry!" Snapped out of her lustful reverie, Rora struggled to help him back onto the bed, but he laughed so hard, he couldn't get up off the floor; it bubbled out of him in a burst of cream and yellow. Unable to help herself, she giggled, too. It *was* funny.

Her hands still tucked under his shoulders, Rydan *felt* her Fountain singing to him in the middle of their shared laughter. Instinct told him to capitalize on it, so he pushed to his feet, twisting around to crawl up and over her. Still grinning, she lay back on the bed and parted her knees without hesitation, hands shifting to caress his chest.

"I love it when you laugh," Rora confessed quietly, not wanting to spoil the mood. Lifting one of her hands to his face, she cupped his cheek. "I want to make you laugh more often."

Turning his head, he smiled and nipped at her fingers. Shifting to settle himself between her thighs, Rydan left her hand in favor of her breasts, circling the nearest tip with his tongue. She sucked in a sharp, appreciative breath, then groaned.

"I wanted to please *you*, not have you please me!" Straining, she reached for his manhood, but could only barely reach the tip of it, given their positions. He caught her hand, pressing it into the mattress off to the side. "Rydan—can't I play with you, too?"

"Later. Right now," he promised, kissing his way up to her throat, "is all for you."

Delving her other hand through his hair, Rora urged his mouth up to hers, where at least she could please him with all the kissing techniques he had taught her so far. Being level with his body allowed her to feel the prodding of his erection against her thigh, exciting her. They were so close to copulating, it frustrated her when he didn't shift into position, and she tugged on his hair.

"Shhh, shhh, this is your time," Rydan soothed between nips.

She tipped her head back, breaking their kiss to voice the complaint, "But it *excites* me to please you."

Her longing and his need wore at his patience. "Rora, I am *trying* to match myself to you. It is I who must please *you*."

Pushing at his shoulders—this time the other way, farther onto the bed—Rora tried to make him roll off of her. Though he was relatively lean, Rydan was muscular, and she didn't make much progress. "Rydan, who says *I* cannot match myself to *you*? Let me touch you!"

His beast grumbled, sensing the shift from desire to frustration within her. Resistance was now counterproductive. Giving in, Rydan sighed and let her push him onto his back. Squirming into place, Rora draped herself over his side. She splayed across his chest, then wriggled a little higher and pressed a kiss to his jaw.

"Now, doesn't that feel nice?" she asked, circling his nipple with her palm.

Eyeing her, Rydan took her wrist, shifted her hand out of the way, and lightly pinched his own nipple. "*That* feels nice. At least, for me."

Her cheeks heated. Hesitantly, she reached for his other nipple, gently tweaking the small, pale brown peak. She wasn't sure just how hard to tweak, though; she wanted to make Rydan feel good, after all, not hurt him. "You, um, like this?"

"Yes . . . and you completely missed my lips, when you kissed me earlier," he added. "You need to work on your technique for that, too."

Realizing his aura now had a peach tendril of teasing in it, Rora narrowed her eyes for a moment, then leaned forward and kissed him. On the side of his nose. Pulling back, she smirked. "You mean, like that?" Darting in, she kissed his cheekbone, then the edge of his chin. "Or that? Or that?"

Burying his fingers in her soft, light brown hair, Rydan guided her kisses to his lips. Sucking on her bottom lip, he let her end the kiss after a moment. "Like *this*."

"Mm. So, like this . . ." And she kissed him, suckling his lower lip, then shifted her fingers over his nipple again, "and like this?"

She pinched it gently, a little harder than before, and Rydan sucked in a sharp breath, letting it out in a hiss. He responded with a pleasure-tinged, "Yesss . . ."

"You really, honestly like that?" Rora asked, bemused by his reaction. "You like being pinched right there?"

Shifting his other hand to cup one of her breasts, he curled his thumb and forefinger into position, and squeezed a little.

Rora's green eyes widened. "Oh! I see." Glancing down at his chest, she pinched him again, then brushed her thumb over the small, taut peak in a quick, manipulative circle. "And . . . that?"

"Mm, yes," he agreed.

"Anything else?" she asked, curious.

"Light touches . . . light scrapes, too," Rydan confessed. When she trailed her fingertips down over his ribs, his breath quickened. A quick, darting touch to his inner arm made him squirm and catch her hand. Giving her a dirty look, he returned her fingers to his torso.

Dragging her fingers lightly down his abdomen, Rora hesitated a moment, then feathered her hand over his erection. A groan escaped him and prickles rose across his skin, generated by the pleasure of her curious, loving touch. Abandoning his manhood, Rora rubbed her palm lightly over his chest and arm, enjoying the new texture of his skin even as she soothed his goose-prickles. Only when they were mostly gone did she glide her hand back down the increasingly tight muscles of his stomach, until she could resume exploring his shaft.

Her hesitant touch was driving him mad. Needing to bring her attention back to the arousing of her own desire, Rydan stopped being passive under her touch. Threading his fingers through her hair, he tugged lightly on the soft strands. Slipping his other hand beneath her arm, he teased her breasts, doing his best to ignore her explorations.

She was getting warm and slick again between her thighs. Rora squirmed, biting her lower lip. Until now, she had ignored her breasts; they were neither so large that they absolutely required an undergarment for constant support, nor so small as to be nonexistent. They were just breasts, a sign of her physical maturity, and designed to one day swell with a mother's milk. But the way Rydan touched them, fondled them, enjoyed them, he made them feel special.

He awakened nerves and connections in her body that she hadn't realized existed, especially the lightninglike paths of pleasure that twisted between nipple and womb. And that thing he was doing with her hair—that caused goose-prickles of her own to rise and scatter across her flesh. It added to the aching need he aroused.

Now that she had felt the pleasure Rydan could instill in her, her womb felt empty, hungry. The only thing that had come close to filling her had been his touch, in specific his fingers, though the rest of it was delicious. Of course, even a maiden of the Plains knew that fingers—her own or otherwise—were no substitute for a husband's manhood. Shifting her weight, Rora swung her leg over his hips, straddling him.

Tucking her hand between her legs, she grasped him again. Positioning him was a bit awkward, though; her aim was untried, or maybe the angle was wrong. Whatever it was, she felt relief when he brushed her hand away and took over, grasping and prodding at the right spot within moments.

There was a stretching ache when he slipped inside, but Rora didn't care. The feel of his flesh rubbing against hers was too good to deny. As he held himself steady, she found her hips rocking briefly, instinctively. Enjoying it, she did it again, and again, until Rydan released his grip and clutched at her hips. Stilling, she looked down at him, wondering what was wrong.

Her teasing was driving him mad. Rydan tugged on her hips, pulling her downward even as he flexed his buttocks, pushing up into her. He could sense her discomfort, but knew it was minor. A shift of his hand slipped his thumb between her folds, permitting him to rub at the sloping peak guarding her folds. Rora shuddered, collapsing over him with a soft cry; thrusting up into her, Rydan sunk himself to the hilt, using her pleasure to ease the rest of his way.

It cost him. Chest heaving, hands trembling, he kept her pressed firmly in place, teetering on the edge of release. The thrumming of her power didn't help; it massaged his nerves, stimulating his inner senses. Thankfully, his beautiful, glorious wife kept herself still. That allowed him time to calm back down while she rested chest-to-chest with him, braced on elbows and knees.

His girth stung; she acknowledged that readily . . . but he did fill at least half of the emptiness within her. The other half, she had already learned, was found in rubbing their bodies together. Regardless, it took her a bit before she felt ready to move. Looking at Rydan as the pain faded, she found him a churning swirl of lust, desire, love, need, and hunger, all in sunset hues of reds and purples and golds. Laced throughout the happier hues of his aura was the dusty blue of patient concern, accenting his feelings.

Licking her lips, Rora finally asked, "Now what?"

Rydan smiled. "You told me at some point how children on the Plains learn how to ride at the age of four. And yet here you are, at the age of . . . twenty?"

"Twenty," she agreed.

"At the age of twenty," he confirmed, "and yet you don't know how to ride?"

"Riding a horse is not the same as riding a man," Rora returned.

"True. There is so much more you can do with a man," he agreed. Caressing her back with both hands, he finally slipped his fingers up to the nape of her neck, urging her mouth down to his. That slid her up the length of his shaft a little.

Curling his fingers over her shoulders, he pulled her fully back onto him, pressing up into her for more depth, prodding until he was stopped by the limitations of flesh. A sharp intake of her breath mixed with a twinge of discomfort, pricking at his beast; the combination told him that she wasn't sure about having him pressing her inner boundary like that. Relaxing his grip for a moment, he pulled down and pressed up again, careful to not delve as deep.

His own pleasure was secondary, compared to the vibration of hers. Working slowly, Rydan focused on re-arousing her. It was imperative he make her sing again, that he align their magics in the aligning of their bodies, and do so quickly, given how much time they had spent so far, versus how long his siblings could hold off that impostor's attack. Yet at the same time, he didn't want to press her farther or faster than she could go.

Concern held him back. Aware of the passing of time, Rora decided to take the matter into her own hands. Pushing herself upright, she sank down deeper onto him for a moment, making her inhale swiftly as he pressed against her back wall, so to speak. She could See his concern peaking at that, but her sharp breath wasn't entirely for discomfort. It felt . . . interesting. Nice, though something was still missing. Something she knew she had to go searching for, if she could only figure out how.

Swiveling her hips, half-blinded by the Sight of his emotions entwining sensually around her, Rora tried to rub him against that spot again and felt a combination of stinging stretch and delicious pressure. It reminded her that motion was part of her pleasure. Flexing her thighs, she rose up, then sank down—oh, yes, that was it.

Eyes closed, Rora did it again, and again, picking up a rhythm quickly. She felt his hands lift to her breasts, cupping and squeezing, then felt his fingers plucking and tugging gently at their tips. Groaning, she reached down, fumbled on his chest until she had to open her eyes, then found and pinched his own.

"Gods!" The shout escaped him, impelled by the sudden clenching of his guts in the desperate need to stave off an ambushed climax. Hissing his breath through his teeth,

Rydan struggled for control, but it was no good. He could *feel* how much his pleasure was exciting her, not just emotionally or physically, but magically. They were so close . . . and yet so far. She was vibrating inside, even singing with the resonance of her desire . . . but she wasn't *releasing* that desire.

Instinct warned him that this was *not* the position for claiming her, body, soul, and Fountain. Pushing her off of him, ignoring her wordless protest at being forced to dismount, Rydan rolled over her as soon as she had sprawled more or less on her back. Grabbing her leg, he doubled her knee up toward her chest, slotted their loins together with a moment of prodding, and thrust himself back inside.

She cried out again, her face twisting into a half grimace, but his beast purred and writhed at her pleasure. *This* was what both of them needed now, not slow, tender lovemaking. That would come later, a surfeit of it. Right now, he needed her to surrender to him.

Rora hadn't realized that having a man take charge so abruptly could be so breathtaking. The new position left her breathless, half-crushed under his weight, half-squashed under her own thigh, but it put a delicious pressure on her womb, and it was surprisingly arousing to be commandeered like this. Rydan rocked into her in deep, thorough thrusts; he ground their loins together, withdrew only to delve hard and deep, and then did it again.

This position allowed him to lean over her to capture her mouth, stealing the rest of her breath, before easing back and focusing on a firm, gliding rhythm. Stimulated, she felt her control starting to slip, and it alarmed her. This wasn't just the minor loss of self-control that came with a bit of self-pleasuring; this was far bigger than that. She felt like she was going to fly apart, like she had sometimes done after the onset of puberty. But losses of that kind of control had usually ended in a release of mage-fire, and that was *not* a good thing; not when she loved Rydan and really, really didn't want to hurt him.

He could feel her struggling to retain coherence, and with it, control. "Let go," Rydan breathed, flexing his hips faster, thrusting into her harder. This was exciting him, too, but he had to hold on; he didn't dare follow his own advice until she herself had leaped. Her resonances were rising, but they were still too contained, too controlled. "Let go, Rora, and give yourself to me . . . Give yourself to me!"

To me . . . to *me* . . . Struggling to hold on to conscious thought through the driving pleasure roused by their coupling, Rora clung to those two words. That was the key—if she fell, if she lost her self-control and fell . . . she wasn't falling free of control. She was falling into *his* control. The only thing she had to do was trust him enough to let him catch her and hold her.

I trust him, Rora thought, and lifted her other leg, wrapping it around his thrusting, grinding hips. *I do—oh, yes* . . . Looking up at him, Seeing his control constraining his bright-hued desire, Rora knew she wasn't the only one who had to fall. Splaying her hands on his chest, she met his dark eyes and smiled. "I'll catch you, too. I trust you—I love you!"

Her smile turned into a gasp, and she threw her head back. Rora convulsed with the pleasure unleashed by that truth. It *rang* through her, a sound that was pure sensation . . . and it was reciprocated, swallowing her whole.

He felt her releasing her control to him, relaxing her mind and tensing her body. Releasing his hold on her leg, Rydan braced his forearm on the bed and cast aside his own control, bucking hard. If he attuned himself to her or not, it didn't matter; *feeling* her complete love and trust was too overwhelming for him to care anymore. Reveling in it, drowning in it, he captured her mouth in a kiss every bit as impassioned and unrestrained as the movement of their bodies.

With the release of control came the unleashing of his beast. But he didn't fear what it would do to her. His passion merged fully, fearlessly, with her power. Blinded by his heart-pounding climax, he vaguely knew his head had arched back, breaking their kiss, that her fingers clawed at his ribs and clutched at his back. Flinging his heart wide-open, Rydan absorbed and embraced her, loved her, until every last ounce of passion and strength were wrung from him.

When he could see again, when he could actually think, he found himself collapsed on her, cradled limply in the tangled grasp of her arms and legs. Aware of the world once more, Rydan guessed he was crushing her, and summoned just enough strength to slip out of her and sag to one side. He didn't want to let go of her—ever—but he didn't want to suffocate her, either.

For the first time in too many years to count, Rydan could not feel his beast. He *could* still feel her emotions, but she was a part of him now. The missing part that made the aching wounds within him finally whole.

Rora murmured and twisted a little, following him to keep her arms and legs wrapped around her husband. For the first time in her life, she felt light-headed, as if she was no longer carrying a massive burden. The weight of her power was still there, but the responsibility for it was shared, and she didn't want to let go of her partner, her lover, her mate.

They cuddled that way for a mindless while, until a ringing noise startled both of them. Blinking, dragging his mind back to full wakefulness, Rydan wormed his left arm out from under her. He squinted at his cryslet, then carefully angled his forearm and opened the lid. His twin's voice. Sizzling sounds accompanied flashes of light on Trevan's face, though his eyes were closed. Respectfully closed, from the emotions Rydan could sense emanating from his twin.

"I really don't mean to interrupt, but if you're done literally making the earth move around us, we need you out here," Trev reported. "Morg got the mirror connected to the communication stream, and managed to get it focused on our foe, only to find that the other mage was using a mirror to try the same thing. And it's a him, not a her; he must have used a voice-copying spell when speaking through the Fountain. Amara says she recognizes him, someone who's been tracking the two of them since practically the Plains themselves."

"Who?" Rora asked, unsettled by that thought. She feared it was the nameless blond, the one whose cruelty had made her skin crawl. He probably was not strong enough to wrest control of her Fountain from either her or Rydan, but what she had sensed from him had frightened her.

"She called him Xenos."

"Xenos?" That woke up Rydan enough to remember. "I know that name . . . Guardian Sheren said he was trying to charm her. He's some newcomer to the city."

"We've met him before," Rora confirmed. "I don't know how he survived the reefs, but then, he is a strong mage."

"Well, he's trying to kill us, not charm us—and he is strong. He's getting closer to succeeding," Trevan relayed, his face wincing from a loud *bang* on the other end of the mirror connection. "Morg thinks he may have infiltrated another Fountain down the line and is pulling power from it as well. I hope you've managed your task, Brother. We need both of you."

"We'll be there in a few moments," Rydan promised. He snapped the lid shut, dropping his arm.

He contemplated their problem for a moment. Touching Rora wasn't like touching his Fountain. He wasn't fully immersed in the energies she carried, but then he realized he wasn't in sole control of it, either. Rora still had some control over the flow of energies within her.

It was a good thing; words had power, within the heart of a singularity. Serina's current situation was the result of attempting to fix carelessly spoken words turned into a spell, thanks to their speakers being in the heart of the Koral-tai Fountain at the time. From the feel of things, he *could* control her energies completely, like being in the heart of a regular Fountain . . . *if* she opened them up to him.

Next to him, Rora inhaled deeply, then sighed. "I think I'm getting some of my energy back. I've never been so drained before, not after, well, pleasing myself on my own." Stretching, she squeezed him with her upper arm. "My sister and I couldn't stop him—Xenos, that is—but then, we're not mages. We could only run. I'll trust you have a plan?"

Thinking of the way he had originally reconnected Nightfall to its fellow Fountains, Rydan nodded. "If we can use up all of his attention with the others' attacks, force him to throw most of his defenses to the front, we can open a Fountainway and strike him from behind."

"Personally, I have no objections to attacking someone like him from behind," she agreed. Pushing up onto her elbow, she gave him a lopsided smile. "Shall we? The sooner we can get this over with, the sooner we can get back in here . . . right?"

Pleased with that thought, Rydan smiled and rose from the bed, hunting for the discarded layers of their clothes.

NINETEEN

Kelly met them in the corridor outside the Fountain Hall. Bright lights and loud noises echoed out of the arched entryway. She gave the approaching pair a little wave in greeting and winced. "Saber kicked me out when things started getting rough."

"What?" Rora asked, as half of the redhead's words were obscured by a sharp sizzling sound.

"He kicked me out! I have no shields, so I'm safer out here! Look, Morg and I figured out how this Xenos character is able to attack and counterattack so well, even though he's only one person and there are several of us," Kelly told them, moving closer so that she could be heard. "He has these little things draped like nets over the bubble-spheres that are sort of analogous to your ribbon-pipes—they're sort of like scrolls attached to nets, only the scroll part is tiny, about the size of a hand," she explained, gesturing, "and they have these bead things dangling from the knotted cords.

"I noticed that each one ripples slightly and the glowing bubble underneath dims a little when a particular attack comes across. Morg thinks they form a combination of rune-magic, knot-magic, and Artificing, which means they're a triple application of magic, making them difficult to defend against. Saber says you're to target those things physically. We haven't been able to mount a direct attack on them magically, but one of the spells Koranen cast was a fire-bomb thing. The other mage deflected most of it, but it managed to crisp and take out one of the net-scrolls."

Rora glanced at Rydan. He nodded. "I have a few spells in mind." Another sizzling sound was followed by a sharp *bang* and a curse from what sounded like Koranen, and a roaring, crackling sound ensued. Rydan raised his voice. "Kelly, I need you to do something for me."

She nodded in agreement, and he pointed behind him. "Go back that way, second left, first right, first left. Open the door, turn right, open that door, and grab the mirror that you'll see mounted on the sitting room wall. Bring it back to the Hall."

"Second left, first right, first left, open door, turn right, open door, grab and bring back the mirror inside. Got it. Morganen's mirror is still intact, though, if you wanted to scry the other Fountain," Kelly told him.

Rydan shook his head. There was a brief lull in battle noise, but it picked up again. "I don't want to scry with it—I want you to toss it into the Hall, as hard as you can, so that it shatters on the floor!"

"You want me to *shatter* it?" she asked, frowning at him in confusion. "Doesn't that give me seven years of bad luck?"

He gave her a dubious look. "Where did you hear *that*?"

"It's a superstition where I come from," Kelly explained. "Break a mirror, and you get seven years of bad luck. If this is a realm of magic, and Curses are real . . ."

"Smashing a mirror gets you shards of glass on the floor, and possibly a few cuts in picking up the pieces, nothing more," Rydan reassured her. "Not to mention the loss of a costly object—look, just do it, alright?"

"Alright, if that's what you want," she agreed, shrugging and lifting her hands. Then she pointed at him. "But if I *do* end up with seven years of bad luck, you're babysitting every last one of my kids." Her stern look faded, replaced by a wistfulness that poked at Rydan's beast, reminding him it was still there. "*If* Saber and I ever have any . . ."

Another loud *bang* made all three of them flinch. Kelly hurried away, and Rora envied the other woman's ability to retreat. She could and had fought to defend the Plains—like any other Shifterai woman, she had learned archery at an early age—but she wasn't a trained and blooded warrior like her twin. The thought of walking into a magical battle zone was even more unnerving than the thought of getting embroiled in a physical fight. But she allowed Rydan to draw her in to the column-lined chamber, putting her trust in him to protect her.

He didn't approach the far end, though. Rydan had something else in mind. Squinting against the flashing, swirling energies, he cupped his hands to his mouth and shouted. *"Morganen!"*

"What?" A figure that looked slender enough to be the youngest of his brothers separated itself from the fray.

"Bring me the mirror!"

The figure lifted a hand in acknowledgment and turned away. Bright streaks of purple obscured his figure, along with a cloud of smoke. Rora arched a brow at Rydan, leaning in close so she could speak into his ear. "First you want Kelly to bring and shatter a mirror, and now you want Morganen to bring you a second one?"

"I just need to see what the targets look like. We can also use that mirror to follow and open the Fountainway path."

"How do we do that?" she asked.

"You open yourself to me, and I do all the work. We'll be like a water pipe; you are the cork, unleashing the power, and I am the faucet, guiding it into the basin."

"And the smashed mirror?" she asked, dubious.

"If Kelly is right—she doesn't have any magic, but she does have a way of observing things—then I think I know how to attack those Artifacts she described."

A tall cheval mirror floated their way between the columns, trailing two thin streamers of coppery mist. Behind it came Morganen, hands outstretched, steadying the levitation charm. Setting it down a short distance away, he winced from a gust of snowflakes that swirled briefly through the hall, then eyed the two of them. "Warring mages aren't pretty, and this one's a clever foe. Do you need me for anything? Mind you, I'm not touching *either* Fountain."

"No, and I wouldn't want you to. I want you to drain the incoming attacks," Rydan told him. Morg blinked and frowned. The sixthborn mage elaborated. "You said there were two types of mages, givers and takers. And that you, as a taker, can drain magic from sources outside yourself. I want you to drain the magic from the incoming attacks."

Morg's brows lifted. "You want me to drain them? But, that's pre-purposed magic."

"If you can drain Rora right through her personal wards—the tightest I've ever seen—then sucking up a couple of spells will be like pulling on a loose string in a piece of knitting. And move closer to the wall," Rydan directed him. "Kelly's going to be tossing in our weapon any moment now."

"Weapon?" Morg asked, glancing between the two of them.

"Don't ask," Rora advised him. A moment later they heard a grunting yell, and turned in time to see a portrait-sized mirror arcing up, then sailing down. It smashed, tumbling a few body lengths across the floor, the wooden frame cracking and twisting as bits of glass scattered across the floor.

For a moment, Morg frowned, then a look of comprehension widened his aquamarine eyes. "You're going to do a Shatter-Cast, aren't you?"

"If the pieces are small enough, they'll slip right through the wardings, at slow speed," Rydan agreed.

"And a delayed Frenzy spell, for shredding the net-scrolls?" Morg asked with rising glee, as Rora looked between the two men, not quite sure what they were talking about. "Dominor does know his sabotage spells."

"He taught us well. How is he holding up?" Rydan asked, glancing at his former Fountain.

Morganen's reply was succinct. "Hurry. I'll prepare the glass, then go see what I can do to attract and ground those incoming spells. You get that connection made."

Nodding, Rydan didn't bother to watch his youngest brother's actions. Turning to Rora, he guided her over to the mirror, positioning her between him and it. The silvered glass didn't reflect the two of them, but rather showed an image of a strange, multileveled chamber streaked with spells and hosting stalagmite-like pillars ending in strange, bubblelike lights that glowed in different hues.

They didn't quite look like lightglobes; their surfaces shimmered and rippled, like watching a bubble rise through water, for all these flexible spheres were stationary. Most of them were draped with scraps of parchment fringed around the edges with a network of cords, beads, and knots that swayed each time a sphere jostled. Just as Kelly had said, when each of the sphere-bubbles jiggled, their lights dimmed . . . and a moment later, some sort of spell either swirled into the room, countering a volley from the brothers, or it surged through the Fountain on the far side of the Hall, attacking them in return.

"Look at the image," he told her, ignoring the sizzling sounds of magical combat at the far end of the Hall. Lifting his hands to her shoulders, he slid his palms slowly down her arms, opening his mage-senses to her resonances. "Ignore the fighting, and anything else transitory. Look at the *room*. Look at those bubbles of energy, focus on sensing them, focus on *feeling* the hues as a symphony of light and sound . . . and concede control of yourself to me."

"Of course," Rora agreed. "I trust you. I'm nervous about the thought of sending shards of glass anywhere near me . . . but I trust you."

His beast purred under the truth of her words. Catching her hands, he interlaced their fingers and lifted their arms, spreading them outward. She leaned back into him instinctively, and he had to pause a moment to remind his body that physical pleasures would have to wait, however warm and willing her curves felt against his frame.

With a sigh he felt rather than heard, she opened herself to him, immersing him in the song of her Fountain. Focusing his mind, Rydan spoke the words of the Seeking chant written on the scroll that Madam Mist had shown to him. He drove meaning and power into the words, aiming to the north by following that coppery thread that connected the mirror to the area it scried.

"*Bela nolva gasthe'kora, kava pujass es'kateyl. Bela nolva gasthe'miikra, zhuma veida ess-traveyl. Bela nolva gasthe'kora, kava pujass es'kateyl! Bela nolva gasthe'miikra, zhuma veida ess-traveyl! Bela nolva gasthe'kora*!" he chanted, voice rising in volume along with his power. Another voice joined his, startling him for a moment, but not enough to disrupt his chant.

"Kava pujass es'kateyl!" Rora chanted with him. She didn't know the exact meaning of his spell, but she could See how he was narrowing the energies of her Fountain into a snaking, driving probe. *"Bela nolva gasthe'miikra, zhuma veida ess-traveyl!"*

Rydan focused harder as he chanted with her. He couldn't See the energies—he suspected Rora could, since she had said she could See such things whenever she focused—but he could Feel them burrowing into the earth, delving deep beneath the sea, shooting north along the curve of the world. Her fingers tightened over his when he sensed them getting near, letting him know that she sensed it, too. Not just the proximity of another Fountain, but lives, hundreds upon hundreds of lives. This other Fountain, it was literally within the heart of a city.

In tandem, they eased back on the intensity of their approach, until they were sure of their target. Rydan guided their right hands forward, stroking their combined fingers against the frame of the mirror. The perspective shifted, sliding to the left, angling down toward the lowest level of the distant room. Rora nodded as the mirror focused on a man, one seen from not quite directly behind; she recognized him, even from behind.

This, then, was Xenos, the mage she feared. Rydan studied the man, vaguely aware of Morganen gesturing at the edge of his vision, indicating that the shards of glass had been enchanted and were ready. The man in the mirror had dark brown, chin-length hair and olive, tanned skin, visible at the nape of his neck and at the rune-embroidered cuff of his loose-sleeved shirt, which draped back with each gesture of his free hand. His other arm was immersed past the elbow in the largest bubble-sphere of all, one that shimmered with half a hundred hues, most of them blue tinged.

Most, but not all. Rydan focused on that with widened eyes. Whatever spell the infiltrator was using, he hadn't completely taken over the Menomon Fountain . . . and that meant it was possible that Guardian Sheren was still alive. Squeezing Rora's hands, he broke off at the end of the next verse.

"Keep chanting!" he ordered her as she started to falter. "Hold it there, keep it going until I say otherwise, but do *not* connect to his Fountain."

Not wanting the Verenai mage anywhere near her, not if he could take over Fountains, Rora nodded. Carefully chanting the strange, rhythmic words, she pushed the channel of magic up to the edge of the odd, pillar-strewn chamber, matching it to the viewpoint of the mirror, until a reddish gold haze started to form over their view. Easing back just a little, she held it there as Rydan lifted their joined arms up over her head, forming a circle.

Abandoning her hands there, Rydan gently tipped her head back. He was pleased by her steady chanting, by the way she had pushed the energies all the way to the edge of the other Fountain Hall, but not forcefully enough to attract their foe's attention. It also pleased him that she closed her eyes, trusting him completely. Snapping his right hand out, he activated the charm Morganen had laid on the pieces; with the left, he traced a sigil in the air between the curve of her arms, careful to keep their bodies touching.

Rora felt her magic swirling, pouring out of her under his guidance, and clung to her chanting for an anchor. She heard a rustling noise. Cracking open her eyes, she watched a shimmering stream of silvered shards, each no bigger than a fingernail paring, streaming into the vortex he had opened over her head. Eyes quickly closed, she concentrated on holding the pipeline of energy stable.

The swirling of her Fountainway eased and faded. Matching the curve of her arms, Rydan lowered them to her sides. He nudged the back of her head, making her lift it and open her eyes. In the mirror, the shimmering stream of shattered glass spread rapidly across the chamber. All around the other room, the bubbles draped in net-scrolls were dimming. Xenos seemed to be shouting and gesturing with both hands, one embedded in the largest sphere, the other slashing forcefully, carving burning runes in the air.

Behind the curve of his back and arm, the slivers darted

into the event horizon of the Menomon singularity. It took the other mage a moment to realize what was happening, then he jerked his arm halfway free of the largest bubble in what looked like shock, before twisting to face the mirror's viewpoint. Brown eyes widened, and power crackled visibly around his free hand.

"Now!" Rydan shouted.

Rora reacted instinctively. The chanting stopped, but her intention didn't. It changed, solidifying into a protective wall. Orange lightning slammed into the air in front of the mirror's viewpoint, but grounded itself before it could touch anything, let alone damage it. The Verenai mage bared his teeth in a snarl—and flinched in the next moment.

Each of the bubble-spheres around the room roiled abruptly, turbulently. Every surface glittered madly. Even the main sphere boiled with shards of glass, and the mage's mouth opened wide in a soundless, agonized scream. Rora gasped as he jerked his left arm completely free; the swirling mass of shards had bloodied him nearly to the elbow. She covered her mouth, feeling sick.

Rydan quickly grabbed her arms, focusing his power through hers, whispering to keep the link between the two locations open, in case his brothers couldn't summon up enough offensive spells to end the bloodied man's invasive reign. If she hadn't faltered, he would have attacked further, but he didn't blame her for it. The bleeding mess of the other mage's arm was gruesome to look at.

Off in the distance, at the far end of the Fountain Hall, the sounds of magical battle had faded, replaced by questioning voices, and a shout of Dominor's name. Footsteps hurried their way, but Rora couldn't tear her eyes from the mirror long enough to see who was approaching. The others didn't have the mirror at their end of the chamber; they didn't see the reddened mess of Xenos' arm, what she and Rydan had done.

Nor did they see the short arrow shafts that slammed into his body, jerking him sideways from the impact, one, two, three. Letting go of her arm, Rydan quickly brushed the mirror frame, readjusting the angle. A round doorway came into view, filled with six figures. Three knelt in front, and three stood in back, each one clad in strange, close-fitted gray leather. Each helmed, masked warrior wielded a crossbow that was aimed at the mage in the distant chamber.

Not arrows, then, but crossbow bolts, Rora realized. The weapons were powerful and relatively easy to aim, but cumbersome to load quickly. Not many women on the Plains chose to wield them, even if bolts were easier to carve from the limbs of the wind-stunted trees found on the edges of the Plains than the longer shafts required for arrows. Three more bolts shot out, striking their target, and the mage Xenos toppled out of the cheval mirror's field of view just as Saber, Morganen, and Mara reached that end of the Fountain Hall.

Rora lifted her fingers toward her sister, but didn't speak a greeting; her attention was focused on the other chamber. As she and the others watched, the bubbles slowed their roiling. Glittering slivers of glass filtered out of the spheres and fell to the floor of the multilevel chamber. The warriors invaded the room, taking up defensive positions behind some of the sphere-peaks for crude cover. A short figure in formfitting blue leather—fitted well enough to leave no doubt that she was female, despite the extremely short, unfeminine cut of her hair—strode into the Menomon Fountain chamber, arms snapping up and light shooting out of her palms.

Rydan quickly stroked the frame, adjusting the view to take in her target. Between one breath and the next, Xenos' glassy-eyed body stiffened and crystalized under the sparkling beam of her spell. The woman curled up her lip in disgust and slammed her fist down while she was still a body length away. Without even touching him, somehow she shattered him, making Rora cover her mouth again.

Turning slowly around, the short woman surveyed the chamber, taking in the shattered bits of glass on the floor. One of the helmed warriors came up to her, saying something. She gestured curtly, and he headed for the door. Rydan realized the man's breath had steamed visibly in close proximity to her. The woman faced in their direction, blue eyes scanning each bubble-topped stalagmite . . . then snapped to their location as if she could see them, though the corner of another mirror was visible in the background, off to the right.

Cupping Rora's hands, Rydan formed her fingers and thumbs into a circle and focused their combined magic through it. The moment coppery mist appeared on the surface of the mirror, he spoke.

"This is Guardian Rydan. Where is Guardian Sheren? Is she still alive?"

The woman twitched, narrowed her eyes, then eased forward warily. Her lips moved, but nothing was heard. Grimacing, Rydan abandoned Rora's hands. Touching the mirror, he swung the view around, positioning it so that it faced the other mirror. They weren't the same shape, and that mirror showed a reflection of copper fog, but that didn't matter. Guiding the viewpoint of his mirror carefully forward, Rydan aligned them and muttered the first scrying-connection spell.

The mirror bucked in its frame. Morganen, hair looking as if it had been fluffed with static electricity, reached out to steady the looking glass as it rocked again, its surface vibrating visibly. Kelly came up beside them, free to enter the Hall now that their magical combat was over. She glanced at the mirror. "What's happening?"

"We'll find out. Trevan! Koranen! Help Dominor and get that communications stream stabilized," Morg called out to the far end of the long, pillar-lined room. One more shudder passed through the silvered glass, making it buzz ominously, then it settled down. The coppery mist cleared abruptly, as if blown away by a sudden gust of wind, revealing a view of a couple of bubble-topped stalagmites and a stretch of curved wall. Morg rubbed his fingers over the frame and spoke a command word. *"Anan!"*

Sound came across the connection, voices babbling in a foreign tongue. Rora grimaced as her ears twitched, adjusting to the new language. The short woman stepped into view, capturing their attention. At this angle, the light from the bubbles fell mostly on her face, allowing them to see that her eyes matched the blue of her strange, tight-fitted clothes and that her inch-long hair boasted auburn highlights.

"I said, who are you? Are you behind this attack? Can you even hear me?" she demanded quickly, blue eyes flicking from face to reflected face.

"I am Guardian Rydan, a colleague of Guardian Sheren," Rydan stated, subtly shifting Rora to his side, so that she wasn't quite so prominently placed anymore. "Where is she? Is she still alive?"

"Barely. She was poisoned," the woman admitted tersely. "By *you*?"

"Hardly," Saber stated. "If you haven't noticed, we just *saved* your Fountain."

"*That* will be judged by the inquest. The Council is demanding answers—and you *will* answer."

"I want to speak with Guardian Sheren, before we'll answer anything," Rydan countered. At her narrowed eyes, he added, "Given what just happened, how do we know *you* don't have anything to do with this mess?"

The woman planted her hands on her hips, staring at him for a long moment. The corner of her mouth finally quirked up. "A touch and point, to you. The Healers are tending to her right now. I don't know how she dragged herself to the doors or summoned up enough strength to let us in, given the condition she's in, but she should be free to speak with you soon enough."

"Is she being checked for other health problems?" Rydan asked next. "She mentioned heartburn, dizziness, and sweating when we last spoke. Those could be signs of a heart attack, too."

"I'll ask. In the meantime, this location is off-limits. You may leave the mirrors linked, but not open—and you'll get rid of that mist-snake," the woman added, gesturing off to her left. "I don't know what it is, and I don't want it in here. I'll contact *you* when Guardian Sheren is ready to speak. Comply, and I'll tell the Council your intentions *may* be benign."

"You're not exactly trusting, are you?" Kelly observed dryly.

The short-haired woman arched one of her brows. "Would *you* be, given what just happened in here?"

"And I believe that's a point for *you*," Kelly quipped wryly.

Again, the corner of the other woman's mouth curled up slightly, showing that she had a sense of humor despite her mostly no-nonsense attitude. "True. Now, back off and wait. I will contact you later, if nothing else."

Morg looked at the others, his gaze finally settling on Kelly. She nodded, and he rubbed his thumb over the frame. The noise from the other side of the connection ceased, though the visual link remained.

Rydan cupped Rora's upper arms again. "Time to close the probe from your Fountain. Picture the energy retreating, but leaving an empty conduit behind, in case we ever need to use it again."

"Couldn't they use the conduit themselves to spy on us?" Rora asked, worried about that possibility.

"Just imagine a series of doors closing and locking at intervals, as you retract the energy. You supply the power, and I'll shape the barricades."

Nodding, Rora closed her eyes, isolating her inner senses so that she could visualize and focus her magic. She had to banish the image of the bloodied Aian mage stiffening and shattering, first. It seemed odd that she could concentrate better in the midst of urgency and chaos than she could in the aftermath of their battle, but there it was. Thankfully, when she felt Rydan joining his efforts to hers, chanting softly in her ear, it became easier to focus her powers.

As soon as their task was complete, she turned to face Rydan. He could feel her need to seek comfort in her husband's embrace and knew she was still upset over the violence she had seen. Wrapping his arms around her, he tucked her head against his shoulder and just held her. In the distance, he could hear the others speaking; among them was Dominor, relieving him that his thirdborn brother was alright.

It wasn't until Dom drew near, floating in a seated position and being guided by both Trevan and Koranen, that Rydan saw just what sort of toll the Fountain had taken on his brother. Dominor looked haggard, with a grayish cast to his skin, dark circles under his eyes, and a hollowed look to his body, as if he had lost fifteen or twenty pounds abruptly.

"What happened to you?" Rydan asked, concerned. Emotionally, Dominor felt fine to Rydan's inner senses, but physically his sibling looked awful.

Trevan answered for Dominor, who had a dazed look in his blue eyes. "The bastard somehow hooked into Dominor's life force as well as the Fountain's power. He'll recover, but we need to get him to Mariel."

"And to a decent meal," Koranen added wryly, giving their brother a worried look.

Lifting a hand, Rydan summoned a will-o'-the-wisp. Unlike the one he had summoned for Dominor months ago, this one would float at a reasonable walking pace, not at a run. Dom wasn't in any condition to be floated swiftly. "This will lead you back to the surface."

Dominor blinked, licked his lips, and focused on Rydan's face. "Fountain . . . will respond to you. Made sure of it."

The two redheaded males barely waited for Rydan to acknowledge that fact with a nod before they guided their brother's floating body out of the Hall. Mara went with them, hovering at Trevan's side.

Kelly faced the others. "Well. *That* was exciting. Let's not do this again, shall we?"

"Agreed." Saber eyed the newly wedded couple. "That was an inventive tactic, Rydan. But why didn't you strike to kill while he was distracted and vulnerable?"

Rydan flicked his gaze to his wife; her face was still buried against his throat, silently answering his sibling's inquiry.

"Right . . . Morg, I want you to stay here, just in case things go southward and your help is needed again," Saber instructed his youngest sibling. "I don't know what you did, but you deflected every attack thrown at us at the end of the battle—try to figure out how to replicate it and write it down, just in case it's something the rest of us can learn. Rydan, Arora . . . good job."

"Quite," Kelly agreed. She peered at the chamber. "So . . . this is where the Convocation of the Gods would be held, if and when we can pull it off? We'll have to haul in a bunch of chairs and benches, if it is."

Rydan opened his mouth to answer her, then closed it, thinking. Lifting his chin at the far end of the Hall, he said instead, "There should be an amphitheater on the other side of that far wall, if my sense of direction is right. But it's not that easily reached from here. The old tales spoke of the Gods seated in a sort of audience or council chamber around the would-be petitioners brought before them at each Convocation. I could carve an opening of some kind, a doorway or corridor to that theater, so that when the Gateway is finally opened, it's just a short walk away."

"That sounds like a plan, though I wouldn't mind seeing it, first," Kelly told him. "And start figuring out where we're going to put Arora's spare Fountain. Not to mention what we're going to do with it when we're not using it to conjure up a mass of Patron Deities every so often."

"To do that, we'll need to know more about the extraction process," Rydan warned her. "Not to mention *how*, exactly, one opens the Gateway."

"We still only have a partial record of what needs to be done," Rora added, finally turning in Rydan's arms so she could join the conversation. She had reached a level of equanimity with the violence she had seen. Shooting arrows into a would-be bandit at a distance wasn't quite the same as this fight had been. "Serina was going to ask some discreet questions about finding a complete version of the scroll, through some Great Library somewhere."

"Guardian Sheren was also going to go looking through her own archives for a possible copy," Rydan said. "But that will depend on whether or not she survives her ordeal."

"Give her our best wishes for a speedy recovery, then," Kelly said.

"Keep an eye on these people, Rydan," Saber ordered. "If this other Guardian falls, her next replacement might not be that much better than the usurper was. Dominor is in no shape to defend Nightfall at the moment . . . and since Morganen *refuses* to help, you're our next line of defense."

Saber's tone spoke volumes of his frustration with his youngest sibling, but Morg merely shrugged. "I have my reasons." Absently, he swiped at his fluffed-out hair, trying to flatten it. "If you'll kindly take note, you didn't *need* me to step up and take over the Fountain, so there's no need to fuss."

Rydan, eyeing Morg's unsuccessful attempts to manage his light brown hair, suspected his youngest sibling needed to discharge some of the energies he had taken at the end of the fight. "Morg, go check the far end of the Hall for any structural damage left over from the fight. I didn't invite you down here just so you could destroy the place, so if you find anything . . . repair it before I see it."

Morg wrinkled his nose at the command, but Rydan could feel his brother's gratitude for the excuse as the younger mage walked away.

Kelly smirked, watching Morg still trying to smooth down his hair. "He looks like he got hit with a static hex or something."

"He'll survive," Rydan dismissed, covering for his sibling. He conjured another will-o'-the-wisp to guide the others out. "Now, kindly remove yourselves to the surface. We may need to stay here to watch the mirror and wait for Guardian Sheren, but I would like to be alone with my wife. Follow the wisp and do not deviate from its path. Now is not the time for sightseeing."

"Just so long as we *do* get the two silvara tour, at some point," Saber warned him, before offering Kelly his arm and following the floating wisp of light.

Watching them go, Rydan sighed roughly once they were out of sight. "I'm going to need to find another place to sleep, if they're going to come trampling through here, in the future."

"As far as I know, all of the caverns I've seen are under the northern mountain range. We could always try digging something out of the southern range, to get you far enough away," Rora offered. "But *some* social interaction would be healthy, too."

"At this rate, we'll be moving back into the northwest wing, up above," he muttered. "It, at least, holds nothing of fascination or worth."

"On the contrary, I think it would hold something very valuable. At least, valuable to me, if you were living there," Rora told him.

Not wanting to argue the matter—since for him, the converse would also apply—Rydan kissed her.

TWENTY

Four days later, Rora knocked on the door, interrupting the voices inside the council room. At a muffled command to enter, she willed the door open and stepped through. Kelly nodded a greeting, motioning with one hand for her to take a seat. "Come in, Arora. Amara, you were saying?

"This will make their third trip to the mainland. Marcas is going to try to convince more sailors to relocate, but not many of them will have their own boats," Mara related as her twin sat down next to her, near one of the ends of the *V*-shaped table. "And it's boats we're needing. He can only bring across two households at a time, three at most if they don't have many belongings, without overloading his ship. But he says they're lining up at the dock in Orovalis.

"Before he sets sail, he wants to take some sort of payment or letter of marque so that he can hire a much larger vessel to transport more people. As it is, he can't take anyone that has more than a few small farm animals, a few geese, or chickens, or maybe a couple goats."

"Saber?" Kelly asked.

"I can't wait until Serina gives birth and comes back," her husband muttered, opening the ledger book in front of him. "We are definitely going to run out of things to sell, at this rate. Remind me to write a letter to the Council about shipping us Artifacts from the Corvis and Devries estates tonight. Marcas and Augur can take it across to the Sea Commerce sub-office in Orovalis City when they set sail tomorrow . . . along with . . . four crates of lightglobes? That should be enough in trade to hire a ship large enough to carry thirty families at a time for, what, a week?"

"I can make three times that many globes in a week," Koranen agreed. "It's a fair price, considering."

"Word spreads fast, in that sort of community," Mariel told the others. "It'll spread fast in any persecuted group, however subtle—or technically illegal—the persecution. It's like the few men who escape from the lands of Mandare back into Natallia. They may not want to discriminate against women, but because of the war, no one in Natallia will trust them, because the Mandarites will sometimes send men into Natallia to try and stir up anti-gynarchy sentiments, so the real refugees have to keep heading east to the Gucheran border."

"At least they can flee to Guchere," Saber returned. "Katan is self-contained, its own continent; the Western Ocean is even bigger than the Eastern, and the Sun's Belt Reefs are a difficult crossing at the best of times."

"Yes, but Guchere is tired of being invaded, even if it's peacefully, and they're rightfully leery of Mandarite philosophy sneaking onto their lands in the form of subversives wandering around in the guise of refugees. So they've been turning them north more and more, forcing them across the water to Sundara," Mariel said.

"That's one of the things I'm here to report about," Rora interjected, drawing attention to herself.

"Go on," Kelly urged her.

"Dominor just received a Fountain call from Serina. The aether over Natallia is apparently not doing well right now, so Mother Naima has arranged for a group of war refugees to camp at the base of the mountains and wait for a break in the weather. As soon as it's clear enough, she says she'll open a mirror-Gate to the top long enough for them to ascend, but she can only host them overnight before they need to be sent on to us."

Saber glanced at his wife. "I've never met a Gucheran, but

I think I'd have to agree with them. I'm not sure I'd want refugees from Mandare, either. Not if some of them are spies."

"Arora, you said yesterday that Rydan was making several Truth Stones for sale, right?" Kelly asked her, and received a nod. "Have Rydan send over several Stones as a hosting gift to the Mother Superior, with the stipulation that she keep and use a few of them on the refugees, before they enter Koral-tai.

"Have her query them about their intentions. If they honestly just want a place to settle and some land to farm, or they have a trade they want to ply, they can come across. If they lie about not being spies . . . well, then that's a problem for Natallia, not for us. Um . . . earmark a couple of those Truth Stones for Marcas and Augur to use, as well. What else did you have?" Kelly asked as Rora took the charcoal stick and sheet of paper Mara passed.

Rora stalled a few moments, writing a note about Truth Stones and Natallian spies. "Well . . . Serina finally heard back from the Mendhites."

"She has?" Mara asked, glancing at her twin. "You don't sound like that's good news, though."

"Well, they refuse to hand over a copy of the Scroll of Living Glory, so I'd say . . . no," Rora returned dryly.

"But they *do* have it, right?" Trevan asked her from Mara's other side.

"Oh, they have it. But they refuse to hand over a copy . . . if we cannot prove we have a true need for it," Rora told them. "Which means telling them that we have a living host, which Serina, Dominor, Rydan, and I all refuse to do."

"You'd better still count me on that list," Mara reminded her sister, golden eyes meeting green. "Just because we've each married and settled down doesn't stop me from protecting you."

"Count all of us as your protectors," Saber amended. "The only reason why they'd demand to know the location of a living host first is so that they can kidnap that living host. As far as the rest of the world is to know, we *don't* have one, yet . . . but we're counting on the Gods providing one for us, since Kelly's petition for an independent, pantheistic nation was clearly accepted by Them."

"That's how Serina said she explained it to them when

she heard the terms, but they won't budge," Rora agreed. "No host, no scroll."

"What about the other chance?" Kelly asked.

Rora shook her head. "Nothing since yesterday's report. Guardian Sheren is stable, but not well enough to return to her Fountain . . . and the people guarding her refuse to go looking for anything for us, without her personally vouching for Rydan as an ally. Which she can't do until she's well enough to come back to their Fountain Hall. She *was* poisoned, with something called *otra vurasifica*."

"It's a mushroom that grows in the forests of Verena, which is where that mage was from," Mara explained to the others. "It's only poisonous to mages—and the more powerful the mage, the more deadly it is—but the victim has to eat a lot of it to die quickly. It's a slow poison."

"That's why it took her so long to fade, and for Xenos to infiltrate and usurp her Fountain. She did get an antidote made in time, so she won't get any worse," Rora said. "But she's not young, so her recovery will be correspondingly slow."

"You are keeping someone on that mirror-link at all times, right?" Kelly asked.

Rora nodded. "Morganen's watching it right now. Rydan's already gone to bed, and I'll be joining him as soon as I'm done here."

"Good. If the Great Mendhi Library refuses to loan us what we want, and we can't get an intact version out of Koraltai, we're just going to have to hope the Gods of this world take pity on us and put a legible copy into our hands. *Someone* has a copy of that scroll," Kelly said. "If it isn't this Guardian Sheren, then we'll need to link directly to Aiar itself, and Guchere, and any other kingdoms or continents we can reach."

"We'll need to start making contacts around the world anyway, to get all the names of the Patron Deities that are out there," Evanor agreed.

"Remember, even if we can't get our hands on a copy of that Scroll, *someone* figured out how to extract a Fountain from a living host without killing him, back when that scroll was first written," Trevan said. "If they can do it once without any help, we can always try to figure it out for ourselves."

"No insult to your intelligence or abilities is intended, Trevan, but I think I'd rather hope that we find a method that's already proven to work," Rora retorted. "It's not *your* life on the line, after all. Now, unless you have something else for me to take back to Rydan, Morganen, or Dominor, I have nothing else to report."

"Just the bit about the Truth Stones," Kelly reminded her husband.

Saber held up a finger, forestalling Rora before she could leave. "How many of those Stones could Rydan have ready by tonight? Depending on how many would-be settlers are waiting for them at Orovalis, Marcas and Augur might need to hire a second ship."

"How many do you want? We've been enchanting them by the dozens while waiting for news about the Guardian of Menomon," Rora told him, then shrugged. "It helps pass the time."

Saber snapped the ledger book shut, glaring at her. "*When* were the two of you going to inform me of this? Rydan *knows* we need more Artifacts to sell!"

"Well, I'm reporting it now, aren't I?" she defended quickly. "We'll get you a box of them by tonight, I promise. Can I go now?"

"Go," Kelly told her, quelling her husband with a hand laid on his arm. "Sleep well, both of you . . . when you get there."

Blushing—and smiling—Rora rose and bowed herself out of the room.

Hope turned away from the whiteboard, hands on her hips and a wry expression on her tanned face. "I can't believe you actually drugged him!"

Morganen gestured with two fingers. The pen floated across the board, scribbling his reply. *It worked, didn't it?*

"That's no excuse, and you know it," she chided him, glancing at his handwriting before looking in his direction again.

The outworlder woman had an uncanny knack for sensing where Morganen's mirror intersected her world, though she rarely found the right spot to seem to be looking into his aqua eyes. This time, her brown gaze missed him by about six inches to the right. Morg wondered what it would be like to have her eyes focus on *him*, one of these days.

Lifting his other hand, he used the eraser to remove the strange ink from the board before writing more. It was an awkward system of communication, but he was used to it by now. Because of the peculiar nature of transdimensional openings—especially into a world with so little magic of its own—he could hear her voice, but he would have had to shout uncomfortably loud for her to have a chance of hearing him.

Writing was much easier, if awkward and power-consuming. With so little magic available in the other world, Morg had to expend more than he could have grasped. It was a good thing he *could* grasp ambient energies, because he wouldn't give up these conversations with her, however awkward they were.

Still, it worked out in the end. I expected him to wake up and be aware she wasn't a dream, he scribed on the white-board. *I didn't expect her to ambush him in his sleep.*

"But he didn't, did he?" Hope retorted tartly. "He grabbed her without asking her, making you a very guilty accomplice to an inadvertent crime."

She didn't mind.

Hope threw her hands up into the air. That caused the skin-tight shirt she was wearing—painted with a plain white mask and a red rose—to ride up her stomach, baring her navel. Between that and the fitted trousers she wore, Morganen admired the view, almost missing her words.

"So *that* makes it better? And how did Rydan react to all of this? *When* he finally woke up, that is," she added wryly.

He was very upset, though neither of them had gone terribly far. Morg erased that after a pause, then added, *He later led me to believe he'd violated her in full.*

Hope read that with a smirk. "Devious. I trust he made you suffer?"

I was literally sick over it.

"I *knew* I liked him from the very start . . ."

Morganen frowned at her odd statement. Rydan *had* a wife. Erasing the board with a few swipes of his left hand, he scrawled with his right, *You are mine, not his!*

Her hands fell from her hips, her mouth sagging open.

Blushing furiously, Morganen raised the eraser. Hope grabbed it, wrestling it back down before he could remove the accidental proof of his jealousy. He slashed with the pen instead, scribbling out the words, only to have her grab the white-and-black cylinder as well.

"Oh, no, you don't! You are *not* taking that back!" She couldn't completely control either item. Releasing them, Hope returned her fists to her hips and spun, glaring at him through the aether. This time, her gaze landed firmly somewhere over his left eyebrow. "Morg, credit me with *some* intelligence? If everything has worked out between them in the end, then I take it he's happily captivated by her, right?"

Removing the crossed-out words, he wrote, *Yes. Very.*

"Then why would I be interested in him, at least like that?" Cocking her hips, she gave the air past his left ear a coquettish look. "Besides, I have *you*. What girl in her right mind would say 'no' to a transdimensional courting?"

You'd be surprised, Morg scrawled, thinking of her friend Kelly's initial reaction to being transported to his world. He started to write more, but a chime from off to the side caught his attention. *Hold on . . . I have a message from the other mirror.*

"Trust her," Hope stated quickly, glancing at his message. "I don't know who it is, or what they want, but . . . my instincts are telling me to tell you to trust her, whoever she is."

I will. Your instincts have indeed helped me so far, he agreed. Cancelling the levitation spells, he moved over to the cheval mirror still attached to the northern communication ribbon. He had brought his favorite mirror down here with him so that he could occupy his time at least somewhat productively while waiting for more news from Menomon. So far, communication from the other Fountain had been sporadic. At least the short, leather-clad woman centered in the mirror was familiar with him.

"Morganen of Nightfall," she greeted, nodding her head, with its crop of short auburn hair. "I apologize for any interruption."

"Danau of Menomon. It's nothing I couldn't set aside. Do you have news of Guardian Sheren's condition?" he asked her.

"Improving, but slowly. It will be at least a turning of Sister

Moon before the Healers think she will be strong enough to step into the Fountain again." She hesitated a moment, then gave him a wry smile. "I'm afraid the Council has come to a decision, regarding the incident. I don't think you will like it very much."

"What did they decide?" Morg asked, curious.

"They're going to seal the city against outsiders. Which includes the Fountain. No one in, and no one out. At least, not voluntarily." She folded her arms across her blue-clad chest. "They're idiots of the highest degree, if you ask me, but they're also xenophobes, and in command of the city."

"Why would they want to do that?" he asked her.

"The idea is to limit how many outsiders get into Menomon. They can't completely cut off those in dire need . . . but they want to interrogate everyone, to discern their motivations. I don't agree with some of the more extreme measures being proposed, nor of the persecution of people who had no choice but to either come here or die," Danau told him, tightening her arms across her chest, "but they're in charge, and they do have a point."

Morg lifted a brow, wondering what situation could arrange such a choice. "What point would that be?"

"When the outsider, Xenos, grabbed control of our Fountain, he drained away a lot of its magics in attacking your own wellspring. Especially at the very end of the battle. Most of the Fountain's magic is used to shelter and protect the city. By draining it, he nearly collapsed the wards sheltering us from an unpleasant death."

Carefully resisting the urge to blush, Morganen skirted around the subject of who had really drained those energies at the end of the last battle. "So this Council thinks that if they seal off the city, they can avoid another attack on the Fountain, or at least hunt down and find someone who might think of attacking it?"

"That's the idea. They don't care that cutting us off from outside contact means that certain foods will stop coming into the city. They don't care that cutting us off from the outside means cutting off access to freshwater as well—they *say* that the Aquamancy Guild can keep up with the demand for freshwater, extracting it from the sea as needed," she added, pacing a little in her agitation, though she kept her gaze on the mirror and Morganen. "Most of them have only thought about the short-term needs and not of the long-term consequences of obtaining freshwater that way. The exterior crops are going to be damaged because of this. I can see it now."

"You said you have an Aquamancy Guild?" Morg inquired. "Would there happen to be a number of single female Aquamancers in this Guild?"

Danau snorted. "A dozen unwed, and two dozen more who are, give or take. It's a common ability here. Why do you want to know?"

"I may have need of an Aquamancer or three in the near future."

"Good luck," she scoffed. "The city will be sealed for months, while they go on their little motivation hunt. Once Sheren gets back to her full strength, she may be able to knock some sense into their heads, but that won't be for at least three months. Even then . . . I don't see the Council budging out of their mistrust of outworlders for at least *two* turns of Sister Moon. Idiots."

"How soon will the city be closed off from outside contact?" Morganen asked her next.

"Technically, at the end of this conversation. Which reminds me," she added. "Guardian Rydan said he was looking for a Scroll of Living Glory?"

"Yes—you have a copy of it?" he wanted to know, anticipation rising within him. "A complete, intact copy?"

"The good news . . . yes. The bad news . . . the Council refuses to give it up. They don't trust outsiders. They're idiots, but I believe I already mentioned that?"

"Yes, you did," he muttered darkly. "I'd call them even worse than that, if I weren't in the presence of a lady."

"Well, I'm sorry. Really. Until Sheren is strong enough to reclaim her mastery of the Fountain, you're out of luck. She's given me instruction on how to close all of the outland connections, which includes this mirror . . . but she also wanted you to know that she'll hold on to a copy of the scroll for you, and slip it to you when she's feeling better. Presuming she recovers on schedule, she'll be able to knock sense back into their heads a few months from now, with any luck."

"We could use it. Danau . . . if anything happens to her, would you make sure we get a copy of that scroll? Just in case?" he asked.

Unfolding her arms, she shifted her hands back to her hips, giving him a skeptical look. "Why? What's so important about that scroll that you have to have it?"

"Nightfall is a new kingdom. An incipient kingdom," he explained. "But not your normal sort of new kingdom. Our Queen won her year-and-a-day incipient status on a pledge in the names of all the Gods and Goddesses . . . which we're interpreting to mean They want us to re-invoke the Convocation of the Gods."

Her mouth dropped open. Blinking, she finally narrowed her blue eyes warily, finding her voice. "You're joking."

"About as much as your Council is, regarding the sealing of your city against all outside influences," he retorted dryly. "We don't know much about the steps required, but we do know we have to gather all the names of the current Gods and Goddesses out there, the kingdoms They're Patrons of . . . and that the information we need to re-create the Convocation is found on the Scroll of Living Glory.

"I do hope you're right about Sheren being able to knock some sense into their heads within the next six months," Morganen added soberly. "The Gods Themselves clearly think it's the right thing to do. If They didn't, They wouldn't have allowed Kelly to make her claim. But the only other place we know of that has a copy of the scroll also refuses to share it with us. Either they don't want the Convocation reopened, or they want to hoard the very idea for themselves, despite how the Gods clearly favor Nightfall. So we *need* the copy that Guardian Sheren promised us."

She looked down for a long moment, then sighed. "I'll see what I can do to rattle a few skulls myself, though I dislike politics. But not entirely for free. I may need some sort of leverage to convince the Council to reopen the city's borders to the outside world—about the only thing going in your favor is that this city is too xenophobic to want to reestablish the Convocation itself . . . not to mention too awkwardly placed."

"What did you have in mind for that favor?" Morg inquired

cautiously. "I can't promise much without consulting with Her Majesty, first."

"Don't worry. I'm mostly just thinking along the lines of fresh food, which will become a priority in a few months," she dismissed. "Of course, that's presuming you have it in sufficient quantity."

"We're working on reclaiming the old, abandoned orchards, but I can't guarantee how much will be harvestable. Certainly not as soon as three months from now, not unless you want sprouts and shoots sent your way. Most of the harvest we did manage to collect got shipped off the island at the end of autumn," he warned her. "The only 'food' we have available in huge amounts year-round are the salt blocks from the desalination plant."

"Desalination plant?" Danau asked quickly, palms slipping off her hips. "Are we talking about the fabled Desalinator of Aquamancer Tanaka Zhou Fen?"

That surprised Morg. "You've heard of him?"

She snorted, fists going back to her hips. "Of course! It's legendary in the Aquamancy Guild, one of the most famous Permanent Magics in our lexicon—actually, that would be *perfect* for my needs," Danau added, switching from sardonic to thoughtful. "Cutting off all outside contact means cutting off more than half the freshwater that supplies the city . . . and *that* means I'll have a compelling argument to contact you sooner, rather than later.

"*I* don't believe in cutting off all outside contact. It's not healthy, physically, economically, or socially," she dismissed. "Unfortunately, I may be a power in the Guild, but I'm not on the Council. I don't have any control over the city wards—you're lucky we've been able to talk this long, but then the Fountain is its own separate system." Squaring her shoulders, she faced him. "Can you *promise* me that I can have access to the Desalinator? Enough to study its secrets?"

"If you can get the other three filtration tanks working again, yes, I think I can swing at least that much," Morg promised her.

That made her frown. She tipped her auburn head. "They're not working?"

"There was a Curse laid on the island, back when Aiar

Shattered. Three of the tanks dried up instantly, and the fourth is running at a mere fraction of its full capacity. I tried running salt water through one of the dry tanks, back when we first came to the Isle, but nothing happened, and none of us is an Aquamancer . . . which is why I wanted to ask you about them," Morganen hedged. It was the truth, for all it was only part of the truth. "If you can promise a group of Aquamancers are sent here to study and repair it—most of them single females—I'm pretty sure I can convince Queen Kelly to let you crawl all over it."

"Why single females?" Danau inquired skeptically.

"It's just a part of the Curse afflicting the island," he dismissed. "The Prophecy that Cursed the island won't be lifted until certain things happen. One of them has been interpreted as a prediction of an unmarried female Aquamancer coming to Nightfall Isle," he explained. "The more unwed lady Aquamancers we host as guests, the greater our chances will be to end the Curse and fulfill Nightfall's Destiny."

"You'll pardon me if I hesitate to send my fellow Guildmembers into a potentially dangerous situation," she warned him dryly.

"Oh, no, it's not dangerous at all," Morg said. "It's just that the Curse involves a bit of . . . well . . . matchmaking."

Her postured stiffened, her expression losing some of its friendliness. "Matchmaking."

"Yes, but *entirely* of their own free will. The Prophecy in question isn't the kind that forces anything unwanted," he reassured her, pushing aside the thought of what he'd done to his sixthborn brother. "It would also give your Guild an excellent opportunity to study a piece of Permanent Magic in their own particular field of interest—an exchange of several favors, each mutually beneficial to the other side."

Distant knocking interrupted whatever she might have replied. Danau looked off to the side for a moment, then faced him with a rough sigh. "I'm out of time. Disengage your mirror from this one. The Guardian of Menomon will contact you when the Council's idiotic ban on outside influences is at an end. That much, I can promise you."

"Thank you for your help—"

The image in the mirror shifted to his own reflection mid-sentence. Sighing, Morganen dismantled the spells connecting it to the communication thread. It was too late to contact Rydan or Rora about the news from Menomon, but he didn't feel it would be right to tell anyone else the news he had just learned before telling the two of them. Moving back over to the other mirror, he re-enchanted the pen, lifting it back to the board. Hope looked up from the newspaper she was reading at the butcher block nearby, smiling first at the board, then in the general direction of his right shoulder.

Well, that was interesting. We can probably get the information we need, but we won't get it for up to half a year.

"Don't worry. You'll get everything you need. I can feel it," Hope promised him. Her gaze slid farther past his shoulder, then she started. "Oh! I'm going to be late for my class!"

Morganen scribbled on the whiteboard as she darted around the kitchen, gathering up the keys to the fancy magical wagon she drove, which wasn't actually magical, but he still didn't quite understand how it worked.

What class is that?

She caught sight of his query as she slung her coat over her arms, shrugging into it. "A gourmet class. I'm taking lessons over in the city—the far side of the city, so it's over an hour's drive from here—and I'm learning how to make chocolate from scratch. All sorts of chocolates, over the next few months."

Chocolate? What's that?

She grinned. "The food of the gods. In *any* realm. You know, I always wondered about Kelly's sanity," Hope added with a mock-thoughtful look. "She never really drooled over chocolate, unlike the majority of people in this world. I suppose that means she was *meant* to be in a universe without it . . . Funny, huh?" Touching one hand to her chest, she held out the other, fingers hovering close to the plane where his mirror intersected her world. "I'll be back in a few hours. Feel free to follow me with your mirror, if you want!"

Reaching through the mirror, Morganen pressed his palm to hers. He lived for these moments, however fleeting the contact. It was fleeting, too; she lingered for only a few seconds, before reluctantly pulling away and picking up her purse. Tempted though he was, Morg didn't follow her with the mirror. Instead, he picked up the jar of powder he had brought with the mirror, and cast a handful of the glittering grit on the mirror's surface, shouting the words that sealed the Portal connecting their two worlds.

If the way to Menomon was now sealed, a vigil over the Fountain mirror would no longer be needed. He would tell the others of Sheren's prognosis and the delay regarding the scroll later, probably over supper. Right now, it was more important to remove himself from proximity to the Fountain, even if he was currently as far as he could get from it while still being in the same vast chamber.

Hope was the only thing he ever wanted to tempt him.

The room was dimly lit at best. Rora could just make out the contours of a body lying on its side, a dark braid draped over one shoulder. Slipping into the dressing room as quietly as she could, she removed her clothes, dropped her dirty things into the basket, tucked her boots onto a low shelf, and hurried back into the bedroom. Rydan had activated the warming sigil, but not at a high level; the air was still a little nippy, shriveling her nipples.

Reaching the bed, she slid carefully between the covers, trying not to jostle her sleeping husband. A twist, and she scooted backward, wanting to spoon with him for warmth. It didn't quite go as planned. The moment she bumped into him, his hand caught her shoulder, pulling her firmly onto her back. Smiling, she didn't resist.

He hadn't been able to sleep without her. Somehow, Rora had supplanted his favorite pillow as the one thing he needed to cuddle in order to have a good night's sleep. Now that she was here, however, sleep was the last thing on his mind. Rydan shifted position, looming over her. Between one breath and the next, he blotted out the rest of the world with a slow, thorough, deep kiss. His hand slipped down her body, cupping her breast, caressing her belly, claiming her quickly dampening flesh.

Unlike their first encounter in this bed, he was very much aware that he wasn't dreaming. Given the enthusiastic way Rora moaned into his mouth and wrapped her arms around him, pulling him down on top of her, he had no doubts about her willingness this time, either. And just beneath his skin, his beast stretched and purred, happily tamed by this woman . . . the woman who had just crept into his Hall.

Rydan didn't give a damn how many hours had technically passed since the sun had risen. As far as he was concerned, it was dawn, and all was right in his world.

Song of the Sons of Destiny

The Eldest Son shall bear this weight:
If ever true love he should feel
Disaster shall come at her heel
And Katan will fail to aid
When Sword in sheath is claimed by Maid

The Second Son shall know this fate:
He who hunts is not alone
When claw would strike and cut to bone
A chain of Silk shall bind his hand
So Wolf is caught in marriage-band

The Third of Sons shall meet his match:
Strong of will and strong of mind
You seek she who is your kind
Set your trap and be your fate
When Lady is the Master's mate

The Fourth of Sons shall find his catch:
The purest note shall turn to sour
And weep in silence for the hour
But listen to the lonely Heart
And Song shall bind the two apart

The Fifth Son shall seek the sign:
Prowl the woods and through the trees
Before you in the woods she flees
Catch her quick and hold her fast
The Cat will find his Home at last

The Sixth Son shall draw the line:
Shun the day and rule the night
Your reign's end shall come at light
When Dawn steals into your hall
Bride of Storm shall be your fall

The Seventh Son shall he decree:
Burning bright and searing hot
You shall seek that which is not
Mastered by desire's name
Water shall control the Flame

The Eighth Son shall set them free:
Act in Hope and act in love
Draw down your powers from above
Set your Brothers to their call
When Mage has wed, you will be all."

—THE SEER DRAGANNA

PROLOGUE

A Bedtime Story

Three centuries ago, there lived in Florence a little girl beloved by her mother, father, and her young brother. Though she was not a princess, as many girls in these stories are, the wealth and power of her family made such distinctions irrelevant.

Unbeknownst to that happy family, their wealth and power also attracted a demon.

When the girl was seven years of age, her father journeyed to Rome and returned a changed man, as if someone else inhabited his skin. The words of love he'd once whispered to her mother became whispers of another sort, until she could bear him no longer. But when he thwarted each assassin she hired and the wounds he received quickly healed, when she poured enough poison to kill an army into his wine and he did not sicken or die, she poisoned her own cup.

Darkness settled over the household. Quiet and frightened, the girl and her brother went largely unnoticed by their father, except for when he subjected them to small torments for his amusement. They noticed him, however, watching his movements as mice will watch a cat until it has left the room, and they saw that he neither slept nor ate. In rare moments, they glimpsed the crimson glow of his eyes, the appearance of scales over his skin, and cloven hooves. They witnessed him move inhumanly fast and fly with bats' wings; they saw him battle and behead a woman who wore wings of white feathers. They watched, and as the years passed, the children understood what their father had become.

The girl shielded her brother from their father when she could, and was relieved when the boy's schooling took him from their home. Though the girl prayed for a similar escape through a good marriage, no happy fate awaited her; eager to form an alliance with a noble family, the demon arranged her wedding to an aged man known for his perversity. The girl fled and found sanctuary in an abbey whose prioress had once been a friend of her mother's, and who pitied her. The girl's father did not pursue her, and she realized that although he had power enough to kill an angel, he dared not cross the Church.

Five years passed. Protected and cloistered, the girl grew into a woman and took her solemn vows. Her brother rarely visited, but they corresponded often, and his missives brought her great joy. Over time, however, his infrequent journeys to the abbey stopped altogether. Dark and melancholy sentiments filled his letters, until they, too, stopped. She still wrote to him daily, begging him to visit her again. Five more years passed before he did, and he was in the company of her father.

They came at night. Despite the hour, she spoke with them in the convent parlor, through the grating that separated the cloister from the outside world. Even obscured by the grating, however, she could see the changes in her brother: his pale appearance, the hunger in his gaze, the teeth that would rival a wolf's—but the greatest alteration was his manner, which had become cold and cruel. He looked upon her with disdain, and she could see no love in him. Alarmed, she began to retreat, but with a few words, her father halted her escape. He told her the abbey offered no protection from her brother and offered her a terrible choice: either she would die by her brother's hand, or all of her sisters would.

Believing that her brother would stay his hand at the ultimate moment, she chose her own death. Though no longer a girl, she could not help but remember the love she and her brother shared when they had been young, and how they had protected one another. He'd been corrupted by her father, his soul twisted, but she could not believe her brother would truly kill her.

She was wrong. He used his fangs to tear open her throat. As her lifeblood poured onto the floor, she watched her brother walk away from the abbey, leaving her for dead. She heard her father laughing.

He did not laugh long. Just as he had once slain an angel, another appeared in a flare of white light and struck the demon's head from his shoulders. The angel lifted her from where she lay dying, told her he was named Michael, and he, too, offered her a choice: to become as he was, a protector who guarded humans against demons; or to die, and face what awaited her in the afterlife. She chose to live, was transformed and taken to Caelum, a shining realm of light and beauty. There, she learned they were not angels, but Guardians. She heard their story, and years later, she would tell it to children whom she called her own:

The Story of the Guardians

Many years ago, when the universe was old but the world was still new, Lucifer the Morningstar led his angels in a rebellion against Heaven. The rebels battled the seraphim, a small order of warrior angels loyal to Heaven, and they rent the skies with their war. But even as the rebels fought the seraphim, they struggled against each other for their place beneath Lucifer, and it was not long before duplicity and betrayal weakened the rebels' ranks. Though vastly outnumbered, the seraphim had but one purpose—to protect Heaven—and with their combined might, they crushed the rebels.

As their punishment, the rebel angels were transformed into demons. Angels were created of energy and light, and although they could assume the appearance of flesh, it was only an illusion; demons were stripped of their light and bound to flesh. They were turned away from Heaven and tossed into Hell, where they dwelled in darkness.

Some angels, uncertain which side to take in the war, hid in the dark corners of the universe until the victor became apparent. They emerged, swearing fealty to Heaven, but they were too late. The weakness of their faith and their hearts had been revealed. These angels were bound more closely to their flesh than demons, cursed with a deep hunger for blood and a need for sleep. They burned at the touch of sunlight. They were called nosferatu, "those who would not be tolerated."

This was the First Battle.

Demons could travel through the Gates to Earth, where humans lived under the protection of the seraphim and the Rules, which forbade both angels and demons from killing humans and from interfering with human free will. Demons could tempt mankind to sin, however, so that when men died, their souls would not ascend into Heaven, but be tortured in the Pit. From those tortured souls, Lucifer drew much of his power. He reigned in Hell, hoarding knowledge, using angelic symbols and blood to perform experiments on lower creatures from Earth and the Chaos realm, from which he drew even more power. He did not rule uncontested, however. The demon Belial, once Lucifer's lieutenant, promised his fellow demons a return to Grace and escape from their punishment if they helped him overthrow Lucifer's throne. Their civil war has been waged in Hell for millennia.

The seraphim, when they were not on Earth, resided in the realm of Caelum—a shining marble city situated in the middle of an endless sea. The creatures of light took human form when they walked among men, but the seraphim's overwhelming beauty and manner eventually led mankind to regard them as gods. Lucifer's jealousy was great. In his rage, he brought a dragon from Chaos to Earth, declaring another war upon the seraphim.

This war, the Second Battle, did not take place in the heavens, but on Earth. The demons rode the dragon, and the seraphim fell before it. The world burned. Mankind saw the battle taking place, and one man—Michael—struck his sword into the great beast's heart, slaying the dragon.

With the dragon defeated, the seraphim regrouped and were victorious. But the angels knew that they could never hide their nature from humans, and it would only lead to more Earth-bound wars between demons and angels, and offer a false truth to mankind. They were not gods.

So they bestowed upon Michael the power of the angels, and gave unto him the ability to transform any other human who sacrificed his life to save another from the temptations of demons and the terrors of the nosferatu. These men and women would be called Guardians. In addition to immortality, wings, strength, and the ability to alter their appearance, these Guardians were given individual Gifts to assist them in their battles. Because they had once been human, they could walk among men without drawing notice, but like the angels, Guardians had to follow the Rules; they could not interfere with human free will or kill humans, no matter how terrible some men were. If a Guardian broke the Rules, he either had to Fall and return to human form, or Ascend and go on to his afterlife.

Centuries passed, and although the numbers of Guardians increased, many also died. Their lives were fraught with danger, and they often had to defend themselves in combat against demons and nosferatu. They avoided bargains and wagers with demons; if left unfulfilled, a demon's bargain would trap their eternal soul in Hell's frozen field. And they fought to save as many humans as possible, all the while concealing their existence from them.

In time, the Guardians discovered that humans who had been attacked by nosferatu might be saved by drinking the creature's blood. Though much stronger than humans—and a vampire created from nosferatu blood was stronger than one transformed by another vampire's blood—they were weaker than Guardians and could not alter their shapes. Like the nosferatu, these transformed humans were vulnerable to daylight and suffered from a deep and powerful hunger—the bloodlust. Fearing discovery and persecution by humans, vampires formed secret communities, living among humans in their cities, but feeding only from each other.

The vampires' souls were not transformed; their characters were the same in undeath as they had been in life. The vampires were not bound by the Rules, just as nosferatu were not, and so the Guardians took upon themselves another task—to guard humans against vampires should the need arise. For the most part, Guardians allowed the vampires to live as they willed, but there were those vampires who had to be watched more closely than others, and who would be destroyed if they broke the Rules.

So the Guardians fought to keep the influence of those Above and Below from touching humanity. There is no end to this story; the Guardians are still fighting. They will keep fighting for as long as they exist.

When the girl heard this she was overjoyed, for it meant that although her brother had become a vampire, he could still be saved. His transformation had not corrupted his soul; the demon had. She persuaded Michael not to slay her brother and allow her the chance to undo what the demon had done.

She could not immediately begin, however—first, she had to complete one hundred years of training in Caelum. Those years were filled with hope. Even the discovery of her Gift to manipulate darkness and shadows, so painful to use beneath Caelum's sun-filled sky, did not diminish her happiness. After a century, she returned to Earth, her hope still bright within her chest.

It took almost two more centuries for her brother to kill that hope. Then he was killed, too.

And so the tale closes with the girl left alone and her hopes shattered, with no one to save—and the demon, though defeated, ultimately the victor. Unlike other stories, this does not have a happy ending.

Not yet.

ONE

The string quartet in the corner the ballroom slipped from a sleepy minuet into a sleepy waltz. Rosalia lifted her champagne flute to her lips to cover her sigh. Thank God for the demons. If not for their conspiring, boredom would have killed her by now.

The small circle of humans she'd joined burst into laughter. Rosalia smiled vacuously in response. She hadn't heard the joke, but no one at the gala would expect a reply, anyway. She'd changed her dark hair to a wispy, baby blond, donned a vapid expression over soft features, and paired them with an insubstantial pink dress for that very reason: she wouldn't be expected to talk. She only needed to stand and look pretty. So she stood with humans she didn't know in the center of a chateau ballroom, watching three of Belial's demons solidify an alliance.

Others watched them, too. Some humans glanced in their direction; some stared. Rosalia could not blame them. Like every demon she'd known, they'd disguised themselves in sinfully handsome human forms—sensual lips and blade-straight noses, black hair glinting under the crystal chandeliers, as if they'd each used an advertisement in a men's fashion magazine as a template. With a backdrop of priceless paintings mounted on gold-painted walls, they formed a would-be triumvirate with Bernard and Gavel as the base and Pierre Theriault at the top.

Of the three, Theriault ranked the highest in both Belial's army and Legion Laboratories, the corporation that both concealed and supported their activities on Earth. Two years ago, when the Gates to Hell had closed, preventing Belial from overseeing the demons that remained on Earth, Legion began to serve as a communication network. Through it, one of Belial's lieutenants issued orders and received reports—until he'd been slain by the Guardians. Now, with no clear successor to the lieutenant and no contact from Hell, Belial's demons were maneuvering for his position, and all of them were arrogant enough to imagine themselves in the spot. But if Bernard and Gavel thought they'd ride the wake of Theriault's ascent, they were as foolish as he was. Theriault's particular brand of arrogance bordered on stupidity.

No, Rosalia amended. Not *bordering* stupidity. He'd flung himself over that line the second he'd begun discussing the alliance in a public room, and using English instead of the demonic language. Good Lord, the idiocy. Though the chateau was just north of Paris, perhaps fifteen people out of the hundreds in the ballroom didn't understand at least rudimentary English.

Even if Theriault imagined that the string music floating over the room and the crowd's chatter would conceal their voices from humans, he hadn't made sure there weren't any Guardians or other demons in the vicinity. Theriault's psychic sweep, though strong enough for Rosalia to feel, hadn't penetrated her shields. At that shallow depth, her mind would seem no different from a human's.

Careless. Stupid. Rosalia had many reasons to slay the demons, but at this moment, making the consequences of that carelessness the last thing they ever saw was the most tempting reason to shove her swords through their eyes.

But she wouldn't slay them. Not tonight. She'd come to the gala to observe Theriault, and to judge how much of a threat he'd be if he led Belial's demons. Not much. But it hadn't been a wasted trip. She'd overheard repeated mention of one demon standing in Theriault's way, one he'd considered too powerful to take on alone: Malkvial.

She hadn't yet learned who Malkvial was, however. Rosalia didn't know many demons by their true name, only by the human identities they used. She needed to find this one out, soon, either by listening in on Theriault or by other means.

A soft crackle sounded in her ear, and her attention shifted. The noise indicated that Gemma had opened the microphone connecting the tiny receiver bud in Rosalia's ear to the surveillance van outside the chateau. Rosalia couldn't perform a psychic sweep without revealing herself to the demons, but she hadn't gone in blind.

Rosalia possessed her share of arrogance. But unlike some demons, she was neither careless nor stupid. At least, not most of the time.

"Mother, infrared is picking up either de Palma or Murnau approaching the chateau. He's moving south across the grounds. On foot."

De Palma or Murnau. Code words for vampires and nosferatu. Though the receiver's volume was probably too low for a demon to hear unless he was standing next to her, Rosalia wouldn't risk drawing the demons' attention. Both demons and Guardians could hear everything said in the ballroom, but they couldn't *listen* to everything. Even if whispered, however, certain words and names pierced background noise like a candle lit at midnight.

To cover her reply, Rosalia turned as if searching the crowd. "You don't know which it is?" she murmured.

Both vampires and nosferatu would register a lower temperature on infrared than a human or Guardian, but nosferatu were huge. Most towered at six and a half to seven feet in height.

"He's tall, but I don't think he's tall enough for Murnau. He's not close enough for me to be sure, though."

"When he is, let me know."

A nosferatu posed a problem. People would notice it. Enormous, with pale and hairless skin, pointed ears, and fangs twice as long as a vampire's, nosferatu were bloodthirsty, evil creatures. Even if it dressed to pass as human—difficult beneath the bright lights in the chateau—and even if people refused to believe what they saw, its presence would stir fear and revulsion. But Rosalia doubted a nosferatu would try to blend in. If one was coming, then it was coming to kill. To protect the people here, she'd have to slay it, revealing her presence to the demons. Then she'd have to slay the demons so they couldn't report that a Guardian had been watching them. She didn't want to give Belial's demons any reason to unite against the Guardians, and she'd prefer not to kill Theriault yet. No matter how little his chances of leading his brethren were, the infighting over the lieutenant's position benefited the Guardians. Even an incompetent demon might provide a distraction for Malkvial and prevent him from quickly uniting the others.

If a vampire was coming, though . . .

Rosalia glanced back at the demons. Bernard and Gavel were taking their leave of Theriault, agreeing to circle among the guests. Satisfaction emanated from each. Demon business finished, now they were conducting Legion business, building human contacts.

Perhaps one of them intended to continue demon business, though. Six months ago, Belial's lieutenant had ordered the slaughter of Prague's vampire community; since then, fewer vampires willingly aligned themselves with the demons. But there were still some vampires who sought either power or protection from the demons—and the demons had their own uses for vampires who were willing to break the Rules in exchange.

The Parisian vampire community had resisted Theriault's attempts to make an alliance, but maybe a dissenter was in their ranks. A foolish dissenter, if he'd come alone. A human crowd provided some protection if the demons turned on him, but not much.

The soft crackle came again. "Mother, I have visual confirmation. It's de Palma."

A vampire. "Anyone I know?"

"Yes." The hesitation told Rosalia that Gemma was thinking of a way to describe him without saying his name. *"Six months ago, he stayed one day in your bedroom and left the same night."*

Deacon. Rosalia's champagne flute tilted in nerveless fingers. Her breath corkscrewed painfully through her lungs. Her mind could hardly comprehend it—*Deacon, here*—but the ache filling her chest said her heart had already taken it in. Deacon was here.

And still alive.

She hadn't known if he was. Once the leader of the Prague vampire community, he'd betrayed the Guardians in a desperate gamble to save his people and lost. Belial's lieutenant and a second demon, Caym, had done everything to destroy Deacon without actually killing him. Caym had beaten Deacon bloody, crushed his bones and his pride, then held his community and lovers hostage in exchange for information about the Guardians. As a result of that information, a Guardian had been killed—a woman Rosalia hadn't known well, but had liked well. After learning of the Guardian's death, Rosalia had watched Belial's lieutenant use Deacon to transform a human murderer into a vampire, then finally break him by showing Deacon the ashen remains of his companions. Though Deacon had managed to slay Caym, Belial's lieutenant had stopped the vampire by stabbing an iron spike through his forehead, and had left Deacon for the Guardians to find and kill. But Irena, a Guardian and the friend Deacon had betrayed, had stayed her hand, and Rosalia had taken him to her home in Rome. She hadn't known what she was going to do with him. She only knew why she'd taken him.

Deacon had rescued her. Once ninety years ago, and again more recently, when she'd had an iron spike through her own head and three nosferatu feeding from her throat. And so she owed him.

When they'd reached Rome, Deacon had still been unconscious, healing from the damage to his brain. She'd taken him to her room and had left him to his daysleep. When she'd returned, night had fallen and Deacon had already gone. Gemma had reported that he'd walked out the door without saying a word.

Rosalia had thought he'd left to die. He'd been broken. She'd felt his despair when he'd realized all that he'd lost; he'd welcomed death when the demon had shoved the spike through his forehead. She'd been certain he'd face the sun the next morning.

He was here, instead. Why? *Never* would he ally himself with Belial's demons. The launch of a new skincare line and this party couldn't interest him. She couldn't picture him mingling comfortably. The people glittered; conversation sparkled. Deacon wouldn't.

Had he somehow known *she* would be here? Rosalia's heart gave a heavy, slow thump. Hope bubbled within her bloodstream. Ruthlessly, she squashed it. Deacon couldn't have known she'd intended to observe Theriault tonight.

Could he?

If he had known, he wouldn't recognize her like this. Not with blond hair and this baby face—

Rosalia closed her eyes. *Stop.* She wouldn't let her thoughts head in this direction. Whatever his reasons, he wasn't here for her.

"He's at the rear of the chateau, Mother. I've lost him on infrared."

A vampire didn't need an invitation to enter a building, but he did to gain admittance into this gala. So did a Guardian. She'd come through the back disguised as one of the caterers. Though Deacon couldn't shape-shift, he could easily climb the exterior wall to the second floor or speed through the doors unseen.

She opened her eyes. The demon Gavel was approaching her group, his gaze fixed on the CEO of a cosmetics company standing beside her. Rosalia excused herself and threaded through the crowd toward the refreshment table, smiling brightly and nodding at anyone who met her eyes. She joined another group of humans at the side of the ballroom. Now that Theriault, Bernard, and Gavel had split up, she needed a wider angle to keep an eye on them. It also let her see both the enormous staircase that led from the second floor, and the main entrance from the gallery—the route Deacon would take if he approached the ballroom from the back of the chateau.

Assuming, of course, that the ballroom was his destination. And if he didn't come, she would *not* seek him out. She'd spent most of her life trying to save her brother Lorenzo from himself. She refused to spend the rest of it on another lost cause, no matter how much she owed him.

But she could thank God he was alive. She'd allow herself that.

She waited. Around her, the humans' laughter and voices

seemed too loud. The musicians finally switched to an arrangement with a quick tempo, but every draw of their bows sawed across her senses.

She glanced at the wide marble staircase. He wasn't there. Disappointment weighted her chest. Accustomed to the feeling, she ignored it.

Returning her gaze to the ballroom, she watched the demons and saw their calculated expressions and conversation win over their companions. Would they recognize Deacon? Only Belial's lieutenant and Caym had used him, but he'd led Prague's community for nearly six decades. Other demons might have seen him before.

If these demons gave any indication that they knew Deacon, she'd kill them—Theriault's alliance and Malkvial be damned. A lone vampire was nothing but sport to their kind. She wouldn't stand by and watch them play.

She looked toward the gallery. Even in this crush of people, Deacon's height would make him easy to spot. He wasn't there.

Had he been delayed? Was another demon or a vampire at the gala, one that neither she nor Gemma had detected? She should wander through the other rooms and see.

Rosalia headed for the gallery, her gaze sweeping the stairs. Sweeping over the vampire descending the steps.

Sweeping past him.

Her heart galloped. She continued walking. *Don't stop. Don't react and draw attention to him.* Her focus traveled the length of the ballroom, but her mind remained locked on that brief glimpse. She'd been right. Even here, Deacon didn't glitter. He stood like an unpolished stone pillar amid sparkling diamonds. His dark dinner jacket stretched over shoulders as wide as a blacksmith's. He'd unbuttoned his shirt at the collar, revealing pale skin that could have belonged to an unfinished marble statue—possessing the strength, but none of the smooth perfection of a completed piece. Before he'd become a vampire, Deacon had earned his money boxing, and his transformation had physically frozen his appearance. His body was still heavily muscled. His dark brows and hard mouth formed uncompromising lines on a face roughly sculpted by both nature and occupation. A beard shadowed his jaw; he obviously hadn't shaved in months. And . . . *had he cut his hair?* She wanted to look again. She forced herself to continue smoothly across the floor. The click of her heels drummed in her ears.

Don't turn around yet. Find one of the servers and—

There. A man in a white jacket and carrying a tray paused beside a matron wearing gold silk. Rosalia downed her champagne, circled the waiter and lifted a new glass from the tray, sliding in next to the matron.

Deacon had reached the bottom of the stairs, but remained on the last step. His gaze searched the crowd.

She glanced at the demons. None were looking toward the vampire, and so she did, studying him from beneath her lashes.

He *had* cut his hair. Though it was longer than the first time she'd seen him, a member of the American naval service and his brown hair regulation short, six months ago the dark length had touched his shoulders. Now he had just enough to slide his fingers through, but not enough to grab a handful. A vampire's hair grew slowly; it'd be another ninety years before it reached his shoulders again.

Though the cut was tidier and less distinctive than his long hair, he still appeared slightly disheveled. With his shadowed jaw and unbuttoned collar, many men would look like they'd just come from bed; Deacon looked like he'd prepared for a fight. One side of his shirt collar had escaped the jacket, as if dragged off his tie just before coming here. Now the points of his shirt collar were uneven. It bothered her. Her gaze kept flicking back to them. She wished he'd fix it, if only because an orderly appearance would make him less remarkable amid all of the glossy perfection. But even if he knew how crooked the collar was, she doubted that it would occur to him to adjust it.

In her cache, she carried a tie for her son, Vincente. It would only take an instant to pull it from her mental storage space and into her hands. She could approach Deacon and offer to tidy him up.

To amuse herself, she imagined his reaction. She was still smiling when Deacon's searching gaze touched her and immediately moved on.

Well. She'd expected that, hadn't she? Rosalia swallowed

champagne past a throat gone tight. He never recognized her. Not his fault, really. Until six months ago, when he'd led the Guardians to the catacombs where she'd been trapped for a year and a half, an endless fount of blood for a nest of nosferatu, she'd never appeared to him as herself; before that, she'd never approached him with the same face twice. The form she used tonight was new, too.

His jaw flexed as if he'd clenched his teeth. After a moment, she realized he was no longer searching the crowd. She looked to see who he'd focused on.

Theriault.

She should have guessed. A man like Deacon would not rest until he'd avenged his people. The two demons who destroyed his community were dead, but not *all* of Belial's demons were. One by one, he would hunt them down and slay them.

For a vampire, it was an impossible task. Perhaps he might slay two, or ten, or fifty. Eventually, though, one of the demons would kill him first.

Deacon had to know that. And so he was not only seeking revenge. He still sought death. It just wouldn't be in the face of the sun. He'd go out fighting, instead of broken.

Good for you, preacher. Rosalia mentally lifted her glass to him as she took a sip of champagne, celebrating his presence here and affirming the similarity between them. She understood the need to avenge her people, no matter how impossible the odds. So she still wouldn't try to save Deacon from himself—she *wouldn't*—but she could help him a little.

And make sure he didn't get in her way.

"My tiny little girl?"

"Yes, Mother?"

She heard the laugh in Gemma's response, as she did every time she referred to the young woman as her tiny little girl. In her bare feet, the lanky blonde stood at eye-level with Rosalia in heels, and Rosalia's current fashion-model height was only slightly taller than her natural one.

"I want to know where he's staying, his financial situation. Where he's been in the past six months and who he's been with." Rosalia hadn't looked before, afraid that she wouldn't find anything. "He came alone, but does he have a new partner? Who is he feeding from?"

He must have been feeding. After two or three days without blood, a vampire began showing it—pale, tired, and thin. None of those described Deacon. Neither did careless or stupid, so he'd likely already fed that night. His psychic blocks were good, but he wouldn't risk the demons sensing his bloodlust by coming in hungry.

So he'd either found a new vampire partner or was using different human women each night. He'd been forced to do that before, while his consorts had been held hostage. *Offer the women so much to drink that they won't remember. Heal the bite, so that even if they do remember, they won't have evidence.* Rosalia thought he must hate that. To her knowledge, he hadn't been to bed with anyone he didn't want since Camille had transformed him. Soon after he and Camille parted ways and he'd taken over the community in Prague, Eva and Petra became his lovers and companions. But the bloodlust wouldn't give him the same choice if he fed from strangers. If the woman was interested, he wouldn't be able to stop his response. He'd have sex with her.

The bloodlust wouldn't always rise and overwhelm his free will, and not every woman he fed from would desire him. So it wouldn't *always* happen—but it would happen often enough that he must feel as if the bloodlust controlled him.

Her gaze fell to his uneven collar again. Maybe that was where he'd lost his tie. Some woman's bedroom. The restroom in a Parisian bar. An alley.

Her fingers flexed. She *needed* to fix that collar.

Gemma broke in, her voice holding a hint of apology. "It will take me longer to send that information to you than it used to, Mother."

Oh, God. Rosalia's throat closed. Grief hit her so hard that only practice and discipline kept it from showing. Once, a team of vampires would have been in the van with Gemma. More would have been at a converted priory in Rome, which they'd all shared and called home. She'd trained all of them, had raised most of them, and had known some for more than a century.

Not just a team. Her family. And they were all gone. Slaughtered by the nephilim, a race of demons that Rosalia hadn't known existed until six months ago. But they'd killed her friends, her family. They'd slain every vampire in Rome, including Lorenzo, and she hadn't been there to protect them. But Gemma had been there. She'd been in the priory when the nephilim had come, and because she was human, she'd been the only one to survive.

Gemma still woke up screaming from the nightmares.

"Oh, my daughter. I was not thinking." Because she could hardly bear to think about it. "Tomorrow morning, we will begin looking together."

"Vin's coming up tomorrow. He'll help."

"And have it all to me before you've finished breakfast." She forced the lightness into her tone. Her son would help, but only because Gemma would ask him to. Ten years ago, he'd left the priory without looking back. He'd still be gone if not for his relationship with Gemma—and if he could convince Gemma, he'd disappear from Rosalia's life again. But he hadn't yet, and she thanked God every day that her son had fallen in love with a woman as bull-headed as he was. "Will he be staying the weekend at the hotel with us?"

"Yes. He will, and he'll like it."

Gemma's determined tone brought Rosalia out of her grief, made her smile. She glanced at Deacon, gathered her calm and her courage. *"I am on my way to speak to de Palma."*

"And I'm turning into a mouse." Except for an emergency, Gemma would keep radio silence until Rosalia put space between them again. *"Give him hell, Mother."*

She didn't have to. Belial's demons had already put him through hell, first when they'd beaten him, then when they'd killed his people. None of those marks were visible, but Rosalia knew they were there. Just as hers were.

Deacon had remained at his vantage point on the stairs, his posture casual, his elbow braced on the wide marble banister. Though he must have been aware of her approach, he didn't acknowledge her until she was a few paces away. He glanced down, his eyes the muted green of a sea lying beneath the darkening clouds of a lightning storm. She put on another dazzling smile and directed it right at him. He looked toward the demon again, dismissing her.

She glided up two steps as if she intended to pass by, then slipped behind him. Propping her hip against the banister, she reached down and rested her hand against his cool fist. Before he could react, she said, "You do not intend to do it here, do you? With so many humans as witnesses?"

His big body stiffened. She could almost feel him weighing his response. Her skin was warm; he'd know she wasn't a demon or a vampire. That left human or Guardian. When he inhaled, she knew he was testing her scent—or trying to, beyond the redolence of perfumes and colognes saturating the air. She'd sprayed her own floral fragrance to conceal her lack of odor, and with every breath, she took in the pine and bergamot that masked his. One so earthy, the other a light tingle lifting through her senses.

To her delight, he raised her hand to his lips and sniffed. The tension leaked from his form. His mouth setting into a hard line, he turned his head, looking at her in profile.

"Of course you would not," Rosalia answered for him, though she guessed he was preparing to respond with, *Haul off, lady*—Guardian or not. She withdrew her hand and touched his back, where she could feel the short swords strapped beneath his jacket. Vampires had no cache to store their weapons. They had to physically arm themselves. "You are just observing him, I think, and plan to finish it later, when the element of surprise is yours. And you will defeat him, because he is arrogant . . . and he could not know how strong and fast you have become."

After Irena had slain the nosferatu who had been feeding from Rosalia, she'd given Deacon their blood to drink. It had changed him, strengthened him, as if he'd been given a second transformation. Though he was still not as strong or as quick as one of the rare nosferatu-born, if a demon only expected a vampire's strength and speed from him—and in their arrogance, most would—Deacon had a brief, important advantage. He was the only vampire to have been strengthened that way, so as long as no Guardians revealed that a second transformation was possible, Deacon would always possess that moment of surprise against a demon, useful for both defense and attack.

She watched his eyes narrow. Had he not expected *her* to know, either? Perhaps no other Guardians knew that the second transformation had been successful. Perhaps he'd only told one—and he had not realized, until now, who had been speaking to him.

Or perhaps he thought that the Guardian he'd told had spread the information to everyone. If so, she forgave him. He had not known her long enough to understand that she would never rip away a friend's defenses. Particularly when he had so few.

"Yes, I know all of this," she confirmed. "Do *you* know that two of his brethren, who have just sworn to protect him, are also here?"

Deacon's face didn't give anything away, but his quick, searching sweep of the room did. He hadn't known.

"If you struck against him tonight, it would be suicide. Suicide compounded by failure, when you did not finish what you set out to do."

Even when he spoke softly, his voice had gravel in it. "Why would you care?"

Some Guardians wouldn't. They'd prefer to see him dead. "I have many reasons. But you are right—foremost among them is not concern for your life." Rosalia lied as well as a demon when she wanted to. "It benefits my kind to keep these three alive . . . for now. Your chance will come again."

He didn't reply. He didn't ask her reason for delaying the demons' deaths. Did that mean he didn't care what those reasons were, or that he was afraid he might care too much and be dissuaded from his course?

"You at least owe us that, do you not?" she pressed.

"I owe my people more."

A fair point, she conceded. And one she wouldn't argue with, so she would leave him to it. Intending to rejoin the crowd, she moved around him and down the steps. "I doubt you will find your opening tonight, preacher. But if you do, take it. I will not interfere."

He caught her hand, palm to palm. She stopped, staring ahead into the crush of chatting, laughing humans. Her heart jumped against her ribs, pounding. If he hadn't guessed before, he must be certain of her identity now. She'd once told him that she'd known he was a chaplain on his ship, and revealed she'd taken vows of her own. No other Guardian knew him that well. Not even Irena, whom he had called a friend before he'd betrayed them.

His grip tightened. His fingers encompassed hers, seemed to draw her into the palm of his hand with that small movement. Rosalia looked back at him. His gaze delved beneath her skin, as if searching for something familiar. She wanted to offer it to him, to wear her own face. *She wanted to tell him, I have known you for so long. I have waited for so long.*

But there was no reason to make such a confession. Deacon didn't want to know her—and she didn't really know him anymore, either. Thanks to Belial's demons, he was no longer the man he'd been. He sought revenge and death. And she was done with waiting.

He glanced over her head. "Tell me who they are."

The demons. Of course. They were his only concern. They should have been her only concern, too. Unfortunately, she'd been cursed since birth with an overdeveloped sense of gratitude.

"Look to the center of the room," she told him. "The silver-haired woman wearing a floor-length red dress and a fortune in rubies. He is on her left. Do you see him?"

Deacon nodded. "And the other?"

"Four meters behind me. He is the only one in his circle who does not hold a drink."

He blinked, the only indication of his surprise that she'd come to him with the demon so close. His gaze dropped to hers. "You live dangerously, sister."

No. She had never risked enough—and thanks to the nephilim, she'd lost it all anyway. She pulled her hand free. And since she had nothing to lose now, she reached up and tucked his collar into place. She doubted he noticed. "If you need assistance tonight—"

"I don't." His tone said he'd already gotten everything he needed from her. He looked toward the demon. "So you can haul off."

Anger jabbed at her. She'd expected rejection and understood his need to go this alone, but she didn't deserve that rude dismissal. "Or, as you once told me, 'Get the fuck out of your face?'" When his startled gaze met hers, she smiled sweetly. "It will be my pleasure. Good luck to you, preacher."

To him, and to her. They were both going to need it.